Danica Winters is a multiple-award-winning, bestselling author who writes books that grip readers with their ability to drive emotion through suspense and occasionally a touch of magic. When she's not working, she can be found in the wilds of Montana, testing her patience while she tries to hone her skills at various crafts—quilting, pottery and painting are not her areas of expertise. She believes the cup is neither half-full nor half-empty, but it better be filled with wine. Visit her website at danicawinters.net

R. Barri Flowers is an award-winning author of crime, thriller, mystery and romance fiction featuring three-dimensional protagonists, riveting plots, unexpected twists and turns, and heart-pounding climaxes. With an expertise in true crime, serial killers and characterizing dangerous offenders, he is perfectly suited for the Mills & Boon Heroes line. Chemistry and conflict between the hero and heroine, attention to detail and incorporating the very latest advances in criminal investigations are the cornerstones of his romantic suspense fiction.

Also by Danica Winters

A Loaded Question
Rescue Mission: Secret Child
A Judge's Secrets
K-9 Recovery
Hidden Truth
In His Sights
Her Assassin For Hire
Protective Operation
Ms Calculation
Mr Serious

Also by R. Barri Flowers

Chasing the Violet Killer

Discover more at millsandboon.co.uk

LONE WOLF
BOUNTY HUNTER

DANICA WINTERS

THE BIG
ISLAND KILLER

R. BARRI FLOWERS

MILLS & BOON

First Published in Great Britain 2022
by Mills & Boon, an imprint of HarperCollins*Publishers* Ltd
1 London Bridge Street, London, SE1 9GF

www.harpercollins.co.uk

HarperCollins*Publishers*
1st Floor, Watermarque Building,
Ringsend Road, Dublin 4, Ireland

Lone Wolf Bounty Hunter © 2022 Danica Winters
The Big Island Killer © 2022 R. Barri Flowers

ISBN: 978-0-263-30354-4

0822

MIX
Paper from
responsible sources
FSC™ C007454

This book is produced from independently certified FSC™ paper to ensure responsible forest management.

For more information visit: www.harpercollins.co.uk/green

Printed and Bound in Spain using 100% Renewable electricity at CPI Black Print, Barcelona

LONE WOLF
BOUNTY HUNTER

DANICA WINTERS

To my family, friends and fans.

May this and all of my books help bring light
to the darkness.

Chapter One

It was a gift, nearly dying. After a lifetime spent on the front lines of her family's many wars, it wasn't until she was wounded and feared dead that she finally found herself with the freedom to really live.

The wound under her left clavicle was Kendra Spade's daily reminder of how close she had come to the edge. Yet it had also been her get-out-of-the-family-business-free card. It was a bullet that she would have gladly taken again.

She slipped on her silk shirt and buttoned it, leaving the top open to expose the diamond solitaire necklace that adorned the base of her throat. Like any shiny thing, it had a way of attracting the biggest fish and the widest mouths. Judge Giuseppe always commented on her necklace after the hearings. She held no doubts, thanks to the look in his evil-dulled eyes, that it wasn't only the necklace he found beautiful. That being said, she would never be the kind of woman who would sell her soul for a judge's favor—there were far better and easier ways to get what she wanted.

She picked up her suit jacket, laid it over her arm and slipped on her blood-bottomed heels. Before walking out of her office, she put on her lipstick and checked her lines in the mirror by the door—as always, she appeared picture-perfect.

It was a good thing the looking glass wasn't capable of peeking into her soul. If it was, it would see all the struggles that came with being a prosecutor and a woman with a past. Everything in her life was peppered with wounds and emotional shrapnel, but the best part of it was the scars—they were the body's way of fusing itself and its weaknesses into a stronger and more resilient space.

She touched the puckered place under her clavicle for good luck and picked up her briefcase. This would be a tough case, but if things went her way—which they usually did—she wouldn't need any luck, just the power of her research and her persuasion. Today was just a bench trial, so she would only have to convince Judge Giuseppe that the defendant had committed the murder he was charged with, and that it was premeditated, not an act of self-defense. The defense had taken a risk, going for a bench trial instead of asking for a jury, and she was all too happy to oblige. Judge Giuseppe was fair and consistent on the law. Juries could be capricious.

The trial would likely last the rest of the afternoon, but it would be dollars in her pocket—money that allowed her to be almost completely free of her ties with her family's private security company, STEALTH. They regularly worked as military contractors and had operatives all over the world, including several right here in New York.

On second thought, she would never be truly free.

Her phone buzzed as she walked up the courthouse steps, and she slipped it out of her briefcase—AJ.

Speak of the devil.

She considered not answering and letting the phone call go to voicemail, but her brother would just keep calling until she did pick up—and that was to say nothing of the rest of the family that he would call to the table and ask to reach out to her as well. They were wolves when they needed to be, and she would always be called back to the pack when pride or lives were at stake.

"AJ." She said his name simply, affectless.

"Glad to catch you. You busy?"

He knew the answer to that question. She was always busy—just like him. "Not too bad. You?"

"Just another day in paradise." AJ chuckled. "I don't know what you've heard about the ranch we're working from in Montana, but we have a situation on our hands."

She could feel a request coming on the flotsam of his words, and she wasn't sure if she wanted to go in for the direct hit and get it over with or if she should make him work for the ask—either way, she would be urged to do his bidding. First, she needed to know if this call to action was because of imminent danger to person or pride.

"What happened?" she asked.

AJ exhaled. "We've had a run-in with a state senator whom we were hired by. He admitted to having his wife killed and his child kidnapped, but now he has recanted and told us that he was coerced into his testimony and feared that STEALTH would kill him if he didn't take the blame."

So, this threat had the bite of both injury of pride and death of souls. "And now he is suing the family?"

"And you knowing that is exactly why we need you to come home and work on our behalf."

"You know as well as I do that I'm not licensed in Montana. I'd be of little to no help. However, I can make a few calls and get you the best lawyer possible."

"No," AJ said, his tone making it clear that there was no argument she could make that would grant her reprieve from his request. "You are the best lawyer I know and the only one we can truly trust. And, if you look, you will notice that you actually *are* licensed in the State of Montana. You can thank Zoey for that one when you get here."

"Just because you had your team…" She glanced around, making sure that no one was listening in on her conversation, but everyone around her kept moving and seemed wrapped up in their own lives. "Just because you *hacked* the state bar and faked documents, it doesn't mean that I will step into line with your plans. What you did is unethical, and if anyone was to find out, I'd be permanently disbarred."

AJ sighed. "The only one who has the power, or could find the proof to get you disbarred, would be you."

She held no doubts he was right—their boss, Zoey, would have done everything in triplicate and spared no expense to sell their ruse. Yet it didn't change the fact she wasn't acquainted with the intricacies of the Montana state legal system and its statutes.

"You've put my reputation, my credibility and my honor at stake, and now you want me to do you a favor? I don't like being strong-armed, AJ," she growled.

"And yet you are still talking to me. We both know that you love me and your family. We have you booked on a flight out this afternoon. All you have to do is go and present your case in front of Giuseppe and secure the guilty verdict that we both know you will get—then go to JFK. We have everything else you will need when you get here."

Damn, they've done their research.

She might have hated being pushed around by her brother, but he was also the only one she loved enough to allow him to get away with treating her like a child despite the fact that she'd grown into a strong, independent woman. No matter how powerful she became or how far she tried to push her family from her world, all he had to do was make a call and prove that he would always have sway—but his most influential weapon to bring her to heel was her love for him and her other siblings. Family would always come first.

"I'll see you tonight," he said, almost as if he could hear the thoughts and the arguments she was having within herself.

"There had better be whiskey and fresh ice in my bedroom when I arrive."

Maybe the only time she would ever truly be free would be when she broke the chains of love she felt for her family—but death would wield that ax, something she didn't want for any of them. Until then, when they pulled the chains tight, she had no choice but to do their bidding.

GETTING GIUSEPPE TO issue the right verdict had been fairly straightforward. A handful of hours later, she found herself seated in a puddle jumper and flying from Minneapolis into Missoula. At least her family had the good sense to book her first-class, but that meant little on the tiny airplane. Basically, she got one extra bag of pretzels and was the first one in line for the cheese tray.

After boarding, she clicked her seat belt in place, and an auburn-haired man with piercing brown eyes smiled down at her. He was wearing cowboy boots, jeans and what she could best describe as something that had come off a ranch supplier's discount rack—though he made that Western-style shirt look good.

"Hey," he said, giving her a nod before stowing his black backpack in the overhead compartment and sitting down.

She gave him a tip of the head and a tight-lipped smile as he clicked in. If she had any luck, that would be where their conversation ended. She didn't mind a little chitchat on a flight, but she didn't like being cloistered next to such a good-looking man for that length of time—actually, any length of time. And this man was definitely good-looking. He had deep-set eyes and the brooding scowl of a thoughtful and intrepid soul.

He glanced over at her, and his eyes picked up the light from her window, making them shine the color of warm caramel. She doubted any woman who'd looked into those eyes had ever felt the ability to say no to any kind of request he made. He was definitely the kind who had his fair share of options when it came to women—and she wasn't the kind who wanted to compete for any man's attention. She commanded respect and, above all, loyalty.

The plane steadily filled with college students, smiling couples and single professionals. She glanced down at her phone. She hadn't even put it on airplane mode yet, and she already had twenty new emails from her office and her clients. While waiting for the flight, she had taken care of what she could and made a few brief phone calls, but her thoughts returned to AJ. He hadn't told her much about what the senator was threatening to do to her family and STEALTH, the private military contracting company that employed them. Well, all except her…for the last few years. *It was a nice reprieve while it lasted.*

"Ma'am?" a flight attendant asked. She hadn't noticed he was standing in the aisle and looking down at her, and his sudden appearance made her jump with surprise.

"Yes?" she asked, her cheeks warming with the thought she had been caught unaware.

"Can you please push your purse farther under your seat?" He motioned toward her leather bag, which was barely showing and, if she had been given a choice, would have never been on the floor in the first place.

She forced a smile, clicked off her phone and dropped it into her bag before reaching to push it deeper under the seat. She felt a snap and her fingernail snagged on the man's bag that was on the floor next to hers, but she barely paid attention as she finished shoving the bag under her seat and sat back up.

The steward didn't crack a smile and moved his way down the aisle, doing his best impersonation of an overworked schoolmarm in the process—she was surprised he didn't have a ruler to rap on flyers who ignored or failed to comply to his standards.

The man next to her cleared his throat. "If you'd like, I can put your bag in the overhead compartment for you."

"Thank you for the offer, but it's fine." And just

like that, she'd had enough of men for the day. The last thing she was going to do was hand her purse over to the care of a stranger so he could put it out of her sight.

A sigh escaped her lips before she had a chance to check the sound.

She could feel the gaze of the man sitting next to her; he must have picked up on her unspoken annoyance. "I am sorry," she said, not bothering to try to deny her actions. "I have had a long day, and it's not even close to ending."

The plane rolled back and taxied out onto the runway, getting in line for takeoff.

The man beside her smiled, his teeth as gleaming and beautiful as his eyes. "You're fine. I get that way, too. Where are you flying out of, originally?"

Her fears of chitchatting were being realized, and she only had herself to blame. It was a good thing her legal cases didn't usually hinge on a single sigh; sometimes she found it only too hard to keep her body language in check.

"New York City." She left it simple, not wanting to have the man continue with his line of questions.

He nodded, pinching his lips together as if he had more that he wanted to ask her but had picked up her reticence. "I'm coming from there as well. Funny, we might have been on the last plane together, too."

His words were innocuous, but something about the way he spoke made the hair on the back of her neck rise.

She turned to him, facing him carefully and searching his eyes for some kind of recognition, but she found nothing but the features of the handsome stranger. "Do I know you?"

He smiled, closed his eyes and let the G-force press his head back against the seat as they took off, forcing her retreat back to her headrest as well.

As the plane leveled out, she had the plummeting feeling that this man was a plant. He could play coy, but she wouldn't put it past her brother to put a tail on her to ensure she made it on the plane and safely to Montana.

He didn't say another word. He seemed to be asleep in the seat next to her—effectively trapping her. Ten minutes ago, she had hoped the man wouldn't talk to her, and now that her wish had come true, she was wishing for exactly the opposite—and to find out if her intuition was right or if she was simply losing her edge.

She battled with herself as she occasionally glanced over at him throughout the three-hour flight. When the surly flight attendant returned with the cart, she hoped the man would stir, but instead the attendant passed him over and gave her the little box of snacks and three minibottles of vodka—two of which she would definitely need to save for later.

After downing the first minibottle, she looked over at the sleeping man. His chin was tilted back, but even in sleep he was sexy. This man, this stranger next to her, was just that—a stranger.

If she was already having to worry about intrigues and plots her family was involved in before her feet even struck ground in Montana, this was going to be one hell of a trip—a trip she would have to work hard to cut short.

Chapter Two

Trent Lockwood could have murdered his assistant for seating him beside their target. She knew his policy—always stick to the shadows—and yet his twenty-four-year-old secretary at Lockwood Bonds had gone ahead and broken the rules. As soon as he got back to Missoula, she would get a talking-to about what exactly it meant for him to be a bondsman and bounty hunter—and the danger that came with his job.

He peeked out from under his eyelashes at the lawyer sitting next to him. She was pretty—prettier than he had expected, based on the pictures he had picked up of her online. In real life, her blond curls were looser and free-flowing around her hard-edged jawline and supple pink cheeks, and they almost worked to conceal the way she occasionally looked over at him.

Did she sense something in him? Or was she just as leery of strangers as he was? People were the most dangerous weapons in the world, and he was only too sure she knew this fact just as well as he did.

He couldn't read too much into her sizing him up. Hell, maybe she was just as bored as he was. He'd been hoping to use this time to catch up on some recon on Senator Clark and his whereabouts, but instead here he was…being scrutinized by the one person he had hoped to never be noticed by. Rather, he hoped she would lead him to the man who had left his company on the hook for a million-dollar bond—a bail bond his brother had signed off on in desperation to make money. Trent had only come to terms with it when Tripp had finally convinced him it was a benefit to have a senator as a client.

Yes, he would definitely need to call a team meeting about expectations and job requirements the moment he got back. As for his seat assignment, it would have to result in a formal write-up of the secretary, if nothing else. She shouldn't make these kinds of mistakes when lives were on the line.

He couldn't have been more relieved when they touched down. Hopefully he had been utterly forgettable. The last thing he needed was her recognizing him outside this airplane. Most women he had met over the years had been only too happy to forget him; he'd never been great at the relationship game. That kind of thing was for people who didn't have to live half of their lives ducking in and out of alleys. As a professional bounty hunter, he lived on the edge of danger every day.

Trent had only been with his last girlfriend for a few months before she kicked him to the curb after he disappeared for a week—four days longer than he was supposed to have been gone. Though he had tried to explain it was for work, he hadn't had the heart to lie to her when she asked how often that kind of thing happened—far too often. It had also contributed to his divorce prior to that, but his ex had bottled up her questions and concerns until it was too late to save the marriage.

Trent was damned good at his job, but that was because he had the patience to wait—a personality trait that didn't work so well when it came to burgeoning relationships in the digital and instant-gratification age. The best thing about his job was the hunt. He could take his time and watch the people he was sent to bring to heel—the people who left his family's company holding the bag when they failed to show up for court and jumped bail.

After landing, he made his way out to his rental truck, carefully keeping an eye on Kendra. From what he'd managed to hear from the grapevine, Kendra was coming to town to sit down and have a closed-door mediation with the senator and his lawyers at the Bradshaw Law offices. He had been sitting on that lawyer's office for nearly a month, and so far come up empty-handed. Hopefully, Kendra's meeting would prove to be as fruitful as they expected, but it meant not losing track of her.

She got into a white Suburban parked just outside the terminal. A man greeted her; he was about six feet and the kind that looked like he worked out at least five times a week. Trent gritted his teeth, and as he caught himself doing it, he wondered why. Kendra was pretty, but what in the hell was he doing being even the slightest bit annoyed about a stranger helping someone who was little more than bait for his intended target?

Sure, she was pretty...*stunningly beautiful*, if he was being honest with himself. Yet he couldn't be, nor was he the type to be, smitten with a woman simply because of her looks. As far as he was concerned, beauty on the outside was a depreciating asset. The only thing that he really looked for in a woman he considered dating was a soul that could speak to him in the night without a word ever being whispered.

He pulled his truck around, keeping his eye on her Suburban. After paying for his parking, he followed her out onto the main road, carefully keeping at least three car lengths behind. Her destination was a mystery; there had been no records of her at any of the local hotels, and he couldn't find anything about the physical location of the company she was representing in the lawsuit, STEALTH Inc.

He wasn't a tech guru by any means, but he'd put in more than his fair share of time in the tech trenches, and he knew how to locate people based on a variety of methods and using a variety of tools—many utilized by law enforcement. Yet he had come up with nothing about this woman besides generic work info and a professional headshot; she was an enigma when it came to her personal life. He'd be lying to himself if he didn't admit that her ability to hide in this world was a bit of a turn-on.

The thought made him fall back slightly more into the mass of traffic after leaving the lot. If her digital protections were that strong, he could only imagine her physical ones were just as robust—ones that would definitely include watching for tails and men who wished to be utterly forgettable.

After driving for nearly forty-five minutes, carefully keeping his distance the entire time, the white Suburban turned off and onto a dirt road that led toward a gulch tucked into the belly of the mountains. The road was barely marked, and he dropped a pin on his map to make sure he could find it again later.

He drove past and didn't stop until he hit the small

town of Stevensville, not much farther down the road. The town was little more than it had been 150 years ago—comprised of a couple bars, a post office and a bank. In fact, the brick facades of the main street seemed straight out of the 1880s, complete with flat roofs and the lawless feel of the old West.

He'd grown up around western Montana, but it never ceased to amaze him when he came into these small towns how much they gripped the past and generational pride.

No matter what came in his life, he would always be pulled back to this world—a simpler place in a simpler time.

Parking his truck, Trent went to work. According to OnX, a mapping app, the road she had driven down led to a four-hundred-acre ranch called the Widow Maker. It had been bought and sold a few years back, and it was registered under a private holding company's name. *That clever woman.*

There were no guarantees that this was the STEALTH headquarters, but his sixth sense was kicking into high gear. Ranches were often kept in trusts or overseen by private holding companies, depending on the size and the owners' desire for privacy, but if he had to guess, this was exactly where he needed to go in order to keep a line on her.

He glanced back at his phone. It would be dark, pitch-dark, in about an hour. He'd have to be vigilant, but as soon as he got what he needed, he could retreat into the shadows. If he had only known they were going to be seated next to one another on the plane, he could have planted a tracker directly on her gear, but instead he was stuck playing a nighttime spy.

From what he'd managed to pull up about STEALTH, they were a private military contracting group…that much he knew. Yet, aside from organizations like Blackwater, he had heard very little of what businesses like this actually did. Blackwater had developed a reputation for skirting the law, killing innocent people and generally leaving chaos in their wake, but he had a feeling that STEALTH wasn't the kind of team that worked at that level. Though he could be wrong.

He pulled up his VPN and started searching for more information. Unlike Blackwater, STEALTH had nothing about them online aside from a monochromatic website that touted their security services—he'd pored through their website before, but it had given him about as few answers as the woman who had been seated next to him.

Closing his eyes for a moment, he was surprised when her face popped into the front of his mind. Had he really looked at her so long that her image had imprinted on him like that? Or was she there because he was paid to have her be his every thought?

It had to be the latter.

He needed to get to the water; that was the only way he could make sense of what he was thinking and feeling—and maybe it would grant him the peace that he so desperately sought. Ever since his divorce, he'd found being on the water the therapy he needed to find tranquility again. The river was silent and nonjudgmental. His ex had been silent and critical.

Glancing back at the map, he noted the river that twisted through STEALTH's property. In Montana, rivers and riverbanks were public property—and damn if he wasn't a member of the public. He smiled.

It was the perfect time for fishing when he got on the river. The sun was a finger's width from touching the top of the mountains that surrounded him, and its golden and pink hues were reflecting off the water. He pulled a caddis fly from his kit and lathered it up with floatant.

There was nothing like fishing with dry flies. An angler had to make them dance just over the surface of the water to lure the trout from the depths, then lace the fly onto the water and wait for the hungry fish to rise. It was the ultimate game of seduction.

He made his way down the riverbank until he was well within the boundaries of the ranch, but he was careful to stay as concealed as possible. Occasionally, he would throw a cast and wait for a strike, but mostly he watched. In the distance, he could make out a line of cabins, like little row houses, where he assumed the ranch hands would have lived, but in this case they were far more likely to be housing trained spies and killers.

It made him wonder about Kendra. Was she a killer? A spy?

If she was, there was no way he was getting the drop on her.

The thought made his skin prickle, and he couldn't help but look over his shoulder. Just because no one had come out and given him the once-over, it didn't mean they didn't know he was here. No one stood behind him, but he looked to the trees, already convinced that he would find cameras pinned on him. Once again, there was nothing.

A woman stepped out of one of the cabins nearest him. He cast his line, looking at her only from his peripheral. She stood, watching him, for a long moment. She was far enough away that he couldn't make out her features, but even without seeing them, he knew it was her… Kendra.

A part of him hoped that she would walk toward the river…that she would walk to him, put her hand to his cheek and say, "I've been hoping to see you again."

She turned away from him, and he found solace in her ignoring him. If she had recognized him, she likely would have confronted him…especially if she was actually a trained mercenary. She wouldn't just shrug him off. Apparently, she was every bit a lawyer.

He watched her walk up the hill and toward the main ranch house until she disappeared. With her absence, a strange and unwelcome loneliness filled him, but he reminded himself the sensation was nothing more than his desire to do his job. That was all she was, a job. He needed to push aside all the superfluous feelings. This woman was all that stood between his family and potential ruin—and he could never let his heart get in the way of their business.

Chapter Three

"AJ, you know you can be a real son of a—" Kendra stopped as the house's front door slammed shut. She'd been home only a day, and they were already yelling at each other. She shouldn't have been surprised, but she was still disappointed.

"All I'm saying is that I think it best if you have a sit-down with the opposing counsel. Maybe we can sort something out before we take this to court and it all goes on the public record. Mediation would be the smartest route here," AJ argued. The water glass in his hand shook, and a bit sloshed over the top as he seemed to forget he was holding anything.

"I came here, against my better judgment, because you wanted the big guns. Now you want me to negotiate? I could have done that over the phone, sitting in my comfortable leather chair in my office in New York."

"I didn't think that they would be game for a sit-down until this morning," AJ countered. "I'd offered before, but they didn't even call me back."

"And yet, they just randomly called you after I hit the state? You are full of crap and you know it. You knew the whole time the mediation would happen—that's why you were in a mad rush to get me back here in time." She was so furious that she could feel her blood pressure rising all the way into her finger-tips. "You know, I always tell my clients there are a lot of things I can do to help people, but the one thing I require in order to be able to do my job is the truth."

"I am *telling* you the damned truth, Kendra. You just aren't listening."

Oh, no, he didn't. She seethed.

There was the sound of laughter from outside the front door, then the latch clicked and Mike and Troy walked inside. Mike stopped, and his face went blank as he looked at her. He stared for a long moment, like he almost didn't recognize her. "Holy crap, look what the cat dragged in. When did you get here, sis?"

She shot AJ a look, making it clear their conversation was far from being over. He was going to get more of an earful about his bringing her here and then putting her in a holding pattern before she would be sat-isfied. "Hey, guys," she said, sighing as she struggled to gain control over her rage.

Troy walked over and gave her a quick kiss to the cheek. "I heard you might be coming back to town but didn't know you would be here so soon. Good to see you. You're looking..." He appraised her tailored pants and formfitting button-down. "Well, you look *New York*–ish."

She gave him a raise of the brow. "You know, not everyone in the world gets to wear tactical gear and hiking clothes for their day jobs. Some of us are ex-pected to look and *act* professional." She glared over at AJ one more time, making sure he heard the admon-ishment in her tone.

He wouldn't glance her way. "I hate to cut this little

reunion short, but we have places to be." AJ smiled. "And so do you. The Bradshaw Law Group office is a thirty-minute drive." He threw her a set of keys. "You can use the ranch truck as much as you need, but keep it between the mustard and the mayonnaise. I know how you drive."

First, he had the audacity to give her orders and push her around, and now he was going to comment on her driving? She could feel her lip curl with disgust as she caught the keys and stuffed them in her pocket.

Though she knew it was likely in vain, she tried to tell herself that AJ's attitude toward her was more a reflection of his love than it was his annoyance. He was just a leader, a typical type-A guy, and with that came traits that were sometimes hard to digest. Though, admittedly, she had that personality type as well.

She'd had more than her fair share of run-ins with her fellow state employees because of her inability to compromise or give any slack when she felt people weren't living up to their potential and doing as she had instructed. There was nothing she had less patience for than a person who ignored her, especially when it came to running a business and practicing law.

Maybe AJ was feeling the same way with her right now.

Logically, she could make sense of all this, but it was like being around her brother—and the rest of her family, for that matter—made her instantly become an eighteen-year-old girl again. Regardless of how much she wanted to fall into the trap of an identity crisis, she didn't have time for that. She could do that when she got back to New York into the safety of her own apartment. The longer she stayed in Montana, the more of a problem this would become, and she wasn't the kind to deal with her own personal drama well.

She turned to Mike and Troy and gave them a tip of the head. Mike smiled, like he knew this was about as close to her saying "I love you" as she would ever get. She wasn't the mushy, gushy kind. "I'll be back later this evening. If you don't mind, would you fit AJ with a ball gag before I get back?" She laughed.

Troy snorted.

"I'm not getting that close to his mouth. After the show you just put on with him, he's likely to bite." Mike chuckled as he opened the door. "Your ranch truck carriage awaits, my lady."

Apparently, all her siblings were looking for a fight. At least she knew Mike was kidding. Regardless, this would be one hell of a long trip.

It had been a while since she had been behind the wheel of a truck, but it didn't take her long to get back into the swing of things. Thankfully, it wasn't a manual transmission or she would have never made it out of the driveway. She definitely wouldn't put it past AJ to stick her with one just to make her look stupid and keep the hierarchy between the two of them clear—he was boss and she was just one of his minions.

Maybe if she handled this meeting well, she could get out of the state by the end of the day.

In negotiations like this, it was always just about finding what was motivating the other party and then capitalizing on personal weaknesses. There was something brutal about it, but that savagery and the ability to go after blood was what had made her an effective lawyer in New York. The attorneys she fought against were sharks. Any scent of blood in the water, and not only would that shark feed upon her, but all the rest would as well.

So far, the best defense she had found against sharks was being the biggest one in the ocean.

She pulled up to the Bradshaw Law office and noticed a dark-colored rental truck driving by the parking lot. She didn't know why it caught her attention, but something about it made the hair on the back of her neck stand at attention. Though she was sure it was just her being back here that was making her paranoid, she'd long ago learned to respect her body's innate intuition. It probably had nothing to do with the truck, but she needed to pay attention.

First, she needed to get her act together. The fates always favored those prepared. No doubt, the Bradshaw Group had received the court filing notifying them she had taken on the case. Which meant they had been doing hours of research on her before she would ever set foot in that office. Aside from the little bit of research she had done this morning and what AJ had told her about the case, she'd not gotten much and hadn't had time to do the level of digging she required.

In the middle of chastising herself, her phone pinged with an email from Zoey, the leader of the STEALTH team. Clicking on it, she wondered if Zoey could read her mind. The email itself was simple: Thought you might need this. Good luck.

Attached was an encrypted dossier on the Bradshaw Law Group, Senator Dean Clark and the lawsuit they had filed against STEALTH.

Most of what Zoey had provided was low-level dirt, the kind anyone could find with a little bit of searching around on the internet. Kendra also knew the senator had jumped bail, missing a preliminary hearing on his trial. The rat was so confident of public approval, he obviously didn't feel the need to abide by the rules. Lucky for her family, this would make defending the defamation lawsuit a little easier.

Kendra needed more information. However, if she played her cards right, the other counselor would give her everything she needed. She'd like to hope she'd get lucky, but over the last few days, luck certainly hadn't seemed to be on her side.

Out of the corner of her eye, she noticed the same dark truck as before, pulling into the parking lot across the street from her. The area was a large industrial complex with a variety of office buildings, but once again she found herself prickling.

She reached down for her purse, making sure that her concealed carry was in place. With a job like hers, she always had enemies. Every so often, ghosts from her past cases would float into her life and haunt her. It didn't seem likely that here in the middle of nowhere Montana one of her ghosts would find her, but complacency was a lawyer's worst enemy.

She stepped out of her truck, keeping her hand on her concealed carry inside her purse, looking as though she was digging around for ChapStick or some other irrelevant item, but she made sure to keep her eyes on the truck.

She couldn't see through the truck's tinted windows, and the realization brought her no comfort. She picked up her pace and hurried into the building, not stopping until she was safely masked by a stairwell leading up. She stopped behind what limited cover there was and looked out. A man in a pair of jeans and a long-sleeve shirt had gotten out, but his back was to her and she couldn't see his face. More than likely, he was just another lawyer going to one of the offices across the street or something.

She was losing her mind.

Maybe this was what she got for trying to trust her instincts. Maybe this level of paranoia had simply been set in motion thanks to AJ and her family. It was really no wonder—every time she was around them, something bad happened.

She gave a long exhale and turned away from the man in the jeans. Something about him reminded her of the guy from the airplane yesterday.

Maybe if she had just talked to the guy on the plane, or made idle chitchat with anyone, she wouldn't be as paranoid as she was feeling right now. Maybe she had needed a single-serving friend to come to take the edge off. Oh well—now it was too late to worry about things like that. Now she needed to put her game face on.

I am the shark.

According to the sign in the main lobby, the Bradshaw Law Group took up the entirety of the third floor. They definitely weren't a fly-by-night firm. They were making enough in the small town to pay for an entire floor in an upscale neighborhood. Not only that, but it said something that Senator Dean Clark was one of their clients.

Having his case was a feather in any law firm's cap, and undoubtedly they would pull no punches and stop at nothing to make sure he got whatever it was that he wanted. In this case, he wanted to take her family down. No matter what, that wasn't going to happen.

She'd faced tougher adversaries in and out of the courtroom than this man hell-bent on revenge. According to what she'd been sent, he was upset after his wife had been murdered and his daughter had been kidnapped—according to the news, he had allegedly been behind the abductions in hopes of swaying public favor to help him get reelected. As such, he had a criminal case pending for his role in kidnapping, which had led to his wife's death and led to him losing custody of his daughter—permanently. Even with those marks against him, he had won his reelection campaign.

When STEALTH had been in control of the daughter's personal security, they'd had very limited control over the family's movements, only tasked with watching the girl outside the home and when and if the wife asked them to do so beyond that. According to the protocol and the contracts between STEALTH and the family, they had done everything by the book.

In fact, she would go so far as to say they had gone above and beyond the call of duty in helping search for the daughter and the wife as well as playing an integral role in bringing the killer down…and learning the senator himself was complicit in the kidnapping. It was the senator's malfeasance that had gotten him in this hot water. This lawsuit was nothing more than some trumped-up malarkey to make it appear STEALTH and her family were inept and had some sort of vendetta against the senator—though nothing could have been further from the truth.

Once again, the senator was just posturing. It seemed to be the only thing he was good at.

He probably wouldn't even be in the office today. If she was sitting on the opposite side of the courtroom on this one, she would've told him to stay as far away from this meeting as possible. It was all about grandstanding and playing head games.

As she reached the third floor, she straightened her blouse and ran a hand over her hair to make sure every strand was in place in her no-nonsense bun. The best defense was a strong offense.

Game on.

She allowed her heart rate to slow and her breath to steady before she reached down and opened the door to the firm's lobby. She was half surprised that an office this high-end didn't have a buzzer system, but then again, this was Montana.

The lobby was reminiscent of a doctor's office, complete with the obligatory white orchid in the corner and a water cooler by the door to the main offices. Behind a pane of glass was the secretary's desk, which was conspicuously vacant. The phone was ringing, and she could hear another from somewhere behind the wall of glass.

The hairs on her arms prickled. Something about the place—perhaps it was the eerie quiet on what should have been a busy day, or the fact that she had been on edge since seeing the truck outside, but something didn't feel right.

She sucked in a breath and made her way over to the secretary's area. Certainly, there had to be someone working. Maybe they had just stepped out for a drink or were running an errand for one of the attorneys. Just because her gut was roiling didn't mean anything. Kendra had been on high alert for two days now. If anything, she just needed to get through this meeting, get things handled for her family and hit the bricks.

Approaching the window, she caught a strange scent. At first, she couldn't quite put her finger on it thanks to the thick and heavy aroma of industrial cleaners they must have used in the office, but as she stopped at the marble ledge in front of the secretary's window, she recognized the smell—it was the acrid, metallic scent of gunpowder.

Her hand instinctively moved to her purse, and she wrapped her fingers around her Glock's grip.

This is wrong.

Something's happened here. Something bad.

She did a quick scan around the secretary's desk. At first appearance, she was alone. No signs of a struggle, and nothing was amiss. She didn't dare let her guard down, but she moved closer to the glass after checking the area for potential threats.

The secretary's tan leather chair was pulled out and pointing toward the back offices. On the seat was a long smear of blood. On the floor leading away from it was a series of droplets, as though whoever this blood belonged to had stood up and run, dripping, toward the back.

She moved closer to the glass, hoping to see where the person had gone. As she did, she spotted the bottom of a high-heeled shoe and a woman's ankle; the rest of the woman was out of sight behind a tall desk-like partition. The woman wasn't moving. Perhaps the woman had hit her head…had a bloody nose and passed out on the way to the bathroom.

Any number of things could have happened. This woman can't be dead.

For a moment, she dissociated and found herself wondering why she didn't also smell blood if what she was fearing was true—if the woman was dead, if she had been shot, there would be more blood. Right?

Was this some ploy the office had set up to put her off her game? Was the woman going to jump up like this was all some kind of sick joke?

The phone rang again, pulling her from her disjointed and nonsensical thoughts.

She knocked on the window. "Hello? Are you all right?" The question sounded stupid as she said it aloud. "Ma'am? Are you okay?" she asked again, her voice getting a bit higher with every passing syllable.

She grabbed the door leading to the back and was surprised to find it unlocked. It was heavy, and she opened it just far enough to slip through. It eased closed behind her, and its sluggishness made her wonder if it was the door or if time had slowed down. It could have been her mind's reaction to trauma—that moment in a fight for life or death in which a person's perception heightened and the imperceptible became a still-life reality.

Kendra moved behind the desk. A pool of blood snaked around and slipped under the edges like it was trying to escape. Moving toward the blood, she found the woman. Her face, or what would have been her face, was misshapen and oddly lopsided. The tilt of her head was like she was confused, as if the last thing she'd seen was so out of place that she cocked her head even in death.

The woman appeared to be in her late twenties, and she was looking straight ahead, her eyes dark and sightless as she stared into death's maw. Her hair was curled, and part of it had slipped down and rested in her open mouth. It wasn't until Kendra blinked and focused on the sight in front of her that she realized what was wrong with the woman's face—part of her head was missing where it was pressed into the gray industrial carpet.

Her phone pinged, and a woman's voice sounded from the device. "Nine-one-one, this is Erin. How can we be of assistance?"

In her many years working as a prosecutor, she'd heard many of these kinds of calls on recordings when they played them for judges and juries. Never had she assumed she would be the one who dialed the number—and strangely, she couldn't remember when she had even taken her phone out of her purse.

"Hello?" the dispatcher repeated. "How can I be of assistance?" she repeated, this time her tone taking on a slightly higher sound as though she could sense the fear in Kendra.

It wasn't the first time Kendra had been this close to a dead body, and as she stared at the dark blood, she picked out the little bits of lighter, fatty pink bits that she recognized as pieces of brain. Once, in a case like this, one in which her key witness had been present at the murder, the woman had described how she had screamed. In that case, she said the sound had come from deep in her lungs and from a place so dark within her that she hadn't even recognized that she was the one who had been making the sound.

She stared at the woman's fingernails. Acrylics. Bright pink with jewels and fresh glitter. No nail beds were exposed. She probably had just gotten them done.

"Do you need assistance?" the dispatcher asked, this time really pulling Kendra from her trauma-induced trance.

"Uh," she said, lifting the phone to her ear and falling back into attorney mode—unflappable in the face of the terrifying and unexpected. "Hello, my name is Kendra Spade, and I have just come upon a deceased woman."

She rattled off the building's address. Her voice was even and her affect was flat. If she was on the stand and sounded like this, no one would believe her because of her lack of emotion—especially in a situation in which she was standing in view of a murdered woman.

"Have you taken the woman's pulse?" the dispatcher asked.

She thought about telling the dispatcher that this woman couldn't possibly have a pulse, but instead she found herself on her knees. She pushed back a bit of the woman's dark hair, pulling it out of her mouth and gently moving it over her shoulder, and then pressed her fingers into the still-warm flesh of the woman's neck. "There's no pulse."

"Okay," the dispatcher said. "I have the emergency crews en route to your location. Stay on the phone with me."

She didn't want to stay on the phone. She didn't want to do anything but get to her feet and leave the office and head straight to the airport and catch the first plane to any place but here. Instead, she did as the dispatcher said. Getting up, she moved down the hallway, where she heard the continuing distinct ring of a cell phone coming from the corner office.

Her stomach clenched as she neared the ringing sound. No attorney she knew would ever let their phone ring for so long without answering it. She tried to convince herself it was nothing, that it was probably just some burner that was left behind and she wouldn't find another scene like that in the lobby. Yet her past and all the horrors she had experienced had her girding her loins. This was one of those times in her life she could pick apart later, but for now she needed to keep being strong and face the reality as it presented itself—gore and all.

The dispatcher was speaking to her, asking her something, but her voice was muffled and drowned out by the fear ringing in Kendra's ears. She held her phone, but her hands drooped to her sides as she nearly floated down the hall.

The office door was open, and she stepped inside. Hanging over the desk was a man. The tips of his brown loafers were grazing the papers on his desk. He was wearing dark blue dress pants and a white button-down shirt with a red satin tie. The brown nylon-looking rope was looped around his neck, his flesh bulging out slightly above the ligature. His skin was bruised and mottled, and his eyes were open and bloodshot— she recognized it as petechia, the breakage of the capillaries in the eye that was indicative of a strangling.

Did this attorney kill the secretary and then hang himself?

Her mind worked fast as she tried to make sense of the scene in front of her. There was no gun on the desk, but some of the man's papers had been pushed off and were scattered haphazardly across the floor. His computer was askew, leaning precariously over the edge, but it was close to his feet. Perhaps he had kicked it and the papers in his attempt to commit suicide? Or was this a murder as well?

Had the secretary seen something threatening—the

murderer? Gotten up to run to the attorney's office? Or maybe to lock the door, but she was shot before she had time to stop the assailant? But why would a murderer shoot her and then hang the attorney?

It didn't make sense.

And then she heard it, a strange keening wail. It was almost quiet at first, and then she dropped to her knees and her phone slipped from her hand to the ground. A feeling of sickness filled her. The sound echoing around the office…was coming from her.

A hand touched her shoulder, and the keen turned to the piercing sound of fear as she jerked away from the touch. Standing behind her was the man from the plane. Without even thinking, she pulled out her gun and pointed it up at his center mass. She stared at his face, looking to see if he meant help or harm, but in his eyes she found only questions.

Chapter Four

Trent hadn't meant to scare his mark. He hadn't even been trying to expose that he had been tracking and following her, but this wasn't a normal situation. Nothing about this bounty hunt had been what he considered average—not by a long way, but here they were.

"It's okay," he said, trying to console the woman and get her to calm down. "I'm not here to hurt you. I heard your screams. Are you hurt?" He glanced down to the phone on the ground beside her.

Her gun barrel didn't waver as she closed her mouth and stared at him. Her eyes were wide with fear, and he put his hands up in surrender. "Put the gun down. I'm not here to hurt you."

The barrel dipped slightly. "You're the man from the plane."

He nodded, but he could feel a faint heat rising in his cheeks. This was the first time he'd been made ahead of schedule, and he felt utterly exposed and at a loss. "Yes, but you don't need to worry. I'm not a threat." He reached down and picked up her phone, clicking it off when he saw 911 was still on the other end of the line.

The dispatcher didn't need any more information—they'd be here soon.

"If you're not a threat, then what in the hell are you doing taking my phone away?" She jabbed the gun at him like it was a knife, giving away her fear.

"You put the gun away and I'll give you your phone."

She slipped the gun back into her cross-body purse. "Phone, please."

"Here," he said, handing it back to her. "Is there anyone else here?" He glanced back out into the hallway. There hadn't been time to clear the rooms once he'd rushed in at the sound of her screams, and he was annoyed with his safety oversight, but it was what it was. At the very least, he had made it to her side without taking a bullet. He'd have to chalk that up as a win—even if everything else had gone a bit assways.

"I didn't hear anyone." Kendra looked around like she almost expected someone else to be standing in the corner of the room.

"I'll be right back. You stay here," he said, holding his hand up. "But you sure you're okay? I know this kind of thing can be a shock."

She furrowed her brow. "How would you know? Are you in law enforcement or something?"

Yeah, he wasn't about to answer that line of questions, at least not yet. "We can talk later. I just want to make sure that the killer, if there is one, isn't still here." He slipped out of the room before she could continue her interrogation.

He shouldn't have come in here, but he couldn't bear hearing her screams and doing nothing. She sounded terrified, just as he would have been if he had walked into a situation like this.

From what he'd seen of her, she wasn't the type to frighten easily or to back down. That made her shouts of horror all the more disturbing. He'd found himself wanting to keep her safe, to pull her out of that fear and get her back to her normal state of no-nonsense confidence.

He owed her nothing, no protections; if anything, he had been using her as a means to his end, trying to get to the senator who was suing her family and leaving his holding the bag for a huge bond.

Ever since he'd sat next to her on the plane and then watched her place last night, though, he'd felt an attraction—or at least a curiosity—growing. He wanted to know more about her.

It hadn't been his first stakeout and it wouldn't be his last, but he'd found himself thinking, often with a smile, of how she'd returned fire when her brother lit into her. He liked a woman who could stand her ground.

Yeah, that was it… Her reaction, her scream… It wasn't the woman he had come to know through his research and short time watching her. She had shown no signs of weakness, not a single one, and yet he had found her huddled on the floor after having fallen to her knees, vulnerable and afraid. That would have made the most hard-hearted man buckle.

As he moved down the hall, he carefully cleared the closest office. It was unoccupied and looked almost identical to the lawyer's office where the man was hanging; books filled the shelves around the desk and there was a series of diplomas adorning the walls. The place was simple, almost austere. He wondered if Kendra's office looked the same in New York City, or if she had pictures of family, something with a sunset, some little article that whispered of the light he sensed in her.

Gah. He was being far too sentimental. It was this scene, the dead bodies, the heightened tensions. Adrenaline spikes could mess with his head.

He focused on the here and now, making sure no threats were still in play.

As soon as they stepped out of this office, there was a high probability that they would give their statements to the police and then never see each other again. There wasn't a damned reason she would want to keep him around, especially after she found out what he had really been up to.

If she had done her research, she had probably already run across documents that could tie him to the senator, this office and, *hell*...probably even the dead bodies.

She hadn't seemed to recognize him as anything other than her seatmate on the airline, but she'd had no real reason to dig into the bond Dean Clark had received, which had allowed him to leave the jail while he was awaiting his trial. She was only here for a civil lawsuit, not for his criminal proceedings.

Maybe, though, it was potentially advantageous to her for him to get his hands on the senator as well.

Yeah, that's it... Make it about her.

That had worked with his ex whenever he had found himself in trouble. Given, the fix was only a Band-Aid as there were a medley of other issues between them.

He cleared the next office and the next. The floor was empty aside from them and the two deceased officemates.

When he came back to Kendra, he found her standing and looking over something in her cell phone. Her clothing and hair were perfectly in place, and her face had taken on the stony look that he had noticed her wearing the first time they had unofficially met.

"Clear?" she asked, clipped.

He nodded.

"So, are you going to tell me who you are before the police arrive?" She gave him the side-eye as she barely glanced up from her phone.

The simple look made him tense. Even when she was pressing for answers he didn't want to give, she was sexy…though intimidating.

He couldn't remember the last time anyone had intimidated him.

Yeah, he was definitely playing ball out of his league with this woman.

"Name's Trent."

"Trent." She said it like it had a bitter aftertaste. "And what were you doing here, Trent?"

"I could ask the same of you," he countered, but he was careful to keep his tone neutral and nonescalating. He wasn't trying to start a fight, only trying to take her sights off him.

"I was here for a meeting with…" She glanced up at the face of the man who was hanging from the bar between two ceiling tiles. "Well, I was here for a meeting with someone I assume was him."

Trent looked at the nameplate on the office's door. It read,

Brad Bradshaw, Esq.
Attorney-at-Law

He nearly chuckled. What parent would stick their kid with a name like that? It made him think of the old country song "A Boy Named Sue."

Maybe Brad's parents wanted him to grow up and be some overstuffed fraternity boy. If so, they had nailed it. Though he instantly felt bad for even thinking such a thing about the dead. He didn't know the man personally. He couldn't pass any sort of judgment against him. If anything, someone already had, and if he thought about the man now, it didn't really matter.

There were the sounds of police sirens and the screeching of tires on hot asphalt as the first responders arrived. More than likely, he'd know a few of the boys who were going to pound up the stairs leading to this place.

He looked out the window, careful not to disturb anything his potential friends would need to piece together the scene and make their case.

"What are you doing?" Kendra asked.

"Looks like you're going to be all right. I'll go catch up with the police. Let them know I've cleared the scene." He knew it wouldn't matter what in the hell he said to them, but he wasn't ready for them to completely blow his cover. Maybe he could still turn this entire situation—and his poor attempt to help Kendra—into something he could work with and keep both of them satisfied.

He moved out of the office and toward the lobby, but as he did, the first of the officers bounded in. "Hello? This is Officer Jared Dell of the Missoula City Police Department. Is anyone here?"

He cleared his throat as he walked out into the waiting area of the lobby with his hands in clear view. "Heya, Jared. How's it going?"

"Trent? What in the hell are you doing here?" Jared asked as his hand moved nearly imperceptibly away from his weapon.

At least he had saved himself from having two guns pointed at him within the hour.

"Looks like there are a couple of people down in the back."

"What about the woman who made the call? Is she still here?" Jared asked, looking around Trent and glancing at the door leading to the offices.

"Yeah, she's down in the last office at the end of the hall. There's a guy hanging back there."

"She have anything to do with these deaths, as far as you know?"

Trent shook his head. "I don't think so. I saw her walk in right ahead of me. She didn't have time."

Jared nodded and his hand moved away from his utility belt. Some of the immediacy seemed to seep from the officer's mannerisms.

"Anyone else you saw?" Jared asked.

He shook his head.

"Good, then I'm gonna ask for you to wait outside for me, and then I'm going to need to ask you some more questions."

Trent sighed. "Actually, I was hoping I could run back to the shop for a bit. If you need me, you know where I'll be. Cool?"

He was aware it wasn't protocol to have a potential witness leave without making a statement, but he also knew they were going to be here for the next few hours poring over the scene and the bodies.

"You see anything, anything at all?" Jared asked.

"Nope. Just found the woman who called it in on her knees screaming from the back office. Cleared the place. Then you showed up." He shrugged.

The door to the waiting room opened, and Jared's hand instinctively moved to his gun as Kendra walked out. She ran her hand over her hair. "If you don't mind, I would like to go with this man as well. I could use some air."

Jared shot Trent a look, like he suddenly was trying to figure out exactly who this woman was to him and why she would press for the same kind of good-ol'-boy treatment he had been requesting.

"I'd like you to stay, if you don't mind. Just for a few questions." Jared looked back at Kendra.

Trent stepped forward. He knew she needed a breather, even if she put on a strong face. "It's okay. She's with me. We're both available, not going anywhere. You know how to reach me."

Jared looked from one to the other. "Well, I suppose it would be all right. I have your contact information, and I will let the detective know. But you need to stay together, understood?"

Trent slipped her a sideways glance, and she gave him a tip of the head. "Looks like you have a deal."

They brushed by three more officers as they made their way down the stairs and out to the parking lot. It was full of cruisers, and the ambulance that was just pulling up to the building was forced to park on the road. Her ranch truck was boxed in, but he didn't say anything. Not only would they be spending what was likely the rest of the day together, she was also going to have to ride around with him—that was until she lost it on him and got a taxi.

This was going to be one hell of a day. It already was one.

"Are we both going to pretend like you aren't going to have to be my chauffeur?" she asked, a smile on her face.

"I didn't want…" He paused, not quite sure what to say that wouldn't make him look foolish.

"We promised the good deputy that we would stick together until we chatted with the detectives. I'm a woman of my word. And you know as well as I do that my truck isn't going anywhere." She shrugged. "Can't say I'm too upset about it. I'm not much one for driving."

It came as a bit of a surprise that she, this woman who so clearly loved to be in control, would be willing to give up the keys and be shuttled around. Maybe he had misjudged her.

"Besides, I need to catch up on a little work." She lifted her phone.

"No rest for the weary," he said, giving her a slight nod as he motioned toward his pickup.

"Your friend back there seemed to know exactly who you were and where we are going. I'd be happy to be brought up to speed." She sent him a warm smile that he was sure had opened many a door.

If he told her the truth now, there would be no going back. Everything would hinge on her being able to accept him and his motives. If she didn't, game over.

He walked to his pickup and opened the passenger side door for her, but instead of getting in, she merely looked at him and waited for his answer.

Here goes nothing.

"I work over at Lockwood Bonds. I'm a bondsman and the occasional bounty hunter," he said, fearing to embellish or expound. He was who he was, and what would come would come.

"Oh?" She cocked her head as she stared at him, their eyes locking. "And what did you say your last name was, Trent?"

This woman was damned smart and definitely someone he was not going to outmaneuver. "Lockwood, ma'am."

"I see." She put her hand on the top of the hood and tapped her nails on its surface with a *clickety-click-thump* sound.

Everything he had seen about this woman had the power to bring her enemies and her friends to their knees.

Without another word, she got in and buckled up.

He closed the door behind her and then let out a long sigh as he strode to the driver's side. Even in his relief, he couldn't help the nagging feeling that he very well could have been heading to the firing squad.

They were quiet as he got in and made his way onto the main road. He was going to have a hard time trying to explain his sudden appearance in the shop, his former mark's bait in tow, to his brother.

"You hungry? Want to get some food before we have to be on lockdown at the shop? I'm sure the detective won't come to see us until this evening at the earliest. This kind of thing, in a small town, tends to take up a lot of time and bandwidth for the police department."

She was looking down at her phone, and he ventured a glance at what she was doing. From what he could tell before she tipped the screen away from him, she was sending emails.

"So, you're from New York?" he asked.

"You know the answer to that. You've been following me for the last few days." She didn't say it like it was a question or an accusation, just a simple observance.

He swallowed back the guilt rising in his throat. There was no way she could have noticed him outside her cabin or at the ranch.

Which made him wonder…if she had known he was following her, how had she not known who he was? Was this just her attempt to fish information out of him and get him to admit something she had no proof of?

"Myself, I'm not much of a New York man. Though your food is something." He sent her a smile, but instead of disarming her, he could sense her tightening up.

"If you don't mind, I'm not one who particularly enjoys small talk. Especially when there are larger issues at hand," she countered, her voice smooth and practiced.

"You're a tough cookie, you know that?" He tried to avoid the jab of her words.

She chuckled lightly as she tapped on her phone. "Not the first time I've heard that one, but thank you for the compliment."

He hadn't meant it as a compliment or a criticism, just as a statement. She was who she was, but damned if he didn't find her confidence and no-nonsense attitude intriguing.

She hadn't answered him about lunch, so instead of asking again, he turned and headed toward his favorite haunt—a little dive bar with cheap beer and prime rib available all day. If he was going to have to do this dance, he was at least going to get his favorite meal in his belly.

The Wolf Lodge was a dive bar in every sense of the word. It had been around longer than he'd been alive. The building listed like most of its patrons upon their leaving. In college, he'd spent more than a few nights in this place with his buddies and his brother. Most of his friends had moved and a couple had passed away—one to a car accident and another to cancer. The thought made him feel old, even though he was only in his early thirties.

It was tough, losing the ones in his life who'd been a part of his growing up. Justin, the friend who'd died in a car accident, had always wanted to be a cop. He would have loved seeing where Trent had gone with his life, and especially all the guns he got to train with and handle.

He parked to the left of the log building's entrance. Kendra finally really looked up from her phone and seemed to be trying to make sense of where they were. She moved to open her door but then dropped her hand to the leg of her suit pants and paused. "Hey, do you mind if we run somewhere first? Before we eat?"

"What do you mean?" He frowned at her.

"There is no way I'm walking into a place like that wearing this," she said, motioning at her bloody clothes. "You know as well as I do that I would stick out even without the blood. Gossip would pick up, and any anonymity I was hoping for would disappear. I'm sure that my family wants me to fly below the radar given what they do."

"I can run you home, if you like." He was careful to avoid the subject of the ranch.

She shook her head. "No, the last thing I want is to go back there."

It was strange, the feeling in his gut when she finally opened up to him. Her admission and little bit of insight made the ambiguity and guilt build within him, but at the very least she must have bought his little white lie—or rather, his avoidance of the truth.

"Where do you need me to take you? There's a mall near the center of town. It doesn't have much by way of high-end brands, but you might find something to your taste."

She chuckled, and the sound made some of his nerves dissipate. Maybe they could be friends after all.

"Why don't you run me to the ranch supply store? They have clothes, right?" She tapped on her phone.

"Yeah, but the fact you are using your phone to look up what they have kind of goes against the spirit of the place," he teased.

"Oh?" She gave him the raise of a brow. "Why would you say that? People don't use the internet here?"

He gave a full, real laugh at the absurdity.

When she smiled, for a split second, he forgot about the horrors that had brought them together and to this moment. She was breathtaking when her face lit up; it was like he could feel the warmth radiate from her when she was happy. Or maybe he had been in the dark so long that being around this woman just did that to him.

Now that she seemed to have recovered her equilibrium, he was losing his. They were two strangers bound together by a horrible tragedy. He wished all they'd just witnessed could go away. He yearned for their respective cases to disappear, too. He wanted to just drive off with her by his side and start the day over—his *life* over. Would she want the same thing?

He shook that thought from his mind.

It wasn't far to the store, where the parking lot was full of ranch trucks, Subarus, prebuilt chicken coops and water troughs for livestock. As they walked inside, they were met with the familiar scent of industrial cleaners, wood chips and horse feed. He'd always loved that aroma; it was a heady mix of everything that was Montana.

As she walked in, he glanced over at her to see if she took in the scent in the same way or if she cringed and wrinkled her nose at the not entirely pleasant odor. Instead, she tilted her head back and closed her eyes, unintentionally inhaling the place as naturally as he had. She really was full of endearing surprises.

"The women's section is over here," he said, motioning to the left.

"Are there chicks here, too?" she asked, an edge of childlike excitement suddenly in her voice.

"It's a little late in the year, but we can walk back and take a peek if you like," he said with a smile. He nearly extended his hand so he could lead her, but he resisted the urge and instead motioned toward the right.

"You've spent a lot of hours in here, I see." She smiled like there was something about the idea she liked.

"Yeah, I grew up on a cattle ranch just east of here in Hall. Ranch supply stores were my mall as a kid."

"Hall?"

"Little town, a coach stop near Drummond. Don't feel bad that you haven't heard of it. Most people haven't."

As they neared the area with live animals, the smell of wood chips intensified. On his left, he spotted large areas glassed in for bunnies.

"So, you are a real-life cowboy who became a bondsman?"

"Odd life path, ya know," he said, though he was sure hers was nothing like his own. She was probably the kind of woman who grew up knowing whom she wanted to be and what she wanted to accomplish with her life and then followed the straightest and most efficient Ivy League path to get there.

"I know a thing or two about those. I've always found as soon as I think I have the right answers, something else comes up—both professionally and privately."

The way her shoulders rose as she spoke made him wonder exactly what had happened in her private life that had made her instinctively move to protect herself. As she seemed to be opening up to him naturally, he didn't push it and instead pocketed the question for another time. For now, all he wanted was for her to feel free to be herself—unjudged and unchecked by him.

Watching her move toward the women's section, he was further reminded how she could change her clothes and she could love what he loved, but she would never really fit in here. All they could ever be was two strangers with a shared target.

Chapter Five

Though she was aware she was only putting off dealing with what she had seen at the Bradshaw offices by agreeing to stay with Trent, Kendra couldn't help but admit she liked the man—liked how he'd given her room and respect. For a brief moment, he had been the oasis in the desert, giving her a respite from the ravages of her life and the reality in which they found themselves.

AJ popped up in her text messages again. Of course, she'd had to let him know what had happened, and of course he wasn't happy about it. He'd even gone so far as to ask her if she'd had anything to do with the deaths in veiled language—but not veiled enough if it were used in a court of law. But she wasn't like the rest of the family—immune, by and large, to death.

If she clicked on his text message, it wouldn't change what had occurred, and right now she had just as many questions as AJ likely did and even fewer answers. He could wait. She wasn't one of his employees he could boss around.

Another text popped up from him.

How did her brothers and sister put up with his constant hounding? They all seemed to get along pretty well, which meant that it was likely only her that had a problem with his authority—or lack thereof. One more reason to hang out with Trent now—so she wouldn't have to face her family after this morning's fiasco.

Maybe AJ was just harder to deal with because he was aware he held no real power over her. Regardless, she needed to catch her breath for a moment before she could give him the attention that he clearly so desperately required.

"You look like you got bad news," Trent said as she got into his car wearing her brand-new clothes and a brown leather pair of Justin boots.

"That easy to tell? I always thought I had a pretty good poker face," she said, covering the truth of her words with a dismissive chuckle.

"I just happen to know the face of disappointment fairly well, given my line of work." He started the car and they hit the road.

She wasn't sure if they were going back to get food or not, but she was hoping for something and so was her stomach, which was rumbling so loudly she wondered if Trent could actually hear it.

"I'm familiar with bounties, obviously, but I can't say I've ever actually met a bounty hunter. What is it that you do...you know, when you are hunting for people who owe your company money?"

He seemed to jerk slightly at her question, and there was something about his reaction that made her suspicions rise. She had tested him before, feeling him out to see if he had been tracking her, but he'd seemed innocent. Had she been wrong?

"Hunting may mean a different thing here than it does in the city. Here it means you are hell-bent on killing something. I'm a lot of things, but a killer isn't one of them."

"I didn't mean any offense, really. My apologies," she said, reaching over and gently placing her fingers on his arm. His arm was thick with muscles, and they flexed under her fingers, feeling like stone. *Damn, he is hot.*

"Don't worry, it takes a lot more than asking about my job to offend me." He sent her a gentle smile, absolving her of any guilt. "As far as my methods, I don't know about in New York, but here we are law enforcement officers and granted the same privileges—with a lot less oversight."

"Did you want to be a police officer?" As she asked the question, she realized he might take it as an admonishment of his profession, as though it was less than, but she was hopeful he would see her intention for what it was—curiosity.

He shook his head. "Nah. If I could start my life all over again, I think I'd be a country music singer. I always thought I sounded a little like Chris LeDoux." He hummed a chorus she vaguely recognized, but she couldn't say she was familiar with country music. For the first time, she wished she was.

She hated this feeling of constantly being a square peg in a round hole and not really fitting in anywhere she went. Try as she might to chameleon her way through every situation, there were times that no amount of changing her clothes could make her quite fit. She picked off a piece of lint that had come from her new blue jeans.

"You look good…*real* good, actually. You don't have a thing to feel uncomfortable about."

There he went reading her again. He definitely was a member of the law enforcement brethren. It raised the question of how rigidly he adhered to the stereotype. From what she had seen of him so far, he seemed like he colored outside the lines and was comfortable with it—but the same could be said of many agents, operatives and officers.

"Do you always do that?" she asked, smiling.

"What is *that*, exactly?"

"Trying to make grown women blush," she teased, trying to take the attention off her visible discomfort.

"Ha! Do you think that's what I'm up to?" He lifted a brow. "I can't say that I think myself capable of making you blush. I bet you've been around better-looking men than me, a cowboy breathing down middle age's neck."

She stared at the little lines that were starting at the corners of his brown eyes. He glanced over at her, catching her gazing at him. He threw his head back in one of the sexiest laughs she had ever just seen. "You see it, don't you?"

She wanted to tell him "not at all," which was absolutely the truth. He was incredibly handsome, but she kept her mouth closed. If she said something like that, she was experienced enough to know it would send them down an ill-advised path of flirting, which would lead to thinking about kissing, then really kissing and then all the things that came after kissing and ended with her getting back on a plane and wishing she hadn't compromised her emotions. As much as she was attracted to the man beside her, and was growing to like him, she loved herself more. This time her need for self-protection outweighed the needs of her belly.

She was wound up tight after the morning's tragedy, and she knew herself well enough to realize it was better to tamp down the high energy coursing through her now instead of letting it run in the wrong direction.

"All I see is a man who is working to do his job to the best of his abilities."

His smile disappeared, and she was reminded that once again she was saying all the wrong things if she wanted to keep this man as just a friend.

The last man who had hit on her had been on the other side of a conference table during a plea deal negotiation. He was the defendant and on trial for first-degree murder after shooting two people in a twenty-four-hour convenience store.

Maybe that was why she was a little jaded when it came to accepting compliments or come-ons, even gentle ones.

It seemed more than possible that her job had set her up for a lifetime of failed relationships. When she had found herself in one, what few there were, she had a way of picking men who needed her to save them—one from his mother and the next from whiskey. She was great at her job, but when it came to being a crutch for needy men, she was less than capable. For once, she would have liked to be with a man who could bring as much determination and intelligence to the table as she did, or at least one who could stand on his own two feet and not only take care of himself but perhaps protect her as well.

"I'm glad you think I'm doing a good job," Trent said, an apologetic look in his eyes as he glanced at her.

"Were you following me from New York? Tracking me?" she countered.

He didn't meet her gaze. It was fine; he didn't have to say anything his body hadn't already—even if she had avoided acknowledging it fully right up until this moment.

She should have followed her gut from the very first moment she had seen this man. Intuition—especially hers, which had been shaped by years of manipulations in the courtroom—was something she relied on, and yet she had tried to ignore it, to this man's benefit. Why? Why had she allowed her emotions to come into play when she should have been running purely on logic and the information that had been presented to her?

This was what happened when she attempted to trust another human being—and not just another human, but a man. Men always let her down. She pressed her fingers to the puckered bullet scar beneath her clavicle. The last time she had trusted a man, he had pulled the trigger and it had nearly cost her life.

Single, all she depended on was herself, and there was less of a chance of being disappointed or hurt. Plus, she was happy enough alone. She liked her private time, her space and her routines.

She needed to focus on the job at hand—protecting her family. They were more important than anything, and should the senator continue his lawsuit—which no doubt he would, albeit with a new counselor—she was the only one with the power to stop him in his legal tracks.

"It wasn't personal." He finally broke the silence.

She simply nodded. They were at an impasse—the best way she could handle the lawsuit was to get the senator alone and convince him it was against his best interest to pursue any further legal action…but that kind of persuading often required a strong arm, one she was certain Trent could provide.

"What is in it for you if you get your hands on the senator?" she asked.

"He owes my family a lot of money—the bond and interest. The kind of money where, if he doesn't return it, it's gonna run our business into the ground." He ran his hand over his face, making her wonder about everything he wasn't telling her.

She filed away the info he'd given her. A bail jumper wasn't exactly an upstanding citizen, and that could help her family in the suit.

"How long you guys been in business?" she asked.

"About five years. Before that it was my dad's business." There was a strain in his voice that told her of family secrets.

Regardless of what those secrets were, he definitely had skin in this game and just as much to lose as she and her family did. For her family, however, it wasn't just about the money—it was also their reputation at stake. They already had a black eye professionally thanks to the senator's family. If they lost the lawsuit, their business was as good as gone. And, no doubt, she would be the family's whipping girl.

"Why do you think someone would want Bradshaw dead?" Kendra asked.

"I hate to say it…" he started, pulling into the lot and parking the car in front of the restaurant. "But the only people I know who could have anything to really gain from his death are you and your family."

Chapter Six

Aside from ordering their lunch, Trent and Kendra had barely spoken. She had been careful to avoid eye contact with him, like she was thinking about all the reasons she hated him and the comment he had made about her family having reason to kill…even if he had a point.

If that wasn't enough, the two-bit bar was clearly so far outside her comfort zone that it might as well have been on Mars. If they were going to have a real conversation, though, maybe making her uncomfortable was to his advantage. She seemed like the kind of woman who commanded every room she entered, but if he was going to get any real answers from her and they were actually going to work together, the only way forward was to know where they both stood—which meant complete honesty.

Kendra was staring off in the direction of the elk shoulder mount hanging over the bar. The massive bull was staring off in the ethereal distance, just like the woman looking in his direction.

"I don't think my brothers would've sent me to that meeting if they had anything to do with that murder." Kendra finally looked back at him, and it surprised him that she must have been thinking about his opinion for this long. In fact, he would've guessed she was looking for an escape rather than for answers.

"But you see where I was coming from, that your family are the ones that have the most to gain by taking out the senator's legal team."

Kendra nodded. "Oh, definitely. But as much as my family and I butt heads, they wouldn't have sent me in there to be the one to discover the murders if they had been behind them. They are pretty protective." She sighed. "That is to say, if this wasn't just a simple murder-suicide. Who the hell knows—maybe the attorney had a breaking point with his secretary? Maybe they were having an affair and there had been a fight. Any number of scenarios could've played out back at that office."

She was grasping for straws, anything that had him looking in another direction than her family. Yet he wasn't the one she needed to worry about. Though he worked with law enforcement, he didn't need to seek justice. Not in the same way as an officer. If anything, if it came out that she or her family was involved, he would have to make damned sure to distance himself from the mess and the eventual fallout.

"I hope your family didn't have anything to do with this. If they did, we're both going to be in more trouble than even we can handle."

"I'm aware—my career hangs on them not screwing me over." She waved at the bartender and motioned for a Bud Light. The man gave her a stiff nod. "What makes you think they'd do something like that? Did someone say something?"

"No—" he shook his head "—I just have found that sometimes it is the ones right under our noses who wish us the most harm." She shifted uncomfortably in her chair, making him wish he hadn't said anything. "Have you always lived in New York?"

She shook her head. "I used to have a more...*active role* in the family business." Her fingers fluttered over a spot near her neck. The bartender walked over and set a bottle of Bud Light in front of her, but he stood there for just a second too long. She frowned and looked up at him. "Thanks, you can put it on our tab."

The man stared at her for a second longer, and his gaze drifted down to her chest before he seemed to comprehend her words. "You got it, doll. Don't be afraid to let me know if y'all need anything else."

She cringed as the man called her *doll*.

Sensing her discomfort, he glared at the bartender. "Hey, man, thanks for the drink, but you need to keep your eyes to yourself," Trent said, waving the guy away.

A faint blush rose in her cheeks as the burly bartender spun around and grumbled something under his breath.

"Sorry about that. I don't think the men around here are used to...well, *women like you*." He cringed at the way his words sounded, but they were the best he could come up with on the spot.

Great, now we're both uncomfortable.

She let out a small laugh, catching him even more off guard. "That's not it. Thank you for...well... Was that a compliment—'women like me'?"

Now he was the one blushing. "You know it was."

She chuckled as she took a sip of the beer and set it

back down. "I just… It's been a long time since any-body's called me anything other than a coldhearted… woman."

He found that hard to believe. "You and me both, sister. Though I guess I've never been called a woman. Way I see it, would be a compliment if I was. Women are a hell of a lot tougher and more resilient than men."

She threw her head back as she laughed. "Now I know you're just trying to get on my good side." She took a long drink of beer, smiling as she did.

"Come now, why would you say that?" It was nice seeing her start to finally relax around him and moving past some of the events of the day and his idiocy.

"You have to know that I'm all about strong women. And you're just using that to get in my good graces. Regardless, well played, sir." She tipped the beer bottle in his direction in respect.

He could've guessed. He liked that about her. "I do like strong-willed women. My mother was one. My grandmother, her mother, was called the battle-ax, but obviously not by me—I wasn't that stupid." He laughed, recalling his German grandmother whose footfalls were as commanding as her presence. There had been nothing delicate about the woman, especially when she started yelling at his grandfather in their na-tive tongue.

"If she was anything like the women in my family, if you had called her anything other than *ma'am*, you wouldn't be sitting here with me now." Kendra sent him an endearing smile. "I don't understand why some men and women need to condemn any female who can conduct herself well in a fight. Not all women were put on this earth to be dependent on others for their own emotional or physical well-being."

He nodded. "None of the women in my life could be called codependent. If anything, for all the ups and downs, our matriarchs were the ones who kept our family from falling apart. My grandmother's the reason my brother and I run the business together like we do." He felt them edging toward a conversation he wasn't sure he was ready to have about how little he and his brother saw eye to eye. Even though he had wanted to have open communication with Kendra, it was far easier when the pressure was on her to tell him her secrets rather than him exposing his own. Maybe it was the drama of the morning that had him opening up. Or maybe it was just her. "But what about your family? You used to work with them?"

She grew rigid. "I used to be a contractor, but I lost my taste for it after I took a round that I should have known was coming. I'll never go back." She touched that spot below her clavicle and then took a sip of her beer. "I prefer standing in a courtroom. So here I am, once again working for my family even though I promised myself I would never be back in the fold."

He could see she knew how to handle herself; when she'd had her gun on him, that had been more than obvious. This woman really was unique. She'd had one hell of a life.

"I won't ask what made you get out of the game, but I understand the conditions out there. I looked into going into contracting a few years out of school, and I couldn't have done the work. I have a lot of respect for what your family does, though."

She took a long drink of her beer. "My family is

tougher than the rest, that's for sure. While we have all done our duty, none of us are cold-blooded killers. We aren't hit men."

He nodded, though he was surprised she would admit he could have been right about them. "I didn't want to offend you earlier, but if it walks like a duck and talks like a duck…" He shrugged. "That being said, it doesn't make any sense for them to send you into a hornet's nest if they are behind this. That is, unless they wanted to teach you some kind of lesson or pin this thing on you…"

She shook her head violently. "My siblings are huge pains in the ass, and we don't get along all the time, but when push comes to shove, they will always have my back. We were raised to be a cohesive unit, even in adversity. Actually, in adversity more than any other time." There was a look on her face that he couldn't quite read, but if he had to guess, it appeared to be some kind of guilt.

He glanced away from her as the server sauntered over, carrying a tray of food. She lowered it on her arm, and as she did, Trent caught a whiff of the prime rib. It smelled like rosemary and cracked pepper, and it made his mouth water. After the waitress got them settled and disappeared, Kendra finally looked back at him. "Are you okay? You've gotten quiet."

He forced himself to smile, hoping to disarm her. "I'm fine," he said, jabbing his fork into the steak and slicing off a bite. "You try your steak yet?"

"Not yet." She looked down at the slab of meat on her plate. It was one degree away from having hooves and mooing, and he wasn't sure, based on her expression, if she appreciated the rareness or not.

"We can send it back," he offered, looking past her to where the waitress had gone, but she was nowhere to be seen. Instead, there was a big dude with a T-shirt with the local railroad workers' union logo emblazoned on its front standing a few feet behind Kendra and looking over her shoulder and down her shirt.

"Hey, man, if you're hungry, you need to order your own steak. That one is the lady's." He could feel his lip curl with disgust. Kendra turned around, glaring at the man.

The dude tore his gaze off Kendra's breasts just long enough to sneer at him, then he looked back at her. "You know you can do better," the railroad guy said with a smirk. "This guy—" he pointed at Trent "—couldn't punch his way out of a paper bag. You deserve a guy who can kick some ass." With that, he placed a dirty paw on her shoulder in a gesture both possessive and menacing, as if he were daring either of them to stop his advances. Trent saw her wince as the man squeezed the spot she'd rubbed earlier.

Kendra slowly turned back to him, pulled her napkin off her lap and set it upon the table. There was a thin smile on her lips as she looked at Trent. He had the sense she was up to something, and he shook his head, but her smile only widened as she stood up. "What did you say your name was?" she asked, her voice as smooth as silk as she faced the man.

"Why? You wanna scream it later?" the guy countered.

"No," she said with a laugh. "I just like to know the names of the guys whose asses *I* kick." She closed the gap with the man.

Before Trent even had the chance to make sense

of what she was saying, the base of Kendra's hand connected squarely with the man's nose. There was a sickening crunch as it snapped under her palm thrust.

Trent jumped to his feet, and the metal bar chair he'd been sitting on dropped to the ground behind him with a metallic *clunk*. He rushed toward her as the man looked in Kendra's direction, but there was a disconnect between the man's eyes and his movements. The guy looked like he was trying to raise his fist to strike her. Without dropping her elbow or giving away her punch, Kendra struck the guy again.

The man crumpled at her feet in a heap of blood and blubber.

"Holy crap. Kendra. Damn," Trent said, shocked at her quick response. He knew women could be vicious and take a man down, but he'd never seen a woman do it so quickly or effectively in anything but movies.

"Who's screaming now?" she said to the man, her voice soft as molten chocolate but cold as steel. "Touch me again, and I'll really make you howl."

"What in the hell is going on?" The bartender charged out from behind the bar in their direction.

The two other men that had been with the railroad worker started to move toward Trent. The fight was going to be on, and part of him loved the idea. The last time he'd taken somebody down—when he wasn't on the job—was in college.

Kendra reached into her purse and threw some money on the table. She grabbed Trent's hand and pulled him toward the door. "Let's get out of here."

Part of him yearned for the fight, to feel the sting of the punch as he landed a hammer fist. The guy's friends were moving toward him, but the bartender swerved into their path, cutting them off as he made his way toward the door behind Kendra. They were bigger than him, but with a few leg strikes he could even the playing field.

As they made it outside, she strode toward his car, unrushed, as if she knew the toughs inside the bar wouldn't follow. "Keys. I'm driving."

There wasn't a chance in hell he would argue. This woman was one major badass.

Chapter Seven

He reached in his pocket and threw the keys in her direction as she rushed to the driver's side. They piled into the car, and there was a spray of gravel as she charged out of the parking lot.

"You told me you were a contractor, but I guess... Well, I thought I would have to save you."

"It's okay." She reached over and took his hands. "Just take a breath. We are out of there."

"No thanks to me. Holy crap. Seriously..."

She shot him a lopsided smile. "I told you I came from the family business. I just didn't tell you about my Muay Thai days."

"Just when I thought you couldn't get any cooler." The words were out of his mouth and flopping around the car like a dying fish before he had a chance to reel them back.

His eyes widened as he tried to think of a way to cover his misstep. "I mean..." he continued, fumbling his words, "you are just so much more than I thought you'd be when I first saw you."

She cleared her throat and let go of him. Opening and closing her fist, she glanced down at her knuckles.

They were starting to swell, and the middle two were turning black and blue.

"I'm rusty." She raised her hand in the air so he could get a better view, but he had no doubt it was also so she could divert the focus from his moronic move of telling her exactly what he thought about her.

"Why do you say that?"

She wiggled her fingers then dropped her hand back to the steering wheel. "If I'd hit him properly, the bruising would be even over all my knuckles instead of just the two. I'm surprised I even made him drop. Only thing I had going for me was the fact I caught him off guard."

He nodded. "It's fair to say you caught us all off our game."

"In my world, and doing what I do, it pays to know how to drop an enemy without them ever even seeing the strike." She smiled. "Now, where's your shop?"

He pointed for her to turn left and head down Broadway toward downtown and the courthouse. "How long have you been doing martial arts?"

She smiled again. "Long enough to know my way around a set of elbows." She glanced over at him. "About the bond. You said you were worried about getting your family's investment back… Wouldn't there have been some sort of collateral that he offered up, or someone who signed as an indemnitor?"

"Yeah," he said, relieved. Work was a safe subject to turn to. Though he knew he shouldn't feel inept in not having come to her rescue, there was still a twinge of something in his gut—he had wanted to save her.

She slowed the truck down. "I can tell something is wrong."

He chuckled, embarrassed that she could so easily read him. "I was just… Well, I should be your protector. I know it's stupid. You know…a *typical* guy kind of instinct."

She gave him a soft smile. "Not stupid, and I appreciate your desire to help. Someday, I may need it." She tapped her fingers on the steering wheel. "The truth is, I've had to learn to be my own protector. I don't know any other way to be. I've gone through so many years of heartache and constant attacks. I've had to fight for every opinion I have and what is left of my personal life and my identity."

He hadn't thought about that, but it made sense. Here was a woman people loved to hate. Even other attorneys probably hated her and worked to undermine her—and maybe they weren't the harshest of her critics. As a prosecutor, she probably had a lot of enemies.

"I'm not judging you," he said, suddenly wishing he was anywhere but stuck in this car with her. He had a feeling anything he said right now would be wrong, and all he really wanted to do was make her happy and get out of this moment somewhat unscathed.

"Yes, you are judging, and that's okay. It's what humans do," she said, an edge to her voice. "You know what really pisses me off, though? It's when someone calls me *too much*." She gripped the wheel tight. "Why is it wrong for a woman to be powerful, to be smart? I shouldn't have to hide that to make people—especially men—more comfortable because they think I'm *too much*."

He could tell where this was going, and he wished he held the answers she needed to hear. "You're not too much for the people who want and need you in their lives."

She chuffed. "No need for flattery. No one wants me unless they can use me. Do you know how tiring that can be? Even now, coming here… I was forced into it. Forced to act for a man who *needed* me."

He nodded, afraid to say anything.

"And here you are—you need me to be on your side…and on your team for this case. But you know what? What if I want to just be on my own personal team, the Kendra team, a one-woman outfit? I just want to get the answers and get back to *my* life."

He reached for the door handle and looked out the window. If he jumped right now and tucked and rolled, they were going slowly enough that he could probably survive the landing.

"Just as an example, I'm sure that I'm intimidating you right now," she said, gesturing at him and his hand clamped around the door handle. "As much as I feel bad about it, why should I?"

"Mmm-hmm," he said, trying to validate her feelings while also not being drawn into her personal problems. He didn't know, nor could he possibly understand, how she was feeling. "I think you are incredible, just as you are. Sure, I bet there are people who are intimidated by you, but why should you care?"

She studied him. "Why do you say that?"

He appreciated that she was coming to him for validation even though she was clearly fighting against herself and struggling with her need for affirmation.

"There will always be people who don't like you, or me. It's just part of being human. There isn't anything wrong with people not liking you—and I think you know that and at a logical level are totally okay with it. Yet I think you are struggling with the emotional toll it is taking on you. You're not alone in your struggle."

"Thanks. What do I owe you for this session?" she joked, then turned serious. "Do you feel the same way—like you are never enough?" She pulled into the parking spot directly in front of the bond shop, parallel parking in a series of jarring motions back and forth.

He laughed. "I just know that no matter what, I'll never please some people. And even though I know that, I still find myself trying to do more—satisfy everyone. But truthfully, what bothers me more is the fact that I'm afraid. I hate being *afraid.*"

She put the car in Park and turned toward him. "You don't have to lie to me to try and win favor. I know you're strong. You're tough. You aren't scared of anything. If you were, there's no way you would travel around the country hunting down criminals—and people like me." She scowled at him.

He could feel her question resting in the air.

"To be clear, I wasn't hunting you. Just following you to my objective."

"Semantics." She waved off the conversation, like it was a hornet threatening to sting them both. "About the indemnitor?"

"You mean the bond cosigner?"

She nodded. "Or was there collateral?"

Of course, she would bring it all back to the task at hand. That was easier than the emotional conversation they'd been having. He got that. "Because of the death of Senator Clark's wife, and her not having a will, most of her assets—including their home—were sent to probate. As such, we had to have a cosigner on the bond in that moment, a woman named Marla Thomas."

"And you've looked into her?" Kendra asked.

He nodded. "My brother Tripp was the one who met her when she came in to sign the papers, but he hasn't said much. He should have done his legwork and done a full-blown background on her, but I've not seen it. Now she's pretty much in the wind. I haven't been able to pull a damned thing about her."

"There has to be something," she said.

"I hear you, but I can only do so much. Besides, I'd rather get my hands on the senator—he's the real piece of work. Maybe the woman just wised up about the guy and hit the road."

"Do you think the senator had a relationship with her, one he could leverage? Maybe he could manipulate her into signing for him because he intended on skipping and slapping her with the debt?" She turned off the engine and put the truck keys in her purse.

He shrugged. "He is a smart man. If he wasn't, he wouldn't have made it as far as he did."

"And you know you guys got worked by him, right?" She gave him a sly smile.

"Oh, for sure. I think that is what bothers my brother the most." He nudged his chin in the direction of the shop. "My brother is on my ass about all this. He straight up wants me to be running down leads every second of the day. You're warned that he may be a real ass when we get in there."

"I'm used to jackasses, in case you didn't notice." She chuckled as they stepped out of the truck and made their way onto the sidewalk.

He went to her side, and she looked over her shoulder at the large, barred window of Lockwood Bonds. There was a big red awning over the window, which helped to keep the hot midsummer sun out of the shop, and it matched the red-and-gold stenciling on the windows. It definitely carried the German feel that had always been a cornerstone of their family's identity. The only thing missing that would have made it the perfect epitome of his family was a pint of beer and an image of broken dreams. Though maybe that was exactly what their entire shop was…broken dreams, which turned into even more broken lives, owners included.

"What's your brother's name again?" Kendra asked, stopping beside the door so he could open it for her.

"Tripp. He's a good guy, I swear, but he is just a—" He paused and gave her a guilty look.

"A ballbuster?" she said, finishing his sentence with a laugh.

He nodded.

"Then he and I should get along swimmingly."

If he agreed, he'd be an ass, but if he disagreed, he was admitting that he didn't think they'd get along. He hated these kinds of situations. "He is definitely one of those people folks either love or hate. Needless to say, he's an acquired taste, but he is one hell of a businessman. If anything, compared to him I might be the black sheep when it comes to wheeling and dealing."

"Are your parents still around?" she asked gently.

He put his hand on the brass pull as he shook his head. "They've been gone for a while now. Just he and I—but I'm the lesser brother." He laughed as he opened the door for her and followed her inside.

"You definitely are," his brother, Tripp, said, poking his head out from under the counter where he appeared to be working with something inside one of the showcases. When he spotted Kendra, he straightened up and smoothed out his shirt. "Well, hey there," he said, his voice a wicked baritone.

Trent had to withhold his desire to roll his eyes at his brother as Tripp continued to glance between him and Kendra. Tripp closed the glass showcase. Inside was a brand-new Rolex watch, no doubt an item one of their clients had used as collateral and then forfeited. "How can I help you, ma'am?"

Kendra smiled. "Well, Tripp, as your brother has graciously let me in on why he's trailing me, we need to locate Marla Thomas."

Tripp's brows rose in surprise. "Well… Ms. Spade—" Tripp said her name with a lilt of earned respect. "I find it refreshing that we don't have to dance around one another. I happen to appreciate getting life at face value for once."

Pointing at Tripp, Kendra replied, "Good. Because you are going to be the one to flush Marla out of hiding. We need her to lead us to the senator."

"Me?" Tripp asked, rubbing his chest like her words had punched him. "How exactly do you think I could do that? I barely know her."

"Doesn't matter. But tell me something…" Kendra leaned on the case and put her fingers over the watch. "Why would Marla sign for the senator?"

Tripp dropped his hands to the edge of the glass—a little too close to Kendra's hands for Trent's liking. "She told us that it was because they worked together and she was the only friend he had left after his wife died."

"So, you knew they were having sex and you thought she was a fool in love?"

Tripp laughed as he looked at Kendra like he couldn't get enough. "Something like that."

Kendra nodded. "I'm not judging. If I was in your business, I would bet on that horse, too."

Trent suppressed a smile. He loved how Kendra was so direct and not afraid to take any situation by the balls. "What does Marla's relationship with Senator Clark have to do with flushing her out of hiding?" he asked.

Kendra sent him a sexy, bloodthirsty grin. "What would a woman who is having a relationship with a high-profile and controversial man fear the most?"

Tripp looked utterly confused. "Is this a rhetorical question or do you really want some kind of answer? Because if you are looking for answers, I didn't pass Women 101—ask my ex-wife."

Kendra let out an audible laugh. "If any man could pass Women 101, I don't think we would be having this conversation."

Tripp snorted.

"As for what this woman fears," Kendra continued, "She doesn't want to lose the man she loves—not if she's signing a bond for a million dollars. Which means that we know what motivates her—and what we can possibly use to get her to come out of hiding."

Chapter Eight

That look, the one of shock and slight intimidation on Trent's face, was one of her favorite expressions in the world—it was exactly what she wanted her enemies to look like when she made her closing arguments in court and slammed down her fist. That being said, it wasn't an expression she wanted to see on Trent's face. Actually, she wanted to see exactly the opposite.

"My family has some connections," she said to him, "if we need to pull strings."

He didn't move; instead he looked over at his brother. "Unfortunately, Detective Baker will be dropping by here shortly to take our statements. We're supposed to be sticking around here until he does."

"Which is fine." Kendra smiled.

"Um…*what* in the hell have you two been up to?" Tripp asked, walking around so he was in complete view.

Trent began to explain the CliffsNotes version of their eventful morning. He wasn't bad-looking, Tripp. He had the long, shaggy hair of a man who didn't have a woman in his life and probably didn't know what day of the week it was—he was likely in the shop every day anyhow, so it probably didn't matter to him unless money was due. He had the same shade of red and mahogany locks and sharp cheekbones as his brother, but he was a little longer in the face, and his nose was a touch wider. They were both handsome, but if she had to choose, there wasn't a question that she would prefer the black sheep. Yet, maybe that was her need to save a man that was once again rearing its ugly head.

The last time she had tried to save a man, it had been her ex-boyfriend. He had been a contractor for her family's company, and after an excruciating operation, one involving crimes against children, he'd lost his battle with depression and despair...a battle he'd never told her much about. She'd come to talk him down after a rambling, fast-paced series of text messages, only to have him pull a gun on her and then on himself. She had been the only one left standing, but she didn't regret trying to help him. She only wished she'd been successful.

Her fingers traced the scar.

"If I told you about our day, you wouldn't be surprised. Let's just leave it with, there was a whole hell of a lot of death and mayhem," Trent said dryly. "The senator's lawyer is dead."

"So, Clark's trial is going to be delayed? Son of a—" Tripp slammed his hand down on the wooden edge of the glass.

What? Tripp doesn't care about the lawyer? His only reaction is outrage that their man isn't going to be coming any closer to their grasp?

Kendra smirked. Yeah, they could be friends. She was an attorney, and she didn't particularly like lawyers, either—but that went mostly for defense attorneys. Then again, that was probably why she made a top-shelf prosecutor.

"Do you think Clark had a hand in the deaths?" Tripp asked.

"Presented like a murder-suicide. Looked like the attorney, Brad Bradshaw, killed his secretary, then hanged himself. But, if you ask me, it doesn't feel quite right." Trent shrugged, but she could feel his gaze work in her direction.

Trent had told the officer that she could be trusted, but from that little glance she could tell he wasn't entirely sold that she hadn't had a hand in the deaths. She felt the sudden need to affirm her truth but stopped herself from voicing it.

Yeah, she was getting entirely too *needy* about this man. She didn't have to care what he thought about her. All they needed was to get to the bottom of the deaths and get their hands on Senator Clark. Though, if he just disappeared, it would be fine by her. No lawsuit against her family. No reason to stick around. Except it would do nothing for this man she was starting to actually like.

Ugh, why do I have to feel? She nearly growled audibly at herself.

Tripp picked up his cell phone. "Let me make a few phone calls."

Kendra paused. "By chance did you guys try and get a location on Marla's phone? Find her that way?"

The men sent each other looks, like there was some kind of conversation they had already had and she'd accidentally fallen into. If there was a secret, she wasn't sure if she wanted to press the issue.

"We couldn't find a device assigned to the number

she gave us, but that doesn't mean she doesn't have a phone—she probably just gave us a false number." Tripp lifted his phone as the screen was lighting up with a phone call. "I'll be right back."

Kendra nodded. There was a tall, metal stool at the far corner of the shop where it looked as though Trent had set up a little makeshift office area. A filing cabinet stood behind it, locked and inaccessible to clients, but still within view. Which made her wonder, why? Why would he want to have files out where everyone could see them? Was it his way of adding legitimacy to their trade? Some show of power, that they really did have themselves lined up? Or was it because they were so far behind that work was always right there and waiting and he needed the visual reminder?

He'd said his brother was a ballbuster about work; if they were behind or not collecting enough, it would certainly help to shed light on why this bond was critical to their survival. He'd talked a bit about the importance of it, but now she was seeing the holes in their facade of professionalism and profitability.

All their futures were on the line.

There was a *ding* as the front door opened. A tall, good-looking man with bleached tips walked in. There was a bulge under his polo shirt in the shape of a badge—it must have been Detective Baker.

"Hey," Trent said, looking at the man and giving him a friendly smile.

"How's it going in here guys?" Detective Baker glanced around the shop as he walked in. Heading to the glass showcase, he stared down at the variety of items, remnants of lives and choices that most likely led straight back to the man who was now looking at them.

For a split second, there was a knot in her stomach, as if she was nervous for the brothers. They were law-abiding men, or so she assumed, but it was always uncomfortable to fall under the scrutiny of a man who had made a life out of picking out flaws and utilizing them to his and his investigation's benefit.

Trent nodded, like he could almost read her mind, though she was certain her thoughts weren't being broadcast on her features.

"We are doing well, considering the circumstances," Trent said, motioning vaguely in the direction of the law group's office. "You here to ask us a few questions? Gotta say, I'm glad you're on the case. Nice to see a friendly face."

Baker smiled, and as he did, she noticed his canine teeth were peg-shaped. She tried not to stare at their distinctive forms. As if he had caught her looking, he closed his mouth. It made her wonder if he was insecure about them.

"My guys told me you all just happened upon the scene when you arrived for a meeting, that right?" Baker asked.

Trent moved closer to her and crossed his hands over his chest as he looked up at the detective. "Yeah, Kendra got there a few moments before I did."

"Mmm-hmm," Baker said, staring down at the case once again. He tapped on the glass like he was thinking, and the normally innocuous action made the hair on the back of her neck rise. "How long were you in there before Trent arrived, Ms. Spade?"

She sent Trent a sideways glance. "Um, I don't know. Not long, maybe a few minutes. Five or so?" Though she had done more than her fair share of taking depositions and asking suspects the tough questions, it didn't make her any more comfortable when the tough questions were being asked of her.

"We are just the ones who reported the crime," Trent said with a frown.

Baker smirked as he turned toward them. "Yeah, you are. However, we were able to determine that the murders occurred not long before you called them in."

"Murders?" The knot returned to Kendra's stomach. "Didn't the guy hang himself?"

Baker shook his head. "Upon first inspection, one would believe so. However, it appears as if he had initially been strangled and then hung to make it look like he had taken his own life. The whole thing was, more than likely, staged." He gave them each a measured glance.

She hated the way he looked her over, peering at her, hoping to find cracks in her demeanor or any little discrepancies he could pry open like an oyster while looking for the pearl of answers. He wasn't going to be getting any answers from her, only more questions. If anything, her entire life was a series of unanswered questions smattered with the detritus of what-ifs.

"When the uniformed officers cut him loose, we found the ligature marks were inconsistent with the presentation of the body."

"And what about lividity?" Kendra asked, her mind going to the postmortem pictures she had often witnessed in her trials. How the blood pooled in a body could tell a good medical examiner or detective—even prove to a jury—the position a person had been in when they had died.

Baker sent her a wide smile, his peg teeth glinting

in the late-afternoon sun. "What did you say you did for a living again?"

"I'm a prosecutor for the State of New York." She met his gaze, unafraid of detectives. She worked with them all the time, and though she understood one little misstep could land her at the top of this man's suspect list, she knew he'd see her on the same team because of her profession.

"Ah. And why were you at the law offices this morning?" Baker rubbed at the tip of his nose, a move she normally attributed to stress.

The little action made her anxiety rise, but she tried to shake the feeling by reminding herself that she was the one who held the power in this situation—she was innocent. He was the one who had to prove anything otherwise.

"I had a meeting with Brad Bradshaw about a lawsuit he and his clients had filed against my client for defamation. They were asking for a large settlement or we were to go to trial. It was my goal to find a middle ground and avoid any further legal action," she said, careful to keep her voice emotionless.

"Would you say it was to your or your client's benefit that this lawyer and his office assistant were killed today?"

She huffed and shook her head. "Absolutely not. With their unfortunate and untimely deaths, I cannot suppress the lawsuit unless I contact the lawyer's client directly. And, as luck has it, he has been working with Lockwood Bonds and recently skipped his court date and left them holding a million-dollar note, which has now been forfeited to the courts."

Baker's eyebrows rose so high that they nearly touched the edges of his blond-tipped hair. She liked his hair, if truth be told. It gave him an approachability that most detectives who she had worked with in the past lacked. "I see." He relaxed slightly, and she could feel the weight of his suspicions dissipate.

"About the murders… What was the man's cause of death?" Trent asked.

The detective stood up straight and ran his hand over his shirt, inadvertently accentuating his badge under the fabric. "Upon closer inspection, it appeared that he died from the same ligature—in this case the nylon rope—that was used to hang him from the ceiling. The initial bruising was low, here." Baker ran his finger near the base of his thick neck. "There was pooling on his back, indicating that he actually died lying down before the killer put him in the hanging position."

"Do you think the secretary could have done it?" Trent asked.

Baker shook his head. "Unfortunately, no. The gun that was likely used was found in his office and had what we believe to be her blood on the barrel. She had to have been killed first."

In most cases like these, the suspect list was generally pretty easy to put together. In her line of work, she would pull together a motive and method of the murders and what the killer had stood to gain in killing those they did—then she would hammer her points home to the judge and jury. She was proud of her ninety percent conviction rate. Yet, in this case, she found herself almost at a loss—the only ones who stood to gain anything in these deaths, at least so far as she knew, were her and her family.

One thing was certain—while she wasn't one to pull a trigger, her brothers and sister were more than happy to take down an enemy—to kill. It was their job.

Chapter Nine

After they gave the detective their statements, Trent dropped Kendra off at her ranch truck. They hadn't said more than ten words to each other since the detective left, but he didn't know exactly why—whether it was the stress of the situation or if she was just looking for the moment that she could finally get away from him and back to her life without him.

She had made it sound like they would make a great team and that they could work together to get their hands on the senator, but when he parked by her truck, she had nearly tripped over herself getting out and away from him. Kendra didn't look back at him as she got into her ranch truck, still parked in the law firm's lot.

He pulled his truck over on the side of the road and watched as she started her car and made her way out. She rolled to a stop beside him. Her eyes were tired and her jaw was set as she rolled down the window. He followed suit, expecting the permanent goodbye that was undoubtedly to come.

He steeled himself—she owed him nothing, even if he had exposed his operation to her and had come to her side when she needed someone the most in the moment. Or maybe she hadn't really needed him—maybe he just felt like he needed to be there for her.

She opened her mouth to say something, but her expression said it all—she wanted to run away to anywhere but where they found themselves. The thought made a strange sensation of refusal twist through him, its forked tongue lashing at the buried softness within him. Apparently, he wasn't as good at steeling himself against her as he wished.

Leaning in, she rested her head on the truck's steering wheel and closed her eyes.

"Are you okay?" he asked, wishing she was still just sitting next to him. It would have made it a hell of a lot easier to console her, and to ignore the fact he might never see her again.

She peeked out from under her eyelashes, and he could see the tiredness in her eyes. "I know this will sound like it comes out of nowhere, but…" She paused.

Here comes the goodbye.

He swallowed back the bitter taste of loss that crept up his throat. He had heard the adage "What is to be, shall be," but damn it if he didn't want to work to keep her in his life at least a little bit longer. Hell, he didn't even want her for his dirtiest naked fantasies—it was just nice having her around, someone smart and brave who didn't take any guff, someone he could talk to and who could confide in him.

Maybe he had just been too lonely, too long.

"Trent?" She said his name softly, like it left sweetness on her tongue that she wanted to savor.

He loved that, the sound of his name on her lips.

"Yeah, Kendra, what do you need?" He tried to say her name like she had said his, with the weightiness of want and yearning while still carrying the rasp of emotional protection he needed.

She sat up straight, and a thin smile appeared. "I know this is strange, and I don't want you to read too much into it, but I don't want to go back to the ranch. And, well… I don't really know where else to go." She sounded slightly embarrassed, like she hated exposing her underbelly to him.

He wanted to tell her it was okay to be herself with him, to show him the real her…the *soft* her that he had so far only seen in brief, sporadic glimpses.

"You can jump in with me," he offered, motioning to the passenger seat. He smiled as he realized he had been the one sitting there last. "If you want, you can even drive. I don't care."

She glanced at the parking lot and nibbled at her bottom lip. "I don't want to leave the truck here."

He wasn't sure if it was because she was afraid of the killer—who definitely wouldn't be coming for them, he hoped—or if she hated the idea of having to look upon the office of horrors, but he didn't allow himself to ask. Not every question required an answer, especially when it came to feelings. Hell, he knew only too well that he couldn't answer for what he was feeling when he looked at her; all he knew with any certainty was that he wanted more of everything she had to offer—but her time most of all.

"Why don't you drop it off at my place?" It felt strange, offering up his private dwelling to her, but at the same time, he liked the idea of her in his house… even just on his property. "You can follow me," he said, not waiting for her to shoot down the idea.

He put his truck in gear and watched to make sure

she was following him before turning down the street and making his way across town. His mind wandered to his kitchen—had he left dishes in the sink? If she came inside, the last thing he wanted her to think was that he was a pig. He was pretty good about cleaning up after himself—he was the only one who was going to do it—but that didn't mean things were as picked up and put away as he would have liked in advance of a woman coming over.

There was definitely dirty laundry sitting in front of the machine. Damn, if his skivvies were sitting out, that was as good as a one-way ticket to her walking out.

He chuckled as he realized how far he had come from his days as a college student. Back then he wouldn't have thought twice about the state of his place when bringing a woman home. Then, however, he hadn't been looking for relationships. Since then, he'd learned that sex was easy. In a swipe-right culture, thanks to dating apps and instant gratification, even in a small city, there wasn't a night that had to go by when a person had to feel physically lonely...

Not that he was the kind of guy whose social calendar was filled with meaningless sex and one-night stands. In fact, he had never had a one-night stand. Lots of his friends had—even Tripp had talked about a couple—but that wasn't Trent's style.

It wasn't that he didn't like sex; he definitely did. If anything, he would say it was one of his favorite pastimes, but there was sex for sex and there was sex for love...and the latter was a whole other ballgame. There was just nothing like looking into the eyes of someone he loved and who loved him back.

It had been a long time since he had one of those

moments, and with an inner wince, he remembered how he'd misinterpreted them when he was married. He'd thought his wife at the time was feeling the same things he was. He'd been wrong. She'd been silently chafing at the restrictions of marriage, and it wasn't long before she threw off what she considered its fetters. He hadn't trusted his judgment in relationships since then.

He glanced back in his mirror at Kendra, who was still following him. He doubted she was the kind of woman who liked one-night stands. And she definitely wasn't the kind of woman who opened herself up and shared herself freely. Sure, they had broken through some of the barriers of emotional vulnerability thanks to the situation in which they found themselves, but it was something else entirely to stand before another person naked both body and soul.

He still had a job to do. He needed to get his hands on the senator, or at least Marla. No matter what was or wasn't going on in his personal life, he had to make his work and his family's business as much of a priority—if not more of one. If he didn't, and they lost the business, what would he have to offer a woman?

And speaking of a woman, he thought of Kendra and how she'd let her guard down around him. He felt himself warm at the realization that she trusted him. Despite her brassy approach to life, she'd allowed him to see a softer side, a side that needed peace and normalcy.

Grabbing his phone at a red light, he did a quick search of local events. He clicked on the first one available. Apparently, there was an Iris Festival at Fort Missoula for the day, complete with food vendors, live music and dancing. He smiled at the thought of holding her in his arms and two-stepping to some good old country music. While the event could hardly make him appear to be at the top of his game, at least it was a whole heap better than showing her around his blast-from-the-past house.

Plus, Missoula was a small town, for all intents and purposes. It was so much so that he was sure he would know at least a few of the people there. He doubted that the folks who came to him for bonds would be hanging out at a flower festival, but he could almost guarantee that their mothers and grandmothers would.

He made his way through the city, passing by mom-and-pop gas stations and roadside stands with tables filled to the edges with Russian breads and canned pickles and beets. Though he didn't have the windows open in the truck, he was sure he had caught the whiff of yeasty doughs and dill in the air as he passed by.

The park was filled with kids playing soccer in a rainbow of different colored jerseys, and there was a family reunion, marked with large signs complete with golden and white balloons, at the main pavilion. The lots were filled with cars, but toward the third row he found two spots that were next to one another and not too far a walk from the museums and garden areas.

Kendra parked and got out of her truck, but she looked confused. "What's going on? I thought we were going back to your place?"

Though he knew why he'd brought her here, he suddenly felt stupid for making the choice, and he shrugged, trying and failing to dispel some of the awkwardness he was feeling. "I thought maybe this would be better. I know you are tired and need a spot to leave your truck."

Her eyes softened, and she gave him a graceful smile. "I appreciate that, Trent."

With an acknowledging tip of the head, he wished she would reach over and touch him or take his hand and they could pretend, for at least a few moments, that they were here as a couple enjoying the summer day instead of running away from horrors and the families.

As they walked, their fingers bumped gently against one another in a way that made him wonder if she was doing it on purpose or if he was just looking for signs that weren't really there. Her fingertips brushed against his again, this time making him glance down. Her fingers were tilted slightly up; she had to be doing it on purpose—sending him a signal. And yet, why? He both feared and found himself exhilarated by the possibilities that came with this simple touch.

He smiled as he thought of what Tripp would say if his brother could see him swooning over her. Tripp had a reach-for-the-stars mentality when it came to women. He chuckled, and as he did, for a split second he forgot about his feelings of inadequacy and his fingers took hold of hers.

Realizing what he had just done, he tried to play it cool and relaxed, but his heart thrashed like a caged jackrabbit. There was no way she was going to keep her hand in his. He tried to grip just an increment tighter without her noticing. Then he relaxed his hand; he didn't need to hold her to make her stay with him. If she wanted him, she *wanted* him, and if she didn't... well, he would have to resign himself to the fate of knowing what a special woman he had lost.

What a hell that would be.

"You didn't get much of your lunch. If you want, we

can get some dinner and then make our way around the gardens." He pointed at the signs, which read 89th Annual Iris Festival, and listed the hosts and sponsors below. "There's supposed to even be a band playing tonight. I think it is Stomping Ground. You like to dance?"

She gave him a look that rested halfway between *"have you lost your mind"* and *"you're crazy if you don't ask."*

"Is that look a yes or a no?" he asked, grinning at her.

"That's an *'I haven't danced to country* music' look," she said with a lightness in her voice. "I'm up for it, if you are willing to teach a girl with two left feet."

Things were looking brighter by the minute. He would dance her all the way to the moon if she would just keep touching him, but he was afraid he would sound stupid saying anything remotely close to that aloud to her.

"I'm not much of a two-stepping cowboy, but I'll be happy to let you stomp on my toes." He gave her hand a gentle, teasing squeeze. As he did, she looked down at their entwined hands, making the happiness he was feeling teeter on the cliff of despair.

Instead of pulling away, though, she readjusted her hand so now even their palms were touching. Her hand was warm and damp with sweat, but it fit in his perfectly.

They made their way to the outlying booths of the gardening festival, complete with displays—everything from weed-mitigation strategies and companies to a stand filled with kitschy watering cans shaped like fat giraffes and squat toads.

"I miss living somewhere I could have a garden," Kendra said as they made their way past a booth filled with cut irises ranging from white to speckled purples and yellows.

Before now, he'd always thought of his grandmother when he saw the flowers. She'd had them out on the edge of the back pasture, brown and purple flowers on tall stalks and reminiscent of bygone days. Whenever he looked out at them from his kitchen window, where he'd often found his grandmother standing, he would always think of her talking about how they were the only things the *damned deer* wouldn't eat.

What she often failed to mention was the fact that she put out all her vegetable and fruit table scraps so the deer could come by and have a nibble on their nightly rounds. In fact, his grandmother had gotten so fond of the *damned deer* that one year, when a fawn had gotten caught up in their fencing around the pasture and the mother had abandoned it, his grandmother had taken to bottle-feeding it in the barn. She'd put on a heat lamp for the little spotted fawn and eventually named the baby Clem, short for clematis. Oddly enough, her deer had acquired a taste for those flowers.

"You're being quiet," Kendra said as they made their way to the next booth. "You okay? What are you think-ing about?" Her mouth clamped shut as if she resented herself for asking the question. "I didn't mean to pry. I just—"

"It's okay," he said, running his thumb over the back of her hand gently to reassure her. "It's not a bad thing to be curious or to want to ask me questions. I'm one of those weird dudes who is comfortable talking about what I'm thinking…hell, even what I'm feeling on occasion."

There was that look again, like she wasn't totally buying what he was selling.

"Really, I'm comfortable not being a stereotypical dude." He hoped that being his true self wasn't going to turn her off, but he was too old to play games and pretend to be someone he wasn't in order to make the other person happy—he'd had that kind of thing in the past and it had gone out in a blaze of glory, including her slapping him so hard he was sure he'd skipped back in the week. Relationships were only truly feasible when both partners were being their authentic selves.

"I would say you have to prove that to me, but the fact that you're even willing to talk about your feelings already does that." She nudged his shoulder with hers. "You know, Trent, you are good people." There was an unexpected warmth in her voice as she looked up at him and smiled. "What happened this morning—it shook up even someone like me, who's seen and heard a lot. You knew that and have been kind to me. Kindness is rare."

"I don't know that I'm good, but I try hard to be," he said as they walked. "The thing about my line of work is that there are a lot of sleazy people who do it. I run up against that stigma all the time. I am trying to do something different, though—be in the business of helping people and not taking advantage of them when they are already at a low point."

She reached over with her other hand and held on to his arm, like suddenly she couldn't get close enough to him. "That is admirable."

His face warmed, but not just from the sun. "I still

brush up against a lot of the worst kinds of people. I have to be tough enough to stand my ground and not be pushed around. Sometimes that involves more than my fair share of violence, but I try to steer clear."

She let go of his arm, and her gaze moved toward the ground. There it was, the look of discomfort he'd been expecting when she finally really got to know him, just like with his ex. He girded himself but kept holding her hand.

Instead of letting go of him completely and moving away, she put her hand back on him. "Sometimes the only answer to violence is violence."

There was a long pause as he thought of her words and what they said about her, and her past. There was so much he still didn't know.

"I'm surprised to hear a lawyer say something like that," he said, breaking the silence. The smell of warm funnel cakes permeated the air, the sweet, warm aroma in direct opposition to their cold reality.

"Why? I can pontificate on how important a safe and just community is to American society. But at the end of the day, results are the same. Violence still occurs, people still get hurt and I find myself back in court."

He didn't disagree with how she was feeling. People, at the basic level, were animals. Many worked off impulse and survival rather than any other cognitive function. He could understand how she would get burned out on fighting what she'd made clear was a losing battle.

"At least you're making a difference. You're putting those who should be behind bars right where they need to be."

"You can't tell me you're not doing exactly the same thing, just in a different way…a way I would never be capable of. I can land a punch and stop someone from hurting me if push comes to shove, but I'm not going to go out there and actively pursue a physical fight."

He chuckled softly, remembering her punching the man at the bar. She must have had the same thought and smiled.

"That fellow at the steakhouse was hurting me," she said in her defense, "and would have kept at it if I hadn't stopped him."

"I'm not judging. I was impressed."

"Hey," she said, letting go of him and staring ahead. "Look at that guy." She pointed into the crowd. In the distance, standing near the beer garden, was a dark-haired man with gray at his temples. He had a strong chin, and sunglasses hid his eyes. "He looks exactly like Senator Clark…" She said the name in barely more than a whisper. "You don't think he would be here, do you?"

If he'd had a warrant out for his arrest and was a recognizable and somewhat notorious public figure, the last thing Trent would have done was go to a public event. Then again, people never ceased to surprise him.

Kendra started to move in the direction of the man, just as he turned away from them and started to disappear back into the crowd of the festival. "No, don't go after him," Trent said, stopping her. "We don't want to rush headfirst into this fight."

She motioned in the direction of the senator. "If I can just talk to him, negotiate… I can put an end to the lawsuit and be on my way. We can take him to the jail, and you and your brother can get your money—plus what's owed."

There was an edge of sadness to the realization that she was right. Just like that, and their time together could be over. She could disappear back into her life in New York, and he could start hunting the next person on the list of people who had done his family wrong.

Though he knew he had a duty and he had to do the right thing, he had never wanted to do the wrong thing more… He wanted to keep Kendra by his side for at least a little bit longer.

Chapter Ten

Though Kendra had seen only a few pictures of Senator Dean Clark, she was nearly positive the man who had just disappeared into the crowd was one and the same. It was hard to mistake the plastic smile that seemed to adorn all the microdermabraded, Botoxed, filler-ridden faces of professional politicians.

At the last Met gala she had attended, she had rubbed shoulders with a former New York senator, and his personality had been more sickening and cloying than his pepper-and-sandalwood cologne. No matter how many showers she took, Kendra hadn't been able to wash the scent or the memory of the man from her mind. That night, the politician had given a small speech about the power of reform and the value of community—while later it had been rumored he had been bedding a Russian operatic soprano in one of the many utility closets.

It wasn't the first talk of his philandering ways and it wasn't the last, but his touting virtuous living and then slipping himself into every woman who would let him in their panties was a level of hypocrisy she would always find morally repugnant. From what she'd read about Clark, he was cut from the same cloth, having allegedly paid for his young daughter and wife's kid-napping, which had ultimately resulted in his wife's death. While he claimed he wasn't responsible for the crimes, a jury of his peers might decide otherwise. She believed in the principle of innocent until proven guilty, but she'd seen enough men and women like him on trial to sense where his case was headed. She assumed he was as guilty as her family proclaimed.

Trent was gripping her hand tightly as she stepped toward the senator, and there was a reticence in the way he faltered behind her, almost pulling her away from the man who could make both of their lives go back to normal. She stopped and turned to Trent.

There was a softness in his eyes, and the way the corners of his lips were raised almost gave him a plead-ing look. When she glanced away and then turned back, that expression had disappeared, masked by the stony front she had first noticed when she had met him. In her turning away at his beckoning softness, it was as if they had gone back to being strangers.

Instantly, she regretted her move. Just as quickly, she had to ask herself why. That kind of closeness with another person wasn't something she had ever really allowed herself to feel. When her ex had pulled the trigger, he had left her with six soul-crushing words: "You will never have true love." She would have rather felt the heat of the bullet than hear those words again.

She'd thought she'd shrugged them off at the time, the last desperate utterances of a desperate man in the throes of mental anguish.

But as time moved on, they haunted her, and it seemed he'd really murmured the phrase to the uni-verse, not specifically to her, directing the fates to make his last wish come true. If he'd said, "You won't find anyone as good as me," she could have easily forgotten it, shaken her head over it. But the words *never* coupled with *true love* seemed to hang over her life after that incident, tainting any relationship or promise of one, making her afraid to pursue closeness.

With Trent, there was something inside her that drew her closer to him, that made her want to spend time with him, get to know him. Maybe it wasn't true love, but it was far better than any moment with her ex.

Standing there, feeling the wisp of possibility dissipate into the sky like a lonely cloud in a hot summer sky, she had to accept her ex's words for what they were—a curse.

"Trent—" She said his name with a tenderness which made the world disappear around them. "We need to go after him. If we take him down…we have the freedom to make any choices we want." She chose her words carefully, giving them just enough inflection that she hoped he understood what they really meant while being retractable if she read this moment wrong.

A smile erupted over his features, and it made a current run through her, filling her with joy. She clenched his hand tighter and almost skipped as she wove through the crowd in pursuit of the senator.

She stopped for a moment and turned, coming back to reality instead of the promises of what the future could bring. "Do you have the power to make the arrest or do we need to call in a uniformed officer?"

"I can arrest him. Besides, if we call the police, we will probably lose him before they get here." He reached down and lifted his shirt slightly so she could see the set of cuffs in a case next to his sidearm.

He walked ahead of her, letting go of her hand as he passed by. Pulling out his cuffs, he hid them in his palm so quickly and quietly that if she hadn't been watching, she wouldn't have noticed. He strode with confidence and quiet strength, a man who knew his mission. Glancing around, she looked to see if anyone in the crowd had noticed, but everyone near them was busy talking and drinking beer and wrapped up in the comings and goings of their own lives. She felt a private connection to Trent in the swirl of the crowd, a silent intimacy.

The senator's brunet head was turned from them and was moving farther away as they tried to gain ground. She was tempted to call the man's name just to slow him down and make him turn, but instead she simply followed Trent's lead. He was the point on this operation, and as such, she just needed to be there to support and call the police if things escalated.

Her throat tightened as she fell back a few steps. If this went wrong and something happened to Trent, she wasn't sure she could emotionally handle it. Not after this morning. Not after realizing how she needed to prove her ex had not cursed her.

She could put on a front like she was strong and completely unflappable regardless of what life threw at her, but she couldn't deny how shaken she was by just the thought of him getting hurt.

She stood still and watched as he reached down and rested his free hand on his sidearm, ever so inconspicuously. It was like he was dancing through the crowd, carefully moving and twisting in the way he readied himself for the battle that was likely to come.

The senator wasn't a man who would go peacefully

or without a scene. The fact he had allegedly been willing to use his wife's abduction and death to help win favor with voters and appeal to their pity was only more evidence that he was total scum. Hopefully Trent realized that as well, and he was prepared for the worst.

Hunting a person was one of the strangest sensations in the world. It was thrilling and exhilarating, knowing that in just a few moments, he would be taking down his prey. Yet, this time there was a different edge to the stalk, knowing the woman he was intrigued by was only a few feet behind him.

Taking down a fugitive was one of his favorite parts of the job, but if Kendra was put in harm's way...

Trent moved faster through the crowd, hoping to create more distance between them while still not making it obvious that he was trying to leave her behind. Kendra likely wouldn't take being left in the lurch well—even if he was doing it to protect her. She'd grown up in a world of militants and violence, so she wasn't new to his world, but it was another thing entirely to see him take down a fugitive in the middle of an American park on a warm early-summer day with kids running around while chomping on shaved ice. He had to be careful.

The festival had a hometown feel, complete with the scent of hot dogs cooking on the grill mixed with the warm, yeasty odor of spilled beer. If he took down Senator Clark, he wasn't sure who would look bad—the senator or himself. He'd probably be caught on someone's camera phone doing the grab, and the senator still had fans in the public. He'd be lucky if a well-meaning passerby didn't jump into the fray and try to kick his ass in an effort to protect the pol.

He moved around the side of the man, careful to keep out of sight lines until the last moment. He wanted to take him by surprise to lower the chances of violent resistance. There didn't need to be a scene. If things went as he hoped, Senator Clark would come along willingly, without him needing to place him in cuffs or take him to the ground at all.

Approaching, he could make out the back of the man's blue polo shirt. He was talking to a woman and gesticulating with his hands to drive home whatever point he must have been making. The woman looked like she had been prisoner to the man's tirade for far too long. If nothing else, at least Trent could save this woman from further annoyance.

As he stepped within a few arm lengths of the man, he paused. As of yet, he had barely caught a glimpse of the fellow's face. Kendra had seemed to think this was definitely the senator, but now that he was closer, he could make out the man's well-kept beard. It wasn't long, but the man he and Tripp had posted for had been clean shaven and the type who went to nail salons for manicures and hadn't stepped into an ordinary barbershop in his entire life.

If we've been following the wrong man...

He nearly shook his head, but then a part of him secretly hoped that they had made a mistake and were going after the wrong person. It would be easier when it came to this *thing* that was happening between Kendra and him. If they were barking up the wrong tree, they would have to keep looking. Which meant they could have more time together—time when she could come to her senses and realize that she was a million times too good for him. Until she did, he was going to soak up every second.

The man he had been tailing started to move toward the stage where a country band was playing a ballad perfect for dancing. The man took the annoyed woman's hand and she resisted for a moment, but he refused to let go. The woman jerked her arm back, trying to break the grip, but the action only made the man's hand tighten, and her skin around his fingers turned white from the pressure.

This was Trent's moment. He moved quickly, cutting off the man's path to the patch of grass that was acting as the dance floor. There were a few dozen couples out there; one of the men was whispering something into his partner's ear, and his date had a nearly blinding smile.

It was a sharp contrast to the imprisoned expression on the face of the blonde who was accompanying their target. He stared at the man's features. His face was obscured by sunglasses and the beard, but he was almost certain the man was Dean Clark. Trent chastised himself for thinking he could have been anyone else. He had apparently come here in this pitiful attempt at a disguise to meet Marla.

Did she know the kind of man who she had laid down her financial future for, the same man who had strapped her with a million-dollar debt because he couldn't face the judge and answer for his alleged crimes?

"Mr. Clark?" he said, stepping directly in front of the bearded man.

As Dean heard his name, he jerked and glared at Trent, like he was trying to place his features.

Dean let go of the woman's arm and her hand moved to where he had been holding her, but not before Trent caught sight of the dark pink lines Dean's fingers had left on her skin.

He would have hated this man even if he didn't owe Trent money. No woman should be treated the way he had been treating her.

"Who the hell are you?" Dean growled, moving behind his date.

The blonde's face relaxed and she moved to step away from Dean, but he put his hands on her shoulders and forced her to stay put.

What kind of lies had Dean told this woman to get her to go out with him?

"Ma'am, do you feel safe?" Trent asked, and he looked over the senator's shoulder to Kendra, who had finally pushed her way through the crowd.

She looked slightly annoyed that he had left her behind, but as she spotted him, the annoyance slipped from her face and was replaced with a quizzical expression of concern.

The blonde with the senator reached up and removed his left hand and then his right from her shoulders. "Actually, I could use a ride so I can get out of here."

Trent nodded and motioned for Kendra to come closer. "My friend Kendra here will be happy to take you anywhere you need to go." He was happy to do anything that could save this seemingly innocent woman from the grips of an accused murderer who lacked any sort of conscience.

Kendra gently put her hand on the woman's back and

waved her hand away from the stage and the throngs of people, several of whom had suddenly appeared to have taken notice of what was threatening to take place.

"Tracy, you stay right there. Damn it," Dean ordered, reaching to take hold of the woman again.

So, this wasn't Marla with him. Of course not. The man was a philanderer and this must have been just another of his many women, but this one was just at the wrong place at the wrong time.

The woman lurched away from Dean's grasp.

"Kendra, get her out of here," Trent said, trying to keep his voice even but firm. He needed both women to get out of here before something really bad happened. He couldn't risk them getting hurt—even if he was more than aware Kendra was strong enough to kick some ass.

"I don't know who in the hell you think you are, but you and that little snatch you're with need to mind your own goddamned business," Dean said.

Trent let out a dark laugh. The man had found it—he had found his crazy switch, the one that flipped him from a person who could open up and talk about his feelings into someone not afraid to kick ass and take names. No one would talk about Kendra that way.

No effing way.

As if Kendra could see the steam that was roiling out of his ears, she grabbed the blonde and began leading her back toward the truck.

"You stop right there," Dean yelled. As he did, the song came to an end and his voice broke the lull between the tunes.

Every face in the area turned toward them and the scene that the senator was creating.

Kendra didn't even look back, but the blonde paused. Kendra shook her head and said something. Trent couldn't quite make out all the words, but they sounded like, "Don't go back to him." Trent hoped they worked. There was nothing worse than watching a person whose spirit had been broken down by a toxic and abusive partner.

"I don't know if you recall, but recently you were ordered to appear in court and failed to, leaving Lockwood Bonds holding the bag for more than a million dollars, plus interest," he said to the senator.

Dean pulled up his sunglasses, putting them on his head as he looked around at the crowd of people that had formed around them. "I have no idea what you are talking about."

"Senator Clark, while I'm sure it was merely an oversight on your part, missing your court date…" He spoke slowly, measuring his words and their effects on the crowd like they were drops of a poisonous elixir. "You know, the felony criminal proceedings for your role in your daughter's kidnapping—a daughter you no longer have custody of—and your wife's kidnapping and murder."

The man's face blanched, and a bead of sweat worked its way down from his hairline and onto his temple; even from where he stood Trent could see the vein protruding beneath it. "I had nothing to do with any of that. And I don't know what court date you are talking about."

"See, I'm sure it is all a misunderstanding, Senator. You just need to come with me and we will sort it all out."

The man's eyes widened—*rabbit eyes* were what he and his brother called them. Dean reached down and touched his shorts like he was going to tighten them, and then he looked the way Kendra and the blonde had gone and around to where there was a small opening in the crowd of people. He was going to run. Trent could sense it.

Trent leaned toward the man, saying lowly in an effort not to cause a scene, "Don't do it. I'll catch you, and when I do, there will be an ass whooping at the end of it."

The man looked him over, like he was considering how bad the beating would be. "Look, I don't know who you think you are, but I can assure you that as a senator I'm an upstanding citizen in this community."

Trent raised his hand, stopping the man's canned garbage speech. "We can stand here and hash this out here in front of all these witnesses, or you can come with me and we can discuss this in private."

The man flexed his hands and balled them into fists, giving him the look of a petulant child.

Trent opened his hand and exposed the cuffs resting in his palm in hopes of avoiding violence. "If you come with me nicely, I won't put these on you…"

He took a step closer, but as he did the man's fist came out of nowhere, and Trent cursed himself for being too trusting as he'd tried to avoid a scene. Before he could react, he felt the crush of bone on bone as the senator's fist connected with his temple. His ears buzzed and a strange floating sensation moved through him. Trent tried to move, to swing in retaliation, but his movements felt like they were being repressed by the tides.

The second hit, a roundhouse, he saw coming. There was nothing his dazed body could do except try to block, but he moved too slowly, and as the hit struck, he knew…he was going down.

Chapter Eleven

From the living room of her hotel suite, Kendra could make out the sounds of sheets rustling on the couch—Trent must have been waking up. Last night, after she had picked Trent up at the hospital, she hadn't wanted to take him back to her family's ranch, and he hadn't wanted to go home.

After the attack yesterday, she'd wanted to be alone, away from his brother and her family, the people who had set them on this course. They needed room to sort out what was going on, how the pieces of their separate cases fit together.

She had lived in many hotels over the years, and the DoubleTree was pretty typical of the nicer ones in which she had resided. She always went for the upgrade at hotels, slipping the front desk staff twenty bucks when she handed them her ID just so she could get a better room. This time it had definitely worked—they had given her the presidential suite. It probably hadn't hurt that she'd had Trent on her arm, black eye and all.

He had definitely taken one hell of a hit. As much as she had known that the senator could cause a scene, she hadn't expected the politician to actually resort to blows. She was as surprised as Trent had been. He'd obviously been working hard to keep the situation under control so that no one would get hurt. He was a good man, so he'd ended up getting hurt himself.

The senator's move seemed out of character. However, this morning social media had blown up and the video of Trent getting the beatdown had gone viral—so far, it had more than three million views. Hopefully one of them was Marla. If the senator was going to keep slipping out of their grip, then they were definitely going to have to focus more on the woman who had cosigned for him. At least, she could act as an insurance policy.

The good news was that, thanks to the video, she could very likely use it against the senator in the event that the lawsuit continued. As it was, she could definitely use it to her family's benefit. The senator was a loose cannon—a man who cared nothing about the safety and welfare of others but was solely focused on himself.

If nothing else, she could thank Trent for taking one for her family's team. The video and propaganda rolled in her favor, and it was always a welcome gift. It wouldn't guarantee a win, but it would make getting one significantly easier. That was, if they even ended up making it to court—as things were going, if the senator didn't make it to the criminal proceedings with a new legal team, well…he definitely wouldn't be following through with his civil action against her family. It had been a ballsy move for him to even file the civil claim before the criminal trial. Usually defamation cases came after not-guilty verdicts, aimed at those who'd painted the defendant as guilty as sin from the get-go.

This case was more complicated than she'd first imagined.

Which once again led her to wonder how and why someone had gone after his lawyer. Now that they knew the senator had likely been in town when the murders had taken place, it put him higher up on the suspect list. Maybe the man was more than just ballsy. Maybe he was relentless in taking down people in his way.

By now Detective Baker had to be aware of the video floating around on social media, and she was surprised they hadn't gotten a phone call or a visit from him. Heck, it was a small enough town that if he wanted to track them down at this hotel, he certainly could have by now.

Perhaps that meant the detective was thinking the same thing she was and was currently on the lookout for the senator in hopes that he could bring him in for questioning about his attorney's demise.

The television in the other room clicked on, and Kendra pulled her hair back and slipped on the white robe that came with the room. Making her way out, she was taken aback when she spotted Trent. He was shirtless, leaning back into the corner of the L-shaped couch, a sheet covering his lower body. He had his arm up, his hand behind his head, and the other hand was lying just under the edge of the sheet on his abs. His biceps were enormous, and a cobra tattooed in black ink wrapped around one of them.

Just when she thought he couldn't get any hotter and she was in fear for her virtue, he looked over at her and sent her a sleepy smile. "I hope I didn't wake you." His eye had taken on a red ring around the iris, and his cheek was still swollen and covered in a black-purple bruise.

She wanted to go to him and run her finger over the bruise and kiss it until it was better, but she resisted the urge. It was already embarrassing to be standing here in front of him in a bathrobe and staring like a lust-filled teenager who was just experiencing her first real crush.

"No," she said, her voice raspy from the morning. She cleared her throat. "I need some coffee, though. You?"

"I'm not a coffee drinker, but if you want, I can get up and make you a cup or go for a coffee run or something." He really looked at her now, and she could feel his gaze move down her like it was his hands skimming over her body.

Yep, he was getting hotter by the passing second. Any man who made coffee for his woman deserved a special place in the bedroom—and any position he wanted.

She smiled at the thought of opening up her robe and letting it fall to the floor in front of him. What would he do?

All of a sudden, needing coffee was drifting from her mind.

He smirked. "You look beautiful this morning. Do you know that?"

She put her hand up to her hair, fussing with a strand that she had forgotten to secure in her bun. "Thank you for the compliment." She paused. Did she throw the bait or did she just take the compliment and retreat? "Though I can't say I probably look half as sexy as you."

She was met with only the sounds of ESPN for a long moment—some team somewhere had won something—but all the words were melting together in a jumble as she thought about the mistake she had just made. It was never a good idea to make the first real move with a man. She had made the first move with her ex, demonstrating that if left to her own devices she always picked the wrong men.

Reaching down, she pulled the edge of the robe tighter, wishing she could disappear into it and end up as just a heap of puffy white cotton on the floor.

"Why are you doing that?" he asked, voicing the question going through her own mind. "If anything, you should come over here, closer to me." He patted the couch next to him. There was a yearning in his eyes, a look of wanting she hadn't seen in him before.

She started to move toward the couch, her walk slow and deliberate.

As she got close to him, he reached out for her hand, motioning to her as if it was an invitation. Yet she had been the one to invite. She slipped her fingers in his, and he pulled her to him in one smooth action.

"When I'm around you, I'm never quite sure why I'm doing anything," she said with a whisper of a smile. "And I'm usually pretty decisive."

"What are you deciding now?" he asked, so softly she barely heard him.

"That I want you, and I suspect you want me." There was something about Trent that called for complete honesty, and she liked the feeling of being able to say what was in her heart and mind.

"How long have you known that I wanted you?" He lifted her hand to his mouth and kissed her open palm, making her knees weaken.

"It doesn't matter to me who wanted who first. I'm just glad to be here with you now." She sucked in a breath as he moved her palm to his cheek and reached around her, wrapping her in his arm.

"You're one of the smartest people I've ever met, do you know that?"

Though she enjoyed being called beautiful, being called intelligent turned her on far more. Being beautiful was nothing more than getting lucky in the genetic draw—that or entirely too much makeup. Intelligence took years of hard work and diligence to acquire, and even then it wasn't a guarantee. She had known many people who graduated from college but couldn't find their way out of a hotel bathroom.

"If you're trying to butter me up, it's working." She smiled at him as she reached up and ran her fingers through his soft reddish-brown hair.

"Are you sure?" Trent asked.

She twisted a lock of his hair between her fingers as she looked at him, confused by his question. "Of course I am. Why do you ask?"

He gave her a devious grin, his eyes sparkling. He reached up with his other arm and pulled her into his lap, exposing her legs almost to her panty line.

"I ask, because if I was doing this right, you would already be kissing me."

Her fingers slipped from his hair down to his sharp jawline, and she slowly moved toward his lips, staring at the sweet pinkness and the lines that adorned them.

The first kiss was dangerous. There were so few

of them in life, ones that mattered. As wonderful as a first kiss could be, for her it always carried an air of sadness. No first kiss had ever lasted long enough. Nor had any of them led to promises of forever. In essence the first kiss was acknowledging temporary bliss and future heartbreak. Even acknowledging that this would almost inevitably lead to nothing, she still couldn't resist Trent. They'd met during a moment of heightened awareness, at the scene of a murder, and ended the day in a moment of heightened tenderness as she'd cared for his bruises. She would have to have a heart of steel enclosed in ice to resist their pull toward each other.

To make this step, and take things between them further, was an enormous gamble. She stopped moving long enough to look him in the eyes. There was no deceit, no hints of broken promises or inconsistency. As he looked at her, she only saw wanting and whispers of what *could be*.

He leaned in, taking her lips and not allowing her to overthink anymore. She wrapped her arms around his neck, holding him close as she savored the flavor of his kiss. Though he'd just woken up, he tasted of toothpaste and promises.

His kiss was luxurious and unhurried, his tongue flipping over her lip gently and reminding her of the sensation of butterfly wings. She could remember no more sensual sensation than when he moved against her. She didn't know how his hand had found her face, but he pushed a wayward hair from the corner of her mouth and let his thumb linger on her cheek.

She was tempted to open her eyes to see the man who was sweeping her away and making her forget about everything and every responsibility. All she could think about was how it felt so good to be kissed by him. To be kissed like he meant it. Like she was his. She kissed him back with the same gentle seriousness. She wanted him to be hers.

This kiss…could it mean forever? She pushed that thought away and lost herself in him.

His breath was warm against her skin, and it reminded her of how the sun felt after a long, harsh winter. She couldn't deny that that was what her life had been right up to this moment—a cold season filled with struggle. In this second, she didn't have to be the strong one.

It was refreshing and freeing to let go of all the pressure and requirements that her life entailed.

Too quickly, he broke away from their kiss. His hands lingered on her face, as did his gaze. His eyes were wide and round, soft, as he looked upon her. She could have melted. Though he didn't say the words, she could feel there was something more to the look than simply lust. In him, she could see a future of languid bliss and relaxed and passionate adventures. If she was right, he was everything she'd ever looked for in a partner.

As much as she wanted him to tell her that he cared for her, to hear endearments that indicated this was more than just quick passion soothing two troubled hearts, she hesitated. There was no need to rush—there was a certain beauty in being patient and enjoying each moment together in this room. As soon as they stepped outside, life would come rushing at them from every direction.

"You are *so* unexpected. You are so different than the man I first thought you were. You are so smart and…so incredibly kind." She didn't dare say what she was thinking—that she would love to dream of a forever with him. A statement like that, in a moment like this, would have exactly the opposite effect than what she wanted. If someone said something like that to her, it would be a giant red flag.

Given how she was feeling, though, she had to question her assumptions and judgments about falling into anything resembling love at first sight. Technically, this wasn't at first sight, but it was close enough. Everything in her life she had made intentionally slow; it saved a person from making impulsive decisions that would inevitably come back to haunt them.

With Trent, however, it felt different. The idea that she could fall in with loving didn't feel impulsive. If anything, it felt complementary. He evened her out and balanced her in ways that she had never experienced with a partner before. He seemed to allow her to work through her feelings without feeling rushed, but at the same time, there was hunger and an unspoken invitation.

Taking his hand in hers and saying nothing, she moved the top of her robe aside and put their entwined hands over her heart. She wanted to tell him that in this moment, her heart beat for him and she would carry him there forever, regardless of what happened in their relationship.

This kind of moment, one in which she was giving herself freely to him, it wasn't something she ever did. Before now, whenever she had been with a man, she had been able to give her body but not her soul. None of the men she'd ever been with deserved to see the real her. She'd feared giving them access to who she really was, because in doing so she also handed them the golden ticket to destroying her.

Hopefully she wasn't making a mistake.

More, she hoped he understood in her simple touch, what she was leaving unspoken—that she trusted him and so much more.

He ran his fingertips over the scar just below her collarbone. "What happened here?" He moved closer, kissing the dimpled skin that carried so much of the past in its ridges and valleys.

She touched his face gently, looking into his big eyes. "I was shot…but it wasn't anything as exciting as what you think," she added quickly as he pulled back.

"What? When? How?" He looked angry and at war with himself as he stared at the scar.

"An ex thought if he didn't have me, no one else should, either… It's why I left him and my family business. I had to run. This life—the people in it, the world around it—wasn't for me. The only way I was going to stay alive and make a difference was by fighting for what was right in the courtroom."

"I am so sorry." He paused. "I know that's not what you want—pity—but I'm sorry that you ever had to go through that. I wish I had found you sooner, stopped that from ever happening."

Her eyes welled with tears as she looked at him. She loved this man's soul. He was so beautiful inside and out.

"Do you know what you do to me, when you look at me like that?" Trent traced the shape of a heart on her delicate skin.

She opened her legs slightly, exposing her lacy black panties.

Trent sucked in a breath, and his fingertips slipped on her skin and moved to the intersection of her thighs. He gently stroked the tender nub at her center. She moaned, closing her eyes as she tilted her head back and enjoyed the sensation of him pleasuring her.

His fingers moved faster, spinning circles on her in all the right ways. It was like he knew exactly what she needed, and there was a comfort with him, as if they had spent many a night together in bed. She wasn't sure why she felt as she did with him; it normally took months of getting to know a man before she could be this comfortable.

He gave her hope that he could bring her to completion. When it came to sexual satisfaction, she wasn't an easy lock to pick. Maybe she was too much in her own head, or maybe it was the controlling aspect of her personality, but releasing for a man was always a challenge.

"Kendra." He spoke her name gently, as gentle as his fingertips felt below.

"Yes?" she whispered between breaths.

"Relax for me." He moved closer to her neck as he spoke, and the words caressed her skin as seductively as his tongue had moved against her bottom lip.

The words in combination with his touch made her grow impossibly wetter. She wanted him. She wanted more than simply his fingers moving over her panties. "Please," she begged.

He shook his head and brushed her hair from her neck as he swirled his fingers faster. He gently kissed the soft spot right below her earlobe, slow and in direct contrast to the speed of his fingers.

He told her to relax, but something inside her was

building. There was an ache for him and an ache for something else… Something deeper.

She wanted everything.

His lips trailed down her neck over the top of her shoulder as he pulled back her bathrobe, and it slipped down her arm, exposing her hardened nipples. He kissed along the top of her shoulder as his free hand stroked her breast. She gasped at the intensity of everything he was making her feel—hot and cool, hard and soft, rough and tender.

He moved to the other side, exposing her completely. The only thing keeping the robe on her was the thin tie around her midsection.

As the pressure to release mounted, there was a knock at the door.

She jumped up, closing her robe tightly around her.

"I'll get it," he said, nodding for her to head to the bedroom. She rushed there, slamming the door behind her. It was a slight overreaction to a silly knock at the door, but she felt like a teenager who just been caught making out by her parents.

Everything…it had all happened so fast. This wasn't her style, and it left her feeling completely off kilter.

From the living room, she heard Trent get up from the couch. There was the click of the peephole opening and closing and then the slide of the latch.

"Is my sister here?" AJ asked.

She had no idea how he had found her, but his being here made her feel like a child who'd stayed out after curfew. Checking that her robe was completely closed, she tried to collect herself as she headed back out into the living room. AJ was standing there with his arms over his chest, looking every bit like their father.

Heat rose in her cheeks, even though she tried to keep it at bay. She was an adult woman with a career and a mind of her own. She didn't need to feel like a kid under her brother's scowl. "Why are you here, AJ?"

He looked her up and down, assessing her lack of clothing. "If you think I want to be here, seeing you in that, you couldn't be more dead-ass wrong." He waved at her with all the condemnation of an angry judge. "I'm here because you need to learn to answer your goddamned phone."

The only thing she needed to learn was how to keep from being found.

Chapter Twelve

There was embarrassed, and then there was being-called-out-by-a-brother embarrassed. Trent was used to neither. He couldn't remember a time when he had been more self-conscious than he was right then, being stripped down verbally by AJ Spade—a man he had never met.

"What do you want, AJ?" Kendra asked.

Though Kendra looked put together and willing to stand up to her brother, Trent was having one hell of a time trying to cover up his discomfort. Both physical and mental.

"I just heard about your run-in with the senator," AJ said, finally looking at Trent's face and seeing him for something more than the man who was trying to bed his sister. "You got your ass kicked."

Trent nodded. "Yeah, but your sister got the senator's date to safety." What he didn't mention was that it had also led to them being in the room where they currently were standing. If getting his ass beat meant that he got to spend one more night alone in proximity to Kendra Spade, he'd gladly take another hit.

"Did you see what was happening on social media?" AJ asked.

Kendra shook her head. "Before we get any more into this, I'm going to go get dressed."

AJ nodded. "Please do." Venom dripped from his words.

Crap. He didn't regret the direction he and Kendra had been taking things, but he didn't want to be in this room alone with AJ. Nothing good would come of that. Before he tried to come up with some excuse to get away from the man, Kendra took him by the arm. "And he'll be coming with me."

He wasn't one to be shuffled around, but for once he was glad just to follow directions. "Be right back," he said with the tilt of the head.

AJ's scowl deepened. "I'm not going to stand here and wait for you guys to do whatever it is you're gonna do. I'll meet you in the hotel lobby. You better not be more than five minutes." He turned to the door and stormed out, letting it bang shut behind him.

Kendra sighed. "Well, that was my brother AJ. And now you know why I wasn't in a hurry to go back to my family ranch."

"He is never going to like me."

Kendra shrugged. "If I was concerned about my brother and his opinion on my life, and the people I choose to bring into it, that would've given me a non-refundable ticket to the psychiatric ward." She laughed. "You know…most people fear their fathers and the judgment of their parents, but growing up I was always most concerned with what AJ thought of me. Thankfully, I've outgrown it. Not to mention the fact that I intentionally isolated myself from this family years ago."

"I'm sure your brother loves you and only wants the best for you, and undoubtedly that includes the men you date. I just wish he and I could've gotten off to a better start." As he spoke, he realized he was referring to the future—one that he and Kendra had never even talked about.

He walked back to the chair in the corner, picking up his shirt and carefully hiding his face. Apparently, today was going to be full of embarrassments. He could hardly wait to see what the rest of it would bring. All he wanted, if he had his way, was to pull her back onto his lap to continue what they'd started. Unfortunately, that moment was gone. Knowing his luck, it was gone forever, and Kendra would soon come to her senses and leave him.

"Regardless of what you and I choose to do," she started, sounding uncomfortable in addressing what might or might not have been the start of a relationship between them, "AJ's opinion is not any of my concern. I'm going to do what makes me happy."

He liked that sentiment and the thought that he made her happy. He hoped he would get the chance to make sure the way he made her feel never changed, but the dark cloud of reality and logic loomed overhead. "You know, I think there are several things that can act as indicators of a worthwhile relationship."

Though it might not have been in his best interest to bring the subject up, he also wasn't going to censor himself. He was too old to play the games he had played when he was in college, pretending to be interested in what the woman liked and to hate whatever it was she hated. He had once gone without potato chips for almost six months to please his ex-wife— never again.

She stepped beside him. There was a frown on her

face. "I'm not sure, with that look, that I want to know." She sounded like she was teasing, but he wasn't quite sure. "Tell me, though. I'm curious to know how your mind works."

He laughed. "Trust me, you probably don't."

She put her hand on his back, and there was a comfort that came with her touch; it was unexpected, but he reveled in it for a second too long and was only brought back to reality when she rubbed her finger over his shoulder blade. "I want to know everything there is to know about you." She gave a nervous laugh. "You know, so I can get a full picture of the man I'm working with."

"Working with?" he asked with the raise of a brow, thinking about how she had opened up and even revealed some of her scars.

"Just tell me what you need in a relationship."

He hadn't said he *needed* anything, merely what he believed was an indicator of something worth pursuing, but he didn't correct her. He needed to trust her, just as she had trusted him. "I think if you are dating the right person, they will help you be the best version of yourself. They will push you to your next level. Together, you should feel like you can take on the world. If they are holding you back or hurting you, in any way—" as he spoke those words, he felt a tug at his heart that told him this was probably him when it came to her "—then you should find someone better."

There was a look of pain in her expression, and her hand moved from his shoulder. "Well, I'm glad we don't have to worry about anything like that," she said, turning away and going toward her room. "I'll be right out. I'm going to finish getting myself together."

She had looked perfect to him, but then she always did, so he wasn't sure why she needed to excuse herself other than he had once again said the wrong thing. If he had made her think he was pushing her away, that hadn't been his intention at all. However, she did need to really and truly consider all that he was before she made the decision to continue down this path. He didn't want to be hurt if he gave her his all and then she came to realize he wasn't what she wanted.

Or perhaps she already knew she wasn't at her best with him, and that was why she needed a moment on her own? He took in a deep breath, trying to center himself.

He slipped into his clothes and readied himself for the day with a quick shave. Coming out of the bathroom, he took one more look at the sheet that he had left thrown on the corner of the couch. Damn AJ and damn his interruptions.

Kendra appeared, wearing a different outfit from the ranch supply store, a black Orvis skirt with a button-down white shirt. He stared at the label on the skirt, impressed that she would wear a fly-fishing brand.

"Did you grab all your stuff?" she asked, and though the question was neutral, there was the underlying implication that she wasn't planning on having him stay with her again.

He tried not to cringe. "Yep, running pretty light these days." He walked over to the side of the couch and picked up his go-bag, which always lived in the back of his truck.

"Something tells me it's not just lately. With your job, and how much you travel, you probably can pack up your whole life into a bag like that," she said, motioning toward his tactical backpack.

Without speaking, he walked to the door and held it open for her, careful to keep his bag out of the way. They strode quietly down the hall, passing door after door. From behind some, he could make out the sounds of television, children talking, and one conspicuous moan, which made him think of Kendra's hotel robe falling open. At the noise, they grinned knowingly at one another, and for a moment, her look made his heart skip a beat. Perhaps she had been brought back to the thoughts of his fingers between her legs.

Before he could decide, she was moving ahead of him down the long hallway.

The hotel lobby was quiet, a few people standing at the concierge's desk, talking with the woman there about restaurants in the area. He grimaced when he spotted AJ behind the bay window that looked out onto the Clark Fork River, which ran through the center of town. He looked just as perturbed as he had in their hotel room—so much so that Trent couldn't help but wonder if that was just AJ's normal expression.

"AJ, thank you for your patience." Kendra's voice had the sharpness of the knife Trent always carried in his pocket.

"Don't give me any of your nonsense. Everyone has been trying to call you. You should have seen Zoey. She was about to load up the baby and come here and get you herself." AJ's scowl deepened as he looked over at him. "And you must be the man of the hour. Because of you and your affiliation with my sister—thanks to the videos on the internet—our family is being dragged through the mud. I'm not sure if you are aware of this or not, but my family isn't one that appreciates a whole lot of media attention."

"You need to stop right there, AJ," Kendra said, stepping between them. "I don't know what happened in the last twelve hours that makes you think you can barge into my hotel room and into my life and start acting like a jerk, but you need to stop. You have no right to treat me or my guest this way."

"Your *guest*?" AJ laughed. "That's one way to put it."

Kendra's dark laugh reverberated through the lobby, and the concierge and the hapless tourists stopped talking.

AJ didn't move.

"Is everything all right?" the concierge asked as she reached for the phone.

"Fine," AJ grunted, and she put down the receiver.

Trent stepped to Kendra's side in a show of support. "Why don't we talk about this outside?" he said, motioning toward the doors that led to the patio overlooking the river.

AJ shot him a look that told him he didn't appreciate being spoken to by him in the slightest, but Trent didn't care. From everything he'd seen, and what Kendra had told him, AJ could kiss his ass if he thought he could get away with treating his sister the way he had been. He had wanted to assume AJ had her best interests at heart and wanted to do nothing more than protect her, but it appeared that perhaps the only thing AJ really cared about was making his sister come to heel.

AJ was clearly an idiot if he thought Kendra would let him get away with that kind of behavior. She was a woman with standards and boundaries that weren't drawn in sand but, rather, in concrete.

The patio was empty, thankfully. They didn't need to make any more of a spectacle of themselves. Ever since they had started working together, he and Kendra had left a wake of bloodied lips and bodies behind them—now AJ was included. Yet he would like to keep things from moving farther downhill.

"So, you were saying that there has been fallout on social media? What has been going on since last night?" Trent asked, trying to dispel some of the tension that was swarming between the siblings like wasps.

AJ cleared his throat, tore his glare away from his sister and exhaled. "First, Kendra, you are right. I do owe you an apology."

She frowned. "If you don't mean it, I wish you wouldn't even fake it. There's nothing worse than being disingenuous."

AJ smiled, apologetically. "No, really, I meant it. And if I weren't already in the doghouse, I would argue that there are several things worse than being disingenuous." He lifted his left hand, which was missing the middle finger. "For example, it's a pain in the ass not being able to flip a-holes off in traffic."

Kendra chuckled and in the sound was the balm of forgiveness. "Oranges and fingertips, hardly comparable, but I'll allow it."

"As I knew you would." AJ sent her a cheeky smile. "As for you—" AJ turned to him as he spoke, his voice taking on a dry tone "—I'm still pissed. However, I do appreciate you looking out for my sister. I know she isn't one to take directions—or criticism—well.

The fact you can work with her at all says something about you."

He wasn't sure if that was a ringing endorsement of either himself or Kendra, but at least no one was slapping anyone.

"Don't ruin a good apology by being an ass, AJ," Kendra said. "Now, what is going on?"

AJ sent him one more wary glance before resigning himself to his sister's admonishment. "My apologies, Trent."

He didn't dare to ask how the man knew his name, considering Kendra had yet to actually introduce them. "No harm, no foul, man." He would take the olive branch where he could get it.

AJ dipped his head in acknowledgment. "So, Zoey might have left you several messages, but there has been a viral explosion on all the social media sites. According to the senator, your boy here—" he motioned toward him "—is being portrayed as some wacked-out religious zealot who had a vendetta against the senator."

"Are you kidding me?" Kendra growled. "Who was behind that stroke of political genius?"

"The senator and his public relations team. They know what they are doing and how to turn what could potentially have been political suicide into a boon." AJ shook his head. "If you had been more transparent with us, we could have gotten ahead of this. Now we are playing cleanup. Zoey, our boss at STEALTH—" he glanced at Trent, filling him in "—isn't pleased."

"Is there a time when Zoey is pleased?" Kendra asked.

AJ smirked, as if that was answer enough.

Trent had to bet all Kendra's siblings were like AJ. He held no doubts that they were a tough lot; given the fact that they were a group of private military contractors, they weren't going to be the kind who walked around patting each other on the backs. Yet, seeing how hard her world could be—and how it paralleled his own, but on a larger-number-of-siblings scale—he could understand her leaving them.

"How can we get on top of this?" Trent asked. He was good on tech, but he wasn't a social media hound, at least not when it came to content creation.

"How can we get the senator pinned down? Or Marla?" Kendra added. "I thought Zoey was on top of this."

AJ shrugged. "She's working on it, but there is no fixing the public perception now. That ship has sailed. Your boy is a bad guy as far as the world is concerned." He shot him a look. "Despite the criminal accusations against the senator, he still has supporters who are willing to use social media to spread his lies."

Trent was used to not being the most liked man in town, because of his job, but being hated around the world due to social media was new to him. He hoped like hell that Tripp wouldn't have to start fielding any nasty phone calls or death threats.

"Was there any mention of me being a bounty hunter?" Trent asked.

AJ shook his head. "No, like I said, they are just calling you a man who had a vendetta against the senator. He's done pretty well suppressing any details about his role in the altercation."

"Of course he has," Trent grumbled.

"Zoey is posting versions of the video with our

audio. We may have made a few key adjustments and added closed captions, but it's all true, and the tide is turned away from us." AJ ran his hands over his face. "Now we just have to hope for the best and keep our name from getting out into the public too much more." AJ started to make his way toward the doors to leave.

"Wait," Kendra called after him and he turned back. "Who is Dean's criminal defense attorney, the one he is using to defend himself against the charges in his wife's death? I've only been dealing with our defamation suit."

"It's a woman named Kate Thomas. Why?"

Kendra frowned. "With Bradshaw Law Group or another firm?"

AJ paused and tapped on his phone. "Looks like she is with the Bradshaw Group."

Kendra shook her head. "I should have guessed. Where is this Kate Thomas, and why wasn't she in the office on the day of the murders?"

Chapter Thirteen

It felt ridiculously good to get back to work. Being with Trent had been more than nice, but with everything going on, it had been foolish to take things where they had. Besides, she prided herself on her ability to look toward the future; she was a planner, and being with a man who had no likelihood of moving across the country to be with her would spell nothing but disaster.

She wasn't one to believe in true love or soul mates—those kinds of romantic notions were for those who had the freedom to make mistakes. Love wasn't something she could ever really dream of having; she didn't have room in her life for a mistake as momentous as falling for the wrong person.

"Are you okay?" Trent asked, but he was looking in the direction of her hands on the steering wheel.

"I'm fine." She nodded. "I'm just thinking about the attorney Kate Thomas. I looked into her law practice, and her office is officially closed for the time being… though there was no mention of the murders."

"No surprise there. Death is bad for business." Trent's expression of concern didn't falter. "What were you thinking about Kate?"

She was relieved to be focusing back on their work

instead of their burgeoning feelings, or whatever it was between them. "I am just thankful we have another way to get to the senator. Marla...she's damned near a ghost."

Trent chuffed. "No kidding. And with your brother breathing down our necks..." He shook his head. "AJ, and, well, your whole damned Spade family...you guys are *intense*."

A thought struck her as she stared out at the Western-style brick building that made up most of downtown and he spoke their last name. They came to a stop at the light. "Did it occur to you Marla's last name is also Thomas?"

He scratched at the back of his neck. "Well, now that you mention it. It's a fairly common name, though. You think they're related or something?"

She put her hands up, shrugging. "It's something worth looking into. A defense attorney's unlikely to share much information with us, but we should try."

"Yeah," he said with a resigned sigh, like he could feel how desperate she was to grasp at straws. "Ever since...well, *you know*...back at the hotel...things have been off. Is there anything I can do make things right with us, or at least make it easier between you and your brother?"

The red light lasted forever.

She had a number of options as to how she could tell him there was no possibility of anything more between them. She just needed to use the method of delivering bad news she felt most comfortable with—that was, speaking like an attorney, cold and devoid of emotion, but not unnecessarily hurtful.

"Let's just not talk about it, okay?" she said.

Trent made a light choking noise, but when she looked to him, his expression was flat and unreadable. It was silly and adolescent, but part of her wanted him to fight. However, Trent remained silent.

She was glad he didn't say anything, because then she'd feel compelled to debate him. It was her greatest professional strength—her ability to counter someone's argument—and in relationships, her greatest personal weakness. Better to leave things alone for now before he realized he'd grow tired of her.

Yes, they couldn't be together. There was nothing about them that was simple—except in the bedroom, but sex was supposed to be easy. She was of the opinion that relationships that fit into a person's life easily and seamlessly were the kind of relationships that were worth having. If things were a struggle, then it was a case of a square peg in a round hole.

To love was to be vulnerable to the biggest cause of suffering of all—loss.

For now, the best thing she could do was focus on the case and not the future.

Without question, now that she had met the senator, she couldn't deny he should have been sitting in a jail awaiting his trial. She hadn't met his criminal defense attorney, but she had probably been more than well compensated for getting him out on bail, even though the crime and his personal wealth should have warranted remand. He was a flight risk from the beginning. And now that he hadn't appeared, the defense team was probably ready to kill him themselves. They had to have told him, in no uncertain terms, that if he desired any chance of being acquitted of all charges, then he would have to be on his best behavior.

Now, even if he did turn himself in, they would be walking into a trial with a strike already against them. From personal experience, those were the kind of trials she loved to take. She had a reputation to uphold, one that included a ninety percent conviction rate for the state. That was fifteen percent better than any of her colleagues. Statistically, if she kept it up, she was on the fast track to run for District Attorney within the next five years.

"Light's green," Trent said, motioning at the traffic that was already heading their direction.

"Oh yeah, right," she said, pressing the gas pedal just a little harder than necessary and sending the truck speeding forward. Her cheeks warmed.

"If you want, you are welcome to run me back to my place. Or you can just let me out here," he said, motioning toward the sidewalk. "It's not too far from where I parked, and I can go get my truck."

Though she was sure she should have let him go, she couldn't bear the thought of being alone. "I was actually just thinking about his attorney. I need to give her a call."

There was a sad smile on his lips, like he had sequestered himself to the friend corner where she had been pushing him.

Trent pulled out his phone and started tapping away. "The Bradshaw Law offices are closed—I think we know why—but I managed to pull a home address."

She frowned over at him. No attorney she knew would have their personal address readily available. "Address for what?"

"As it so happens, she posted on social media."

"And?"

"I wasn't finished." His smile widened. "As it so happens, I saw her house in a picture she posted and was able to pull an address."

"Damn," she said, impressed.

He puffed slightly. "It helps to have friends who are in the trenches." He pressed a few more buttons. "Take the next right and head toward Pattee Canyon."

She followed his directions until they were parked in front of a well-kept house. The place had a manicured lawn, raised flower beds in the front and large flower baskets filled with pink and purple petunias adorning the wraparound porch. The house itself was beige, somewhat unremarkable, but freshly painted with a new asphalt roof. It spoke of money but in a way which wouldn't draw attention—just the kind of home she would have expected.

"Let me think about my approach for a sec," she said, looking at the house and pondering how she would feel if someone brought work to her doorstep without announcing themselves first. She liked using the element of surprise, but the attorney probably had a gun sitting right beside the door; Kendra did.

"It will be okay," he said, waving off her concerns like they were inconsequential. "She probably has couriers running back and forth. Whether or not there was a disaster at her office, she still has work to do."

That she knew. While she could get continuances to put off trials, they could only wait so long before she would have to be in court or in a meeting room working out plea deals. "All I'm saying is that I'm sure two people who are standing on the opposite side of her client's best interests aren't likely to be welcome."

"I'm not saying she will click her heels when she

sees us, but she also won't really know who we are," he countered.

She huffed. "That is, unless she has been on social media today. By now, she has to be more than aware of the fight between you and the senator."

"Oh," he said, sounding like she had just punched him in the gut. "Here, I'll give her a call." Not waiting, he dialed. Even from across the car, she could hear it click straight to a call service. He left his name and his number, but he gave her a look that spoke of the fact he knew he would never be receiving a return phone call.

"So, yeah." She tapped on the steering wheel, weighing their options. "You are definitely going to be our weakest link in trying to make contact with this woman."

"Agreed. But I don't think we should give up now. In fact, I would say it won't hurt anything if you go and knock on the door. I can stay in the car, if you need me…" He held out his hand for her phone, and she handed it to him, unlocked. He put his number in. "Now, if you need me, you can get ahold of me."

He couldn't think that if she was in trouble, she wouldn't have time to send him a message, and as such, his action was sweet but ineffectual. At the thought, she chastised herself. She was searching for weaknesses instead of looking at intentions. He had already proven to her on more than one occasion that, if she needed him, he would come running. The same couldn't be said of any of her exes and barely of her siblings—not that she had ever really run to them in her time of need.

Actually, she couldn't think of a time other than when she had been a child when she had really needed anyone—besides this trip. Even when she'd been working in the family business, she'd been ferociously independent and capable of taking care of herself, even in cases where self-extraction had been a necessity.

Yet it did feel good knowing that he would have her back if she required help.

"If you don't hear from me in five minutes, come inside."

He nodded slightly, but she could see from the tense way he moved that he was afraid. There was no denying that his fear wasn't for himself, but her.

It was getting harder to ignore the pressure in her chest that was growing for him each time he looked at her like he was now. Before she second-guessed her choice in pushing him away, she turned off the truck and opened the door. "Five. Minutes."

"You got it, boss."

She wanted to hate the nickname he used, but given the circumstances, she liked it. The name reminded her that she was the one who was in charge, not her heart, him or her family. There was nothing stopping her from going to the front door of this house and asking the questions that needed to be asked.

Stepping out of the truck, she made her way onto the sidewalk and strode toward the door. She pressed the button on the security camera–equipped doorbell and waited. There was a long pause, and she pressed the button again.

A voice erupted from the speaker. "I'm sorry, we do not accept solicitors."

"I'm sorry to bother you, Ms. Thomas, but my name is Kendra Spade, and I'm here to ask you a few questions about your client Dean Clark." Saying it aloud, she was sure that the woman would, in no uncertain terms, tell her to get off her doorstep.

There was another long pause.

"I am deeply sorry about your colleagues at your office. I had the unfortunate misfortune of finding their bodies." Kendra tried another tactic to get the woman to talk to her.

The microphone crackled. "Yes, I'm aware of who you are. You've been all over the news since you arrived in the state. If you don't mind, I have a few questions for you as well."

That made the hairs on the back of her neck rise. It wasn't a hackle response—rather, one that told her no good would come of whatever the woman wished to ask her.

"I'm sorry for coming to your home. I just wasn't sure of any other way to reach you. We tried to call."

Pause. "We?"

Of course, the attorney would pick up on that kind of misstep. "I'm here with a friend."

"You mean the bondsman who physically assaulted my client in the park yesterday?"

Oh, this chat was going downhill quicker than she had anticipated, though she hadn't really expected much. "I would prefer to have this chat in person, if you wouldn't mind."

If she had been in the woman's shoes, she would have been laughing at her request.

"Unfortunately, I'm not at the house right now. If you'd like, you can come to my temporary office space. It's on 410 East Essex. It's in the Sherman Law Offices. They were kind enough to offer me a place." The woman sounded open to the idea of meeting. "I will be available in an hour."

It wasn't a surprise that the woman asked for time. Just like any good lawyer, Kate Thomas needed to collect her thoughts and get her questions in order before she was put on the spot. Plus, sometimes it helped to slow down the pace when it came to forced meetings; it allowed for the host to gain more of a power position. Time had a way of increasing tension. Even though there had been no real direct confrontation between the women, there was still the game of intimidation in play.

"An hour?" Kendra said, looking at her watch and making a show of thinking about her schedule. "I may have to move a few things around, but I think I can make that work. We will see you soon." She gave the woman and the camera a slight wave and walked away, not waiting for a response—two could play the power game.

Chapter Fourteen

From inside the truck, Trent had been able to tell Kendra had been speaking to someone, but he couldn't make out what she had said. She had a perturbed expression when she made it back to him.

"She didn't let you inside. Not a shocker." Trent had been hoping that something would come of their trip up here aside from making themselves look like stalkers, but he couldn't say he was surprised with the way things had turned out.

"No, it was good, though. She's at her temporary office. We have a meeting with her in an hour." Her words and her facial expression didn't align, but he wasn't sure if he should press or just let her open up to him naturally. She pulled out her phone and started clicking away. "According to the map, we aren't far from the offices."

If he had his way, they would have been spending their downtime wrapped in each other's embrace and taking things between them to the next level, but now to even imagine such a thing seemed like some kind of medieval torture device.

Once, he had been ambling around a museum to kill time on one of his many bounty trips—he couldn't remember where—but he had come across a room filled with all kinds of instruments used during the Dark Ages. He shuddered as he thought about the pilliwinks, or thumbscrews, which at this moment he would have endured if it meant they could go back to this morning, before they were interrupted.

She was tapping away on her phone, and after a moment she looked up. "The senator is on social media right now, doing a livestream. Look," she said, lifting her phone for him to see.

The man was talking animatedly, using his hands to make a point. The captions rolled across the bottom of the feed, and from what he could make out, Dean was talking about the "attack." He had a puffy left eye, like he had taken a hit, even though Trent had never landed a punch.

Trent gritted his teeth. "Are you effing kidding me?" He took hold of her phone, and, trying to ignore the lies the senator was saying about him, he studied the background.

"Oh, I'm sure my family is going to have a similar response. I'm actually surprised I haven't heard from them again."

"If we don't move, we will both be getting the what-for from our kin. Luckily, if we hurry, we might be able to catch up with the senator." He pointed at a sign in the background of the video. "Look, right there. He is standing in front of the Missoula Club. Let's go."

She started the truck, and the tires squealed as she punched the gas. He pointed her in the direction of the Missoula Club that had come to serve as one of the key fixtures in the town—it was where everyone went on Griz football game days and the place locals came to talk about anything of importance that happened in the town.

They weren't far from the place, but thanks to the awkward silence, the drive seemed like it took an hour. Things were tense between them, and they were about to go in to what could turn out to be a den of snakes. He should've been mentally preparing himself, as she appeared to be doing, but he found himself only staring at her.

"About this morning—"

She didn't even look away from the road, and yet her expression puckered and put a stop to his attempt to talk things out.

"Trent, there's no question that I'm attracted to you, but we can't really make anything more happen. Sure, we could have some fun, but we both know how these things work."

It was the first time she'd admitted she was attracted to him. Though he knew she was merely trying to soften up her rejection with a compliment, he couldn't stop himself from trying to convince her they could be something more. "Tell me, how do you think this could work? What do you see happening if we give this thing a shot?" She shook her head as though she didn't want to give even the idea a chance.

"Sometimes the things we need most in our lives are the things we have to fight the hardest to get. If you told me you'd want to do this thing, I hope you know I would fight for you."

"We are both capable, intelligent adults who have had relationships before. You can't tell me that our being together would be a good idea." She looked over at him with the raise of a brow.

"I have had relationships. So have you, but I can't say that I've ever been in a situation quite like this before," he said. "Though, since my divorce I haven't really dated a whole lot, so my experience with women is limited."

"I'm sorry about your divorce. I know how hard something like that can be." She gave him a long, appraising look, but he wasn't sure that she wasn't just trying to avoid his offer by being kind.

"Have you gone through it before?"

"Me?" She touched her chest. "No. I never found anyone who wanted to share their life with me."

"Now, I find that hard to believe. What man wouldn't want to spend a lifetime with you? You are incredible."

There was a pink hue on her cheeks. "You are giving me far more credit than is due. I'm as big a mess personally as anyone else."

"We're all just doing the best we can." He chuckled, and some of the strain between them slipped away with the sound. "Things don't always go as perfectly as I would like in my life, either. In my opinion, people and relationships don't have to be flawless…in fact, good ones shouldn't be."

Kendra smiled. "You say I'm incredible, but I honestly can't imagine why you wouldn't have women all over you. In fact, I bet you do." She gave him a sidelong look before pulling her gaze back to the road.

He laughed aloud. "Yeah, right."

He didn't often talk about his divorce, or any of his relationships—what few there were. He knew it was part of developing a relationship with others, talking about each other's pasts and hoping to find common ground to build a new foundation from, but it made him uncomfortable.

"I've not dated much since I've been single." He laughed awkwardly, thinking about the blonde who had broken up with him after learning how his job kept him on the road. "My last girlfriend was not impressed with my life."

It was uncomfortable admitting that aloud, especially to Kendra.

"You don't seem to have any problems communicating with me," Kendra said, and her smile made his heart skip a beat.

"I can't say we have any problems at all." As he said that, he felt ridiculous. There was a slew of problems and impediments standing in their way. "At least… I don't think that any of the problems we have are because of how we feel about each other."

He was met with road noise.

Just when things were getting better with her. He was so ridiculous sometimes. Even now, when he was chastising himself for saying too much, he still wanted to tell her there were at least a hundred things he found attractive about her, starting with how her mind worked. She was so incredibly smart and capable. He really couldn't imagine being a lawyer who had to go up against her in court; she had to be intimidating as hell up there.

A possibility dawned on him, pulling him from his churning feelings of lust and wanting. "I don't think I really asked you, but are you dating anyone?"

She tapped the brakes, sending the truck lurching slightly. "You have to be kidding me. Are you really asking me that now?" She huffed. "I'm not the kind of woman who would have a boyfriend and then try to seduce another man."

Though he knew it was the wrong reaction, a huge smile erupted on his face. "So, you *were* trying to seduce me?"

"What?" She sounded flustered. "Wait. That wasn't the point I was trying to make."

"Doesn't matter. You said it. It's on record." He laughed. "Regardless of what you want to call it, it happened. I know you think we can't have a relationship because we are from different worlds, but I don't agree."

"You would hate New York if you had to live there." She waved her hands in the direction of the quaint Western buildings that surrounded them. "If I lived somewhere like here, I would never want to leave."

"I never said I wasn't willing to move or that I loved this place. It's beautiful, but I'm not here for the scenery." He tried to sound at ease with the idea, but in reality, Tripp and their business sprang to the front of his mind before he was even done speaking.

"Regardless, we are putting the future ahead of the present. It's probably silly to worry about who would move where when really you should be asking yourself whether or not you really are compatible with me. I've been honest with you about who I am and what people think of me. Obviously, I'm direct. I know it can come off as brash and rude sometimes, and it can push people away."

He shrugged. "I don't think you're rude. If anything, I appreciate you just addressing things head-on. My ex-wife was notorious for masking how she really felt. I'm good at a few things, but I'm not particularly good at reading minds. It was the nail in the coffin of our relationship—her failure to communicate." He sighed. "I blame myself. I should have been more direct. It's a lot of work having to constantly press someone for answers about what they're thinking and feeling, especially when I wasn't there all the time. Yet, I should have worked harder if I wanted to save us. I didn't, though, and whether or not I want to admit it, I let my relationship die."

She nodded slowly. "I know what you mean. Relationships take two people, and no matter what happens—staying together or falling apart—it's the responsibility of both," she said.

He loved that about her…the fact he didn't have to explain himself to her to make her understand what he was thinking. That he could be so open with her, even though he hadn't known her long. "Have you always been direct?"

"I was never particularly shy, even when I was young. My last boyfriend said he loved that I was straightforward, but it didn't take him long to realize while it was great in theory, it was another thing in practice."

"How is it possible that we've had the exact opposite relationship problems?" He laughed as he looked out at the city around them. The downtown area was bustling with people out walking and window-shopping at the variety of pop-up stores that lined the road.

"I'm never going to be a submissive in a relationship. I want to stand beside my partner."

They stopped to let a person cross the road. "Look," Trent said, pointing at the crowd down the street.

In front of them was a large group of people. Most

were standing on the sidewalk, bustling about like they were trying to see someone standing in the doorway of the nightclub in front of them. While he couldn't see what they were looking at, or whom, above the crowd was a large red-and-white '50s-style sign that read Missoula Club.

He hadn't really thought they would catch the senator here, especially given the fact it'd taken them so long to drive over, but it appeared like they were going to have another opportunity to get their hands on the man they so desperately needed to find.

"Before I go running headfirst into this thing, we have to be smart," Trent said. He wasn't always one who was metered in his responses, especially when it came to this kind of work, but he had to protect Kendra and do the right thing by her family even if things between them ended there. Hell, even if they weren't dating, he needed to do right by her.

"What're you thinking?" Kendra asked.

"Honestly, that I don't want to do anything that would upset your family. I don't want to set you back in what little progress you've managed to make with your brother." Trent paused. "I'm sure Tripp doesn't want any more drama when it comes to our business, either."

Kendra nodded. She tapped her fingers on the steering wheel. "Why don't we call the police on this? I mean, all you need is him back in jail, right? We could keep a watch on him until they arrive and take him into custody."

It wasn't a bad idea. Things had a tendency to go all kinds of sideways when he got anywhere near this guy. "I'll text Tripp and see if he thinks we should call it in." He picked up his phone and sent a quick message about the senator's location with their request.

His phone pinged with a message from his brother almost immediately. It simply read, Don't cause nothing. Hold back.

Trent turned his phone for Kendra to see, but he pulled a baseball cap on like it was his best attempt to conceal his identity. "I guess we have our orders. We need to try to disappear."

She parked the truck a block away, and they made their way over to the bar. They could hear laughter as they approached the crowd. Standing on the step, puffy left eye and all, was the senator. He was holding a microphone.

Always the showman.

Kendra leaned in close to Trent. "This guy could give the slickest politician a run for his money. Can't say he doesn't know how to work the crowd."

"You can say that again." He sighed. "This guy is a real piece of work. I don't know how, given his level of popularity—even considering his current murder charge—the jury is going to convict him."

He hated this man who seemed to always be above the law. Hell, he hated anyone who was. He'd had clients at the bond shop who he'd really thought were innocent of crimes, who were later convicted. And yet, here was a man who was almost certainly guilty, and he'd probably get a slap on the wrist—if he was even found guilty. If anything, it also proved the power of media.

"I never try to give the public too much credit. I've seen some crazy things," Kendra said. "But if there is a good prosecutor, he is definitely going to go down for his crimes."

"We'll see. Clark is a snake. He could wiggle his way out of this thing."

On each side of the senator stood two thick men, each wearing scowls. The men were scanning the crowd as if they were looking for threats. He knew the body language of the predator well. These men were there as bodyguards, and also as a show of strength.

He stepped deeper into the shadows and out of the senator's line of sight. He pulled Kendra back with him.

The senator hadn't been here doing a livestream by accident. He had set this up. Guards and all. Had he intentionally been hoping Trent would come for him again? That kind of game seemed right up Clark's alley.

The guard closest to him was thick-jowled, and his face reminded Trent of a pockmarked wolverine. The man looked familiar, but he couldn't quite place him. More than likely, he was someone they had once bonded out. It happened more often than he liked, running into past clients. From the look on the guy's face as he glanced over at him, the man recognized him as well. His scowl deepened.

The guard turned to the senator, and the man instantly stared in Trent and Kendra's direction, but then he returned to addressing his crowd. "It is a sad day for Americans when we are not safe in our own streets," he bellowed into the microphone. "And when we cannot be provided an adequate trial. Instead, we are hunted down like dogs."

The senator shook his fist in the air like he was morally outraged, but it was nothing more than an act. "The America I knew as a child, one built on equality and a justice system that could be trusted, is no longer the America of my adult life."

Trent's resolve at not making a scene or causing problems for the families dissipated. He stepped out of the shadows, and Kendra tried to pull him back. Shaking his head, he pulled free of her grip. He'd had his fill of this man. He couldn't stand idly by for another second—with or without AJ's approval.

"Do you know what I believe is unjust and morally repulsive?" he yelled, pulling the crowd's attention away from the man. "A senator who touts family values and pulls at the heartstrings of his constituents through manipulation tactics that would make most people cringe."

The crowd opened up in the direction of the senator as Trent spoke. The senator's face blanched.

"Why don't we talk about your using your wife's death to gain votes? Or how about the fact that you had her and your own daughter kidnapped?"

"You need to get him out of here!" the senator ordered. "I apologize to those in attendance today. This man is a nuisance. Just yesterday he attacked me without so much as a warning. Some of you may have seen the video! Don't be alarmed, but he is a danger." The senator pointed at his puffy cheek.

The guards charged toward Trent and Kendra. He was tempted to tell Kendra to run, but that would only make it appear like the senator was telling the truth and he was out to get him. Clark was damn good at using the victim card. Trent couldn't play into that.

"I ask that no members of the public put themselves in harm's way," the senator said, his voice nauseating and cloying.

"Senator, what actually happened to your wife?" Trent countered.

The senator's main guard grabbed Trent by the arm and tried to throw him to the ground, but Trent stopped him with one well-timed jab to the throat. He barely looked away from the senator as his hand connected. As the guard dropped to the ground clutching his throat, Trent regretted having touched the man, but it had to be done. "I'm sorry I had to defend myself. But it is important for the public to know about your role in a murder. Not to mention the fact you didn't appear at your last court date. You are a con man, a bail jumper. You are nothing but scum. These people and all the people who voted for you deserve to know exactly what kind of person you are!" His rage pumped through his veins like lifeblood.

Looking to the guard on the ground, the senator smiled. As quickly as the smile appeared, it was replaced by the look of concern. "I am deeply saddened that you would accuse me of such crimes. I'm innocent in the eyes of the law until proven otherwise. There is no evidence. I did nothing wrong." Tears welled in the senator's eyes as he put on the show.

As Trent was about to counter, a police officer approached him.

Kendra's face softened as she looked to the cop. "I am so glad you're here. This man, the senator, has a warrant out on him," she said, pointing up at Clark.

The officer looked to the senator and then back at them, but instead of moving in the direction she was pointing, the officer stepped closer to Trent.

"Sir, there have been reports of a disturbance. Did

you just hit this man?" he asked, pointing at the guard on the ground at Trent's feet.

Trent's entire body went numb. "What? No... I—" The officer motioned for silence, cutting him off.

"Sir, do you wish to press charges against this man?" he asked the guard, pointing at Trent.

His former client looked up and sent him an evil smile. "Officer, I most certainly would."

The senator was moving along the building's facade, disappearing into the crowd and no doubt running from the justice that should have been served.

In an attempt to save what dignity he had left, Trent turned and put his hands behind his back. There was no fighting to clear up this misunderstanding with the officer. He should have never laid his hands on the guard, out of self-defense or otherwise. He looked to Kendra, and there were tears in her eyes.

This time, they both knew the wrong man was going to jail.

Chapter Fifteen

This would all get straightened out. It had to. Kendra watched as the patrol car drove away with Trent handcuffed in the back seat. His eyes locked with hers, and he mouthed the words *It's okay.*

Okay was the last word she would have used when describing what had just happened. Nothing was okay, and in fact, things were consistently getting worse and more confusing as each minute passed by.

She was equally angry at the police officers who'd ignored her demand to arrest the bail-jumping senator, telling her they had no information on that warrant.

Ha!

She didn't believe that for a second and wondered if Dean had paid off someone to look past his crime. They'd also ignored her description of Trent's fight, despite her willingness to swear an affidavit attesting to his acting in self-defense.

Making her way back to the pickup, she felt her purse, making sure her gun was still inside. If she found the senator, this man was as good as dead. She'd never thought of herself as a killer; it was more her siblings' jobs. Yet she was willing to make the sacrifice for Trent. She wasn't sure exactly what that meant about her feelings toward him, but depending on the perspective it was either wonderful or extremely inconvenient.

Starting the truck and pulling out onto the road, she searched the sidewalk for any signs of the senator. If she just looked hard enough, she could find the man. He couldn't have made it that far. She went one block, then two and three.

This man was from the area. If he didn't want to be found, there was little chance she, an out-of-stater, was going to find him.

The meeting with Kate Thomas was in ten minutes. The last thing she wanted to do was go sit down in a lawyer's office, not with everything going on. Trent needed her.

She wished she could be actively helping him, but until he was processed, there was little she could do. They had driven by the police station on the way to the Missoula Club, so it wasn't too far, but the booking process could be tedious on a busy day. He had to have been freaking out. She would have been—especially given the fact it had all just been a terrible mistake.

She thought of the way he had looked at her when he'd been making his way to jail. It tore at her heart to think about the injustice that was being done.

While she couldn't say with a hundred percent certainty that the senator was guilty of all the things she'd heard, he was far more guilty than Trent. Trent was a good man with a tough job, one that took a special kind of person to perform. It was strange how he could be so self-deprecating when she could find no real fault in his work. Just like everybody else, he had a job to do—a job that didn't always make him beloved. However, she was in the same boat. Everybody was just trying to do the best they could, all while trying to be the best people they could be—that was, except Dean Clark. He seemed to have made a profession out of toeing the line between morally bankrupt and illegal.

She drove by the police station slowly, looking at the large brick building as though its walls were the only thing keeping Trent inside.

The only way she could help right now was by speaking to Kate Thomas and finding out what she knew. Kendra was an attorney through and through. She loved the thrill of standing in a courtroom and convincing the judge that the defendant was guilty. It was such an incredible thing to feel the energy in the courtroom shift in her favor. Often when the defense attorneys questioned her witnesses, there was a ripple in that energy—and that spark of contention and drama was a feeling she sought and could only find in those moments.

Perhaps it was that competitiveness that kept her going. There was so much drama and so much intrigue, but ever since coming to Montana, she hadn't been able to decide whether her job or this place was more interesting.

She could only imagine what would happen if she stayed here for any real length of time. She'd just been here a few days, and already she had found herself embroiled in a set of deaths and Trent had been arrested— the morning after she'd nearly slept with him.

Trent.

She pictured his brown eyes, his strong shoulders and solid physique. The way he made her laugh—even with everything that had been going on since they had first met… Even though how they met was unusual and she should have been leery of him because of his initial secrets, she'd found that she just wanted to be around him.

She shook off the thought. She was fine. *Independence* should have been her middle name.

She slammed her hand against the steering wheel.

That was a lie. She wasn't fine.

She was at a loss without him.

Stopped at a traffic light, she couldn't think of what to do next. If he had been with her, he would've had some clever idea about where to look for the senator or Marla, but on her own she felt like a fish out of water, a new sensation for her. She was usually confident in her abilities.

It wasn't just that she wasn't from here. The town wasn't that big. Basically it was made up of four zones that she had seen so far, and then a medley of suburban developments. She could find her way around, but the problem was knowing where to start and whom to go after first. She had her family's lawsuit to think about, and now she wanted to help Trent bring the senator in so his family business didn't lose money on the bond.

The light turned green, and Siri told her to turn left—as if the phone itself had known she was in need of guidance. Unfortunately, just because it could tell her how to get somewhere, it didn't mean it would provide her with the answers she so vitally needed.

At the bottom of it all, she just wished she could do something more to help Trent.

It's okay. She could still envision him mouthing those words to her.

He must've known exactly how she was going to

feel as he was being taken away. Which meant that he had been worried about her when he should have been worried about himself. He was so selfless.

Driving down the road, she saw a heavyset man walking down the sidewalk with his black Lab on a leash. The man had his back to her, but the way his shoulders were shaped reminded her of the guards.

Were they looking for her?

The thought frightened her. With what had just happened with the senator, she was definitely going to be on the senator's guards' radar. For all she knew, she wasn't the one doing the hunting; rather, they were hunting her. It's what she would have done if she had been in the senator's position. Right now, it seemed as if she and Trent were his biggest enemies. With an enemy, the best defense was often a strong offense.

She had a feeling that was something Trent would have said to her, and the thought brought her some peace.

With a few more turns, she found herself around high-end offices and the start of a residential area. Lush, green maple trees lined the road, casting their shade onto the summer lane.

To her left was a large brick building adorned with white windows and black shutters. The building had a colonial feel, as if one of the Founding Fathers had originally constructed it. It was beautiful, with ivy growing up the brick walls around the front entrance. The building was inviting and a far cry from what she had expected to find when going to meet the senator's criminal defense attorney. On the other hand, this wasn't Kate's office.

After parking, Kendra stared down at her phone. Tripp probably needed to know what happened.

She searched for the number for the bonds company. She pressed call, and a young woman answered on the first ring. "Hello, this is Lockwood Bonds, Emily speaking. How can I help you?" The woman sounded far too chipper for Kendra's liking.

"This is Kendra Spade. I was calling to get ahold of Tripp. Is he available?" She had her hackles raised, but as much as she tried to talk herself down from her annoyance, she found she had no control over it when confronted with this twentysomething-sounding girl who must've worked with Trent nearly every day.

She wasn't the kind to be jealous, but oddly enough, it was undeniable. What did that mean?

"Hold on one moment, hon." Emily sounded one step off from giggling.

The fact that the girl had just called her *hon* set her teeth on edge. If Emily had worked for her, she'd have been fired already. There was a time and a place for a jovial and nonchalant manner, but working in a business that controlled the destiny of its customers was not that time.

The phone clicked, and she was sent to the dreaded hell of late-'80s lobby music. She wasn't sure when Mötley Crüe had gone from being edgy and on the forefront of music to becoming so mundane that it could be played while a person was on hold.

After what felt like ten minutes, Tripp answered the phone. "Hey, what's going on?"

Hearing Tripp's voice, which sounded far too much like his brother's, she felt a lump rise in her throat.

Now she was getting emotional, too? What was going on with her?

"Hey, so, your brother was just picked up by the local PD. He is being charged for assault." The words came out like they were weighted and they sank in the air.

"Holy crap, are you kidding me?" Tripp laughed, as if he actually thought Kendra was playing some ill-advised and poorly timed prank.

"No, seriously. We ran into the senator. Things went downhill rather quickly." That felt like an understatement. "Is there anything you can do to get him released?"

She could hear Tripp typing away on a keyboard. "I'm looking at the police scanner data now. The boards are pretty empty. We might get lucky, but I have to make some phone calls. I'll keep you posted."

"Thanks, Tripp, I appreciate it." She could hear the relief in her voice.

At least I'm not completely alone.

The thought reminded her of her family. It was odd, but she hadn't even thought of calling them and instead had chosen to call Tripp. She would have liked to say it was merely an oversight and she would call them soon, but as she thought about dialing, AJ popped into her head. He would be absolutely livid if he heard how everything had been going. It was probably a good idea not to have him in the know—not until everything played out and she was back in control and at the top of her game.

"I gotta say, you must really like my brother." Tripp was still clicking away, and he spoke the words like it was no big deal or even slightly surprising.

"What do you mean?" She kept her voice light, as if she didn't really care, even though she hung on his words.

"Seems to me, your family's lawsuit is probably on hold about now. The senator's lawyers were murdered, after all. You could probably head on home to New York and come back and still be ahead of the ball. Yet, you're choosing to stay here and help us out. You're a busy woman. It must be costing you a pretty penny to hole up in Montana like this. Which could only mean a couple of things."

"My family wanted me here."

Tripp chuckled. "And I know my brother is interested in you—or he certainly seems to be. You're definitely his type."

"What type is that?"

She could feel Tripp's self-satisfied smirk even though he was on the other end of the phone. "He likes a woman who takes charge and pulls no punches. As for my brother, he isn't one who normally hangs out with anyone for more than a couple of hours before seeking to be back by himself. He is a lone wolf, so the fact that it doesn't seem like he's left you alone… well, it's telling me all I need to know about his feelings toward you."

"We are just friends, that's all." She wasn't sure why she said it, but something inside her drove her to want to protect their burgeoning relationship…or whatever it was.

"That's good. Trent needs *friends*," Tripp said, a shard of ice smattered in his words. "And I guess I'm glad there ain't nothing more between you two…considering my brother's got a girlfriend. If for a minute

I thought you were into him, I'd have to warn you off. As it is, it would be in your best interest to steer clear of him."

Her stomach dropped. Of all the things she'd thought the man was going to say, him telling her about Trent's love life in a context that didn't involve her came as a surprise. Trent had told her—or at least she thought he had—that he was single. She definitely remembered him telling her about his ex-wife, but that didn't mean that he didn't have a new girlfriend.

"I have to go." She hung up the phone, not waiting for Tripp to speak another word out of the fear that what was left of her heart would be ripped to shreds.

Chapter Sixteen

The steel handcuffs were chewing at his wrists like hungry hound dogs. It wasn't the first time he'd been booked, and it wasn't going to be the last—at least, he solidly doubted it. That being said, this was the first time he felt like he was innocent. He had done a hell of a lot worse and never been caught, so to find himself here sitting on the bench and waiting for them to take his fingerprints was almost laughable. Hell, he would have been laughing if it hadn't been for Kendra.

He couldn't forget that look on Kendra's face after they cuffed and stuffed him. She'd looked absolutely terrified. He would've done anything—or gone back in time and made a whole hell of a lot of different decisions—if only he could wipe that expression off her face. She was far too beautiful to look that scared. From the moment he had met her, she had been nothing but confident. Yet somehow, he had broken her.

He'd never really liked the senator, but now he hated the man.

If he ever found the senator's guards in a dark alley, they would get an ass whooping that they would never forget. When he told Tripp about this, his brother would probably want to tag along just to lay down the hammer. His brother could be one hell of a pain in the ass, but when it came to things like this, he was a good man to have standing at his side.

When Trent got his one phone call—which wouldn't be for a while—he wasn't sure exactly whom he should call: Tripp, a defense lawyer or Kendra.

By now, if he was Kendra, he would've been on the first plane back to the city. She didn't have to put up with his crap. She didn't owe him anything. It was crazy how much they had been playing this delicate game of so close, yet so far. Right now, he was farther away than ever.

He was so angry, he could spit. For just about the first time in his life, he was doing the right thing for the right reasons, and yet here he was paying the price for all his other misdeeds. And, of course, he had been made to look the fool in front of her... Would she even stay?

Kendra definitely wasn't his girlfriend; she wasn't even his lover. Though they had come damn close. He would never forget the way she had felt sitting on his lap, the robe slipping from her shoulder, exposing that little puckered scar. If he hadn't been able to see any part of her but her shoulder, he still would've been harder than pine.

The thought made him squirm on the hard wooden bench. Now wasn't the time or the place to think about Kendra naked. It would lead to some odd questions if his body responded. Though, if he had to guess, there were probably people who enjoyed this kind of thing. He had definitely met a few who would get a rise out of being handcuffed and dominated, but he wasn't one of them. He had to really trust someone to even allow them access to his world, let alone have any real control over it.

The officer who arrested him hadn't said any more than what was absolutely necessary during the booking process. Now he was filling out paperwork on the computer, but he kept glancing over at Trent, making sure he wasn't going anywhere.

The guy should've known better. He would've done about anything just to get out of this place right now, and acting up would have been against his own self-interest. He needed to get back to Kendra. She needed him. He'd seen it in the way she looked at him, and now sitting here, powerless, was far more torturous than anything they could do to him inside the jail.

He leaned his head back against the concrete wall behind him and closed his eyes. He tried to calm himself, reminding himself that Kendra was one of the most capable women he knew, but his heart was thrashing in his chest. If only he had gotten his hands on the senator. At least then he would've known where the man was and if he posed any real threat to Kendra.

So far, the man only seemed hell-bent on taking him down and hadn't even really seemed to notice that Kendra had been with him. It could have been an oversight, or it could have been that the senator didn't even know she was gunning for him. Trent hoped for the latter. If the senator wasn't after her, she stood a chance in getting out of this entire fiasco without too much more going wrong.

Yes, that had to be it. She wasn't in danger. She had anonymity on her side. Hell, even her family's lawsuit was probably moot now, too, since the senator was a bail jumper.

The arresting officer made his way over to Trent. "You ever hear the story about the jackrabbit?" The man looked down at him, but even from where he was sitting, he could make out a thin sheen of sweat on the man's brow. The guy even smelled of sweat, the dank, hormonal kind that came after a long day's work and heavy stress.

They had been in the bucket for about an hour, so he couldn't imagine why the man was sweating so profusely.

"Well, have you?" the officer inquired.

Trent shook his head.

The officer sighed. "My grandmother always told me a story about this one jackrabbit. Lived on my family's ranch in North Dakota."

Given the start of the story, he wasn't sure why the man would've thought he'd ever heard it. However, being snarky and picking a fight didn't seem like the greatest idea when he was sitting here at this man's mercy.

"This little rabbit found itself in our family's barn. Wasn't a bad place for a rabbit. In fact, he thought it was real perfect. He could play all around the combine and big machines and stayed one step ahead of any little predators that liked to look outside the barn. At night, the little rabbit would slip under the door and nibble on the grass around the barn and do what rabbits do."

The man looked at him, assessing, like he was making some odd metaphor about how Trent was the rabbit. The man failed to realize Trent wasn't playing—this wasn't some goddamned game to him.

"Sure enough, one day this rabbit got picked up

by a little fox. That fox got it in its mouth and moved to start shaking it about, but lo and behold, that rabbit wasn't alone. Out came another one from the barn. Instead of running or turning back and going back in that barn, that rabbit came charging after that fox, forcing it to drop the rabbit in its mouth." The officer sounded annoyed.

If this guy was talking about them, Trent couldn't imagine who would have already come to his rescue and forced the man to let him go.

"Are you saying you're releasing me?" Trent asked.

The officer crossed his arms over his chest, making him look even wider than he already was. The guy was stocky and thick, and the last thing he would've called the guy was fox-like. If anything, he was more like a tank, thick and blocky, the kind of guy who would have no problem taking any dude to the ground.

"Hold your horses, I wasn't done with my story." The officer smirked.

Trent could see this man was enjoying his little show of power. He didn't totally understand why the guy was going after him like he was. For all intents and purposes, they were fighting for the same side when it came to criminals. Or was this guy trying to warn him about something?

"While that little rabbit and his compadre got away, that fox was smart. Now he wasn't just going after one rabbit, he was going after two. So, he hunkered down and waited. It wasn't a day later that those hungry little rabbits poked their heads out, and he devoured both of them. The only thing he left of them was tufts of fur." The officer bristled with the threat.

So, the man *was* going to have to release him. This

couldn't have been the first time the guy was faced with something he felt wasn't right or fair, but if the cop had just talked to him and seen his side of things, maybe he could have helped him to understand that he wasn't the villain here.

He looked at the officer, studying him. The guy was young—if he had to guess, he would've said he was probably about twenty-seven. He was just getting to that age where a person was starting to figure life out, but with figuring it out came a complete lack of humility. Life was just about to slap him down. Trent didn't particularly want to be the guy that was responsible for that with this kid, but his own self-interest had to come first.

"Who told you that you had to release me?" Trent made sure not to smile, keeping his expression neutral in an attempt to keep the kid from reading him.

"Who said anything about releasing you?" the young man countered.

Trent tried to stifle his annoyance. The fellow was just learning the ropes. "What sergeant's on duty today?"

"Why do you care?"

"I'm not sure if you're aware of this, but I'm friends with quite a few of your brothers in blue. In fact, I work closely with most of the men here. Detectives really like me." He tried not to sound full of himself, but the kid needed to know that it wasn't Trent who was playing with fire here.

"It's funny, but every time I arrest somebody, they seem to get some new friends around the department." He smirked again. "So, before you go throwing out any names, you need to make sure that they know I'll be giving them a call."

He was growing tired of this kid's game. "I'm currently working with Detective Baker on a murder case. If you wanted to give him a call, I'm sure he'd be more than happy to come down here and talk to me and explain the situation." He didn't really want the dude to call the detective; he was nothing more than a witness for the man. However, if it sped up the process of getting him back to Kendra, he would pull out all the stops.

The young officer dropped his hands from his chest and started fiddling with the latch on his utility belt. He tapped his fingers on the set of handcuffs in the hard plastic shell, making them rattle. It was almost like a nervous tic.

Finally, maybe they were getting somewhere.

The kid pulled out his cell phone and started tapping away, and without saying anything, he went back to his computer.

Trent smiled; he'd be back to work in no time. He'd never been more amped up to get his hands on a fugitive before.

Trent was tired of men like Dean, the kind who never found themselves staring down the barrel. Instead, they were always the one holding it.

The officer answered a phone call. He turned away, shielding his face from Trent's view, and it made him wonder who exactly he was talking to—if it was the detective or whoever had led him to having the conversation about rabbits.

The phone call didn't last more than thirty seconds, and the kid's hands were shaking as he slipped the device into his back pocket and turned again to his computer.

A few minutes later, the door at the end of the hallway opened, and Detective Baker came strolling out. He looked at Trent and gave him a stiff acknowledging nod before making his way to the office area where the patrolman was standing. They had a quick, hushed conversation.

Detective Baker made his way over to Trent and took out a handcuff key. "Why don't you go ahead and stand up and we can get you out of here," he said with a lift of the hand, motioning him upward.

Trent stood and turned toward the wall, holding his arms out behind him so Baker could take the cuffs off. With a quick flip of the key, Baker removed them and tossed them on the floor in the direction of the patrolman. While Trent wasn't sure what they had said to one another, the toss made it clear the two weren't going to become friends anytime soon.

Trent turned back around, rubbing the red welts on the outsides of his wrists where there had been the most pressure from the cuffs. Though he was flexible, it was amazing how much damage a set of cuffs could do to a fully grown man in a matter of hours.

"Sorry about this," Baker said, motioning him in the direction of the door from which he had first appeared.

"It isn't your fault. If anything, I should have made more of an attempt to control my temper." He walked beside the detective as they made their way down the hall, but as he neared the desk where the patrolman was standing, he found the kid wouldn't look him in the eye. "I appreciate you helping me out. Thanks."

"Oddly enough," Baker said, "I've actually been

fielding a number of calls about you and Ms. Spade today. Sounds like you guys have been up to your knees in crap since I last saw you."

Trent reached up and ran his hand over the back of his neck. "Well, hell. It wasn't like we were aiming to cause problems. We were just trying to do the best with what the world has given us." He gave a nervous laugh.

Baker shook his head admonishingly. "You're just lucky that a pair of reporters caught your little scuffle with the senator's guard on film. Otherwise, there would have been little we could have done to get you off being booked for an assault charge. As it is, after reviewing the tapes, Officer Daniels," he said, pointing in the direction of the kid, "and I were able to conclusively say that you were acting in self-defense and no charges could be filed."

He silently thanked his lucky stars. Maybe Baker had been in his corner all along and he hadn't needed to make the young officer call him in. "So, you talked to Daniels earlier?"

Baker chuckled. "No, but it didn't take me long to get things straightened out after I was told you were here. You and I, we have bigger fish to fry than some little pissant coming after you on what was little more than a miscommunication and you being in the wrong place at the wrong time. Weren't you at the wrong place, Lockwood?" The way he said his name made it clear that he wasn't really asking him a question.

"Yes, sir." He felt like he owed Baker more, but he was sure the favor would come full circle someday when the man would need him.

"A mistake was certainly made by our teams in letting the senator go, but they are now combing the streets looking for the man. We are hoping we can bring him in on his warrant by tomorrow. Which means, maybe you can…and *should*…keep your head down. There aren't many more strings I can pull for you today."

He nodded appreciatively. "Again, thank you. You know I owe you one—especially if you bring in the senator." He probably shouldn't have said that last bit aloud, but he couldn't help it. He really would owe this man more than he knew if he was to put an end to the manhunt.

Baker scanned his key card and opened the door that led to the main lobby. "Before you go home—and, I repeat, *go home*—I do need to ask you a few more questions about the scene you found at the lawyer's office. Do you have time to chat?"

He didn't have time. He wanted to get back to Kendra, but he would have to do whatever this man asked. It was primarily because of him that he was standing where he was.

The lobby featured a couple of rows of blue plastic chairs, the kind that looked like those in high schools across America, except these had been welded together. "Why don't you take a quick seat?" Baker motioned toward the chairs, glancing around quickly as though he was looking to make sure that they were alone and out of earshot of anyone who cared to listen.

He did as asked, and Baker sat down in the chair one down from him. There was a strange twitch at the corner of his eyes that made Trent wonder if this was going to be less than a friendly little chat and more of an interrogation.

"What's going on? Did you get a lead on your murder investigation?" Trent asked, unexpectedly nervous. "I'm telling you, you need to start looking into Clark's guards. He is obviously willing to use them to get whatever it is that he is after. Now, I don't know why he would kill—"

"Stop." Baker raised two fingers, silencing him. "I know you have a vendetta against the senator, but just because you dislike the man—"

"It's a whole hell of a lot more than just a vendetta. The guy is trying to destroy my family's business, and he is probably going to get away with it. Lockwood Bonds has been in my family for forty years. I can't let him take us down with him."

"You know," Detective Baker started, his voice low and soft, "in my line of work, what you just said could best be called a motive."

"Motive for what?" Trent asked, put out. "All I want is to get our money back."

"You're a friend. If you weren't, I'd let you keep on talking... But, as it is, I think you need to be very careful about what you say next."

The blood rushed from his extremities and pooled down in his feet as his central nervous system kicked into high gear and deep-seated fear took hold. "What do you mean? Am I being investigated for something? What do you think I did?" The questions came out in a single breath, and for a moment he felt like he was fifteen years old again and his dad had just found out he had totaled the family's car.

"We received some new information about the secretary's and lawyer's deaths. As such, there are a few more things you and I need to discuss." Baker leaned forward in his chair and tented his fingers together, his elbows on his knees. His hands were pointing directly at Trent, which made him wonder if somehow he had become their primary suspect.

Here he had been, feeling all too proud of himself for getting out of the assault charge thanks to his connections in the law enforcement community, when in reality he was being looked at in relation to a homicide. His fingers went numb.

"About you and Ms. Kendra Spade… What would you say is the nature of your relationship?" the detective asked.

Trent was surprised by the direct question; up until now, he'd been asking himself the same. "Baker, you know me and women… They're a mystery."

Baker chuckled. He leaned back slightly, as though he was taking some of the pressure off in his questioning. "You're not the only one who doesn't understand them, Lockwood. I'm just lucky to be married to one hell of a woman. I don't know how you still do the dating thing." Baker sat back and scratched his chin. "I know you and Kendra probably haven't defined the nature of your relationship, clearly, but would you say that you are friends?"

"We haven't slept together, if that's what you're asking." Trent was careful to avoid mentioning the fact that, yes, they were definitely more than friends.

Baker nodded. "Would you say that you're a friend of mine, Lockwood?"

Trent nervously ran his hand over the back of his neck, as though the dead lawyer wasn't the only one who had once felt a noose. "I've called you a friend, and I've helped you through more sticky situations than either one of us can probably count."

Baker smiled. "You're definitely right there. So, given the nature of our friendship, if I were to ask you some questions about Kendra, would you be able to tell me the truth?"

Trent couldn't imagine what Baker would ask that would compromise anything he had going on with Kendra. There was definitely nothing to lie about, other than their rendezvous in the hotel room. Trent wasn't one to kiss and tell.

"I have nothing to hide from you, Baker. You know how I work."

Baker dropped his hands back down to his knees. "You know I'm glad to hear that."

"Fire away." Trent wasn't sure he was really ready for whatever Baker was going to ask, but sometimes it was just better to get it over with.

"Well, like I said, some new findings came to light about the deaths." Baker shifted in the chair. "We did find some spent brass near the secretary's body, and while the fingerprint analysis won't be coming back for at least a week, based on some other items we found in relation to the murders... I have a feeling those fingerprints are going to be Kendra's."

It's impossible.

Kendra wouldn't have had anything to do with those murders. First of all, there hadn't been enough time. Not only that, but he couldn't imagine Kendra being able to take down the lawyer and then hang him. Yet, she had a family whose livelihood was at stake. If it came out that STEALTH actually did have a role in the senator's wife's death and his daughter's kidnapping, it would be the end of them.

Maybe she had known Trent was following her and

had brought him to the scene of the crimes on purpose to hide something she or one of her family members had done. It was a nearly perfect alibi.

Up to this point, he had thought Kendra was sticking around to help him find the senator out of the goodness of her heart. However, when he really thought about it, there were few people in his life who did anything out of the kindness of their heart. Had his attraction to her blinded him to her ulterior motive?

On the other hand, she very well may have simply touched the casing when she had found the body. It could have been an accident. He was struggling to make heads or tails of what little the detective had told him. "If her fingerprints are on that brass, there are explanations for it."

Baker's face pinched into a scowl. "That was my first thought, too. She doesn't seem like the kind who would kill anyone in cold blood." Baker paused. "That being said, though, did you notice if she was wearing acrylic nails? Gray or silver?"

Trent thought about holding her hands. They hadn't done it much, but he could remember her fingernails against his skin. "I think she does, why?"

"Do you remember if she was missing one? Or if one had been broken?"

Trent shook his head. "I can't say I ever looked at her hands that closely."

"Well, the next time you see her, you'd be doing me a favor if you paid attention."

"So, I'm assuming you found a broken fingernail on scene?" Trent asked.

Baker nodded. "Not just on scene. We actually found a woman's acrylic nail embedded in the lawyer's neck, almost directly below the rope that was used to string him up. All we have to do is match up that nail and we will know the name of our murderer."

Chapter Seventeen

Kendra was rarely annoyed when faced with the fact that others were just as busy and manically scheduled as she was. However, after she had been sitting in the criminal defense attorney's office for more than an hour and a half, she was about to lose it. The woman had set this meeting, and yet after Kendra had checked in with the secretary in the lobby, the woman had disappeared and she hadn't seen anyone again. It was as if she had been forgotten or intentionally waylaid.

It reminded her that when she got home, she would need to send in a plant to her office to see if things ran more smoothly. If people were being treated like she was here, heads would start rolling.

Taking out her phone, she called the attorney, but there was no answer. She called the office number, and the phone rang not far from her in the lobby at the secretary's desk.

Screw this.

She hung up. Something was going on. She could feel it. If she stumbled onto another crime scene, she would definitely go crazy. Looking at the secretary's desk, all she could think about was the Bradshaw office where she'd first seen the woman's high-heeled shoes and known she was dead.

Her stomach churned.

She wasn't sitting here for another minute. She blew out of the office, anger and a slight trepidation pushing her forward and out of the damned place.

Getting into the truck, she thought about Trent. If personal favors had been called in, he would've been out of jail by now. Yet, he hadn't reached out. That had to mean he was still inside. And, if he was still inside, he was going to be there overnight.

Hopefully, he was okay. Jail could be a rough place, a world where people were frightened and vulnerable. When shame and isolation came into the picture, people turned either inward or outward. And when they turned outward, it often came out in the form of violence. While she was certain Trent wouldn't be the one causing fights behind bars, she held no doubts he would defend himself if put in a situation that required him to. On that point, he was definitely more than capable of taking down any opponent. He was her protector.

She needed someone as strong-willed as she was. She would just walk all over a weaker man. Mild-mannered men could be sweet and kind, but she knew that while they treated her extraordinarily well, they also bored her.

If this, the time she spent with Trent, was any indicator of what was to come between them, she would definitely never be bored. She smirked, and the silly reaction to the thought made her shake her head. While she needed a challenge, what woman wanted that in a relationship? What was wrong with her?

She'd always thought she was the kind of woman

who valued stability and reliability when it came to relationships. Yet she had never thought it was possible to have those things in combination with a man who kept her on her toes. In her experience up to now, all men were either one or the other. Perhaps she had found the last unicorn, or the Holy Grail of men. Or she had found a man who was her perfect fit…someone who perfectly complemented everything she was while allowing her to be her authentic self.

A message popped up on her phone from Tripp. It read, Talked to arresting officer. Didn't make a lot of progress. Keep trying. Making follow-up calls.

She wasn't overly pleased, but at least it was something. The thought of going to the jail to get Trent popped into her head again, but if Tripp hadn't made any real progress, there was no way her showing up would likely have any sort of sway. It was better if she just went back to her hotel.

Besides, as much as she liked Trent and could imagine having him in her life, he had a girlfriend. She could leave his rescuing up to that woman.

Then again, that was assuming Tripp was to be trusted. She had only just met him, while she and Trent had been talking so much—he'd even admitted he'd been ghosted. Maybe Tripp had misunderstood or something. There were a thousand things that could have gone askew. Or maybe Tripp really was telling the truth.

If and when she saw Trent again, she wasn't sure she would give him what for, or if it was best just to pretend like she didn't know about another woman and let things lie.

She made her way back to her hotel, picking up

some Taco Bell along the way. She loved Taco Bell. It wasn't something she would admit to a lot of people, but it was her comfort food. There was nothing better than one of their quesadillas on a bad day.

Her hotel room was quiet. Everything was as she had left it; her suitcase was in the closet beside the white robe. She sat on the couch staring at the robe as she ate her food. She would never look at a hotel bathrobe the same way again. Actually, even though she was more than sure that she wouldn't sleep with Trent, she'd have to make a point of taking that robe home with her. It could be the one positive reminder of Montana.

Though this trip had gone wrong in every way, when she glanced out the window, she was met with the river view. She realized she had started to love this place. It was becoming a respite.

Finishing her food, she undressed and stepped into the shower. The water ran down her back, relaxing her. Right now, everything was in the air. Yet, the next time she talked to AJ, she would be able to tell him things were going their way. Though there were no definitive outcomes with the litigation, she had hope her family was in the clear. How could the senator complain about his character being defamed when he was jumping bail?

Getting out of the shower, she put on the white robe. It carried the faint sense of Trent. The smell was intoxicating, and she closed her eyes as she took him deep into her lungs.

There were many scientific papers on how true desire could be tested based on the level of attraction one felt to a potential mate's scent. In fact, she had even seen it on one of her nerd shows—one of a number of documentaries and YouTube videos about science and technology—on which they performed a blind scent test in which women were asked to rate the scents according to level of attraction. The results were intriguing.

Though the olfactory senses were incredible and one of the best when it came to inducing and recalling memories, it was hard to know if that particular skill set was a blessing or curse when it came to Trent.

Regardless, she doubted she would be close enough to him again to delve too deeply. For now, she could just enjoy this moment, this place and the aroma.

She lay down on the bed and, closing her eyes, she let her fingers lace over her damp skin at the edge of the neck of the robe.

Her robe drifted open. It delicately grazed against her leg, reminding her of Trent's fingers. She could have lived in that moment forever. She untied her robe and let it fall the rest of the way open. Her fingers moved down to her center, and she gasped as she thought about Trent and how he knew how to touch her even in her fantasies. Maybe she couldn't have him in real life, but he could be hers in her dream world. If anything, at least in her dream world there would be no drama and no other women to compete against.

She smiled as she thought about him moving down between her thighs on the bed. She could just about imagine how his tongue would feel on her. Damn, it would've been nice to know how that felt in real life so she could have had that memory to pull from. Maybe he was the kind to run figure eights with his tongue, or perhaps he was the kind who buried his face. She had to guess he was the latter. He was not the shy type. He seemed like a giver.

Her fingers moved faster, and she could think of nothing but him and how he would have felt pressing inside her.

As she grew close, there was a knock on the door. She had no idea whom it could be; the previous time it had been AJ. He was the last person she wanted to see right now, especially since she'd finally found a few minutes to herself.

She tied her robe closed, making sure she was properly covered before she moved toward the door and looked out the peephole.

Standing outside in the hallway was Trent. She gasped as she threw open the door in excitement. "What are you doing here? Did they let you out already?"

He chuckled. "What, did you want them to keep me there longer?"

She shook her head. "Of course not. I just thought that you'd be there at least overnight. Your brother said he tried to get you out but he couldn't make it happen."

A shadow fell over Trent's face. He couldn't have possibly known what his brother had told her. Yet he looked guiltier than ever. As much as she wanted to avoid the topic of him having another relationship, addressing it seemed inevitable. If they were going to move forward, even as friends, she needed to know some truths.

"Come on in." She motioned him inside, careful to pull her robe tighter as he walked by her.

He stepped inside, and she let the door close behind him.

"Thanks." He shuffled his feet as though he was just as uncomfortable as she was at the moment.

If he just told her the truth without her prompting, at least they could move forward as friends. But, if she had to pry out information from him, she wasn't sure he was the man she had assumed.

"How did you get out?" she asked, her voice cracking slightly as she thought of how hard it had been watching him being arrested and loaded into the cop car.

She hadn't realized how much she'd missed him until he was once again in her presence. It was as if part of her was restored and she was whole once more. She hated to think about how she would feel when she would have to let him go when they found the senator…or when their time came to an end.

"The prosecutor dropped the charges. Though I think he may have had a little help in making his decision." He smiled, but the action didn't move into his eyes.

Something was bothering him. As much as she wanted to be direct and push him, he needed to tell her his truth on his own time. "Who pressed for that? Tripp?" She could just imagine his brother finding the guard and strangling the man into submission.

Trent shook his head and looked down at her robe. "Actually, Detective Baker had a hand in it."

She frowned. "Why don't I get dressed and we can go down to the lobby and talk about this or something?"

His expression of concern deepened, and he stared at her for a long moment. "Okay. It's fine if you don't want me here." He sounded hurt.

His reaction both confused and somewhat annoyed her. He couldn't have really thought that she would stay in the dark forever, had he? "It isn't that." She crossed her arms over her chest, preparing herself for the inevitability of getting her heart broken. "Did you see your girlfriend today?"

He laughed, the sound so loud and out of place that she was taken aback and a little hurt. Why was he being dismissive of her? "What are you talking about? Where's this coming from?"

She frowned, as she tried to read him to see if he was lying, or if there was a legitimacy in his being offended. "I know the truth, Trent. It's okay for you just to admit you have a girlfriend." Her throat tightened as all the fears and thoughts she was having bubbled to the surface. He couldn't have a girlfriend. She wouldn't be hurt or humiliated in this way.

"First, I don't know who you've been talking to, but I don't have a girlfriend. And second, I told you that I don't have a woman in my life, so I don't know why you're questioning me." He stepped closer to her, like part of him was hoping to touch her, but when he looked her in the eyes, he stopped moving.

She wanted to believe him. To give herself completely to him and trust in everything he said, but she couldn't. If he was lying to her… Merely the thought of it made her want to break down and cry. "Trent, people lie to me every single day. You can't expect me to just buy what you're saying." She stepped back from him and moved toward the bedroom where her clothes waited. "Tripp told me you have a girlfriend. So, if you do, just tell me, because if I find out on my own after this conversation and learn that you lied to me, whatever friendship we have is done."

She sat on the edge of the bed. He couldn't see her be weak, and right now her knees were threatening to give out on her. She didn't like it, and she didn't know why she was having such a pathetic reaction to confronting him. She was stronger than this. She could handle asking the hard questions…usually.

He walked over to her and pressed on her knees with his, gently nudging her to open her legs. For a second, she didn't dare move, but when he reached up and brushed her hair behind her ear, she melted into his touch. She opened her legs, and he moved closer to her. He took her face in both his hands and looked her in the eyes. "I have no reason to lie to you, Kendra. And I would hope that you would never lie to me."

Though she was aware he was the one on the spot here, she looked up at him. "I've been honest with you since the first moment we met." She wanted to point out that she was the only one here who had been. Yet she remained quiet.

He nodded, but there was something in his eyes that made her wonder what he was thinking about. She believed him about not having girlfriend, but he was still hiding something.

Leaning in, he took her lips with his. His kiss was sweet and gentle, and his lips tasted of watermelon, like he had been chewing gum on his way over to see her. Which made her wonder if he had been thinking about kissing her and being close. It was probably just a nervous tic, but the thought brought a smile to her lips as he pressed his forehead against hers. "Do you know how beautiful you are?"

She looked away from him coyly. "You don't have to say anything to me you don't mean," she said, her voice sounding airy and breathless.

He moved her chin gently with his finger, forcing her to look at him. "I only tell you what I mean. And Kendra...you are the most beautiful woman I have ever laid eyes on. You are incredible."

She didn't know where this was coming from, but she liked his sweet candor. Reaching up, she took his hands and opened them away from her face. She kissed the inside of his left palm and looked into his eyes. "I know we are different, and I know this might only be a temporary thing, but I can't tell you how glad I am that you are a part of my life. I couldn't have made it through this without you."

He moved to his knees and hugged her. From where he knelt, he leaned down and rested his head on her chest, like he was listening to her beating heart. She soaked it in. Right here, with his skin against hers, she forgot about everything else. This was all that mattered. This moment. Being here. With him. In his arms. Touching him.

He pushed back the robe. "I'm glad to see you were ready and waiting for me," he teased, looking up at her with a playful smile.

"You think this was for you?" she countered, giving him a mischievous grin.

"If it wasn't, then I'm the luckiest man on the planet to have shown up at your door at just the right moment." His smile widened as he pressed back the fabric just a little bit more and exposed the inside mound of her breast. His lips found the exposed skin, and he kissed her slowly, like he was savoring the flavor of her body and the lingering aroma of her shower. "You smell so damned good," he whispered, his hot breath tickling the wetness left by his kiss.

"You know, this is all I've been thinking about. When you got arrested, I didn't know what was going to happen or if I'd ever see you again..." As his lips trailed down her skin, she was reminded of her phone call with Tripp. As much as she didn't want to stop his kissing her, she needed to know the truth. "Trent, why would your brother tell me you were seeing someone?"

"My brother was trying to get under your skin. Don't let him."

Her skin prickled with anger. "Why would he want to upset me?"

"Remember when I told you my brother was an acquired taste?" Trent looked annoyed. "I don't always understand his thought process. But if I had to guess what he was thinking, he was probably trying to help me out by trying to make you jealous—maybe he wanted to see how you would react."

It was strange, and it didn't make her like Tripp, but she believed Trent.

"My only question is—" a large smile took over his face "—did it work?"

"You know, this isn't helping me to like your brother." She scooted away from Trent, inspecting him. There was a light in his eyes that made her no longer need to question anything with him. He wanted her. Not just for sex. If it was just for sex, they would have already been deep into the throes of ecstasy in her bed. Instead, they were actually talking. He was reassuring her. He cared for her.

Looking at him, it struck her how crazy it was that

life could change so rapidly. There was no denying that she was falling in love with him. And while she didn't know if he felt the same, she knew what she wanted—all of him.

She pulled at the bow that secured her robe and the tie slipped free. She let it drift from her fingers as her robe fell open. His gaze went to her nakedness. She could hear his breath catching in his throat, and he mumbled something she couldn't quite hear but that sounded like a thank-you being sent upward. He took a step toward her, but she stopped him with a wave of the hand. "No."

The smile on his face vanished. "What?" He sounded utterly confused.

"Take off your shirt." It wasn't a request.

He followed her order and unbuttoned his shirt and pulled it off. Beneath was a white T-shirt.

"That, too," she said, pointing at it. "Then your pants."

His smile returned. As he realized the game, his motions became relaxed. He lifted up the bottom of his white shirt and slowly drew it over the top of his head. Then, reaching down, he unbuttoned his jeans. "What about my boots?" He pointed down at his cowboy boots.

She smiled, knowing he was teasing her. "You can leave those on, if you can get your pants off around them."

He laughed, throwing his head back. Collecting himself, he slipped them off and gently set them on the floor in the corner.

"What? Are you afraid your boots are going to get in the way?" Kendra gave him the raise of a brow.

"What kind of gymnastics are we going to do around this room?"

"Excuse me, miss? I don't know what you think is going on here, but I'm not a man who can easily be seduced," Trent teased.

"Well, that's good, because I never wanted anyone who is easy." As she said that, she knew the truth in her words. Whether she liked it or not, everything about this—being with Trent—had been a challenge. "Now, take off your pants."

He did as he was told. In fact, he seemed to enjoy being ordered around by her. Perhaps he had to be so in control with the rest of his life that it was a relief to be with a woman who wasn't afraid to ask for what she wanted in no uncertain terms.

"Now sit." He stepped toward her, and she pushed him down onto the bed.

The robe she was wearing slipped down her arms and fell to the floor atop his clothes. For a long second, she stood there in all her nakedness and let him stare. He reached for her, and she moved into his hands. He cupped her breasts and stared at them as he ran his thumbs over her delicate nubs. She threw her head back as he drew them into his mouth, making her moan.

He reached between her thighs, and her knees grew weak as he felt the folds between her legs. Gently, he stroked at her wetness until he pressed his fingers inside and made it nearly impossible for her to stand. "I have to finish what I started," he whispered, kissing the skin between her breasts. "I want to kiss every inch of you until you are the only flavor on my lips for the rest of my life."

She swooned at his words and the pleasure of his

touch as he swirled his fingers around her. He wrapped his free arm around her and gently turned her and helped her lie down on the bed next to him. He slipped between her thighs and got down on his knees. Moving her to the edge of the bed, he kissed the inside of her thigh.

All she could think about was the way his kiss felt on her skin and how badly she wanted him to find her center with his tongue. She lifted her hips as his mouth moved closer to her. He wrapped his arms over her legs, holding her still. His fingers dug into her skin with just the right amount of pressure to mean business, but gentle enough for her to want more.

He ran his tongue on her opening and probed inside her. "Trent." She spoke his name like it had its own set of wings.

His tongue moved deeper, and his fingers spun circles on her. Faster. Slower. He moved upward and sucked on her swollen mound. She gasped as he pulled at her. That feeling. She loved that feeling. This man. This moment.

Stars formed in her eyes, and she could feel the pressure for release building inside her with every passing flick of his tongue and swirl of his finger. He knew what he was doing. There was nothing better than a man who could work a woman without having to be instructed through the course.

"Oh my…good…effing…" She moaned sounds that she didn't even know she could make as the end found her and she succumbed to ecstasy.

This man… He was everything she had ever wanted. No matter what was to come, she wanted him to be her everything.

Chapter Eighteen

It felt strangely natural to be sitting at the end of the hotel bed in the chair and watching her sleep the next morning. She was so goddamned beautiful. Even as confident and powerful as she was, he doubted that she could possibly comprehend how gorgeous he found her. If he didn't know better, he would have thought she was actually a goddess. There was no question that she was almost too perfect to be real, and there was no damned way that he deserved a woman as good as her.

She rustled in her sleep and cracked open one eye. Seeing him, she sent him a tired smile.

"Good morning, beautiful," he said. "When you are ready, there's a Starbucks and a croissant on the nightstand." He motioned to the table beside her.

Her smile widened, and she stretched, letting out a loud yawn. "Have I told you today how sweet you are?" Her voice was hoarse and thick with sleep, making her words that much sexier.

"Babe, I'm definitely not the sweetest one between the two of us." There was no doubt in his mind that he was falling in love with this woman, but he couldn't help the nagging doubts he had in his mind about her role in the lawyer's and secretary's deaths.

He stood up and made his way over to the side of the bed and sat down next to her. There were black shadows from yesterday's makeup underneath both of her eyes, and there was white powder on the edges of her lips from sleep. She would've probably thought herself imperfect, but these little details only made her more beautiful. It was a gift to see a woman in the morning. Hell, it was a gift to see a woman in bed.

He was a lucky man.

He reached down and took her hand in his. He ran his thumb over the back of it gently. With his left, he brushed a stray hair from her face, letting his fingers graze against the soft skin of her cheek. She leaned into his touch and closed her eyes. As she did, he glanced down at her hand. The silver-colored nail on her right index finger was snapped in the middle. The sight made his gut clench as he was brought back to the reality of what might or might not have happened and her role in it all.

"When did you break your nail?" he asked.

She opened her eyes as he pulled her from the gentle playfulness and safety that had been his touch. "I noticed it felt odd when I got off the plane. It might have snapped off when I grabbed my bags, but I don't really know when I lost it." She lifted her finger and ran her thumb against the ragged edge of the broken nail. "I haven't been too worried about it. I'll get it fixed as soon as I get back."

She wasn't exactly rambling, but she was definitely talking more than she usually did, which made him wonder if somehow her broken nail had made her nervous. Then again, she was so hard on herself, and this little imperfection could have been making her uncomfortable since he had pointed it out. That, or she really had had something to do with the murders.

She'd had a motive to kill the guy, but he just couldn't bring himself to believe that she would've done such a thing. It was strange—or maybe it wasn't—but he felt compelled to ask her outright about the broken nail and how it would have come to be located in the man's flesh.

"Did you lose it before your meeting with the attorney?"

She looked down at her hand and tucked it into her palm. "I remember seeing it was gone when I left the ranch, but like I said, I think I lost it before that. I've just been so busy." She paused and stared at him for a long moment. "What is going on, Trent?"

He wanted to ask her straight out about her role in the deaths, but he held back.

If she did have something to do with the murders, maybe she needed a safe place to talk about it. Maybe she even had a reason that things had gone as they had with the man, a reason she had never expressed to him before. Trent wasn't a cop, so if she did tell him that she murdered the man and his secretary, it wasn't as if it would change what had happened. The only difference would be that he would have become an accessory after the fact. That was, unless he turned her in to the authorities and told Baker what she had done.

He chewed on the thought. He wasn't sure he wanted to be thrust into a position of holding her freedom in his hands, but he had to protect her and help her in any way that he could. Was she really capable of killing those people? He couldn't believe it. If she had done the deed, he needed to know why. And if she hadn't, they needed to figure out if it really was her fingernail that had been found at the scene of the crime.

"Talk to me." She reached over and took his hand in hers. "If you and I are going to be something…something more than sex, you need to be honest with me. No secrets."

There it was, the call to arms.

He wanted it all. All of her. All she had to offer, and he wanted it all to himself.

"Kendra, Detective Baker told me something…" He ran his finger over the edge of her nail. The edge was dulled from wear. "Apparently, they found what they believe was one of your broken acrylic nails under the man's noose."

Her mouth dropped open, and she sat up in bed. "There's no goddamned way."

"That's what I thought, but then I got to thinking about it…"

She gripped his fingers, hard. "No. I didn't have anything to do with their deaths." She sounded breathless and hurt. "What would make me even want to take them out?"

He looked into her eyes, trying to read her and make sure she was telling him the truth. The vein at the side of her neck was pressing against her skin, and he could see how quickly her heart was racing. She was stressed, but that didn't mean she was lying…only that this was making her uncomfortable.

He could understand her feeling that way; he felt the stress, too. He hated drama and theatrics. More than anything, he hated that they had to be having this discussion. Life was never easy, and hell if love wasn't even harder.

"If Bradshaw and his secretary disappear, it sure makes it a hell of a lot harder to continue Clark's litigation—at least that is what the detective is thinking."

"Well, then, he is an idiot. I'm a good enough attorney that I don't need to kill people to win my case, especially one as weak as the senator's. It's just a defamation case anyway—hardly worth breaking a nail over, let alone killing someone for." She spoke wildly, throwing her hands in the air.

"I know, but there is nothing more damning than physical evidence."

She deflated, and her hands fell into her lap. Dropping her head, she rubbed the space between her eyes. "You're right. I know you're right."

They had broken her. They had hurt her. Once he found out who *they* were, he was going to kill them.

"Who would want to kill these people and pin it on you? It had to have been someone who could get close to you without you noticing."

"Why do you say that?" she asked, looking up.

"They had to have been watching you. Saw you break your nail. Picked it up and planted it. I don't think they intended on hanging the attorney, but they went with it when the opportunity to plant your nail appeared. If anything, I bet they didn't intend on the secretary being there. That was a fast kill, but she had time to get out of her seat…like she was going to run. They shot her, then went after the lawyer."

"Don't you think the lawyer would have heard the shot and come running out of his office?"

Trent tapped his fingers on his leg as he thought. She was right. There was no way the lawyer would have sat still. "He had that second ligature mark on his neck. Someone had to have strangled him first, then hung him."

"And you have to know, there's no way I could have lifted him."

Trent nodded.

"Then again," she started, rubbing her face once more, "I'm sure there could be some kind of circumstances, counterweights or whatever, that a prosecutor could use against me. It all depends on what the scene presented. Bottom line…this doesn't look good, Trent."

He chewed at the corner of his mouth.

"Please tell me that you don't think I had anything to do with this. Really," she pushed, but her expression was pained, and he could tell she was nearing her breaking point.

"I don't think you did, Kendra. Not only are you not the type, but I just don't see how you could have made it work." He paused for a moment. "That being said, though, I do think it's possible that your family could have set you up to take a fall."

She sucked in a long, audible breath. "I… My family and I, we have our problems. There is no denying that our relationship is contentious, but I don't think they would do that to me. We are a fighting unit, and if they wanted to take me down or hurt me, there have been any number of other opportunities throughout the years."

"I know, but you would make one hell of a scapegoat in this situation. If they were responsible for those murders and are setting you up, it wouldn't surprise me at all."

She sat up from bed and took a long drink of coffee, like it was some magic elixir that could make all the confusion and stress drift away. *If only life was that easy.*

Standing up, she made her way to her clothes and slipped into her jeans, doing a little butt jiggle before zipping them closed. It was amazing how something so seemingly inconsequential could be such a damned turn-on.

"I'm tempted to run out to the ranch and talk to AJ and see if there is any validity to what you are thinking. I mean…" She looked over at him. "I can definitely see where you are coming from with this. Sure, my family wanted Bradshaw out of the way…" She paused. "I just can't see them killing him and trying to pin it on me, though. My family is more of the type that, if there is *collateral damage*, the bodies would likely just disappear and no one would be the wiser."

She slipped her shirt on over her head and then pulled her hair back into a ponytail. She moved to the sink and mirror and scrubbed her face before she dabbed on touches of makeup. As she worked, she kept glancing over at him.

"Does it make you uncomfortable if I watch?" he asked, not wanting to bug her.

She shook her head. "If you've seen me without makeup and you are still around, I guess you can watch the magic it takes to make me beautiful once again." She smiled, brilliantly.

"You are always beautiful."

Her hands stopped moving, and she walked over to him and gave him a quick kiss on the lips.

As she moved back to the mirror, he had an idea. "I know Baker wanted to talk to you. Let's head him off and be proactive. Show him you have nothing to hide. That will help him to see you're not guilty and get him moving in another direction while he waits on forensics."

Kendra nodded. "Good idea. I don't want to have anyone breathing down my neck any more than necessary. And you know I have no problems answering any of his questions."

His only fear was that if they did see Baker, it would go downhill and she would end up arrested, just as he had been the night before. They didn't need any more jail time between them, or any false charges. They'd have to be smart about this. He knew she was a powerful attorney familiar with all the legal traps a suspect could fall into, but she was emotionally involved with her client—herself—and that could skew her actions.

Finishing up, she grabbed a sweatshirt, and they made their way out of the hotel and to the pickup. Getting in, he dialed the detective.

"Hello?" Baker answered his phone on the first ring.

"I'm with Kendra, and we were hoping to meet up with you this morning, if you have time." He wanted to add that she hadn't had anything to do with the murders and that they were going to prove it one way or another, but he stopped himself. The detective was going to be picking apart everything he said or didn't say, so he needed to be careful about his words.

"Right now, I'm just heading over to chat with some witnesses from last night's little run-in with the senator. If you'd like, I'll happily meet up with you afterward. I do need to ask you both a few questions."

Trent nodded. "We will be more than happy to answer anything you have for us."

"Great, let's meet up at the Double Front Café for lunch. We can sit down and talk. One o'clock?"

"See you soon." Trent hung up the phone and peered over at Kendra. "Did you hear that?"

She nodded. "Let's go see if we can track down the senator." She put the truck into gear, and they made their way out of the parking lot.

He didn't bother to ask her where she was taking him; he trusted her, and he loved the fact that she was happy to lead this fight. She pulled out her phone and fired off a text while sitting at a red light. "AJ is going to have my ass about this, but I have to tell him about the nail. If he finds out from anyone else, I will have hell to pay."

There was no doubt that she didn't think her family was in on this, especially if she was telling them about the murder investigation. If she felt so strongly that her family didn't have a role in this, then he would have to trust her judgment.

He was hoping that she wasn't mistaken.

Her phone pinged, and she sent another text. After a series of pings and texts, she threw her phone down on the console between them as the light turned green. "You keep saying your brother is a piece of work—well, I'm coming to the conclusion mine isn't a whole hell of a lot better." She sighed. "Let's just send them both out to some deserted island without any way to communicate. The world would be a better place."

He laughed as she smiled over at him. Though he knew she was kidding and she loved her brother down to the bone, he could definitely understand how she was feeling.

"What did he say?"

"AJ said he is taking point on this. Apparently he thinks we aren't doing enough, and that's why I am finding myself in trouble here. He didn't want to hear anything in my defense. Needless to say, he is a little amped up. I can't stand it when he gets this way. He is in a full rage."

"Well, he is definitely a type-A."

"They are a special breed, and anyone who is consistently around them deserves a medal," she said, laughing. "Don't get me wrong, I love him and I love my family, but he does drive me up a wall sometimes."

She parked the truck in front of a large brick building. "The senator's criminal defense attorney is working out of this office. She blew me off yesterday. Today I'm not going to give Kate the chance. She, more than anyone, may have a line on where to find the senator. At the very least, we can maybe get her to talk to the man. I've been thinking about it, and he will probably be only too happy to throw us Marla in order to get us off him. I want the defamation case thrown out the window, your bail money returned and this jerk in jail. And any information he has on the murders would be nice, too."

"After last night, this isn't just about the money to me anymore." His anger rushed back as he touched the bruise on his wrist left by the cuffs.

She nodded. "This guy needs to be brought to justice—and be taught a lesson. He's been getting away with crimes for far too long and using everyone around him to skirt the law." She sent him a vicious grin. "I promise you, though, babe, I'm not going to stop going after this man until he pays for his crimes."

She stepped out of the truck and waited for Trent to

follow her. Slipping her hand in his, they walked into the brick building and climbed the stairs up to the law offices. A woman was sitting behind the desk in the lobby. She looked up as they walked in and sent them a warm smile. "Hello, how can I help you?"

There was something about the woman that seemed familiar. He tried not to stare at her as he struggled to place the woman, but he found it a challenge.

"We are here to see Kate Thomas. I had a meeting with her yesterday, and unfortunately it didn't quite work out." Kendra sounded civil, but there was annoyance in her tone that made even him feel like he'd done something wrong.

The secretary's eyes darkened, and her entire demeanor shifted, as if she was closing herself off. It made him wonder how much she had to do with Kendra being stood up. "Let me call her, see if she is available. She has been exceedingly busy."

Oh, he didn't doubt that. The woman had to be elbows-deep in all the crap the senator was bringing into everyone's lives.

Kendra moved around the desk as the secretary picked up her phone. "Actually, we are just going to make our way down there. I'm sure she will understand."

"No! You can't go back there." The secretary stood up, but as she moved to stop Kendra, Trent stepped between them.

"No, we are going to let her handle this." He put his hands up, but the secretary moved to step around him. "I said *no*." He blocked her advance with his body. "You just need to sit down, right there." He pointed at the secretary's chair.

"I'm calling the police."

"Perfect. We've already talked to them," he said, shrugging as he followed Kendra down the hall.

Baker is going to be pissed, but screw it. Kendra comes first.

She rushed to the last office on the left and opened the door. Looking inside, she covered her mouth with her hands and turned to Trent, shock on her face. He closed the gap and moved beside her.

Sitting inside the office, across the desk from the female attorney, was the senator. Beside the con man was Tripp.

"What in the actual hell is going on here?" Trent was instantly pissed as he tore into the office.

Tripp stood up and moved closer to Trent. "Hold up, bro." Trent paused, shocked, and without another word, his brother's fist connected with Trent's kidney, dropping him to the ground with the cheap shot. Pain rattled through him. His brother knew how to land a damned punch. He wheezed as he tried to get back up to his feet. Tripp leered down at him. "Stay down, damn it. You know I've got you whooped."

Trent put his hand on the edge of the desk and staggered to his feet. "Not hardly. I was just catching my breath." He moved to swing, knowing full well that even if he landed the punch, his brother was right.

He could count the number of times he'd beaten Tripp on one hand, and those times had only been on the nights his brother was about knock-down drunk.

"Stop. Right there." Kendra had a gun and was pointing it at Tripp. "If you lay another finger on Trent, I will pull this trigger."

Tripp tipped his head back with a laugh. "We all

know you ain't got the balls. You may be some high and mighty big-city attorney, but here you ain't nobody, and you damned sure aren't the kind of woman who knows how to run that gun."

Kendra smirked. "Take another step closer and believe me, you'll find out."

Trent tried to straighten up, but his kidney throbbed and his knees threatened to buckle under him. Tears had welled in his eyes, but he tried to blink the unwelcome bastards back. "Tripp, why did you do it?"

Tripp looked down at him, and his lip curled. "Do you know how much money we lost last year? Nearly two million dollars... I told you I wanted to go into the pawn business and you were against it—you didn't want to make 'blood money' from people who were coming in to get money for drugs by selling crap that wasn't theirs to sell. That's when I realized we ain't never going to make this business work. All we are doing is struggling from one day to the next and running our asses ragged. All because you don't want to be the bad guy. But guess what? Bad men make good money."

His brother was right—he didn't want to be a bad man...no matter what kind of money it would bring in. "So you sold me out to the worst man of all? You know he killed his wife. He is a low-life criminal, and yet you would choose him over your own flesh and blood?"

Tripp flexed his neck. "If you hadn't fallen for that little slit," he said, pointing at Kendra, "you might have seen this coming. You and I know we haven't been getting along for some time. The senator can make things happen for me and our family's business with a stroke of the pen."

"Why did you send me after Kendra if you had no intention of ever bringing him in?" He was so hurt and confused. "What about the money he owes us?" The pain of his brother's betrayal inflected his voice.

"Got you out of my hair for a few days before I worked out the final deal with the senator here." Tripp smirked. "And that money ain't nothing but water under the bridge as soon as you're gone."

Dean started to move toward the door, but Kendra pointed the gun at him. "Sit your ass back down. The police will be here in a minute."

"If they are on their way here, it isn't me who needs to run," the senator said, putting his hands up as he stopped moving. "You're the one with a gun pointed at a senator."

"You know, Clark, you can threaten any number of people and perhaps make them do what you want, but I'm not one of them," Kendra said, her finger moving down to the trigger. "There is nothing I would like more than to put a round in you."

"I'm sure that's true, especially since you have to cover up your role in my civil attorney's death." Clark sneered.

"You and I both know I didn't have anything to do with that," she spat.

"Oh, really? Just wait until they check the security cameras at Bradshaw's office. I'm sure that they will see you shooting that poor secretary. Unfortunately, there isn't a camera in the attorney's office… He really took entirely too long to die." Clark looked from Kendra over at his attorney and sent the woman a malevolent smile. "You know, you two look a little bit alike. Isn't that right, Kate, my love? Very convenient."

The attorney walked over to him, and Clark slipped his arm around the woman's back. "Be quiet, Dean," she said, her voice just one step above a whisper.

"Your love?" Trent choked on the name like it was shards of glass. "But you're his lawyer."

She smiled. "I am. And, Trent, you're not the only one who can have an alias. It is convenient when signing for bonds—especially when the bondsman is on your side and is willing to help you cover your tracks."

He rarely worked under an alias, but of course his brother would have told her that on occasion he would. He had never hated anyone, not even the senator, as much as he hated his brother right now. Tripp had knowingly let Kate Thomas sign as Marla, and then he'd pretended he didn't know her.

Trent moved closer to Kendra, his kidney and back throbbing in pain, but he refused to let it control him for another second. "You are all going to jail."

Clark looked over at him, bloodlust in his eyes. "You will never have to worry about that." He moved his arm from behind Kate, and in his hand was a snub-nosed revolver. He pointed it at him.

The cylinder started to turn as Dean pressed on the trigger. It was crazy how slow time moved as he watched the *click, click, click* as the cylinder moved into place and the round moved into the chamber and waited for the hammer to strike.

As Kendra pushed Trent out of the way, a shot rang through the air.

Trent waited for the rush of fire from the bullet ripping through his flesh. Waited for the pain. Yet, nothing came.

Dean's finger was still on the trigger, but the revolver wasn't fully cocked. Blood was beginning to seep from a wound at the center of Dean's chest. He turned the gun toward Kendra. Another shot rang out.

Dean slumped to the floor, the gun slipping from his hands and falling on the floor.

Kate moved to pick it up.

"Don't you dare," Kendra seethed. "I'd be more than happy to take down an attorney like you—you give us all a bad name. Just give me an excuse to pull this trigger, please…"

The woman stepped back and raised her hands.

"Drop your weapons!" Baker's voice sounded from down the hallway, accompanied by a cacophony of footfalls Trent assumed were from other officers.

Kendra set her Glock down on the ground and raised her hands, sending Kate a vicious smile. "I will see you in court."

Tripp put his hands up in the air.

The police officers burst into the room, Baker at the front of the team. The detective rushed to Dean, who was lying motionless on the floor. He dropped to his knees and pressed at the senator's neck. Baker's face pinched, and he looked at the officer who had come in behind him and shook his head, slightly.

The senator was dead.

Finally, justice was going to be served and evil would be eradicated—but Trent had never imagined his brother was one who had fallen on the wrong side of the spectrum.

Chapter Nineteen

Two months later

It had been a nice break while it had lasted. Kendra hated the idea of going back to the city, but work and life there waited for her. She had done as much as she could remotely, and she had gone back and forth three times from Montana between making statements to the courts and meeting with the investigating officers.

Baker had gone above and beyond in working with her in clearing her name. The fingernail had been the hardest part to explain—but thanks to Baker, she had been cleared when Baker had gotten Tripp to confess to having found it. He hadn't been sure it was hers, but had taken it and planted it in an effort to muddle the murder scene.

From banking records and depositions made by the remaining Bradshaw employees, they discovered Brad and Kate had been arguing about the management and handling of the senator's cases. Kate had a contentious relationship with the man—especially when he refused to make her a partner in the firm. Unfortunately, the secretary had been collateral damage.

Love could be a cure, or it could be a curse—and

in the case of Kate and Dean, it had led to more deaths and mayhem than even she could have imagined when she had first set foot on Montana soil.

Kendra stared out at the river as it flowed through the back stretch of her family's ranch. Trent was standing in the water near the bank, his arm moving forward and back as he sent out his cast. Watching him fly-fish was like seeing a ballet in the city; there was a beautiful grace to the way he worked the line over the sparkling, nearly translucent river, twisting and turning and letting his line drift to the surface with a series of gentle waves.

She had tried to let him teach her how to do it on her last trip, but after three lost flies, she had handed his rod back to him.

Picking her way down the rocky path to the river, she stopped to the left of him and waited for his line to settle on the water and for him to meld his line before she spoke. "Trent, I need to head to the airport."

He moved toward her. As he did, he smiled, and the simple action pulled at her heart. How could he smile when her heart was breaking over the thought of leaving him?

"Are you sure you have to go? The fish are biting." His smile widened, but all she could do was stare at his oh-so-kissable lips…lips she wouldn't be seeing for another three weeks.

Stepping out of the water, he put his rod down on the bank and reached down to the pack against his chest.

"Babe," she started, "this is getting harder every time I have to leave you." What she didn't want to say was that she wasn't sure how much longer they could keep doing this before one of them made a change—

she couldn't keep coming back here as she was. Yet, she couldn't think of a future that didn't involve this man.

"I know..." His smile faded. "It's not getting any easier for me, either." He pulled out his phone. "That's why I got a ticket for New York. This time, I'm coming with you."

She rushed to him and wrapped her arms around his neck. He took her in his arms and lifted her off her feet as he looked up at her. "I love you."

Putting her hands on each side of his face, she looked into his eyes. "I love you, too." The words she really wanted to say rested on her tongue, but she was unsure if she should say what she was feeling.

"What's on your mind?" he asked, lowering her to her feet but not letting her go.

"I'm thrilled you're coming this time..."

"But..."

She gave him a sad smile. "But I want it *all* with you. I want you to move to New York. To be a part of my everyday life. I want you to live with me..."

His smile reappeared, and there was a sweet, mischievous glint in his eyes as he reached back into his chest pack. "Well, Miss Kendra Spade, if we are going to live together... What if we were engaged?" He lowered to his knee and pulled out a blue Tiffany's box.

This man knew her favorite color. He clicked open the lid. Inside was the most beautiful diamond solitaire she had ever seen.

"Will you marry me?"

Through it all, she hadn't shed a tear, but looking at him, she felt a single drop slip down her cheek. This man, this incredible, badass man, was on his knee for her. He was her present, her future...her everything.

"Yes, Trent, I will marry you."

He reached into the box and, taking out the ring, slipped it onto her finger. As the cool metal touched her skin, she was warmed by the sensation of forever.

* * * * *

THE BIG ISLAND KILLER

R. BARRI FLOWERS

In memory of my beloved mother, Marjah Aljean, an ardent fan of Mills & Boon romances, who provided me the tools needed to find success in my professional and personal lives. To Loraine, the true love of my life, whose support has been unwavering through the many years together; and to the loyal fans of my romance, mystery, suspense and thriller fiction published over the years. Lastly, a nod goes out to super editors Allison Lyons and Denise Zaza for the opportunity to lend my literary voice and creative spirit to Mills & Boon Heroes.

Prologue

Ever since she was a little girl, Liann Nahuina had rebelled against the conventional order of life and living. Growing up on the Hawaiian island of Oahu, she had been struck by the overreliance on all the things that smacked against doing for yourself, as if there was no other choice. By the time she had relocated to the Big Island of Hawaii two years ago, Liann knew otherwise. Living off the grid suited her. Being self-sufficient and liberating herself from dependency on public utilities and the materialistic world was like a breath of fresh air. Fortunately, she found a like mind in the man who swept her off her feet, and it seemed as if they would be together forever, living a minimalistic lifestyle while enjoying the lay of the land.

That was, until disaster struck unexpectedly and her whole world came crashing down like a castle made of sand. The thought gnawed at Liann, like one of her migraine headaches, with regret and what in many respects seemed like an inevitability. Now, once again, she was left to fend for herself and try her best to make the most of a bad situation she was left with. Maybe in the spiritual world, he was still with her, trying to convey in his own way that he wished things had turned out differently. But then, neither of them could have imagined that a common adversary would come between them, resulting in the unthinkable.

Liann pushed aside the disturbing reverie as she approached the place she called home, a small remote cottage on Komohana Street with solar panels and a propane generator. She ran a hand haphazardly through her long, thick dark hair as she entered, stepping onto gray laminate wood flooring. Immediately, as if she was being warned of looming danger, Liann sensed another presence, even though her locked-in brown eyes saw no one. Who would have come there uninvited and made themselves right at home, as if owning the place? One person did occur to her, leaving Liann unsteady on her feet. A feeling of dread permeated throughout her entire slim body like a killer virus.

When she spotted movement to her right, Liann pivoted in that direction. Before she could shield herself, something hard slammed against the side of her face, knocking Liann to the floor, her chin taking the brunt of the contact. Dazed and bloodied, she tried to get up, while attempting to focus on her suspected attacker. She fell short on both counts, as an object came down on her head forcefully, and Liann went out like a light that quickly faded into darkness.

Mercifully, she was unable to feel the subsequent and persistent bludgeoning by a determined and menacing foe, for Liann Nahuina was already dead.

Chapter One

Before they could serve a warrant, the door had burst open and the domestic-violence suspect had opened fire with a semiautomatic handgun, striking Police Detective Hideo Zhang in the face at point-blank range, killing him instantly. That horrific image of his Chinese American partner being gunned down before his very eyes haunted Detective Logan Ryder of the Hawaii Police Department's Area I Operations Bureau, Criminal Investigations Division, on the Big Island. The fact that he then shot and killed the perp before Logan could become his next victim, in what was clearly an ambush, was not enough to shake off the memories of the tragedy almost three months ago. Internal Affairs had cleared him of any wrongdoing in what was self-defense on his part. But even that did little to erase Logan's belief that if he had only acted sooner, or anticipated things beforehand, then maybe Zhang would still be alive today. Instead of leaving his young wife, who was just as torn up about the loss as Logan, a widow.

His mind moved in another equally disturbing direction as he sat up front in a faux-leather chair in a conference room in the Hawaii PD. Located in the *moku* of Hilo, divided into North and South Hilo districts, it was the largest city and county seat in Hawaii County on the Big Island's east coast. It overlooked Hilo Bay, at the base of the active Mauna Loa and dormant Mauna Kea shield volcanoes. Logan folded his arms as he contemplated the murder of two young women in Hilo in the last four months. Both had been the victims of blunt-force trauma to the head. The press had gotten ahead of the investigation in presuming them to be targets of one unsub murderer, dubbed the "Big Island Killer." Though the women had apparently been bludgeoned in different ways, somewhat unusual from the normal predictability of single killers and their modus operandi, Logan was inclined to agree that this was likely the work of a serial killer.

He listened as Police Chief Richard Watanabe spoke about the new task force that had been established to that effect, and included representatives from the Sheriff Division of the State of Hawaii's Department of Public Safety and the FBI. Watanabe, sixty-one and a veteran of the PD in various roles, had been appointed to the position by the Hawaii County Police Commission. "With the unsettling nature of these violent deaths," he said, his forehead creasing below a short head of gray hair with a V-shaped hairline, "it's best to get out in front of this. While the killings thus far all fall within the Area One Operations Bureau jurisdiction, including East Hawaii districts of North and South Hilo, along with Hāmākua and Puna, they could just as easily spread beyond that into Area Two, if we don't stop what seems to be one unsub..." His medium-sized frame seemed to squirm beneath his full police-chief uniform "With that in mind, for those of you who haven't had the pleasure, let me introduce you to the point person for the FBI's participation in the investigation, Special Agent Aretha Kennedy—"

Logan watched as she shook hands with the chief. African American and around his own age of thirty-four, the pretty FBI agent was tall and slender, with big coal eyes and long black locks in a protective hairstyle. Though she was new to them, the PD had worked with the FBI on different cases in the ten years he had been with the force. The Bureau even had a field office on the Big Island, making cooperation between the two law-enforcement agencies that much easier. Rather than view them as adversaries, Logan welcomed any useful input from the FBI, so long as they didn't overstep their bounds for an investigation in which he was the lead investigator.

"The Bureau is glad to be of service to you in any way we can," Aretha said in a pleasant but straightforward voice. "I know that with only two murders currently being investigated in relation to one another, the tendency is not to want to jump the gun in labeling the unsub a serial killer. That's perfectly understandable. It wasn't all that long ago that federal law defined serial killings as a minimum of three murders or more with common features that were believed to be perpetrated by one or more individuals." She paused. "Today, the Bureau's National Center for the Analysis of Violent Crime is listening to its law-enforcement partners across the country in constructing a definition of serial murder more in line with the practicalities and predictabilities in investigating such crimes in modern times, and the need to identify as early as possible for the necessary resources and manpower to combat. Toward that end, the current trend is to look at serial killings as, at minimum, the murder of at least two people by one or more perpetrators on different occasions. As such, I'd say your current unsub qualifies as a serial killer loose on the Big Island."

Logan nodded with approval, knowing instinctively that whoever had murdered those women was more likely than not to kill again in sowing the seeds of serial homicidal behavior. The Bureau, with its experience in dealing with serial killers, got this. He would see to it that the task force was fully supportive as they moved forward in solving the case.

"We're all on the same page here, Agent Kennedy," he assured her, having exchanged a few pleasantries earlier. "Whatever assistance you can give in nailing the perp, we'll take it."

"Mahalo, Detective Ryder," she uttered cheerfully.

"I think it's safe to say that whoever we're dealing with here, the unsub's violent tendencies have us all on edge," Detective Ivy Miyamoto said. The newly single and petite but tough-as-nails Japanese American had been with the force for five years. At twenty-nine, she had short brunette hair in a textured pixie cut and small brown eyes. She had picked up the slack in the investigation since Hideo's death, allowing Logan more time to pursue new angles in the case. "It's not a good feeling, especially when having to confront our neighbors, who want this solved in a hurry."

"No one wants that more than I do," Watanabe stressed. "Hopefully, the task force will bring this to a satisfactory ending as soon as possible and we can all go about our business in working other cases." He eyed Logan. "Take it from here, Ryder, and bring us up-to-date on where we're at in the investigation."

"Will do." Standing to his full height of six foot three inches over a solid frame, Logan gave his boss and the FBI agent a nod, then made his way to the large format display. He grabbed the remote off a table, then aimed it at the screen, cut it on and jumped right in. A photograph of an attractive young woman with long, straight dark hair appeared. The sadness in her brown eyes seemed to foretell her fate. "Liann Nahuina, age thirty-one, single and a store clerk. Four months ago, her body was found inside the cottage she lived in alone, off the grid. She was the victim of blunt-force trauma to her face and head. An aluminum baseball bat, identified as the murder weapon, was left behind by the killer as though it was inconsequential once the deed was done." Logan sighed as he considered the nature of the attack. "Unfortunately, we were unable to collect any DNA, fingerprints, or other evidence that could lead us to Ms. Nahuina's killer."

He replaced her image with that of another pretty young woman, this one with blond hair styled in a long shag. "Daryl Renigado, age twenty-six. Three days ago, the registered nurse, recently divorced, was found not far from the Hilo Public Library. She, too, had been bludgeoned to death on and around the head. Her ex-husband, Roy Renigado, a contractor, was questioned, but had a solid alibi and is not considered a suspect in the murder. Outdoor surveillance cameras picked up a tall and slender person of interest wearing a black or dark gray hoodie, dark clothing and dirty white tennis shoes running from the area near where the victim was discovered. Forensics has not as yet been able to give us anything useful from the murder weapon—a wooden mallet left beside the dead woman—apart from the victim's DNA. Or the crime scene itself…"

It was not from lack of trying, Logan knew. He glanced at forensic scientist Shirley Takaki, who headed their crime scene investigation unit and had gone over the scenes of both homicides with a fine-tooth comb, but had come away empty-handed insofar as pointing them in the right direction. The slim, twenty-seven-year-old Pacific Islander had a brown asymmetrical bob and sable eyes, which stared back at him apologetically from her chair. He acknowledged this, but respected the work she did and had no doubt that if this investigation continued, it was only a matter of time before the killer left behind something that would crack the case.

He sucked in a deep breath and said calmly, "So what we have are two women under the age of thirty-two who have generally similar racial and ethnic characteristics of a Hawaiian persuasion, along with being slender, long-haired and attractive. Neither one was sexually assaulted. The manner of death leads us to believe that the killings are related. Or, very likely, the work of one perp.

"If nothing else, the killer is obviously someone full of rage against women," he said with a catch to his voice. "And bold enough to taunt us with these brazen attacks and a clear indication that there will be more to come, unless we can put a stop to it." He gritted his teeth, hating that this was happening under his watch with the pressure building to catch the killer.

Logan presented an illustration of a giant question mark, symbolic of where they presently stood in the investigation. "Who and where is this unsub…?" He let that sink in for a second, then said in clear and precise terms, "It's the duty of everyone in this conference room to work together to come up with the answer. When we have it, we'll be able to put the brakes on the killings before this blows up in our collective faces—" While admittedly being a little overdramatic, he understood that the department expected no less in a case of this degree. Logan felt the same, and didn't wish these types of deaths on anyone. Certainly not if he could help it.

After the meeting ended on a positive note when one of the task-force members mentioned the Merrie Monarch Festival—an annual cultural festival in Hilo next month, with arts and crafts, hula dancing and a grand parade—Logan felt a firm hand on his shoulder. He turned and saw it was Chief Watanabe. "Good presentation," he said tonelessly.

Logan nodded while sensing there was more to come. "I just want to keep things running as smoothly as possible."

"I'm afraid the bumpy roads come with the territory in our line of work."

"I suppose," Logan conceded, still suspicious. *Just what type of bumpy roads are we talking about here?* he asked himself.

"Can I talk with you a sec…?" Watanabe's eyes darted around—they were the only ones left in the room.

"Yeah." He locked eyes with the chief. "What's up?"

Watanabe narrowed his gaze. "How are you doing?"

It was obvious to Logan that he was asking about his mental state in dealing with his partner's murder. "I'm hanging in there," he responded, figuring it was best not to be too high or low in a response.

The chief pondered that for a moment or two, then

said, "Losing Hideo Zhang the way you did can be tough to handle, even for someone who has seen his fair share of homicides over the years."

"I won't let it come between me and the job." Logan felt that he'd needed to say it, as though there was an insinuation on the part of his boss.

"I'm sure you want to believe that, but something like this can eat at you like a cancer, no matter how tough you think you are."

Logan jutted his chin. *Where is this going?* he asked himself.

He got his answer when the chief said frankly, "You need to talk to someone, Ryder…"

Logan lifted an eyebrow. "Like a therapist?"

"I was thinking a grief counselor," Watanabe told him.

"Aren't they one and the same?" Logan eyed him defiantly.

"I suppose they are in some ways and not others. A licensed grief counselor specializes in dealing with the pain of loss among other things, such as depression and anxiety." He put a hand again on Logan's shoulder. "I happen to know a good one. Her name is Elena Kekona. I saw her a couple of times last year after my sister had a stroke. It really got to me."

"I remember," Logan said of her illness. He hadn't known about the stroke.

"Elena helped me," Watanabe said thoughtfully. "I think she can help you, too."

"I'm not sure I—" he began, still reluctant to expose his feelings to a total stranger, but Logan was cut off.

"This isn't a suggestion, Ryder." The chief stood his ground. "We need you focused on this Big Island Killer case with a clear head. That can't happen if you're unable to better process the death of Zhang." Watanabe sighed. "I've made an appointment for you to see Ms. Kekona this afternoon. Let me know how it goes…"

On that note, he walked away, and Logan knew from the chief's hard-line demeanor that if he was to continue to take the lead in the investigation, he needed to see this through, begrudgingly or not. Maybe it wasn't such a bad thing if the woman had been able to help the chief deal with his sister's stroke, which she had since recovered from. There would be no such luck here, as Hideo Zhang was gone for good and no amount of therapy was going to bring him back.

An hour later, Logan headed to the grief counselor's office in his department-issued dark sedan. Since Hideo's death, he had been riding solo during a period of adjustment, as the police chief had put it. This was fine by Logan. In fact, if it was up to him, things would stay this way. He preferred his own company since he'd lost the strong presence and dependable friendship of his late partner. Logan wondered if Elena Kekona could somehow lessen the pain of losing someone he was so close to as he still tried to shake the sorrow he felt like a persistent headache.

The office was located on Waianuenue Avenue. After parking, Logan walked by some swaying *loulu* palm trees that lined the sidewalk and made his way inside and up a flight of stairs to the third-story suite. Having never before sought mental-health counseling, if that's what this was, he wasn't quite sure what to expect. He vowed to keep an open mind. But once he stepped inside, he began to have second thoughts. *Maybe this wasn't such a good idea*, he mused, a natural resistance getting inside his head. He glanced around the reception area, noting its warm ambiance.

Those misgivings swung in the opposite direction the instant Logan's eyes landed on the tall and streamlined gorgeous Hawaiian counselor as she flashed him an incredible wide-mouthed smile beneath big olive-brown-colored eyes and a dainty nose, and uttered smoothly, "Aloha, I'm Elena Kekona."

"Detective Logan Ryder." He saw that her long black hair was styled in a braided updo above a heart-shaped face and imagined what it might look like down and loose. She wore a mixed-color, ruffle-neck shell and brown pencil skirt, and honey-colored slide sandals. Seeing that she had extended her hand to him, he reached out and shook it, immediately sending sparks his way. Did she feel it, too?

Removing her hand from his, Elena said in a sincere manner, "I'm happy to be of service to you, Detective Ryder. Why don't we step into my therapeutic office and talk?"

"Okay," he agreed, following her into what looked more like a comfortable living room, with a cream-colored rustic chenille sofa across from two white grace chairs, separated by a rectangular black coffee table with two potted succulent plants. Sunshine filtered in through a picture window.

"Please, have a seat," she offered, eyeing a grace chair.

Logan sat down and watched as she took the other chair. He suddenly couldn't help but wonder if this—the counselor—was just what he needed to get over the hump regarding his partner's murder.

As a Native Hawaiian, Elena Kekona had always known she wanted to put her master's in psychology from the University of Hawaii at Mānoa to good use. What she hadn't expected was to lose her husband, Errol, a software engineer, to a heart attack three years ago. Dealing with her own unimaginable grief gave Elena a purpose in trying to help others who were going through similar loss in their lives. Becoming a grief counselor in Hilo, where she and Errol had had seven good years together, was a smart decision. Using tried and true methods, such as cognitive behavioral and nature therapy, and newer treatments such as brain-spotting, she had successfully treated most who had come to her to confront their issues. In only one instance had her efforts failed miserably—when a depressed and suicidal man took his own life, in spite of the therapy and Elena's belief that they had made good progress in getting him back on track. Though left wondering if there was more that she could have done to save him, she had come to the conclusion that some people were simply too far gone in their grief to be brought back from the brink.

Elena had no reason to believe her newest client was at such a tipping point in his life as she studied him. In his early thirties, as was she, at thirty-two, he was tall and certainly as fit as a fiddle, as the saying went, with regard to physical health. The detective was above and beyond good-looking and dripped masculinity, with a square-jawed face featuring hard angles. He had arresting deep-set ocean-blue eyes beneath slightly crooked thick eyebrows, an aquiline nose and a crescent-moon-shaped mouth. His dark hair was cut short on the sides with a layered top and side swept. A short-sleeved blue polo shirt and black straight-leg trousers fit nicely on his frame, with black loafers. With that appraisal out of the way, while ignoring the hot sensations that shot back at her, Elena turned her attention to the purpose of Logan Ryder's visit. According to his boss, Police Chief Richard Watanabe, the detective was struggling to come to terms with the death of his partner, who'd been killed in the line of duty nearly three months ago. She recalled hearing about it and could fully relate to the pain experienced not only by the detective, but also by his late fellow detective's widow.

"I understand that you counseled Chief Watanabe a while back," Logan said casually, snapping Elena out of her reverie.

"Yes," she said simply, but knew that was something she shouldn't discuss, even if the chief had sent the detective her way. She gave him a well-meaning smile and said, "If you don't mind, I think it's best that we keep the session on what's troubling you."

Logan nodded, scratching his chin. "Understood."

Good to see he's not fighting me on this in order to detract from his own burden, Elena thought. She gazed at him squarely. "Why don't you tell me why you're here…?"

He paused, as if trying to decide whether he truly wanted to be there or not. Finally, he met her eyes and explained, "Three months ago, I witnessed my partner, Hideo Zhang, being shot to death. Though everyone in law enforcement knows the inherent risks that we face each and every day as part of the job, I haven't been able to let it go. Some, or at least my boss, believe that it's affecting my ability as a homicide detective to perform my duties effectively."

Seemed reasonable to Elena. "And what do you think?" she asked curiously, knowing that denial was often a big part of the problem in coping with loss.

"I think that I'm more than up to the task of doing what I do for a living," he responded sharply. Logan took a breath. "That being said, I admit that differentiating the death of Hideo from other homicides I've encountered has been daunting at times. Or, to put it another way, I miss my buddy and hate the thought of losing sight of who he was and what he stood for when grappling with new murders that are every bit as grating on the nerves."

"I don't think you'll ever forget him and what he meant to you, Detective," Elena told him, almost wanting to reach over and touch his hand as a show of physical support, to go with emotional understanding. "You have every right to grieve for the loss of your partner. It's a natural means of coping that any of us who have had to deal with the same issue understand all too well."

Logan faced her, thoughtful in his gaze. "Do you mind if I ask who has been lost in your life?"

Elena batted her curly lashes. This usually came up sooner or later, but this early on? She supposed this came with the detective in him. And maybe was his way of sizing her up. "I lost my husband three years ago," she admitted solemnly. "It was quick and not of a criminal nature, but no less traumatic."

"I'm sorry for your loss." He seemed to speak from the heart. She wondered if he was currently married, or ever had been. Somehow it wasn't hard to picture the handsome detective as good marriage material for some lucky woman. Or was she getting ahead of herself in evaluating him in intimate terms?

"Thanks. I've come to accept it as something that neither of us could have prevented." She paused, having wondered more than once if a change in diet, more exercise, or earlier medical intervention might have made the difference. "Anyway, getting back to you, I believe that I can assist you with better coping techniques in dealing with the death of Detective Zhang. This should go a long way toward making you feel whole again and getting on with your life in the ways most important to you, including your career."

He nodded. "I already feel as if something weighty has been lifted from my shoulders."

And very broad shoulders they were, she mused. "I'm glad to hear that." Maybe his treatment wouldn't take so long after all. Elena used the next thirty minutes to further probe into his psyche, as well as what his traumatic experience had taken away from him like a thief in the night, and how it might be restored, short of bringing Hideo Zhang back to life.

Logan appeared to accept everything she brought to the table. But at some point, his mind seemed to wander, even while his eyes were unflinchingly leveled on her. Elena found herself feeling self-conscious and wondering if something about her appearance was embarrassingly off. "Something wrong?" she asked.

Only then did he lower his gaze ponderingly, before lifting again to meet her eyes—this time with a softer edge. "I'm currently working on a serial murder case," he stated tentatively. "Are you familiar with the so-called Big Island Killer…?"

Elena cocked an eyebrow. Who hadn't heard about the murders of two young women, beaten to death, that the press had labeled the work of a single individual they had given the moniker to? Why was he asking? "Yes, I'm familiar with the murders. Not too much that's happening on this island goes unnoticed by its inhabitants."

"Figured as much." Logan lifted his chin. "The victims have, thus far, been in their mid-twenties to early thirties, and had your general features, more or less, and build, with long hair."

"What exactly are you saying?" Elena narrowed her eyes, while reading uncomfortably between the lines.

"Only that, without meaning to frighten you, as long as the killer is still at large, you might want to watch your back," he said in no uncertain terms. "Be aware of your surroundings and if you see or hear anything unusual, it might suggest danger."

Elena took a breath. She certainly hadn't considered that someone out there could be targeting her. Or someone who fit her physical characteristics as a member of the Hawaiian Islands Indigenous Polynesian people. Never mind that Native Hawaiians, such as her, were second cousins to other Pacific Islanders, as well as Filipinos, Puerto Ricans, Portuguese and Japanese, and even Mexicans and Spanish, and thereby opened a wide range of potential female victims who looked alike. Still, living her life in fear in what was supposed to be paradise for what might well be a misleading hypothesis was not an option. She had taken up kickboxing with Errol, mainly for sport, but hadn't remained active in it with him gone. Besides that, she never left home without pepper spray. And since running was one of her favorite pastimes, it was also a way to put some distance between her and a potential assailant. "I'll keep that in mind, Detective," she said coolly, standing. "Thanks for your concern. I'm sure I'll be fine."

"I agree." He grinned crookedly and rose above her, then took a card out of his pants pocket and handed it to her. "All the same, if you find yourself running into any problems with anyone, don't hesitate to call me, day or night—"

Elena glanced at the card that had his work and cell phone numbers. Even if she felt it was unnecessary, she found having access to the good-looking detective reassuring. Did he really mean day or night? The notion of getting to know him outside their occupations was somehow appealing, if not practical, as things stood. "Mahalo," she told him softly.

Chapter Two

More than an hour after he had gone to the counseling session and less than half an hour since Logan had interviewed a coworker of murder victim Daryl Renigado, accompanied by FBI Special Agent Kennedy, he still found himself thinking about Elena Kekona. Apart from her good looks and appealing demeanor, much to his surprise, Logan felt that she had actually helped him in just one session. Or was it more that he was so taken with her that this made everything else she was selling seem like something he was more than happy to buy? Either way, his mind was certainly more open to the notion of needing someone to help him in addressing Hideo's death than before. More uncomfortable was the belief that Elena fit the general profile of the victims of the Big Island Killer, in terms of being part of the ethnic Polynesian group on the island. Whether she believed this or not, the therapist was not safe so long as the unsub was free to pick and choose women who looked or carried themselves like her. And for that reason, if no other, Logan welcomed the upcoming encore meeting as a chance to get a better handle on the woman and her ability to protect herself from an unseen but deadly enemy.

He glanced at the FBI agent in the passenger seat—she was busy texting someone. *Business or personal?* he wondered. Maybe, like him, she had no personal life. His had ended, romantically speaking, more than a decade ago, when the supposed love of his life had decided it was just a one-way street. He could only hope the day would still come when love worked both ways for keeps. Had Elena given up on love and all its magical properties with her late husband no longer in the picture?

"So I imagine you've come across other serial killers like the one we're chasing?" Logan got the agent's attention, mindful of the FBI's updated view on what constituted a serial killer in the modern era, with two murders and counting.

Aretha shut off her phone. "Yeah, there's been others the Bureau has gone after that were prone to one degree or another to bludgeoning their victims to death, as opposed to strangling, shooting, torturing, poisoning, or whatever," she pointed out matter-of-factly. "Infamous names that come to mind as perpetrators of murders mostly by way of blunt-force trauma include Ted Bundy, Terry Rasmussen and Gerald Gallego, to name a few."

"Figured as much." Logan considered some of the familiar serial slayers, keeping his eyes on the road as he drove down Kapiolani Street, wondering what made such killers tick. How were they largely able to seem perfectly normal on the outside and so capable of such brutality whenever the dark spirit moved them from within? "Is there any method or madness to the time between one murder and another? Or, in other words, does the fact that the first two murders attributed to the

Big Island Killer occurred nearly four months apart buy us some time?"

"Not necessarily." She sighed. "The time frame may be more a reflection of opportunity or circumstances that prevented the killer from killing sooner after the first kill than anything. If you ask me, the Big Island Killer is more likely than not to pick up the pace now that the unsub has two killings in the bag. Making it even more critical for us to identify and apprehend."

"Could the killings have been stalled because the perp simply was lying in wait to find a suitable target, no matter how long it took?" Logan asked, pondering out loud.

"Yeah, it's possible. But since it's not all that difficult to find beautiful women of Hawaiian descent or similar on the Big Island to kill, the urge to do so, or not, may be less about homing in on the perfect victim than other triggers, such as stress, along with influences like alcohol and/or drugs."

"Okay." He wondered what some of those additional triggers might be. Hatred? Lust? Prejudice? Revenge? Or something else? Whichever way he sliced it, Logan still couldn't help but believe that the unsub was on a mission, and that, for whatever reason, Hawaiian women in particular appeared to be singled out for victimization. Meaning his counselor, Elena Kekona, even if not necessarily being targeted, per se, was still vulnerable to attack.

After arriving at police headquarters, Logan caught up with Detective Ivy Miyamoto, who was seated at her desk in the middle of the large room with cubicles. She faced him as he walked up to her. "Hey," he said inquiringly.

"We've released the still shots and surveillance video of the person of interest in the murder of Daryl Renigado to the media and all law enforcement on the island," Ivy said, a look of optimism in her eyes. "Though the suspect is moving away from the camera, meaning we can't see the face, there's still the body shape and clothing that, hopefully, will get the ball rolling in leading to an opportunity to talk to this individual, if not make an arrest."

"Yeah, that would make our job a little easier, if someone recognizes the person in the video and comes forward." Logan was optimistic, but was realistic, too. This was hardly a clear-cut road map to solving this case. If, in fact, the suspect running from the crime scene was the killer and not a passerby who'd panicked. "Too bad the video is pretty grainy and doesn't exactly give us any facial characteristics or hair style and color of the person in it," he muttered. "What is clear is that it's an obvious attempt to disguise oneself with the hoodie and dark clothing. If I didn't know better, I might think that the suspect even planned to be captured on the video, as if to toy with us, while knowing it would give an incomplete picture for us to grapple with."

Ivy twisted her lips. "I doubt the unsub is that clever. But we'll see if the video and picture yield any results." She shuffled a stack of papers and looked up at him. "What did you come up with on the victim's coworker?"

"Not much," Logan admitted. "According to the woman, Candace Piena, also a nurse at the Hilo Medical Center, Ms. Renigado left work at approximately six p.m. to drop some books off at the library. There was no indication that she was being followed or otherwise in fear for her life."

Ivy frowned. "Oh, well—we'll keep digging."

"Yeah." Logan headed to his own desk, while wondering when the killer might strike again, assuming they didn't get to the perp first. He was cut off by Chief Watanabe, who asked, without diffidence, "How'd it go with Elena Kekona?"

"Pretty good, actually," he confessed. "You were right—I think the counselor might be able to help me overcome whatever issues I'm having with Hideo's death. In fact, I have another appointment with her tomorrow."

"Glad to hear that." A pleased look brightened the chief's face. "You can thank me later."

Logan grinned. "Will do." His thoughts turned to Elena, as he wondered how things would go for the wilderness therapy session she had planned. She didn't exactly strike him as someone who was necessarily as much at home with nature as not. But then again, he didn't know what he didn't know, and may have been selling her short. Maybe she would give him the opportunity to discover more about her beyond that she counseled troubled people like him.

ELENA STEPPED INSIDE the Prince Kūhiō Plaza, the Big Island of Hawaii's largest enclosed shopping mall, feeling the air-conditioning hit her face after the humid outside air. She made her way past stores, restaurants and a movie theater, then reached an open area, where a children's hula dance group was performing as free entertainment for tourists and locals alike. Elena smiled as she watched the youngsters dance to the sound of the song, "Hawaiian Hula Eyes," before she turned to the trio playing the music. Or, more specifically, her brother, Tommy Nagano, who was playing a ukulele. It was a part-time gig to supplement his full-time job as a tour guide.

At twenty-nine, Tommy was three years her junior. Tall, lean and handsome, he had their father's brown-gray eyes and short black hair in a tight fade cut, with a stubble beard on his round face. He was wearing his usual attire of an orange Hawaiian print shirt, relaxed-fit jeans and sneakers. In his youth, Tommy had had a few run-ins with the law for minor infractions. Elena was thankful he seemed to have gotten that out of his system. With their parents dead and no steady relationships, they only had each other to lean on, as was traditional in the Hawaiian culture when it came to family.

When the show went on break, Tommy came over to her with a big grin on his face. "Hey, sis."

She gave him a little hug. "Thought I'd check in on you after work before heading home."

"What did you think?"

"As always, I think you're great," she admitted, as a sister would. "The kids really seem comfortable with their routines, which are made easier because of the music."

"I was thinking the same thing." He ran a hand over his head thoughtfully. "You know, you look more and more like Mom with each passing day."

Elena blushed, knowing that many, herself included, considered their mother—or *makuahine*, in Hawaiian—beautiful. "I'll take that as a compliment."

"Would it be anything else?" He chuckled evenly.

She smiled and glanced at his fellow band member who played the keyboard—she was an attractive and shapely twentysomething Hawaiian with long raven hair in voluminous waves. "Who's the new girl?"

"Her name's Kat," he said simply.

Elena wondered how long it would be before he hooked up with her, knowing that he seemed to have a new bedmate every other day. "She's pretty."

"And she also has a boyfriend," Tommy pointed out, as if that had ever stopped him from going after someone who captured his fancy. Elena sometimes wished she could be as free in romance. The better part of her knew she was a one-man woman. Since Errol's death, there had been no one else. She was ready to move on, but only with the right man. For some reason, Detective Logan Ryder entered her head. She wondered if Tommy could ever be all right with her dating a cop, given his negative view toward police officers. Maybe if he kept an open mind…and she did as well—

"Well, the show's about to start again," Tommy said, breaking her reverie. "I'd better head back."

"All right." She gave him a hug. "Catch you later."

In the parking lot, Elena got in her blue Subaru Outback, started it and took off. A few miles later, she was pulling into the private driveway of her two-story, two-bedroom custom redwood house on Laimana Street. It had a porte-cochere entry and French door. Stepping inside and onto a travertine-tile floor, she took in the spacious interior, with its open concept and floor-to-ceiling windows, great room with vaulted ceiling, proper dining area, gourmet kitchen that had solid wooden textured cabinets, granite counters and a farmhouse sink. There was a mixture of modern-and-retro-style furnishings and transitional ceiling fans throughout the home. The wraparound lanai opened to tropical landscaping that included banana, lemon, papaya and tangerine fruit trees, along with plumeria and coconut palm trees, and a Balinese two-story gazebo. Located not far from the Wailuku River, Elena had purchased the place with her husband. It was supposed to be their dream home, but had ended up being a place where she lived alone. A detached *ohana* unit that was accessible by way of its own private, gated lava-rock-walled entry yard was being rented out to Tommy.

After kicking off her shoes, Elena went to the kitchen and poured herself a glass of white wine. While tasting it, she found herself pondering the not-so-subtle warning by Detective Ryder.

You might want to watch your back.

Could she really find herself coming face-to-face with this so-called Big Island Killer? Or was she getting carried away at suddenly being paranoid over the notion that someone could try to take away the very life she'd built while destroying any future she might have? Elena sipped her wine as a more proper perspective crept in. She understood that the detective was merely doing his job in telling her to be on the lookout for danger, and she very much appreciated it. But there was really no cause to be alarmed. At home, she had Tommy around the corner much of the time, should trouble come calling. And elsewhere, she was around enough people in public places to make it unlikely that a murderer would single her out.

With those calming thoughts, Elena finished the wine, then tried to decide what to have for dinner.

THE NEXT DAY, she was up bright and early looking forward to her session with Logan Ryder, perhaps more than she should have been. After all, it wasn't like this was a date. He was her client for now, and needed a bit more of a push to get past his partner's death. And never mind that she had an earlier client before their 10:00 a.m. outing. The fact that she'd chosen to meet him at Wailuku River State Park instead of her office was more about using ecotherapy as a more relaxing environment to tackle his issues. Anything else was being premature, in spite of feeling a connection with the detective, even if she was unsure what it meant. If anything.

After dressing in a pink boatneck top and green twill shorts, worn with casual sneakers and sunscreen, Elena put her hair in a low ponytail and headed to work. When the time came to rendezvous with the detective, he was already waiting for her at the sixteen-acre park, just west of downtown Hilo.

"Hey." His voice was soothing and his grin infectious.

"Aloha." She tried to maintain an even keel in spite of his strong presence, if only for professional integrity.

"Thought I'd arrive a bit early to soak it all in."

Elena smiled, studying him. His clothing was similar to what he'd worn yesterday and was just as form-fitting on his muscular body. Only this time, he was wearing black athletic sneakers. "In case you're wondering about the location, I like to bring clients to one of my favorite places on the island as a therapeutic way to balance nature with delving into emotions."

"Works for me," Logan assured her, a comment that Elena took to heart in continuing the journey into self-discovery.

"Let's walk," she said. As they did so, Elena ignored the sheer force of his manly presence and focused on the purpose of the visit. "Why don't you tell me more about your partner. What was Hideo Zhang like?"

"Where do I start?" Logan pondered thoughtfully. "On the job, he was dedicated, but didn't take it so seriously that he forgot what was truly important in life."

"Which was?" Elena asked.

"His wife and marriage," the detective said matter-of-factly. "Hideo understood that their love would always be front and center, with his career needing to take a back seat to family and everything it meant to him."

Elena choked up at hearing the heartfelt words. Neither she nor Errol ever lost sight of those principles. While the extended family never came, the intent was always there before it was so cruelly taken away. She wondered where Logan stood when it came to family and work. "Are you or have you ever been married, Detective Ryder?" she asked, hoping he didn't consider this too intrusive.

Logan rubbed his chin. "I was married once a long time ago to a botanist named Gemma. Didn't work out. Seems like she couldn't handle being married to a cop." His gaze fell. "I blame myself for that, at least to some extent. I didn't always put her first, the way I should have. But I can't go back. If there's a next time, I'll do it the right way—"

"Good for you." She admired his honesty and assumed he was currently on the market. Or was she reading him wrong? They reached the 80-foot Rainbow Falls just in time to see a rainbow created by the combination of mist and sunlight.

"It's beautiful," Logan remarked, peering at the falls.

"Yes, I agree." Legend had it that the cave below the waterfall was home to the ancient Hawaiian goddess, Hina. Elena gazed at the scenery in awe, sensing the setting was accomplishing its purpose in softening him with the therapy.

Their shoulders brushed as Logan commented, "Hideo was an adventurer. He loved to hike, scuba dive, ride horses, you name it."

"Sounds like he led a full life," she said, feeling the electricity pass between them like a bolt of lightning.

"Yeah, I think he did."

"As such, that's all any of us can ask for in the short time we're here."

"You're right." Logan flashed her a sideways grin. "Good way of looking at it."

"Grief has a way of making us draw on the worst rather than the best in coping with loss," Elena pointed out. "I'd like to think that your partner understood that on some level."

Logan nodded, as if this idea had begun to take shape with him, as well. They began to walk again in silence. Oddly, Elena saw this as part of the process. The quietness broken only by the calming sounds of nature allowed a person time to reflect internally. They reached Boiling Pots, a sequence of large, terraced pools that connected by way of underground currents, with bubbling, rolling water, that gave the appearance of boiling.

"I was thinking that Hideo's widow, Leilani, has had a difficult time as well coming to terms with his death," Logan said, gazing at the water. "I believe she could benefit from your counsel."

"I'd be happy to talk with her," Elena said, quick to offer her services.

"I'll bring it up to Leilani." He turned toward Elena. "If we're almost done, do you want to grab a bite to eat?

I missed breakfast and could use something in the system before heading back to work."

She, too, felt hungry, while at the same time having butterflies in her stomach at the thought of spending more time together. Was it a good idea? Or not? "What did you have in mind?" she asked cautiously.

Ten minutes later, she had followed his vehicle to the Tastes of Hilo Food Truck on Kilauea Avenue, where Elena ordered a grilled-cheese sandwich and Logan a club sandwich.

"So, are you any closer to solving the Big Island Killer case?" Elena had decided to ask the detective out of curiosity, and maybe a little uneasiness about the murderer being on the loose, since he had brought it up the day before.

"Wish I could say we were." Logan used a napkin to wipe mayonnaise from the corner of his mouth. "Unfortunately, the investigation is still ongoing and the killer still at large."

"I see." She bit tentatively into the sandwich, wishing he'd had better news on that front.

His eyebrows knitted. "Why? Have you seen anything or anyone that was suspicious?"

"Not that I can recall," she said thankfully. "But don't worry, Detective, I'm keeping my eyes open for any signs of trouble."

"Glad to hear it." His cheeks rose. "By the way, call me Logan if you like. I'm not on duty right now, as such."

"All right, Logan." She smiled. "As long as you call me Elena, even as a grief counselor."

"Elena, it is." He finished off the sandwich. "And when do we meet again for the next session…?"

"Actually, we don't," she replied, surprising herself by saying it.

Logan lifted an eyebrow, apparently puzzled by her statement. "Excuse me?"

As much as she wanted to continue to see him, Elena felt she needed to be honest about it as a professional. "I don't really see a need," she said sincerely. "Usually, I only need to counsel a person for one to two sessions—unless there is a need for more. In your case, I believe I have done my job by giving you several things to work with in coping with your partner's death. The rest is really up to you."

"I understand," he muttered.

"Do you?" She gave him a questioning look. The last thing she wanted was for them to part on bad terms. But she wouldn't have felt right taking his money and time as an excuse to continue spending time with him. Didn't he get that?

"Of course." Logan finally put a smile on his handsome face. "I'll do my best to cope using the pointers you gave me." He paused. "Guess I'd better head back to work now."

"Me, too." Elena made herself smile back, while wondering if it was a mistake to watch him walk away. Or was it the right choice for the right reasons? *Am I really ready to have a love life again?* she asked herself. Maybe it was time to move on. With any luck their paths might cross again. If so, Elena only hoped it wasn't just because she needed Logan's help as a crime victim, but because she wanted the chance to explore where she and the police detective could go on a more personal level.

Chapter Three

Why didn't you just ask her out already? Logan chided himself, a beer in hand and a frown on his face that next afternoon. He was standing on the covered lanai at the back of his two-story house, surrounded by mature hibiscus, plumeria and Fiji fan palm trees. His home sat on a four-acre parcel of rural land, bordering the Waiākea Forest Reserve. His eyes strained to see the Pacific Ocean beyond. He had asked himself the same question maybe a thousand times since yesterday, when Elena had released him from his compulsory counseling. Though pleased to be given his walking papers, insofar as being fit for the job as a homicide detective, even if the grief of losing his partner still lingered somewhat, Logan hadn't been quite ready to break contact with the striking counselor. But something had held him back from pursuing her on a more personal level. And he knew what that something was. The truth was he wasn't sure if she was up to dating a cop and all that it encompassed any more than his ex was. And he wasn't ready to risk getting his heart broken again. Maybe he never would be.

Logan took another sip of the beer before stepping back inside the country-style, three-bedroom home in a gated community on Kulaloa Road. He had purchased the completely fenced property a year ago. On the main floor, the living room was spacious with a coffered ceiling. A formal dining room led into a large kitchen with a breakfast bar and stainless-steel appliances. There was engineered hardwood flooring and picture windows throughout. Tropical-style furniture and decor made the place feel like home, with brushed-nickel ceiling fans in every room. But even with that, Logan knew that he wanted someone to share it with someday before it could ever be complete. He imagined that Elena could be that person. Maybe if they had met under other circumstances, at a different time and place…

The chiming of his cell phone caused Logan to lose his train of thought. Lifting the phone from his pocket, he saw that the caller was Detective Ivy Miyamoto. He connected her. "Hey."

"I just reviewed surveillance video from the Aloha Hardware Store on Keawe Street in Hilo," Ivy said. "The day before Daryl Renigado was killed, a man identified through his credit card as Glenn Sewell was seen purchasing a wooden mallet and latex gloves. It could be coincidental, but it's worth checking out."

"I agree," Logan told her. "I'll meet you there."

"Okay." She texted him the address.

Though they were hardly at the point of probable cause, much less ready to slap on the cuffs, for now Logan definitely considered Sewell a person of interest in the death of Daryl Renigado and, by extension, Liann Nahuina. Checking to make sure his Glock 17 semiautomatic pistol was still safely tucked away in the duty holster attached to his belt, in case it was needed, Logan headed out.

Ten minutes later, he pulled up behind Ivy's official vehicle outside a small, two-story plantation house on Hualilili Street in South Hilo. Logan got out and met the detective halfway between their cars. "See anything?" he asked her.

"No one's gone in or out." Ivy tucked her hair behind an ear. "But since the Range Rover Sport in the driveway is registered to Sewell, I'm assuming he's inside."

That was good enough for Logan, so he said, "Let's go."

They crossed the street and walked up to the door, where Logan rang the bell. He was tense, as always, when confronting a potential suspect in a murder investigation. At the same time, he understood it was a process and that not everyone they encountered was an offender. This time around remained to be seen. When the door opened, a twentysomething Latina female with midlength feathered blond hair was standing there. "Yes…"

Logan flashed his badge. "Detective Ryder of the Hawaii PD," he told her, and added, "And Detective Miyamoto. We'd like to speak to Glenn Sewell."

She looked noticeably uncomfortable. "What has he done?"

"Maybe nothing," Ivy said ambiguously. "What's your name?"

"Julie," she said succinctly.

"Julie, is he here?"

"Yes." She paused. "Wait just a moment."

"Actually, I think it would be best if we waited inside," Logan insisted, wanting Sewell to feel their presence, should he want to make a run for it.

Julie nodded reluctantly, stepping aside as they

moved into a small living room that was traditionally furnished. Ill at ease, she yelled upstairs, "Glenn, the police are here. Can you come down?"

Momentarily, a muscular man in his early forties, with a short blond faux-hawk haircut, came lumbering down the stairs. He looked warily from Logan to Ivy, before settling on Logan. "What's going on?"

Logan studied him, deducing he wasn't carrying a piece. "We need to ask you a few questions."

"About what?"

Ivy stepped forward. "A purchase you made six days ago at the Aloha Hardware Store," she said bluntly. "Surveillance video picked you up buying a pair of latex gloves and a wooden mallet."

"So…" He wrinkled his bulbous nose. "Is that a crime?"

"Only if used to commit a crime." She peered at Sewell suspiciously. "The day after your purchase, someone using a wooden mallet bludgeoned Daryl Renigado to death, leaving the murder weapon behind. Mind telling us where you were the evening of March eighteenth?"

"I was at home with my girlfriend, Julie." Sewell chewed on his lower lip. "Ask her."

"We will. Right now," Ivy told him, "We'd like to see the mallet you bought…and the latex gloves."

The suspect ran a hand across his mouth, seemingly breathing a sigh of relief. "No problem. I didn't use the mallet to kill anyone. Come with me…" He led them out the back door to a workshop behind the house. A wooden mallet was on a steel workbench. "It's been right there since the day I bought it," he said. "See for yourself."

Logan and Ivy examined the mallet without touching it. It looked new and was obviously not the one used to murder someone. Still, Logan considered that the suspect could have simply replaced one mallet with another. "Where are the latex gloves you bought?" he asked him, knowing they could potentially contain DNA from the crime.

"Right here," Julie answered, having followed them into the workshop. She held up the gloves. "Glenn bought them for me. I needed them for my gardening. I can show you…"

Logan recalled the tropical garden they'd passed before entering the workshop. "That won't be necessary." He glanced at Ivy, who was in agreement, as both of them realized that they were likely barking up the wrong tree here. Still, to be on the safe side, Logan asked Julie to verify that Sewell was with her on the day in question, which she did. For now, the detectives had no solid reason to believe otherwise. "We won't take up any more of your time," Logan told the couple, as he and Ivy saw themselves out.

When back at her car, Ivy groaned, "Looks like a big nothing burger."

Logan didn't exactly see it that way. "We both know we have to go through a few detours to get to the finish line."

"I suppose," she muttered in agreement.

Logan blinked, thoughtful. "See you later."

Ivy cocked an eyebrow. "Where are you going?"

"To the cemetery," he stated, leaving it at that as he headed to his vehicle.

A short while later, Logan was at the Hilo Memorial Park, making his way across the damp grass until he came to the grave site of Hideo Zhang. He observed someone already there, as expected, with flowers lying against his headstone. The woman never looked his way, as though too caught up in the moment to hear him coming.

"Leilani…" Logan called out softly.

In her midthirties, Leilani Zhang was small-boned and attractive, with delicate features on an oval face, hazel eyes and long dark hair with blond highlights, styled in zigzag curls. Like her late husband, Leilani was Chinese American. She turned his way and just stared, as if in a trance, then uttered, "Logan—"

"Figured you'd be here," he told her, knowing it had been exactly three months to the day since Hideo had been gunned down. She started to bawl and Logan took her in his sturdy arms.

"I miss him so much," Leilani spluttered, crying into his shirt.

"I know you do." Logan fought hard to keep his own emotions in check. "So do I." He thought about how Elena had helped him better process things and believed she could do the same for Leilani.

Half an hour later, after paying their respects to the fallen detective, Logan followed his widow back to her town house on Kumukoa Street in central Hilo. The carpeted, roomy place had natural lighting, cathedral ceilings and a warm ambiance, with sleek contemporary furnishings. The only thing missing was the usually upbeat presence of Hideo. Instead, Leilani was left only with a Tonkinese cat named Mona to keep her company. Along with the memories of Hideo.

Logan shared those as she made them a cup of *māmaki*—Hawaiian herbal tea. After taking a sip, he said to her casually, "I've been to see a grief counselor in dealing with Hideo's passing."

Leilani looked up from her cup, as they stood in the U-shaped kitchen. Mona sat on a rattan stool, quietly observing them. "Really?"

"Yes. Her name is Elena Kekona. She's helped me in ways I didn't think possible." He paused to gauge Leilani's reaction, knowing her to be a private person when it came to dealing with her emotions.

"Maybe I should go to see her," she suggested.

Logan nodded. "Yeah, I think that's a good idea. I can call her and set it up."

"Mahalo." A weak smile played on her lips.

While he hoped Elena could work her magic on Hideo's widow, Logan also looked forward to having an excuse to reconnect with the attractive counselor. Not to mention check on her, hoping to keep her out of harm's way with a serial killer on the loose.

ELENA GREETED LEILANI ZHANG as she stepped into the office, after Logan had called to make an appointment for her. "I'm so glad you came," Elena said.

"I nearly chickened out," Leilani confessed. "But since you came highly recommended by Logan, I figured that maybe there is hope for me in trying to carry on without my husband there to hold my hand."

"There's definitely hope for you, Leilani." Elena realized this was precisely her own mindset after losing Errol. Her entire world seemed to crash in on her at that point, making it seem like there was no more tomorrow worth pursuing. Thankfully, she'd been able to get over that difficult hurdle and get to the other side, realizing there was still a whole world out there that she deserved to be a part of. The same was true for Leilani. And Logan, too, for that matter.

Elena led her latest client to the therapy room, where she did everything possible to make her feel at home. That was always the key to reaching a level of trust that was good for both sides in addressing the grief that could make or break a person if it wasn't harnessed properly.

"I understand that you also lost your husband early in life," Leilani said evenly.

"Yes, three years ago." Elena realized that it was still painful to talk about. But she had to, if she hoped to get Leilani to do the same. "Heart attack. It came on very suddenly and…that was it. I never saw it coming. I doubt that he did, either."

"That must have been devastating to you." Leilani fluttered her lashes. "I mean, it isn't exactly something you can prepare for, is it?"

"No, it isn't," Elena admitted, no matter how strong she tried to be and realistic in the knowledge that someday they would all leave this earth. But the focus should not be on her life and loss, as she pivoted back toward the detective's widow. "Why don't you tell me about what you've been going through these past months since you lost your husband."

Elena listened as Leilani went through the typical emotional roller coaster experienced by survivors, empathizing with her every step of the way. How could she not feel for Leilani in losing someone you had given everything to?

"It's been tough," Leilani concluded, finishing on a sigh.

"It's perfectly normal to feel the effects of grieving,"

Elena pointed out to her. "What's key is to be able to keep things in a proper perspective."

Leilani frowned. "How do I do that?"

Elena answered by giving her tips on positive reinforcement, compartmentalizing and thinking in terms of moving on, as her loved one would have undoubtedly wanted. Leilani seemed amenable to these techniques, giving Elena confidence that she would be able to get past the death of Hideo Zhang and make her own life count for something.

When the session had neared an end, Leilani brought up the Big Island Killer investigation that was currently underway. "I hope they catch the person soon," she remarked.

"You and me both." Elena shuddered at the thought of being the victim of a serial killer. "Log— Detective Ryder seems determined to solve the case."

"I know." Leilani nodded thoughtfully. "Hideo was working with Logan when the first victim was killed." She sighed. "I only wish he had lived at least long enough to be around when an arrest was made and we could all breathe easily again on the island."

Elena found herself reaching out and touching her hand. "Maybe part of him is still alive in the spirit of Hawaii, as a sort of angel on Detective Ryder's shoulder in carrying on in law enforcement without him."

"I think you're right." Leilani offered her a tender smile. "I'm glad Logan talked me into visiting you."

"So am I." Elena imagined that she would be a great person to hang out with beyond the therapy sessions, with their similar storylines. Along with the common link in Logan.

After she had seen the client out, Elena called him

to let him know the session went well and that Leilani had made an appointment for a second visit. He seemed pleased, thanking her for, as he put it, "coming to her rescue." Though flattered, Elena saw this as her calling and was always happy to help those in need.

Then, abruptly, Logan said in a level voice, "Do you want to get together for a drink?"

She didn't need any time at all to think about it, as Elena was ecstatic to spend time with him in a non-therapeutic way. "I'd love to."

That was all he needed to suggest they meet at a place not far from her office in an hour. She was all in, even if a part of Elena wondered exactly what that meant, in terms of expectations. Or should mean in terms of where they might go from there, when it came to possibly starting something with the gorgeous and dedicated police detective.

ADMITTEDLY, LOGAN FELT like he was sixteen again, looking forward to his first date, as he waited at Veronica's Lounge on Kanoelehua Avenue for Elena's arrival. The difference was, while those high-school dates were largely forgettable, there was nothing about the gorgeous counselor that he wouldn't always remember. Whether anything could come out of this remained to be seen. He would take it one step at a time and see how things played out.

The moment she walked in the door, Logan's heart skipped a beat. Apart from her pleasing appearance overall, Elena had her long hair down for the first time, making her all the more appealing to him. "Hey," he greeted her.

"Hey." She walked up to him and smiled.

"Let's get a table." Logan followed closely behind her as they found a spot and sat. After she had met with Leilani, his partner's widow had called him and had nothing but good things to say about Elena. Seemed as though the two women might actually come out of this as friends. Maybe the type of friendship he and Hideo had. Or, Logan mused, the kind he could have with Elena himself, assuming it never reached that of a romantic nature. "What would you like to drink?" he asked her.

"I'll have a Lava Flow," Elena told him.

"Good choice." Logan ordered it and went with a Kiwi Colada cocktail for himself. He found he wanted to know everything about her. Or at least anything relevant in shaping her into the person she was. "Do you have family on the Big Island?" he asked after the drinks had come.

"Yes, my brother, Tommy, lives in Hilo," she said. "He's currently renting an *ohana* on my property, separate from the main house."

"And your parents?"

"They passed away some years ago." Elena tasted her drink and Logan immediately regretted bringing them up, knowing that she would then think about her late husband. "I believe they're still together in some spiritual realm, which is a good thing."

"I agree." He leaned back in his chair.

"What about your family?" She met his eyes.

"My parents split up when I was very young," he recalled. "My mother is still alive and living in Northern California, the Bay Area, where I grew up. A few years ago, I reconnected with my father before he died of liver disease."

"Sorry to hear that," she said.

Logan was thoughtful. "Yeah. At least we were able to form some sort of relationship toward the end."

Elena regarded him curiously. "Any siblings?"

"No siblings," he responded with regret, believing that it might have made his life easier if he had brothers or sisters to lean on during difficult times.

"How did you end up on the Big Island?"

"To make a long story short, I was recruited by the Hawaii Police Department to fill an opening, after working with the California Department of Justice's Human Trafficking and Sexual Predator Apprehension Team. Guess I had become burned out at that point in investigating trafficking cases, often involving the sexual exploitation of women and children, and decided I needed to move in a different direction."

Elena took another sip of her drink. "Any regrets?"

Reading her mind, Logan supposed she wondered if going after human traffickers and sexual predators in favor of serial killers and other homicide-related offenders was much of a trade-off. He saw both as equally heinous in nature, but the incidence was much greater with the former than the latter. Rather than delve too deeply into those dynamics, instead, he told her earnestly, while appreciating the view across the table, "From where I'm sitting at this moment, I'd have to say no regrets whatsoever."

She blushed and uttered, "You're smooth, I'll give you that, in skillfully dodging the question."

He grinned, enjoying this easygoing communication between them. Where else could it lead? "On balance, having the opportunity to live and work in Hawaii, even if it's less than utopia, I'd gladly do it over again."

"I'm glad you made that choice, Logan," Elena said sincerely, meeting his eyes.

"So am I." In that moment, it seemed like an ideal time to kiss her—those soft lips that seemed ever inviting. Leaning his face toward her, Logan watched for a reaction that told him they weren't on the same wavelength. Seeing no indication otherwise, he went in for the kiss. It was everything he expected—sweet, sensual and intoxicating. Only when his cell phone chimed did he grudgingly pull away. He removed the phone from his pocket, glanced at the caller ID and told Elena, "I need to get this."

"Please do," she said understandingly.

Before he even put the phone to his ear, Logan sensed that he would not like what he heard. He listened, anyway, as Ivy spoke in a near frantic tone. Afterward, he hung up and looked gloomily at Elena, and said, "The body of a young woman has been found." He paused, almost hating to say this, considering the concerns he still had for the safety of the grief counselor and not wanting to unnerve her. But there was no denying the truth or sparing her what she needed to hear. "It appears that the Big Island Killer has struck again."

Chapter Four

Logan took the coastal drive down Kalanianaole Avenue toward Onekahakaha Beach Park, where the victim had been discovered. From his brief chat with Ivy Miyamoto, the woman appeared to be Hawaiian, and fell into the mid-twenties to early thirties age group, similar to the others targeted by the Big Island Killer. This made it all the more disturbing to Logan, especially now that he was starting to feel something for Elena Kekona, who matched the general description of the dead women. But he couldn't exactly ask Elena, even with the kiss that had seemed to up things a notch between them, to put her life on hold until they caught the unsub. Even if he could, he doubted she would listen. Not that he could blame her. He just didn't have enough to go on at this point to start making demands on her, or any other woman who could potentially be in the crosshairs of a killer.

All I can do right now is try to catch the perp and end this nightmare for Hilo and the Big Island once and for all, Logan mused with determination, as he turned onto Onekahakaha Road, soon coming to the parking lot. After getting out of the vehicle, he made his way to where the activity was, with crime-scene tape cordoning off the area where the body had been found. He flashed his identification to a thin officer with a French crop, who allowed him through, before Logan rendezvoused with Ivy and FBI Agent Aretha Kennedy, who were both wearing nitrile gloves.

"Sorry to have to get you down here," Ivy told him. "But it looks like our serial killer is back at it."

"When duty calls, the job comes first." Logan frowned. He'd known it was just a matter of time. After all, serial killers never seemed to stop—until they were taken down.

"If this is our unsub, that makes three," Aretha said, as if to validate their categorizing of the previous two murders as the work of a serial slayer.

"Point taken." Logan gritted his teeth. "Where is she…?"

"Right this way," Ivy answered, leading them past crime-scene investigators at work collecting possible evidence, and other law enforcement officers who were actively engaged in the investigation. They came to a section of grass beneath a clump of evergreen trees. "That's how she was found…"

Logan eyed the female lying on her side in a pool of blood, as though positioned as such. Nice looking, or would have been were she still alive, she had long, multilayered brown hair, was slender and around five-five or five-six, he deduced. The victim was fully clothed in a purple tie-front T-shirt, gray terry shorts and black running sneakers. Her vacant russet-colored eyes were open, as if for a final look at her killer. Logan grimaced at the unsettling image and could only imagine what had gone through her head as she was being killed. "Who is she?" he asked.

"According to the driver's license found in a handbag near the body," Aretha responded, "the victim's name is Yancy Otani, age twenty-five. It looks like she was jogging before being accosted by the unsub." The agent muttered an expletive. "The killer probably caught her from behind while she was still on the move."

"It was certainly a brazen attack," Ivy remarked, raising her eyebrows. "A witness reportedly saw a tall person wearing a dark hoodie and dark clothing running away from the scene."

"Same as the last victim," Logan muttered thoughtfully. "The unsub is getting reckless—making the attacker even more dangerous."

"Tell me about it," forensic analyst Shirley Takaki said dramatically as she approached the group, wearing protective equipment. "The perp really went to town on the victim." With gloved hands, she was holding a large evidence bag containing what looked to be a big, blood-stained lava rock. "We think this is the murder weapon."

Logan smirked, troubled that the unsub seemed capable of using all manner of weapons to attack the victims, as though to keep them off balance. What would be next? "Hopefully, you'll come up with some DNA we can use," he declared pessimistically.

Shirley made a humming sound. "If it's there, I'll find it."

"I know you will." Logan had no doubt that she and her team welcomed the challenge of putting their scientific expertise to the test with each criminal investigation. But would that be enough to catch a crafty killer?

"Hey, get over here, Campanella," she barked at Martin Campanella, the thirty-year-old crime-scene-and-evidence photographer who was new to the team. His predecessor, Joan Gonzalez, had quit after getting in with the Bureau of Alcohol, Tobacco, Firearms and Explosives.

Campanella, tall and lanky with crimson hair in a topknot, walked over with camera in hand and said, almost apologetically, "I'll try not to get in the way."

"I think it's more the other way around," Logan stated aptly, as they made room for him to photograph the deceased and surrounding potential evidence.

"Only a matter of time before the unsub slips up," Ivy said, removing her gloves.

"In this instance, time is our enemy," Logan indicated sourly, taking in the surroundings for what was supposed to be a family-friendly park and not a place of murder and mayhem. "The more time goes by, the greater likelihood the killer will strike again and again."

"I've got agents fanning out with your officers," Aretha reported, "looking for anyone who fits the description or otherwise may know something."

"Maybe we'll get lucky." Logan wanted to believe this, knowing that sometimes a good break was all they needed to find the perp and solve the case. More likely, they would need good old-fashioned legwork, modern technology and forensics to arrest the culprit.

"Whatever it takes to end this nightmare," said the forensic pathologist, Dr. Bert Swanson, who came to claim the body. The sixtysomething subspecialist in pathology was of medium build, with gray hair in a comb-over style and a salt-and-pepper ducktail beard. "This trend is something none of us, least of all me, want to keep putting up with as the bodies start to pile up."

"Tell me about it." Logan curled his lip cynically. He thought about Elena and dreaded even the possibility of her suffering the same fate. He watched as Swanson crouched down and lifted the deceased's severely damaged head with his gloved hands and manipulated it a bit, as if a rag doll. "Did she die the same way as the others?" Logan asked anxiously, realizing it was possible that it was a different killer, in spite of the similarities in the manner of death.

"My preliminary finding is that she succumbed from the injuries sustained from the solid blows to the back of her head," the pathologist said tonelessly. "I'll be able to give you a more definitive answer when I complete the autopsy, first thing in the morning."

"See you then," Logan said, if only to confirm what they all pretty much knew. Yancy Otani had been bludgeoned to death the same way as the other victims of the Big Island Killer. Meaning they had their work cut out for them if they were to make any significant headway in identifying the unsub and getting the person off the street before anyone else was added to the collection of murdered women.

IT HAD BEEN a couple of hours since Logan had left Elena at Veronica's Lounge, after learning that someone else had been murdered. She was admittedly spooked by the whole notion of a serial killer in their midst. This frightening reality undercut the kiss she shared with the man, nice as it was. Logan's tender lips were amazing. It left her longing for more. Whether they would get the opportunity to build upon that kiss or not, she couldn't say. Was she really up for getting involved with a police detective, especially at this time? Would his job always come first? Would hers?

As she grappled with those thoughts from the comfort

of her great room, Elena leaned back on the burgundy velvet sofa and rested her arm against the wingback shoulder. She had checked the local news and not gotten much information about the body discovered at Onekahakaha Beach Park, other than it was a young woman, who appeared to have been the victim of foul play. Was she another victim of the Big Island Killer? More than a little curious, Elena wondered if it would be appropriate to ask Logan directly about the investigation. *Given his concern about my safety, and a vested interest in the case as a resident of Hilo, where the murders were occurring, I say yes*, she told herself. Lifting the cell phone she had been holding, Elena called the detective before she lost her nerve.

He picked up on the second ring. "Hey, I was just thinking about you," he spoke in an ultrasexy voice, as though picking up where they left off at the lounge.

"Really?" She knew the same was true in reverse.

"Yes, I just wanted to make sure you made it home safe and sound." His more serious tone brought Elena back down to earth.

"I did," she assured him. "That's kind of why I'm calling. I was hoping you could update me on the body found—if only for my peace of mind."

She sensed some hesitancy on the part of the detective, as if he wasn't in a position to share sensitive information. But then he said straightforwardly, "A young woman is dead—murdered in a manner similar to the others victimized by a serial killer. I'm sorry to have to lay this on you, but you have a right to know—especially since the victim, like the others, bears a strong resemblance to you. Not to say any could have passed as your identical twin, and all were a bit younger, with varying heights. However, what they share in common with you besides being attractive and long-haired with a slender frame, is that all are Hawaiian, as far as we could determine."

Elena sucked in a deep breath while mulling over his weighty words. "What do you think that means?" she asked, putting herself into the proverbial shoes of the victims.

"Not sure at the moment," he told her frankly. "I'm guessing the perp has some particular beef against Native Hawaiian women and is targeting them."

She tried to imagine what that beef might be. Why them and not others? Was there a method to the killer's ostensible madness? Who knew what went on in the minds of psychopaths? Elena thought, assuming the killer was operating with such a mental disorder and not fueled purely by hatred. "I'll do my best to be on guard," she said, sensing he was thinking that very thing. Even then, she wasn't under any illusion that she could ever be totally safe from a determined foe. No matter the safety measures taken. Still, she had no desire to be a sitting target for a killer, any more than the next woman living on the island. "I do have my brother around for added protection," she stated. "Tommy's not exactly a bodybuilder, but he's fairly fit and protective in his own way."

"That's good to know," Logan said in a level tone of voice. "But should he or your self-protection not be enough, I'm just a phone call or car drive away."

"I appreciate that, Logan." The kiss between them flashed in Elena's head. She wondered if it was still registering with him, too. Or had the investigation already made it little more than a distant memory. "Well,

I should let you get back to it. Thanks for the update, sad as it was to hear."

"I think it's best to be up front on things like this," he insisted defensively. "Knowing what you're up against can sometimes make all the difference in the world."

"I agree." How could she not, all things considered? "Talk to you later," she told him and hung up.

After taking a moment to reflect on Logan, the murders, the kiss and her own reality, Elena figured she would pop over to see Tommy, feeling in need of some company and maybe reassurance that everything would be all right. She grabbed her keys and left the house, locking the door behind her, and headed through the open gate and down the lava-rock entry yard. She spotted Tommy's black Volkswagen Atlas in the driveway before arriving at his front door. Elena listened in to see if he might have a woman inside, or otherwise be entertaining friends. Hearing nothing, she rang the bell.

When the door opened, Tommy appeared in dark jogging attire and gym shoes. His hair was damp, as though he'd been working out. "Hey," he said in his usual easy tone, studying her.

"You busy?" she asked.

"Nah. Was just fooling around a bit in the exercise room. Everything all right?"

"Yes, I'm fine." Or at least as fine as could be expected after learning that someone like her had been found beaten to death.

Tommy tilted his head. "Come on in."

The inside was a two-bedroom guesthouse, with an en suite and full kitchen. Tommy had converted one of the rooms into his own home gym. The style of the *ohana* was much like the main house architecturally, with an open feel and travertine-tile flooring, along with modern vintage furnishings.

"Want something to drink?" Tommy asked, even as he headed to the refrigerator and took out two cans of strawberry guava juice. Elena took one from him and sat on a dark blue retro sofa, then watched as he flopped onto a wide brown barrel chair. He looked at her and asked perceptively, "So, what's up?"

She sighed and opened the juice. "Did you hear that another woman was killed in Hilo?"

He cocked an eyebrow. "Really?"

"Her body was found at Onekahakaha Beach Park," she told him. "She'd been murdered like the other women purported to be victims of the Big Island Killer."

"Damn. Sorry to hear that." Tommy took a gulp of his strawberry guava. "Did they arrest the killer?"

"Not that I've heard." Elena paused, thinking about Logan. Was there any chance that he and Tommy would get along, if it came down to that? "I understand that the police and FBI are pulling out all the stops in trying to get to the bottom of this and put someone away. Until such time, truthfully, it's got me feeling a little unnerved."

He gazed at her with concern. "Why, has someone been threatening you?"

"No," she responded quickly.

"Do you suspect someone of being this killer…?" His voice raised an octave.

"No. But apparently all the victims look basically like me." Elena tried to process that in her own head.

"Says who?" he asked point-blank.

Without bringing Logan into the conversation, she responded evasively, "It's in the news. I've seen their pictures. The killer is targeting pretty young women of my racial and ethnic persuasion. It doesn't take a rocket scientist to realize that I could be next on his list, at least in theory."

"I doubt that." Tommy waved his hand nonchalantly. "No one's coming after you, sis."

"You sound pretty confident about that." Her lashes fluttered. "I'm no safer from victimization than any other native Hawaiian female on the island. Not while the killer remains at large."

He frowned. "So, what, you think that all young Hawaiian women are suddenly at the mercy of some psycho?"

Elena considered Logan's views on the subject. As a lead investigator on the case, she had a feeling that his observations and instincts were probably spot on. "I wish I could say otherwise," she told her brother. "I'd just like to err on the side of caution until this is over." She paused while regarding him. "Having you nearby is comforting…at least when I'm at home."

Tommy's features eased. "I don't think you have anything to worry about, but since you are clearly worried, you can count on me to be there in a snap if you sense any trouble, wherever you happen to be."

"Mahalo." She smiled at him, glad to know he had her back. Just as she knew that Logan did. But would either be able to protect her from a determined killer? Or would that ultimately fall on her?

"In the meantime, just keep your guard up," he said with earnest. "Killers usually like to catch victims unprepared and aren't too interested in those who are observant and actually willing to fight back."

Elena laughed. "Looks like someone has been

watching too many episodes of *Hawaii Five-O*," she teased him.

"Just telling it as I see it." Tommy drank some more of his juice. "Honestly, sis, what I think you really need is a man in your life."

"Oh, really?" Her eyes popped wide. This should be interesting.

"Yeah. Errol's been gone long enough. Time for you to get on with your life. I know you're a strong independent woman and all, but c'mon. There's someone else out there for you to share and share alike. I'm just saying…"

"Look who's talking," she challenged him, even if the thought of sharing her life with someone special was appealing. A man like Logan would probably fit the bill, she imagined, if they were ever to give it a go. "Coming from a guy who seems to have a different woman on his arm every other week."

Tommy grinned crookedly. "What can I tell you, I'm just trying to find the right one to give it a go with."

"When you do, let me know." Elena gave him a sarcastic look and sipped her drink.

"Ditto," he told her, before getting to his feet. "I'll walk you back to the main house."

"Okay." Though she felt fairly safe in the upscale neighborhood, and her own residence in particular, Elena welcomed the offer. But could anyone ever feel safe enough in the current environment in Hilo, in spite of Logan and his colleagues being hot on the trail of a serial killer?

Once inside her home, Elena locked the door behind her, while Tommy headed back to the *ohana*, claiming he planned to make an early night of it for an early start with a guided tour the next day. Given his penchant for partying sometimes into the wee hours of the morning, she was suspicious of just what his plans were for the evening.

As for herself, Elena took a quick shower before bed, having eaten earlier. After putting on a chemise nightgown and applying moisturizer to her face, she walked into the master suite, with its rustic furnishings and large windows. After climbing onto the panel platform bed, she tried reading a few chapters of a novel she had started, but could not seem to focus on anything but the latest poor woman who had been murdered, ending any dreams she had for the future. Elena imagined the grief her loved ones would experience, having been on that side of the equation in dealing with such loss. Turning her thoughts to Logan, Elena wondered what type of stress he was going through in trying to solve the case, over and beyond having to deal with the recent death of his partner. She was sure Logan was strong enough to adjust accordingly. Elena was not as confident where it concerned becoming romantically involved with the detective, in spite of the potency of a single kiss and its rippling effect on her body. Could he handle a relationship while pursuing a serial killer? And beyond? Could she? Or were any possibilities between them doomed to failure, even as she tried to move on with the hope of finding love as a widow, as Errol would surely have wanted. These disquieting questions lingered in her mind as Elena fell asleep.

Chapter Five

Even though it was ten at night and he dreaded having to be the bearer of bad news as he arrived at his destination, Logan would not shirk from his duties as a lead homicide detective. Unfortunately, this included being assigned to informing loved ones about those who passed away. In the case of Yancy Otani, that sad news had to be delivered by phone half an hour earlier, given that the murder victim's parents lived in Sacramento, California—the family had relocated there a few years ago from the island of Maui. He had few answers to give them, apart from the obvious. As soon as the autopsy was completed, the body would be released to a funeral home and any arrangements for transport could be made then. For now, the victim's remains were still evidence in a murder investigation, one which Logan hoped would lead them to a killer.

Among Yancy Otani's belongings was her University of Hawaii at Hilo campus ID card. Her parents verified that she was an out-of-state graduate student seeking a master's of science in tropical conservation biology and environmental science and resided in an apartment on Aupuni Street. Logan knocked on the sixth-story door. Opening it was a thin young woman in her early twenties with blue eyes and light auburn hair in a graduated style with curtain bangs. She was clad in a pink peplum top and denim shorts. Flashing his badge, he said in an equable voice, "Hi, I'm Detective Ryder of the Hawaii Police Department. And you are…?"

"Shailene Leclerc."

"Are you Yancy Otani's roommate?"

"Yeah." Her eyes narrowed. "Did something happen to her?"

"Mind if I step inside for a minute?" Logan asked, hoping not to have to discuss the matter in the hallway.

She stepped aside and he walked into a small living room with neatly arranged country furniture. "Where's Yancy?" Shailene persisted.

Always the hardest part, Logan thought. But there was no getting around it. Especially when he still needed to question the roommate about the victim. "I'm sorry to say that Ms. Otani is dead—"

"Dead?" The color seemed to drain from Shailene's face. "How…?"

"She was murdered." Logan paused. "Her body was found at Onekahakaha Beach Park."

Shailene's shoulders slumped. "It was that Big Island Killer, wasn't it?"

"The investigation is still underway." He didn't want to be too presumptuous before it was confirmed. "I can assure you that whoever did this will be brought to justice." Logan hoped the words didn't come across as hollow. Especially since he had said the same thing to family and friends of the other victims, more or less. But he still believed this to be true, if he had anything to do with it.

"Have you gotten in touch with Yancy's parents?" Shailene's eyes watered.

"Yes," he told her with regret. "Naturally, they're broken up by the news." How could they not be? Logan considered how he felt when witnessing the murder of his partner. And how Elena felt in losing her husband. These things would be tough for anyone to take. That included the victim's roommate. "I need to ask you a few questions…"

Shailene wiped away tears. "Okay."

"We believe that Yancy was jogging in the park when she was attacked. Does she often jog there?" He noted that it was a few miles between the apartment complex and Onekahakaha Beach Park.

"Yes, she jogged there a few times a week—usually after her shift was over at the Pizza Isle on Punahoa Street, where she worked part-time."

Logan considered that someone who knew her routine, including an employee at the restaurant, could have followed her to the park and killed her. "Was Yancy seeing anyone?"

"No," Shailene said swiftly. "Between school, work and staying in shape, there wasn't much time for dating."

"Did she have any enemies, stalkers, or anyone she seemed to be concerned about?" Logan asked routinely, but still needed to know for the record.

"Not that I can recall. She got along well with everyone." Shailene's lower lip quivered. "I can't believe she's gone…just like that."

"I understand what you're going through," he told her. More than she knew. "Look, if you need to talk to someone, I know a grief counselor who could help you deal with this." When she seemed to be open to the possibility, he gave her Elena's name and contact info, knowing that her office welcomed anyone coping with loss and other traumas. Finally, Logan asked Shailene gingerly, "Do you think you're up to IDing the body?" Though they were fairly confident that the murdered victim was Yancy Otani, this would make it official, given the distance and time it would take for her parents to get there.

Though she looked to be barely holding up on wobbly knees, Shailene agreed to accompany him to the morgue. Another punch in the gut for Logan in the course of a murder investigation. After the mission was successful, unfortunately, he dropped the victim's roommate back off at her apartment and called Ivy as he drove off, putting her on speaker. "Yancy Otani worked at the Pizza Isle restaurant. She left her vehicle, a red Hyundai Sonata, there while she went jogging at the park. We need to have it dusted for prints and see if any DNA collected will point a finger at someone."

"I'll get the CSI unit over there right away," Ivy told him.

"I'm heading over there now to speak with employees and check out surveillance video," Logan said. "Whoever killed her may have been at the restaurant and trailed her to the park, before catching her off guard."

"I'll meet you there." Ivy sighed. "The rising body count is starting to get to me. The unsub is almost daring us for a showdown."

"We're more than up to the task, believe me." To suggest otherwise would be handing the perp a victory. That wasn't going to happen, as far as Logan was concerned. He doubted Ivy felt any different, in spite of the frustration he heard in her voice.

"I do," she stated flatly. "One person—even such as this serial monster—can't come out ahead of an entire task force that's pretty pissed off right now."

"Couldn't agree more." Indeed, they were all fully committed at the Hawaii PD, along with their partners in law enforcement, to working overtime to bring the unsub to justice. No matter how long it took. As if he needed any more reasons to that effect, Logan had one, anyway. Elena Kekona. Yes, he knew that her brother was around for her to lean on right now and help safeguard her from danger. But was he really equipped to take on a serial killer if push came to shove? For that matter, was Elena even safe while at work? What would prevent the unsub, if the perp believed she fit the profile of his other victims, from spotting her by chance and going on the attack when Elena least expected it? The mere possibility of losing her shook Logan to the core, even though he and the counselor had yet to even go out on a proper date. Much less become involved in something akin to a real relationship.

Calm down, Logan ordered himself, having disconnected from Ivy as he neared the restaurant. *Don't freak out prematurely.* Elena was a grown woman and smart enough to take precautions to ensure her own safety, wherever she happened to plant her feet. As much as he wanted to be her protector with a murderer at large, Logan didn't want to do more harm than good in being worried about Elena. The last thing he wanted was to come across as more of a hardheaded cop than a man who had genuine feelings for her, but not obsessively so. His best bet at this point was to take it slow and let things play out naturally. At least where it concerned Elena. There was no slowing down in the hunt for the unsub. The sooner they put an end to the perp's reign of terror on the Big Island, the sooner Logan could concentrate more fully on the woman who was unknowingly making his heart patter.

STUDYING THE SURVEILLANCE VIDEO, Logan saw Yancy Otani leave the restaurant on foot, en route to Onekahakaha Beach Park. She gave no indication of anxiety or belief that she was being followed before she disappeared from view. No one appeared to be following her. "Let's back it up and watch again," he told the manager, Karen Foxworth, who was in her midthirties with orange hair in a diagonal fringe cut.

"Sure thing," she said, and rewound the video.

"Doesn't seem like anyone's on her tail," Ivy stated tonelessly.

Logan frowned. "Maybe the unsub met up with her later." Or not. "Rewind until a couple of minutes before Yancy comes into view." The manager complied. "Stop!" Logan ordered when he spotted some movement in a corner of the screen. "There's a person standing by some bushes—"

"Yeah, you're right," Ivy said. "They seem to be going out of their way to stay inconspicuous."

Logan felt the same thing. "Can you zoom in on the person?"

"Yes, I can do that." Karen brought the image closer. The person was tall and slender, wearing dark clothes and a hoodie. Logan couldn't make out the face or hair, covered in shadows.

"Looks like our person of interest," Ivy remarked.

"It does, doesn't it?" Logan concurred, locking in on the suspect.

"You think he went after Yancy and killed her?" Karen's mouth hung open in fury.

"That's what we intend to find out," Logan responded tersely. "Does that person look familiar at all?" He eyed the manager, thinking it could be an employee. Or a regular patron.

She peered at the image for a long moment. "I don't recognize them. Sorry. Maybe one of my staff can help you identify the person."

Logan pursed his lips. "Why don't you fast-forward the video past when Yancy disappears from the screen."

"Okay." Karen did as he asked.

"Stop!" Logan snapped as he spotted the person in the hoodie begin to move in the direction the victim had gone. "The unsub's following Yancy, presumably in the process of tracking her down in the park and murdering her."

Ivy muttered an expletive. "We'll see if we can match this up with other surveillance video that leads to the park. Could give us a better description of who we're looking at."

"Do it," Logan told her. "Maybe some eyewitnesses can help us ID the unsub." The better part of him believed they would unmask this perp eventually, surveillance video or not. But could they do so before the killer decided to strike again?

Eight hours later, after a mostly sleepless night, where his head was filled with thoughts of the Big Island Killer, the unsub's victims and Elena, not necessarily in that order, Logan got dressed and settled on coffee with a little cream and a bagel for breakfast. Then he headed for the forensic pathologist's office to get the official autopsy report on the death of Yancy Otani.

"I was expecting you," Bert Swanson said the moment Logan stepped into his domain. The office itself was spacious with modern furnishings and equipment.

Not wanting to beat around the bush, Logan asked, "So what are we looking at on the death of Yancy Otani?"

Swanson scratched the hair on his chin, then responded authoritatively, "Just as I suspected, Ms. Otani died of the injuries sustained due to blunt-force trauma."

"Can you be a bit more specific?" Logan had no desire to hear the gruesome details. But as a homicide detective, he needed to believe they were talking about the same killer here.

"Of course. The victim's death was caused by blunt trauma to the back of her head and neck. The killer likely pummeled her repeatedly with the lava rock that I, along with your forensics department, determined to be the weapon used to kill Ms. Otani. It dealt something akin to a crushing blow that the poor woman simply had no chance to survive."

Logan furrowed his brow, the thought of such a violent ending playing on his emotions. "In your professional opinion, do you think she was killed by the same unsub we believe bludgeoned to death Liann Nahuina and Daryl Renigado?"

Swanson took a breath and locked eyes with Logan. "That's ultimately your call, Detective, but based on the autopsy results from all three homicides—illustrating severe trauma with blunt force—I'd have to say that we're almost certainly looking at a serial killer with a thirst for extremely vicious behavior."

Logan nodded. "I expected as much," he muttered, wondering if he would have felt any better had there been three separate killers. The fact that they were looking for a single individual did, if nothing else, allow them to focus their investigation in one direction.

"Unless you want us to keep doing this song and dance," the pathologist warned with a catch to his voice, "I highly recommend that you and your team find this killer and stop the madness."

"I hear you." Logan gave him a sincere salute, meant to show that they truly were on the same page in knowing what needed to be done if the female residents on the Big Island were ever going to be able to rest easily again. That included Elena, whom he was still keen on getting to know much better, even in the midst of a serial-killer investigation. He wondered if she was up to having dinner at his place. Or would that be more than she was ready for at this point?

ELENA HAD A restless sleep before morning came. She had a disturbing dream in which the Big Island Killer was chasing her in the dark of night. Just as the faceless, hooded killer was about to descend upon her maniacally, Logan seemed to come out of nowhere to her rescue, stopping the villain cold. Afterward, Logan scooped her in his arms, kissed her passionately and, she supposed, they lived happily ever after. Awakening, Elena blushed at that last thought, which was purely speculation. She only knew that the detective saved the day in her nightmare and she was eternally grateful for that, even if it was only a dream that Logan would never know about in the real world.

Guess I really let the latest murdered woman get

to me, Elena thought, reclaiming her equilibrium and sense of reality, before climbing out of bed. She needed to keep a proper perspective as she began her day. Last thing she needed was for an unidentified serial killer to both invade her dreams and drive her crazy with fear while awake. Wasn't that what all serial killers wanted at the end of the day, to get into the heads of vulnerable women like those being targeted, giving the offenders a psychological boost over and beyond the killings?

Declaring that she wouldn't allow herself to become a victim, Elena freshened up and dressed, put her hair in a French twist updo, had cereal and black coffee for breakfast, and was out the door for work. She noted that Tommy's car was gone, indicating that he had already left for the Hilo tour he was guiding this morning. She was glad they got to talk last night, as they didn't have heart-to-hearts nearly as often as they did when they were younger.

After getting into her own vehicle, Elena started it and took off. At 9:00 a.m., she had her first session of the day with a woman named Marybeth Monaghan. In her early thirties, she was tall and lean, yet big-boned. Her jet-black hair was in a pixie bob cut, surrounding an angular face and blue eyes behind geometric-shaped beige eyeglasses. She was wearing a floral print midi dress and brown ankle-strap sandals.

"Aloha," Elena greeted her with a smile.

"Thanks for seeing me," the woman said politely.

"How can I help you, Ms. Monaghan?"

"Please, call me Marybeth," she insisted. "Ms. Monaghan was how they always referred to my mother, who was a single mom, until she passed away recently…"

Elena showed appropriate sympathy. "I'm so sorry to hear that."

"It's the reason I'm here." Marybeth's voice shook. "Guess I just needed someone to talk to about it."

"I understand. I'm happy to offer my services." Elena recalled when she lost her own mother and then her father. Both deaths were devastating, taking a piece of her away forever. Obviously, Marybeth was going through much of the same journey of grief and transitioning to life afterward. After the payment had been taken care of, Elena said, "Why don't we go into my therapy room and talk?"

She led the way and sat across from the new client. "How did your mother die?"

Marybeth smoothed an eyebrow. "Cancer." She paused. "Pancreatic."

"I'm sure it had to be devastating for you." Elena could only imagine how difficult it was to watch someone die a slow death from the hideous disease, while being helpless to do anything about it aside from hoping to make them as comfortable as possible.

"It was." Her head slumped. "Still trying to come to terms with it, you know."

"It's a process that will take some time." Elena knew this both from experience and the many stories she had heard before and since becoming a grief counselor.

"Having you to help walk me through the stages of grief, or whatever, would be a big help," Marybeth said thoughtfully.

"I can do that," Elena promised her. "Together, we can deal with this head-on and find solutions that should get you past the worst of it and back on an even track."

Marybeth touched her glasses timidly and managed a tiny smile. "I'd like that."

After finishing up with Marybeth, and then two more clients, Elena thought about taking a walk before her afternoon session. Though the area was usually bustling with locals and tourists alike during the day, given the fact that a serial killer was on the loose and targeting women who resembled her, she thought maybe that wasn't such a good idea. Or was she being overly paranoid, putting a dent in her independent spirit?

When her cell phone rang, Elena looked at it and saw that it was Logan. Her heart did a little leap and dance. She answered. "Hey."

"'Hey' back to you," he said and waited a beat, making her curious if there was more news on last night's victim. Or worse, if someone else had been murdered. "I was wondering if I could make you dinner tonight since our outing last night was cut short."

"I'd love to have dinner with you tonight," she answered enthusiastically. *So he can cook—how nice,* she mused. "But I'd like to bring the wine."

"Feel free to. Pick whatever color you like." Logan's voice sounded amused. "In fact, I'll be heading over to the farmers' market on Kamehameha Avenue to get some fresh items for the meal. If you're free later, say around three, three-thirty, we can get a head start and meet up there and you can help me pick out what works for you."

"Sounds like a plan." Elena actually thought the timing was perfect, as she had no clients scheduled after two o'clock. Plus, it might be fun to pick and choose the ingredients for the meal together. Almost like a real couple, even if they weren't there just yet.

When three o'clock came around, Elena did not see Logan at the agreed-upon spot. She suspected that he may have gotten tied up with work, so she decided to check out the latest at the farmers' market on her own. She looked with interest at some *hamakua* mushrooms, hydroponic lettuce, organic spinach and rambutan—all appetizing. Just when she was about to move on and check out other vendors, Elena spotted out of the corner of her eye a tall figure wearing a hoodie. The person barreled toward her and, before she could react, in an instant she had been shoved hard to the ground at the same time her handbag had been grabbed by the assailant. The last thing Elena remembered just before her head slammed into the concrete was the sound of Logan's powerful voice, though she could not make out the words, and his rushing toward her like she was the most important person in the world, his handsome features an interesting mix of concern and anger.

Chapter Six

The moment Logan saw the tall male, wearing a dark hoodie and dark clothing, moving toward Elena at a brisk pace, he knew she was in trouble. But he was not close enough to them to thwart the danger. Instead, Logan could only warn Elena of the impending threat, even as he raced to get to her. She seemed to respond to the sound of his voice, but barely had time to look in his direction as the assailant body-slammed her. As she went down, the man in the hoodie snatched the handbag she was holding and took off.

Caught between a rock and a hard place, Logan was furious that the brazen daytime robber should target Elena, who was only at the farmers' market at his request. *Damn you*, he cursed within. This made him all the more determined to nab the culprit. But first things first. He needed to make sure Elena was all right. Lifting her up into his arms, he could see that she was shaken up. "Did he hurt you?"

"My pride more than anything," she joked, and put a hand to her forehead. "I am feeling a little dizzy, but I think I can stand on my own two feet."

Taking her at her word, Logan stood her up. She didn't appear to be wobbly. That was a good thing.

"I'm sorry this happened," he said, feeling guilty that he couldn't get to her in time.

"I was just in the wrong place at the wrong time. I'll be fine," she insisted, "provided you can get my handbag that he took. It's expensive and my cell phone and other things I'd rather not have to buy again were in it."

"Say no more." Logan led her over to a bench and demanded that she stay put, even if she felt perfectly okay. Given that she seemed to have hit her head pretty hard, he saw no reason to take any chances before she was checked out. But he needed to make things right, and so he honored her request to retrieve what was taken from her. "Be right back—"

With that, Logan took off in the direction of the thief. At the same time, he got on his cell phone and reported the crime, described the suspect and demanded that the arrest of Elena's assailant be given top priority. *Assuming I can't get to him first*, he thought. Being familiar with this particular farmers' market, which he liked to go to for fresh fruits and vegetables, Logan considered the escape routes a suspect might take. He sensed that this wasn't the perp's first time stealing. Success gave him the confidence to stay the course, as he believed himself to be nearly invincible. More troubling to Logan was the fact that the suspect's clothing and hoodie matched the description of the unsub seen running away from the scene of two of the murders attributed to the Big Island Killer. Could they be one and the same?

With an even greater sense of urgency, Logan took a shortcut, anticipating the suspect's escape route. Bingo! He spied the perp, still clutching the berry-colored designer leather shoulder bag as though his life depended on it, as he moved casually through the crowd inconspicuously. Logan suspected Elena's attacker was only biding his time before bolting to safety to enjoy the fruits of his labor. *Think again*, Logan mused. Without warning, he charged toward the suspect like an angry bull, taking him down hard and giving him a dose of his own bitter medicine. Easily gaining control of the suspect, Logan wrapped his arms around his back and, after handcuffing him, announced with rancor, "You're under arrest." He read the perp his rights and hauled him up without incident at about the same time the cavalry arrived in the form of two uniformed officers.

Forty-five minutes later, Logan was in Elena's hospital room at the medical center, where she was taken for precautionary measures. He was still peeved that the robber had laid a hand on her. The good news to Logan was that he was able to return Elena's handbag to her. As far as he could determine, it still had all its contents, which she had verified. "How are you feeling?" Logan asked again, as if she hadn't heard him before and indicated she would survive.

"Terrific!" Elena flashed her teeth convincingly. "Just a slight headache, but nothing I can't overcome with a good night's sleep."

Logan wondered if that meant their dinner at his place was off tonight. Probably so, he figured, given that he needed to interrogate the suspect as both a thief and possible serial killer. As Logan gazed at Elena on the hospital bed and contemplated whether or not the universe was trying to tell them something, the doctor came in. An African American, Dr. Wellington was in her thirties and slim, with long brunette hair in large and low curls. After checking Elena out, she told her, "You've suffered a mild concussion, Ms. Kekona."

Elena lifted an eyebrow uneasily. "That's good news, right, considering?"

"Yes," she said in earnest. "Especially after you apparently took a nasty blow to the head, according to Detective Ryder."

"Must be that hard head of mine. It worked in my favor this time," Elena quipped.

"Must be." Dr. Wellington smiled. "You won't need to stay in the hospital overnight, but I recommend you take one or two days off from work to rest—the best medicine for this type of injury."

Elena frowned, as if the thought of being away from work was tough to bear. Logan understood where she was coming from, as his work had become his life over the years. He was beginning to wonder if that was a good thing for either of them. Particularly when life could be snatched away so quickly. Smelling the roses, so to speak, had become even more important to him. But only if he had someone special to smell the sweet fragrance with.

"Whatever you say, Doctor," Elena said acquiescently.

"Do you have someone who can drive you home?"

Logan was just about to volunteer for the job, having driven Elena to the hospital in his car, when he heard a strong male voice say over his shoulder. "I will…"

Pivoting to his right, Logan saw a tall and slender man in his late twenties with dark hair in a tight fade cut and a stubble beard walk up to the bed. "Hey, sis, you look like crap."

"Thanks a lot." Elena gave him a disapproving look

and turned to Logan. "This is my brother, Tommy." She paused, seemingly ill at ease. "Tommy, this is Police Detective Logan Ryder."

They sized each other up and Logan had the distinct impression that Elena's brother was not too fond of cops. He wondered if there was a story to that. Sticking out his hand, he said in a friendly tone, "Nice to meet you, Tommy."

"Yeah, you, too," he responded with a less-than-enthusiastic inflection, but shook hands, anyway, before turning to Elena. "So, what exactly happened?" She had phoned him en route to the hospital and tried to convince him it wasn't necessary to come. Apparently, he'd thought otherwise.

"I was accosted at the farmers' market by some creep," she explained. "He stole my handbag." She drew a breath and gazed at Logan. "Detective Ryder was able to arrest the thief and return my handbag. Nothing seemed to be missing, thank goodness."

"Mahalo, for helping my sister out," Tommy told him genuinely.

"No problem." Logan wanted to say that his interest in doing so went well beyond an official capacity. But something told him that Elena would rather break the news of the personal nature of their involvement to Tommy in her own way and time. He had to respect that, given that he had no siblings to deal with when it came to matters of the heart. He only hoped that they could get past this awkward moment and continue to move forward in getting to know one another in romantic terms. "Well, I'd better get back to work," he said, wishing otherwise. "I can have someone bring your car home, if you like…"

"I'll take care of that," Tommy volunteered, almost territorially.

Logan nodded. Eyeing Elena, who looked uncomfortable, he said, "When you're feeling up to it, we'll need you to come down to the station to provide a statement regarding the attack."

"I will." She smiled tenderly at him. "Thank you, Logan, for everything."

He nodded again, happy to hear her refer to him by his first name, suggesting a more personal involvement between them for her brother to contemplate and deal with. That would have to do, for now. Logan left the hospital, already making plans to reschedule their dinner date, if Elena was willing. At the moment, he was eager to grill the suspect, while considering if he could actually be the Big Island Killer as well as a common thief.

ELENA SAT QUIETLY in the passenger seat of Tommy's Volkswagen Atlas, still reeling from her rather harrowing experience with the robber at the farmers' market. She still felt a little sore, but counted her blessings that things hadn't ended up much worse. At least she would live to see another day. The same couldn't be said for the three women who'd died at the hands of a serial killer terrorizing the Big Island. *I could just as easily have been one of them*, she thought, knowing the similarities among the victims. She was glad to know that Logan was out there trying to track down the culprit, sworn to do his duty as a member of law enforcement; even while grateful that he had been there to witness her attack, protect her from further harm and nail the thief before he could rob another unsuspecting person.

Her mind wandered to the date they had planned that evening that went awry, through no fault of either of them. She wondered if Logan was as disappointed as she was that they were unable to have dinner at his place. Did he believe the forces were somehow working against them? Or was it more a case of "if at first you don't succeed, keep trying"? After all, if things were meant to progress between them, wouldn't they still be able to give it a go and see where it went, no matter the hindrances? Could one of those hindrances be her brother? She had seen him tense up when introduced to Logan as a police detective, as though he would be his natural enemy. It was for that reason she hesitated to go further in trying to fix what was likely a nonexistent division between Tommy and him—she hoped to ease into the topic. And there was no time like the present to start.

As if reading her thoughts, Tommy broke his silence. "So what's up between you and the detective?"

"We're friends," Elena said simply, which was true, since they hadn't gone much further than that up to this point, no matter how strong the vibes were between them.

"Since when did you start hanging out with cops?" he asked hotly, peering over the steering wheel.

Not liking the tone of his voice, she responded tartly, "I don't *hang out* with cops. Logan just happens to be in law enforcement. There's a difference."

"Where did you meet, anyway?"

"We met in the course of my work." Elena saw no reason to get into specifics in divulging the confidential nature of their initial meeting without Logan's approval. Besides, there was no reason to justify their friendship to her younger brother, no matter how much she loved him and wanted him to at least like anyone she became involved with, were that to ever happen with Logan in a serious way.

Tommy grunted. "You like him, don't you?"

"Yes, I do." Might as well put it out there and make her brother grow up at the same time. "While we're just getting to know each other, I think I'm old enough to choose my own friends or whatever."

"Never said you weren't," he huffed.

Elena decided she may as well seize the moment. "In fact, if my memory serves me correctly, I seem to recall you telling me recently that it was time I start dating again. Not to say that we're dating," she added quickly, even if they were leaning in that direction.

"Yeah, I know." He paused. "Do what you want. It's your life."

They picked up where they left off once inside her house. Elena ignored some grogginess and told him, "Yes, it's my life. Just as it's your life. I don't tell you who to go out with. So, please, don't try to tell me."

"All right, all right. I get it." Tommy bobbed his head yieldingly.

"Do you?" She fixed him with a hard stare, though believed she had made her point.

"Yeah, I do." He ran a hand across his mouth. "Just be careful," Tommy warned. "I don't want to see you get hurt."

"Logan won't hurt me," Elena insisted. "He's a nice guy. You might actually like him, if you can just get past your prejudices against the police."

"Not sure that's going to be happening anytime soon." Tommy wrinkled his nose. "Too much history there. Anyway, I'll hitch a ride with a friend and go get your car."

"Thanks." She forced a smile.

"If you get sick or anything, let me know."

"I will," she agreed, "but I'm sure I'll be fine."

Elena saw him out and all she could think of after her experience was wanting to soak her aching bones in a nice hot bath. *I'll also need to go and give a statement to the police about my encounter with the thief,* she told herself. But for now, in following the doctor's orders, she needed to get some rest before rearranging her counseling schedule for the next two days. It would give her plenty of time to read and think about how she could make up for the lost dinner occasion with Logan. Now that she had smoothed things over with Tommy somewhat, as far as the detective was concerned, the time might be right to flip the switch and invite Logan over for dinner. Then the ball would be in his hands as he continued on the offense in search of a serial killer.

"WHAT DO YOU THINK?" Aretha Kennedy asked Logan, as they gazed through the one-way window at the suspect. He had been identified as thirty-six-year-old Gregory Roarke, and had a long criminal record of assaults, robberies and drug-related offenses in Hawaii, California and Nevada. Authorities had been seeking his arrest on a number of charges, including a string of local break-ins and thefts. Though they had him dead to rights on these offenses, Logan was less certain that he was the Big Island Killer. In spite of his penchant for violence related to robberies, Roarke did not have a history that suggested he was prone to being a serial killer. But then, not all serial murderers left a road map that was predictive of future behavior.

"Let's just see what the perp has to say," Logan responded noncommittally, wanting to keep an open mind, even while keen on making sure the suspect felt the full weight of the law for attacking Elena.

"He's definitely not going to be able to worm his way out of this," Ivy Miyamoto said confidently. "At least not for the crimes where the forensic evidence and witnesses point directly to him."

"You've got that right." Logan furrowed his brow and entered the interrogation room with Aretha. Handcuffed, Gregory Roarke sat at a metal table. He was tall and gangly. With the hoodie down, he had slicked-back brown hair, parted in the middle, and gray eyes. He glared at the investigators.

Logan stared back at him with equal rancor as he took a seat next to Aretha across from the suspect, who had been read his rights, including the right to a lawyer whenever he wanted one. "You're in a boatload of trouble, Roarke," Logan said, making himself clear, while seeing how much they could get out of him. "The charges you face are off the charts." The suspect remained mute, as if this would somehow get him out of the jam of his own making. *Not a chance*, Logan thought resolutely. "Robbing someone at a crowded farmers' market. Not your smartest move, pal. The fact that I witnessed the crime taking place makes it even dumber, as I'll be your worst nightmare when you go on trial for this."

Roarke scowled. "You're scaring me to death," he hissed sarcastically.

"You should be scared," Aretha argued, peering at

him unblinkingly. "You're facing hard time and it's not very nice where you're going." She paused. "Being a serial killer is a whole different ballgame…"

The suspect's eyes grew wide. "What?"

"You heard me. We've been looking for someone wearing a hoodie and dark clothes, like the ones you have on, who's been going after young women in Hilo and beating them to death. If you're ready to confess to being the Big Island Killer, it would certainly make our job a whole lot easier."

"Whoa," Roarke spluttered nervously. "I didn't kill anyone. I'm not the Big Island Killer!"

Logan leaned forward. "I'm afraid your word alone isn't good enough in this case. Convince us we're way off base—we need rock-solid alibis and more."

By the time they were finished with the interrogation and some verification, Logan and Aretha had come to the conclusion that Gregory Roarke was a serial offender, but not the serial killer they were after. The suspect was turned over to other detectives in the Area I Criminal Investigations Section who focused on burglaries and home invasions.

Logan sensed they were on the wrong track in attributing the serial murders to Roarke, but it was incumbent upon them to not leave any stone unturned in the pursuit of the unsub. At his desk, Logan gave Chief Watanabe a brief update prior to tomorrow's task-force meeting. "We hoped we had him, but as of now the Big Island Killer remains at large," he explained.

Watanabe jutted his chin. "So, you stick with it until the right perp is taken into custody—hopefully, sooner than later."

"That's the plan." Logan was glad they saw eye-to-eye on staying the course, even if there were detours along the way. He told him about Elena's encounter with Roarke, but left out the fact that they were starting to get involved. At least for now. Logan knew that he was free and clear to date the counselor, should they go in that direction, which he hoped for.

"Good thing you got the perp." The chief's nostrils flared. "And glad to hear that Elena's going to be okay."

"So am I." Logan couldn't hide his relief that she hadn't been hurt badly by Roarke in the process of stealing her handbag.

"By the way, I meant to tell you that Elena sent in her report indicating that you were successful in managing your grief after losing Hideo Zhang, meaning you're able to go about your job with the PD without being distracted in that way."

Logan grinned, happy that Elena had made it official. "Good to know. Elena was a big help in getting me to come to grips with my emotions. I owe her a ton of gratitude."

Watanabe laughed. "Well, that is her paid profession, so I wouldn't have expected any less from the counselor."

"Point taken." Logan left it at that, not wanting to get too carried away. Especially when it was the woman herself that was capturing his fancy even more than the grief therapist.

When he got home, Logan called Elena. "How are you feeling?"

"Better." She sounded good. "Just had a hot bath."

"Great." He conjured up erotic thoughts of them bathing together, before putting them in check. There would be other times, hopefully, to go down that road and back. "Thanks for letting the chief know that I'm no longer mentally unbalanced," Logan joked.

Elena chuckled. "You were never that. Just in need of some rechanneling of your emotions."

"Whatever the case, it worked. I can mourn the loss of my partner and play the role of police detective at the same time." *And can also manage a relationship*, he told himself.

"Exactly," she concurred.

Logan gave her a rundown on where things stood with the man who attacked her. "Since we have other witnesses to the crime, including myself, it won't be necessary for you to come and give a statement after all," he told her, wanting to take the pressure off, as well as give her more time to recover from her ordeal.

"Are you sure?" Elena asked.

"Positive. We've got it covered." Logan took a thoughtful breath. "Sorry this whole thing ruined our dinner date."

"Me, too." Her voice was filled with sincerity.

"I was hoping I could make it up to you." He thought about the cold shoulder he'd received from her brother. Would that impact Elena's willingness to go out with him? Logan wondered.

"I think it's more the other way around," she said, surprising him.

"What did you have in mind?"

"Dinner—Friday night. Only I'd like to cook for you."

The notion lit Logan's face with excitement, even if it was two days away. "I accept your invitation, as long as I get to bring the wine," he said with a chuckle.

"It's a deal," she agreed, chuckling back at him and

the nice role reversal from their failed first attempt at having dinner.

Logan got her address and, though he loved talking to her and probably could have done so all night, he didn't want to stand in the way of her beauty sleep and full recuperation. "I'd better let you go," he told her persuasively.

"All right," she said. "See you on Friday at seven."

"I'll be there," he promised.

After hanging up, Logan made dinner for himself, using what he had picked up before going to the farmers' market. The chicken long rice and lomi lomi salmon went down easier knowing that he and Elena would have another shot to do it right. He planned to make the most of it, wherever that led, and refused to allow a killer at large to take away the basic things of life, such as trying to see if there was someone out there Logan could connect with. A person such as Elena.

Chapter Seven

The following morning at the task-force meeting, Logan stood before the large screen display, where he used the remote to show the faces of Liann Nahuina and Daryl Renigado, the first two victims of the Big Island Killer, as a prelude to the third victim, Yancy Otani. He put her image on the screen and immediately couldn't help but see the resemblance to Elena, albeit a few years younger and a different hair color. "Her name is Yancy Otani. Two days ago, the twenty-five-year-old graduate student was accosted at Onekahakaha Beach Park in broad daylight. The murder weapon was a large piece of lava rock used by the perpetrator in an act of blunt-force head trauma to the victim. It's similar to the bludgeoning deaths of Liann Nahuina and Daryl Renigado, though in each instance the murder weapon was different. Nahuina was attacked with a bat and Renigado a wooden mallet. But the MO is close enough that the likelihood is high that we're dealing with a single unsub here—"

Logan put on the screen a still shot of a tall, slender person wearing a dark hoodie and dark clothing, with dirty white tennis shoes. "This person was seen running from the scene of Daryl Renigado's murder. Unfortunately, we can't see the suspect's face, or even hairstyle and color." After taking a breath, Logan said, "A person with a hoodie, clothing and body type matching the description of the person of interest was also seen running from the area where Yancy Otani's body was found." He switched to another image of a tall and slender individual wearing a hoodie and dark clothing and continued, "This was taken by a surveillance camera outside the restaurant where Otani worked part-time and was at, prior to jogging to the park. As you can see, the unsub is hiding in plain sight with the face obscured by shadows and the hoodie. We believe this person of interest followed Otani to the park, beat her to death with a lava rock, and is the same one spotted fleeing the crime scene."

Logan's brow creased, as he felt the frustration of everyone in that room. "Whoever this unsub is, we need to uncover their identity and bring them to justice, with more Hawaiian women vulnerable to being targeted for death." On that note, while the sense of urgency settled in, as if this wasn't already a priority, he called FBI Agent Kennedy to come up.

After she gave a briefing on the Bureau's actions in working with the task force, Aretha introduced a former FBI criminal profiler turned serial-killer crime consultant named Georgina Machado. A Latina and a bestselling author in her early forties, she was on the slender side, and had long black hair in a brushed-out curls style. With three murders and counting attributed to one killer, leaving no ambiguity in defining it as serial in nature, she had been asked to come in to provide a general profile of the Big Island Killer for some added perspective on the unsub to assist in the investigation and apprehension. For his part, Logan wanted to hear what she had to say, having read her book on serial killers with interest. He was open to anything that could add to the investigation in an effort to nab the killer before others had to die needlessly.

"Thanks, Agent Kennedy and Detective Ryder, for inviting me to join the task force pursuing the Big Island Killer," Georgina said coolly. "I've had a little time to study the homicides and behavioral pattern of the unsub in creating a profile of the person we're looking for that I hope will be helpful in the ultimate capture of the killer. First of all, let me say whether it be such monsters as Albert Fish, Henry Lee Lucas, Arthur Shawcross, Jerry Brudos and Robert Hansen, or black widows Belle Gunness and Lydia Trueblood, or even prostitute-turned-serial killer Aileen Wuornos, virtually all are sociopaths who don't need much to get them going.

"In the case of the Big Island Killer, the unsub is fueled by rage over some real or imagined wrong that's been done to them," she asserted, "be it a jilted lover or otherwise failed romance, irrational obsession, workplace-motivated assault, or a simple act of revenge on steroids, as one is never enough. This disturbing behavior caused by the pain and internal conflicts is being relieved through the malevolent and largely unprovoked attacks. Given the similarities between the victims, obviously the killer is targeting women of Hawaiian persuasion, whom the unsub blames for whatever significant event or circumstances triggered the homicidal tendencies…"

Logan listened as members of the task force posed relevant questions to the criminal profiler, before he asked one of his own. "So what, if anything, can potential targets of the unsub do to avoid getting caught in the crosshairs?" If he could do anything to keep Elena out of harm's way, Logan would certainly pass it along to her.

Georgina angled her head musingly. "You can't change who you are, unfortunately," she said candidly, "as it relates to the vulnerable group. That being said, I'd say the best way to avoid this serial killer is to not make yourself an easy target, such as walking around day or night alone, or being isolated for a killer to strike and leave with no one being the wiser or little to no resistance. Last, but certainly not least, one should never be too trusting of strangers or let their guard down in situations where it should be just the opposite. Could mean the difference between life and death at the hands of a serial murderer."

"Should all else fail, being able to legally protect oneself is a must when confronting a predictable enemy such as this one," Aretha added knowledgably. "The Bureau certainly doesn't encourage violence or use of firearms by or against anyone. Or, for that matter, taking the law into your own hands. But if it comes down to surviving a serial killer or succumbing to one, it's pretty much a no-brainer."

Logan agreed. He also understood that not everyone was mentally or physically equipped to fight fire with fire. Which played to the advantage of killers, such as the one they were hunting. How might Elena fare if confronted by the Big Island Killer? Would she be able to adequately defend herself?

"So why pick on Hawaiian women?" Ivy asked the consultant. "As a Japanese American, I'm not too far removed from my Hawaiian female friends. Are we talking about prejudice for the sake of it, or what?"

"I doubt it," Georgina responded with an air of confidence. "It's not about prejudice, per se. I believe it's personal. The unsub has chosen women who, perhaps by chance, best fit the narrow window at the center of the attacks. It could have been any racial or ethnic group, but does give us a gateway through which we can pinpoint our focus in the investigation."

When the task-force meeting was over, Logan felt they were still on the same team and of the same mind in their pursuit of a relentless killer. Though that was a good thing and Georgina Machado had given them added insight into the unsub's warped mind, this did little to allay Logan's concerns that the worst of this might not be behind them. If the perp's actions were a ticking time bomb, they needed to do everything in their power to keep the unsub from detonating it one victim after another.

AFTER A DAY and a half being cooped up inside her house while recovering from the mild concussion she had suffered at the hands of a robber, Elena welcomed an opportunity to get back out and on with her life. Friday afternoon, she arranged to meet with Leilani Zhang at the Liliuokalani Gardens, a nearly twenty-five-acre, attractively landscaped Japanese oasis in Hilo. It was lush with arched bridges over fish ponds, gazebos, pagodas, rock gardens, and meandering paths over lava flows and tide pools. Throughout the park, there were Japanese stone lanterns and sculptures, and torii gates with amazing views of downtown Hilo, Hilo Bay and Moku Ola, or Coconut Island, a small islet within the bay. Elena saw this as an ideal and safe setting for some nature therapy, as well as an opportunity to get to know a new friend.

"I can't believe you were attacked at the farmers' market." Leilani's mouth hung open with shock as they crossed a bridge.

"I know, right?" Pushing up her sunglasses, Elena could barely hide her own disbelief, knowing the market was normally a hospitable environment. "I guess he thought of me as an easy mark and went for it. Apparently, he had been responsible for a string of similar attacks in the city and elsewhere."

"Just glad you weren't seriously hurt." Leilani tilted her canvas bucket hat, further blocking the sun.

"So am I." Elena considered the person perhaps most responsible for coming to her aid, or at least in taking the perpetrator into custody. "Logan played a big role there. I honestly think the attacker freaked out when he saw him coming his way, fleeing before any more damage could be done."

"Guess it pays to be in the company of a handsome detective who can cook," teased Leilani as they moved past the bridge and enjoyed more of the setting.

Elena blushed, though found it hard to argue the point. She had told her about the dinner date, knowing that Logan and Leilani had gotten closer as friends following the death of her husband, Hideo. "I suppose so," she concurred. "But his cooking for me will have to wait a bit longer as I've invited him to dinner tonight."

"Oh, really?" Leilani fluttered her lashes. "Sounds romantic."

"It's just dinner." At least Elena tried to keep telling herself that. The truth was she was attracted to Logan and felt it was mutual. So why not let it play out and see if there was any fire after the smoke. Especially now that things were out in the open with Tommy and he had begrudgingly chosen not to make waves based on his own experiences with the police.

"Even if you two went beyond a nice meal, there's nothing wrong with that," Leilani told her. "Logan has been on his own for a long time and so have you. There's no harm in seeing how compatible you might be."

Elena laughed. "No harm at all." She hoped someday Leilani would be able to find someone new in her life, and realized it was too soon for the widow to look past losing Hideo. The thought of going it alone for the rest of one's life was not something Elena would wish on anyone. She used the short pause to turn the conversation back toward Leilani as they headed down a winding path, where a gecko put on the speed to cross over ahead of them. "So how are you doing?" Elena asked, as they passed by a stone sculpture.

Leilani sighed. "I have my good and bad days," she confessed. "Talking with you has definitely helped me find ways to be more creative in getting beyond the hurt."

Elena took that as a good sign that the therapy was working. "In my personal experience with loss, I certainly found that using my creative juices constructively was an excellent means to move on."

"And what directions have those creative juices sent you in?" Leilani eyed her curiously.

"I'm reading a lot more these days," Elena said. "Also love to hike, run and swim."

"Not much of a reader, runner, or hiker, but I do

enjoy swimming and scuba diving, though I haven't done much of either lately."

"Maybe you should." Elena took this opening. "We can swim together and you can teach me how to scuba dive."

Leilani beamed. "I'd love to."

"Then it's settled." Elena thought about a neglected pastime she hoped to get back into: kickboxing. She wondered if that was something Logan might be interested in as a hobby. Or was his life way too busy to think and act too much outside the box?

After picking up items for a traditional Hawaiian dinner, Elena went home. She was admittedly a bit nervous about cooking for someone other than Tommy for the first time since Errol's death. But she was more excited about the prospect of having a quiet meal with Logan, hopefully without the drama of duty calling or being a victim of a robbery. *Is that really asking too much?* she mused half-jokingly.

Using cooking and food skills she learned from her mother, Elena prepared kalua pork, poi, squid luau and purple sweet potatoes, with haupia for dessert. She hoped it all met with Logan's approval. Realizing she had run short on red alaea salt to season the food, Elena expected she could get some from Tommy, assuming he was home. She let the meal simmer and stepped out to go to the *ohana*. Spotting his car, Elena breathed a sigh of relief. *Good, he's here*, she thought.

As she approached, the door opened and Tommy came out with a woman. Both were giggling like children. When her brother saw Elena, his eyes widened and he said, "Hey. What are you doing here?"

Feeling somewhat embarrassed for dropping in unannounced, she responded, "I was hoping I could borrow some alaea salt."

"Of course. Help yourself." He grinned awkwardly and faced the other woman. "This is Kat. She's with the band—"

Elena gazed at the lovely young Hawaiian woman, remembering her from the children's hula dance group at the shopping mall, where they provided the music. She also recalled that the keyboardist had a boyfriend. Her long black hair was in a fishtail braid and her brown eyes sparkled like jewels. "Aloha."

"Aloha." Kat faced Tommy and her eyes popped wide, as though she was eager to leave.

"We're going dancing," he said, reading Elena's mind.

"I see." Elena wondered if Kat had moved on to Tommy as her romantic interest.

"You can come if you want." Tommy eyed her guiltily.

Elena smiled thinly. "Mahalo, but I already have plans for the evening."

He raised his chin contemplatively. "Well, have fun. I know we will."

"I'm sure you will." She wondered just how long this one would last. "I'll go get that alaea salt."

"No problem. Be sure to shut the door on your way out."

"I will." Elena watched briefly as they walked away, before heading inside the *ohana*. Judging by the empty beer cans strewn about, it was evident to her that Tommy and his bandmate had started the party before going dancing. Elena wrinkled her nose in judgment, but pushed back on her assessment. Far be it for her to try to micromanage her younger brother's life, any more than he had the right to dictate whom she decided to spend time with. He was entitled to his choices in companionship, just as she was hers. It was on that last thought, with Logan in mind, that Elena smiled while getting what she came for out of the wooden kitchen cabinet.

She headed back to the main house and continued preparation of the meal, before heading upstairs for a change of clothing. Elena hoped it would be an evening where they could get to know each other better without any interruptions.

Chapter Eight

"You clean up nicely," Elena told him, her cheeks lifted in a sexy smile as she stood in the entryway.

Logan grinned at the compliment, having ditched his detective wear to put on a blue striped dress shirt and khaki pants to go with a pair of brown monk-strap oxfords. He'd even shaved for the occasion, wanting to look presentable on what amounted to their second attempt at a real date. "So do you." He drank in the sight of Elena in a body-flattering fuchsia bandage dress and black mule loafers. Her long and layered dark hair was loose and fell over her shoulders attractively.

"Mahalo." She flushed. "Please come in."

If Logan had been impressed with the outside of the property, with its lush landscaping and fruit trees, he was just as enamored with the house's interior in one sweeping glance. "Nice place."

She smiled, thoughtful. "Sometimes I think it's too big for one person."

"I can relate," he said sincerely. "My house is the same way, albeit a different style." *I'd love to have someone to share it with*, Logan thought. He stretched his arm out, holding a bottle of Hawaiian guava wine. "This is for you."

Elena took it from him, studying it. "Good choice."

He was glad to hear her say that. "I thought so."

"The food will be served shortly, along with this wine," she said. "Why don't you make yourself at home."

Logan nodded. "I will." He watched her head to the kitchen and was tempted to follow. Instead, he took her up on making himself at home, and walked around a bit, admiring the place. It occurred to him that she must have lived here with her late husband. Instantly, a streak of jealousy shot through Logan at the thought that Elena had been in love with another man. He realized how dumb that sounded, considering he was her husband and Logan hadn't been in the picture to win her over first. But maybe there was a chance that he and Elena could both get a second shot at love.

After the food was laid out, they sat on upholstered cappuccino-brown chairs around a retro wooden table in the dining room. A stationary gecko made itself at home on the wall, barely noticeable to Logan as he dove in to the meal. "Delicious" was all he could think to say in defining the meal in one word.

"Thanks." Elena beamed. "All the credit must go to my mother, who taught me the finer things on traditional Hawaiian cuisine."

"She taught you well." He smiled and thought that this was something he could get used to. As long as Elena came first and foremost with the food. Logan imagined any such involvement would also need to include Tommy as her next of kin. "So, what's with your brother?" Logan hoped this was a good time to clear the air.

Elena kept her fork with squid luau in the air. "Excuse me?"

"I could be wrong, but I got the feeling he didn't like me very much when we met," Logan told her. "Is it a protecting-big-sister thing…or just me?"

"It's not about you in particular," she said with a catch in her voice. "And has nothing to do with protecting me from getting hurt."

He regarded her. "Then what?"

She paused thoughtfully. "When Tommy was younger, he had a run-in or two with police officers. Since that time, he doesn't really trust the police."

"Sorry to hear that." The last thing Logan needed was to be looked upon as the enemy by a sibling of the woman he was attracted to. "He has nothing to fear from me."

"I know," she said confidently, setting her fork back on the plate. "Deep down, I think he knows it, too. We talked about it and Tommy won't be a problem for us. Trust me."

"Good." Logan showed his teeth as he sliced into the tender kalua pork. Maybe he had gotten carried away with his analysis of her brother. "I do trust you, Elena, and feel comfortable being around you."

"I feel the same way," she gushed, lifting her fork again, this time with a couple of slices of purple sweet potatoes.

Logan felt as though they had cleared a potentially major hurdle in moving forward. He wouldn't kick a gift horse in the mouth, but he was feeling good again at the prospect of having someone in his life. The only obstacle left was a serial killer who didn't seem to want to give the Hawaii PD a moment's peace. And, by extension, the native Hawaiian women of Hilo.

As if reading his thoughts, Elena asked over her goblet of wine, "Anything new with the Big Island Killer investigation…?"

After dabbing a napkin at the corners of his mouth, Logan decided he should be frank with her. "Other than the latest victim, we're at a standstill as far as identifying the unsub," he admitted.

"Sorry to hear that." She frowned. "I've seen the creepy image of what looks like a man wearing a hoodie. Sooner or later, I'm sure someone will come forward who recognizes him."

"I sure hope so." Logan ate more food. "We thought the man who attacked you could be the Big Island Killer. But that didn't pan out." He watched as she appeared to be reliving her ordeal. "The good news is the perp faces multiple charges and, with any luck, will be put away for a long time."

Elena's features eased back to normal. "Good. He deserves everything he gets."

"I couldn't agree more." Logan wanted to avoid the evening being turned upside down by talking about crime and criminals, so he tilted the conversation back to more personal topics. "Tell me what your interests are."

He listened as she talked about being a hiker, runner, swimmer, kickboxer and avid reader. When his turn came, Logan relayed his love for hiking, too, as well as riding horses, snorkeling, working out at the gym and traveling.

Elena jumped on that last passion. "Where have you traveled?"

"When I was working with the California Department of Justice's Human Trafficking and Sexual Predator Apprehension Team, I spent time in Central America and Eastern Europe working with our partners to try and keep a handle on the flow of international trafficking. It gave me an opportunity to see the good side of people living in the countries I visited."

"Sounds fascinating," she said, sipping her wine.

"It was. I hope to visit Australia and New Zealand someday if the opportunity presents itself."

"I'd love to visit those places, too." Elena smiled at him and Logan thought it sounded like she might be open to visiting them together. "And maybe Japan again, having visited there when I was in college." She looked across the table. "I hope you saved room in your stomach for dessert. I made haupia."

"Sounds good." Logan grinned. "Think I can handle it."

Elena smiled back. "I was hoping you'd say that." She stood and cleared the plates to make room.

After finishing dessert, they stood with their goblets of wine and moved to the great room. "This was nice," Logan remarked, grateful that there had been no interruptions, as they stood close enough to kiss. He could feel his heart pounding, as desire to be with her threatened to overwhelm him.

"I agree." Elena raised her chin, as if daring him to claim her mouth with his. "Kiss me," she demanded before he could react on his own.

"With pleasure." Logan set their wineglasses on a rustic side table, then cupped her taut chin and brought their lips together. This time, there was no stopping him from probing Elena's full mouth deeply with his tongue, tasting her wine and naturally sweet juices. Their bodies hugged tightly and Logan felt Elena's breasts and hard nipples pressed against his chest, making him all the more eager to take her to bed. Was she ready for that, as well?

Several minutes of going at it breathily only heightened his libido, then Elena pulled away. Her eyes locked on his ravenously. "Do you want to take this upstairs?"

He held her gaze. "Do you have to ask?" The urgency in his voice, Logan hoped, would tell her everything she needed to hear.

"Who's asking?" She gave him a coquettish look. "Let's go."

Elena took his hand and he followed her as they scaled the curved wood staircase, moved down a hall and into the spacious master bedroom. Logan gave a cursory glance at the antique furnishings before locking in on the king-size platform bed. Elena took away his view by grabbing his face and giving him another passionate kiss. Unlocking their mouths again, she murmured with anticipation, "Do you have protection? If not, I—"

"I have it," Logan told her succinctly. He had been prepared in case such an occasion arose. It had, and he fully embraced what was about to occur between them—taking their relationship to a whole new level. They kissed again lustfully, as the storm of unbridled passions overtook them.

SINCE WHEN HAD she become so assertive sexually? Elena wondered boldly, as she unbuttoned Logan's shirt, exposing his well-developed upper body, as if to tease her for what he brought to the table with the rest of his package. She slid the dress from her own body, exposing herself to him in only underwear and bare skin. His blue eyes darkened with the expectation of seeing her nude. Though she would normally have felt self-conscious at the very thought of being naked for someone other than her late husband, Elena felt just the opposite with Logan. Something about him and his attraction to her made her feel not only comfortable in showing him everything, but it was also a big turn-on that seemed to bring her sexuality to life. This carnal instinct rose a notch or two in her own overwhelming desire to see him from head to toe.

When they were both completely naked and standing before one another, on full and inviting display, Logan said in a throaty voice, "You're absolutely gorgeous."

Elena took in his rock-hard body and handsome face with equal fascination. "So are you," she uttered unblinkingly.

"I want you," he declared bluntly.

She quivered at the prospect, knowing she wanted him just as badly. "You can have me."

As though this declaration unleashed everything they were holding back, without prelude, Logan gripped Elena's shoulders and angled his face to kiss her ardently. Opening her mouth to meet his head-on, she felt the potency all through her body as their lips joined as if belonging together in a perfect fit of delightful sounds of yearning. Grabbing one of her buttocks, Logan brought the two of them even closer together as the kiss intensified. Elena gasped as her hardened nipples brushed stimulatingly against his chest, causing waves of delight to radiate through her. She wasn't sure how much more she could take before she exploded with joyous release. Surely he felt the powerful need as well to be inside her and make love to her.

As if reading her mind, or perhaps sensing her bodily

reaction to the mouth-to-mouth intimacy, Logan broke the lip-lock and yanked aside the double-brushed micro-fiber duvet cover, exposing the sateen-cotton sheet. He then lifted Elena off her feet and gently put her down on the bed. Sliding beside her, Logan said smoothly, "I want to make sure you're pleasured first before losing myself to desire in making love to you."

Before Elena could argue, wanting them to experience the orgasm together, she found herself succumbing to Logan's skillful hands as they caressed her breasts and nipples, making her want to scream with sensual delight. That wave of satisfaction tripled when his fingers moved down between her legs and began to fondle her there with torturous precision. The climax that followed both surprised and thrilled Elena in its intensity and the need to complete it with him inside of her. "Please, don't hold back any longer," she cooed urgently. "Let's do this together—"

"With pleasure." Logan's face was contorted, indicating the difficulty in showing such willpower. He got to his feet and swiftly retrieved the condom from his trousers, placed it upon his erection and came back to bed ready to finish what he started.

Going in for the kiss, Elena seized his lips, exchanging tasty tongues, as Logan sandwiched himself between her splayed legs and lowered his trembling body onto her. They locked eyes lustfully as he drove deep inside and she cried out when he repeated this process of undulating pleasure time and time again, until they climaxed simultaneously. Their ragged breathing slowed down gradually as their heartbeats returned to normal. Only then did they separate and lie side by side, regaining their equilibrium.

Afterward, Logan kissed Elena's damp shoulder. "You were incredible."

She blushed and responded truthfully, "So were you."

"Helps when you're so in sync with another person."

"Now we're in sync, huh?" Elena said teasingly, even while agreeing wholeheartedly. She wasn't sure she had ever been more in sync with someone sexually in her entire life. What did this say about her marriage to Errol? What didn't it say?

"Yeah, I'd say we definitely are." Logan ran a hand along her thigh. "And to think, I nearly balked at the idea of seeing you for counseling." He grinned salaciously. "Glad I didn't let stubbornness get in the way of what might have been the biggest mistake of my life."

Elena laughed, though she was touched by his words. "Not sure that would have qualified as your biggest mistake, but I'm happy too that the chief convinced you to come my way." She giggled. "Of course, I'm sure this wasn't exactly what he had in mind when recommending my services."

"Probably not." Logan chuckled, resting his hand on her knee. "But some things in life require taking your own initiative."

"Oh, you think so, do you?" Elena's eyelids fluttered flirtatiously as she ran her fingers across his chest.

She got a reaction out of him. "Yeah, without a doubt."

"And what might that initiative be telling you now?" she asked, noting that he, like her, was starting to get aroused again.

"That a second go-round might be nice—very nice, at that." Logan's voice sizzled with renewed desire.

"Hmm…" Elena shivered at the prospect of a repeat

performance. Only this time, she imagined it would be even more rewarding, now that the elemental urges of the first time had been thoroughly quenched. "I can hardly wait," she murmured, happily giving in to mutual desire and the gratification that promised to come as a result.

To say he wasn't more than ready to make love to Elena again would be unimaginable to Logan, as he fought to contain himself while they kissed, caressed and stimulated one another. He started on top but wound up on the bottom as they went at it hot and heavy, like gladiators doing battle in the arena of sexual attraction. With his hands latched on to her slender hips, Logan guided Elena over him, filling her with the solid heat of his manhood. He let her take charge from that point on as she rode him like the type of dependable stallion he hoped to own one day on his plot of land. He fondled her breasts, perfectly sized as they were, and taut nipples, and heard Elena's breath quicken at the stimulation. His own breathing became erratic as the sex brought her down and their bodies molded into one, moving frenetically while climaxing in lockstep. When it was over, they lay there, her on top of him, for a long moment while catching their breaths, and then slowly returned to the world they had managed to block out like a shade from the sun.

Afterward, still exhausted, Logan held Elena in his arms and they remained silent, as if no words were truly necessary to describe what spoke for itself in their hot and hotter actions. He wanted to ask her where had she been all his life, but knew it was too clichéd. She had been with another man and, for a time, Logan had been with another woman. But that was then and this was now. Whatever the past, he knew that he wanted a future with Elena. Logan believed by her reaction to him that she would be open to this, too. And, hopefully, her brother would give it his blessing. If only for the sake of making Elena happy.

As Logan mused about this, his mind wandered to the Big Island Killer investigation and where it stood. Three women were dead, victims of blunt-force trauma. And one killer was still at large looking for more women to target for the kill. It was something Logan was determined to bring to a halt, if his skills as a homicide detective meant anything. He would return to it full throttle tomorrow. For now, he just wanted to relish the moment with a gorgeous and sexy woman in his arms sound asleep.

Soon Logan joined her in slumberland. Until the sound of his cell phone ringing snapped him into consciousness. Glancing at Elena, whose pretty head rested comfortably on his chest, he noted she was beginning to stir. Wishing they could just remain that way forever, reality told him otherwise and Logan managed to slide from beneath her without Elena waking fully. He took a few steps in the nude to his pants on the floor, where they'd wound up last night, and found his phone. The caller was Ivy Miyamoto.

"Yeah," he answered, while watching as Elena's eyes opened and she gazed at him apprehensively, as if sensing that the call was related to the case he was working on. After listening to Ivy, Logan responded laconically, "Okay. I'll be there as soon as I can—"

"What happened?" Elena's brow creased with worry

as she leaned up on one elbow, and her naked upper body caught his eye.

Logan swallowed thickly and said in a flat tone, "A woman, identified as a native Hawaiian, has been reported missing. Apparently, she never made it home last night…"

Chapter Nine

"Her name is Kakalina Kinoshita," Ivy said over the speakerphone as Logan headed to the missing woman's address. He had just come from his own house, where he'd taken a shower and put on a fresh set of clothing. "According to her parents, Daniel and Valerie Kinoshita, whom she lived with, Kakalina was out with a friend, but always checked in through phone calls and text messages to let them know she was okay. When they heard nothing at all from her by morning, they became worried and filed a missing-person report. Could mean nothing," she emphasized. "But given that the missing woman apparently fits the description of the Hawaiian women targeted by the Big Island Killer, it seemed worth checking out—"

"You're right." Though in most instances they preferred that a person was missing for at least twenty-four hours before devoting manpower to investigate what usually turned out to be someone who was not really missing at all, but simply hadn't bothered to inform anyone of their whereabouts, Logan understood the necessity and urgency of investigating right from the get-go, in case the disappearance may have been connected to their serial-killer case. *For her sake, I just hope she's safe and sound somewhere*, he thought. "I should be there in a couple of minutes," he informed Ivy, who was meeting him at the home on Hawaii Belt Road in North Hilo.

"All right," she said and disconnected.

Logan gazed contemplatively through the windshield. Yes, he lived for the hard cases, never backing away from a challenge that required relying on his investigative skills to solve. But the Big Island Killer case was one that was starting to get to him in more ways than usual. It was becoming personal, making it all the more critical that they catch the unsub. Logan thought about Elena, the main source of his added uneasiness in the investigation. The night they had shared had been everything he could have asked for and so much more. She was as wonderful in bed as out of it. The closer they got, the more he couldn't bear the thought of anything happening to her. They had a chance to build something special. He would be damned if he let a serial killer destroy that.

When Logan drove up to the residence, Ivy was already outside, ignoring a light rain that had begun to fall. He got out and walked up to her. "The missing woman didn't happen to show up by chance, did she?"

Ivy shook her head. "Afraid not."

No harm in wishful thinking, Logan told himself. "You never know in these types of cases."

"True." Ivy studied him curiously. "Hope I didn't take you away from anything—or anyone—this morning, Ryder."

Logan imagined that he and Elena might have had another round or two in bed had his overnight stay not been cut short. But being in law enforcement and its, at times, frustrating demands was what he signed up for, so he couldn't complain. At least not openly. "Nothing I couldn't handle or hadn't expected," he responded coolly. "Let's see what the parents have to say."

They walked past swaying palm trees onto the covered lanai of the single-story country-style home on a cul-de-sac. Before the bell could be rung, the door opened. "You the police?" asked a short Hawaiian man in his early fifties with a shaven head and a black chevron mustache.

"Yes, I'm Detective Miyamoto," Ivy said, "and this is Detective Ryder. And you are?"

"Daniel Kinoshita. Please come in."

They stepped into a sunken living area with colonial-style furniture and vinyl plank flooring. A thin Hawaiian woman in her late forties with thick short black hair in a blunt cut entered the room. "This is my wife, Valerie," Daniel said, moving up to her, as if to keep her from falling on shaky knees.

"You reported your daughter, Kakalina Kinoshita, missing?" Logan asked, eyeing the couple.

"Yes, she didn't come home last night," the father pointed out. "That's not like Kakalina."

"We're afraid something bad may have happened to her." Valerie's voice shook.

"That may not be the case at all," Logan assured them, knowing he had little to go on at this point to give them false hope. "How old is your daughter?"

"Twenty-eight," Daniel said matter-of-factly.

Old enough to go off and forget or choose not to inform her parents, Logan considered. "I understand that she went out last night with a friend?"

"Yes." Valerie wrung her hands.

"Male or female?"

"Male," she answered tersely.

"Does this male friend have a name?" Ivy peered at her intently.

She shook her head embarrassingly. "We've never met him."

"But you're sure the person is a male?"

"All of her friends are male," Valerie claimed un-apologetically. "She just gets along better with men."

Meaning any one of them was a potential suspect in her disappearance, to Logan's way of thinking. At the top of the list would have to be the man she went partying with, or whatever Kakalina got herself into. "Maybe she chose to spend the night with this friend," he suggested. It sounded reasonable to him, all things considered. *Friends with benefits*, Logan mused, assuming it was all innocent and aboveboard and not something nefarious.

"Kakalina has a boyfriend," Daniel said suddenly, as if this somehow made her immune to infidelity. Or making a mistake. "They love each other. He's just as worried about her as we are. Kakalina would never cheat on him…"

Ivy glanced skeptically at Logan and back. "Even if we give her the benefit of the doubt on that front, it still doesn't mean that your daughter didn't crash at this friend's place and simply forgot to let you know she was okay."

"Kakalina wouldn't do that without letting us know," her mother insisted, her eyes watering. "We've given Kakalina her space, but she's never let us worry about her safety. Especially now, with women being terror-ized on the island by a killer…" Valerie's voice broke.

"Something has happened to her. You have to find our daughter. She may be hurt…"

Or dead… Logan read between the lines of her frightened tone. He was sympathetic, if not entirely convinced that this was truly a missing-person case. Much less, the work of the Big Island Killer. How many young women going out with a male friend—and who liked hanging out with male friends in general—showed up a day or two later with a hangover, but otherwise not the worse for wear? Still, she was missing, and until located safe and sound, all bets were off. "We'll do the best we can," he promised them. "But we need more information to go on. Such as, where did Kakalina go last night?"

Daniel scratched his chin. "They went to a night-club."

"What nightclub?"

"She never told us." He looked at his wife, as if to back him up.

"We don't know which club," Valerie stated. "She liked dancing at different clubs."

"If you can give us the names of any clubs she's mentioned, that would be helpful," Ivy told them levelly.

They named a few of the places and Ivy made a note of each on her cell phone, before Logan asked, "Does your daughter own a car?"

"No, she likes to walk or ride her bicycle," Daniel replied.

This told Logan that it likely meant the friend drove them to the club and wherever else Kakalina may have ended up. Or she met someone else there and went off with them. Then there was still the boyfriend, who may not appreciate his girlfriend spending time with other guys. They needed to talk to him. "What's the boy-friend's name?" Logan gazed at the father.

"Henry Pascua."

"Do you have a number where we can reach him?"

"Yeah, hold on." Daniel took a cell phone out of his pocket.

Logan took down the number on his own phone and asked, "Do you have a recent photograph of Kakalina on your cell that you can send me?"

"Yeah." The father nodded and pulled it up. "Just took this last week."

When the image came onto his cell phone, Logan saw an attractive and slender young woman of Hawai-ian descent with long, wavy black hair and hazel eyes. She definitely fit the bill of those in the crosshairs of the Big Island Killer, with respect to their general char-acteristics; apart from the victims' long hair coming in different colors, whether natural or dyed. Had the unsub gotten to her? Logan turned to the parents and tried to put on an optimistic face. "We'll investigate your daughter's disappearance with the seriousness it deserves. In the meantime, if you hear from her or oth-erwise learn of Kakalina's whereabouts, be sure to con-tact us right away."

"We will," Daniel Kinoshita promised and put an arm around his trembling wife's shoulders, pulling her closer.

"Please bring Kakalina home," Valerie cried, as if a mother's instinct feared that this might already be a lost cause.

"We'll do our best," Ivy told her, exchanging glances with Logan, as if weighing whether or not their best would be enough. Outside the house, she asked him, "So what do you think?"

"I think we need to locate Kakalina Kinoshita," he said simply. "She's old enough to know better, but young enough to be taken in by a charming man and potentially a killer."

"My feelings exactly."

"I'll track down the boyfriend," Logan said to her. "Why don't you see if we can pinpoint which club she may have gone to, and who was with her."

Ivy nodded. "Will do."

As they went to their cars, Logan had a sinking feeling about the disappearance, even as he found himself pivoting to Elena as someone whose health and well-being had become a priority to him, if it hadn't been before.

ELENA SHOULD HAVE been caught up in the afterglow of the amazing sex she'd had with Logan last night. He had reawakened her own sexuality and imagination in ways she would not have thought possible as a widow who had, at one point, mistakenly believed that with Errol's death that part of her life might be over for good. That obviously was not true. Logan had seen to this with his tender and magical touch, which had brought her to new heights in the bedroom. But as exciting as this was, and where it could eventually lead them as they navigated the waters of uncertainty in moving forward, Elena's thoughts, as she drank coffee in the kitchen, were on the missing woman that had sent Logan off as a police detective. The moment he received the call, she could tell by the tension in his handsome face that he feared the Big Island Killer had struck again. Had he? Or would they find that the missing woman wasn't actually missing after all?

Elena could only hope for the best, as all Hawaiian women would, given that none of them wanted to die prematurely at the hands of a killer. *In my case, I have too much to live for with Logan now a part of my intimate life*, she thought dreamily, pouring the remaining coffee that had grown cold in the sink and rinsing the cup. She went upstairs, brushed her teeth and put her hair up in a low bun, while imagining Logan running his hands sensually through her loose locks last night and seemingly enjoying every moment. When would there be an encore? And what then? Was he ready for anything steady between them? Was she, when the reality of their separate lives set in? She tried not to get too carried away with the twenty questions, thinking it best to allow nature to run its course, wherever that might be.

Leaving the house, Elena noted that Tommy's car was parked outside the *ohana*. She imagined he and the keyboardist he hung out with yesterday made a late night of it. *Hope you know what you're doing, little brother*, Elena thought, mindful of Kat's supposed boyfriend.

Half an hour later, Elena was in her office for her first session, happy for the distraction from Tommy, Logan and the unsettling thought of a missing woman. Nelson Schultz, her client, was seventy-four and grieving over the death two weeks ago of his wife of fifty years, Gwyneth. The retired cultural anthropologist was wiry, and had short and textured backward-swept white hair. He and his wife had settled on the Big Island a decade ago, moving from Arizona.

"I swore to her that I would just keep on living to the best of my ability once she was gone," Nelson uttered painfully, pushing up his rimless eyeglasses. "But that has proven to be much more difficult now that I truly am on my own for the first time in half a century, putting aside three children, ten grandchildren and three great grandchildren…all of whom I love dearly."

"It was never going to be an easy transition," Elena told him as they sat in her therapeutic office. "Couples who have been fortunate enough to be married as long as you have have earned the right to grieve a bit longer than the rest of us." With her own marriage lasting just seven years, a fraction of the time her client had spent with his late wife, Elena found herself as envious of him as she was sympathetic to him and his loss. What she wouldn't have given to have had five, ten, twenty, or more years with Errol before their marriage ended, way too soon. Along with children to reflect their love and bond. She wondered if a second chance, in the form of a new romance, could be just as gratifying over the course of time and the inner workings that came with a committed and successful relationship and the possibility of a family to go with it. "Your wife was lucky to have you, Mr. Schultz," she told him. "And from the way you've described her, you were certainly most fortunate to have had the pleasure of her companionship for so many years."

"You're right about that." The creases in Nelson's face softened. "Gwyneth was the best wife and mother of our children that I could have asked for. I just wish we'd had more time…" He paused emotionally. "But then, isn't that what we all want—just a little more time?"

"If only that were possible." Elena leaned forward

and couldn't help but think about those poor women who had lost their lives to a serial killer. Now there was a possibility that another woman could have met the same awful fate. Like her client's wife, they, too, deserved better. "Unfortunately, it doesn't always work that way." She spoken the sad truth and hoped he got it in the way intended. "What's most important now is that you hold on to the treasured memories you have and try to forge new ones with the help of family and friends." These were words Elena tried to live by in her own experience, no matter how difficult the journey.

LOGAN ENTERED THE Pascua Realty office on Kinoole Street. He was immediately approached in the spacious, carpeted suite by a tall, slender man in his early thirties with dark hair in a windblown bob. The man was dressed in sleek, business-casual clothing. "Hi, I'm Henry Pascua," he said. "You must be Detective Ryder?"

"Yes." Henry extended an angular hand and Logan shook it warily, having spoken to him briefly over the phone and not gotten a good read on him as the boyfriend of the missing woman.

"Why don't we step into my office?"

Logan followed him through the lobby and to a door that led to a good-sized office with modern furniture and a picture window. Without asking him to sit, Henry said tentatively, "You wanted to talk to me about Kakalina, or Kat, as she prefers, which is short for the non-Hawaiian variant of Katherine…"

"As I explained to you over the phone, Kakalina was reported missing by her parents," Logan said, standing flat-footed. "Do you know anything about that?"

"Wish I did." Henry lifted his chin. "The truth of the matter is Kat and I broke up last week."

Logan regarded him with misgiving. "And why was that?"

"She was into another dude," he said straightforwardly. "I don't like competing for a girl's affections, no matter how hot she is. Especially when she made it clear it was over between us."

Logan tried to decide if being dumped by her had made Henry angry enough to do her harm. Or did it merely free him to move on with someone else? "What do you know about the other guy?"

Henry shrugged. "Not much. Only that they met at a club and he got her a part-time gig playing hula music at the mall."

"Which mall would that be?"

"The Prince Kuhio Plaza."

"Do you happen to know his name?" Logan asked, wondering if this was the same person Kakalina had gone out with last night. Or could it have been one of her other male friends?

Henry ran a hand across the top of his head. "No, sorry. She never bothered to tell me."

Logan frowned and became curious. "Did Kakalina— or Kat—ever go missing when you were together?"

"Yeah, you could say that." He snickered. "When we were together, one time we flew over to Kauai and spent the night without telling her folks. They went nuts. Guess she managed to smooth things over with them when we got back."

Logan wondered if Kakalina could have decided to go island hopping again with another man. They would check into that. "According to her parents, Kat's only friends were men."

Henry wrinkled his nose. "Yeah, that seems about right. I knew that going in, but we seemed to hit it off, so I looked past her always wanting to be the center of attention with every guy who looked her way."

"Do you think any of them might have wanted to harm her?" Logan asked, an edge to his tone of voice.

Henry shook his head, maybe a little too quickly for Logan. "I know her folks are worried about her, maybe thinking Kat's fallen into the clutches of this serial killer running around. If you ask me, I think Kat's just being Kat. When she's ready to surface, she will. I wouldn't worry about it too much if I were you."

Giving him the benefit of a hard gaze, Logan took umbrage at Henry's rather cavalier attitude regarding his ex. "When women like Kakalina are being beaten to death by a serial killer, I take it very seriously. Maybe you should, as well."

"Didn't mean to give you the wrong impression." His shoulders slumped. "I hope she shows up, alive and well."

"So do I." Logan's nostrils flared. "Until such time, I'd advise you to stick around in case we need to talk further."

"I plan to," Henry insisted. "If you have more questions, you know where to find me." He pulled out a business card. "And after this is cleared up with Kat, if you're ever in the market for a house, give me a call."

Logan glanced at the card, knowing he wouldn't have any use for it in the foreseeable future. "I can see myself out," he said succinctly, and walked away still feeling empty-handed as far as a solid lead on the whereabouts of Kakalina Kinoshita. He knew that with every minute she remained unaccounted for, the less the chances that she was still alive.

Chapter Ten

In the afternoon, Elena got a text message from Logan informing her that they were still investigating the apparent disappearance of a Hawaiian woman. In noting that less than twenty-four hours had passed since she'd gone missing, and with no signs of foul play thus far, Logan seemed less than convinced that the woman had been abducted. Or was otherwise absent against her wishes. According to the missing woman's ex-boyfriend, this disappearing act wasn't something new for her, making Logan believe she may have gone somewhere of her own accord.

Elena breathed a sigh of relief. Deciding you wanted to get away without informing anyone may have been selfish, but it certainly wasn't a crime. Whereas, abducting a woman against her will was one. Not to mention if the missing woman had fallen prey to the dreaded Big Island Killer. Still, Elena hoped she resurfaced soon, if only to let her parents know she was okay. *That wasn't asking too much, was it?* Elena thought, having seen her last client for the day. It would also give Logan and the others working the serial-killer investigation one less thing to worry about. She could only imagine the stress they were under in dealing with this case, even if Logan did a good job of masking it. The sooner they could put an end to this nightmare, the sooner things could get back to normal on the Big Island.

As she drove home, Elena pondered what it might mean for her and Logan once they could focus more on them and less on their individual lives. Was this what he wanted? Did she really see a future with the detective after one intense night of intimacy? Or had she somehow lost her perspective and misconstrued sex, mind-blowing as it was, with wanting something much more substantive with a man in her postmarried life? *Guess I'll just have to find out where we go from here and not overthink it*, she told herself, while considering whether or not to invite Logan over tonight for a repeat performance. The thought of making love to the man again made Elena hot and bothered. Or would it be best for him to make the first move after what happened between them last night?

AFTER LOGAN WAS forced to abruptly leave Elena's bed this morning, he'd been more than happy to alleviate, if not squelch altogether, her concerns about the disappearance of Kakalina Kinoshita. The last thing he wanted was to have the Big Island Killer case hanging over them like a dark cloud, which was where all roads seemed to lead whenever a Hawaiian woman went missing. Until proven otherwise. No matter how this ended, Logan did not want it to get in the way of the solid foundation he and Elena seemed to be building. That was the worst thing that could happen. If he hadn't known it before, after last night with Elena, he knew he wanted more between them. Much more. She wanted it, too. He could sense that much. Making it work, given their histories and current lives apart, would be challenging. But since when had he ever run away from difficulty? As far as he was concerned, Elena Kekona was more than worth fighting for. He hoped she felt the same way about him.

That evening, Logan met Ivy at the Southside Pub on Waianuenue Avenue. Kakalina Kinoshita had apparently been seen at the club the night before, accompanied by an unidentified man.

"Yeah, I'm sure she was here," said the fortysomething bald owner who sported a grayish circle beard, Marcelo Tahutini, as he studied the photo of the missing woman. "She was dancing up a storm after she'd had a few drinks."

"What about the man she was with?" Logan asked interestedly.

Marcelo scratched his chin. "Hmm, let's see… He was Hawaiian or Latino… Mid-to-late twenties, tall, slim, dark-haired, with some hair on his face…" He sighed. "Just a regular dude."

Ivy looked at him. "Do you have surveillance cameras?"

"Yeah. Have to, these days."

"Mind if we take a look at the video from last night?" she asked.

"Not a problem."

Logan followed them into a cluttered back room, where the owner pulled up the video and got to the approximate time Kakalina was thought to be present. For a while, it looked as if they would come up short, until someone resembling her appeared on the screen. "Stop it there," ordered Logan as he peered at the image and compared it to the picture from his cell phone of the missing lady. "That's her," he decided.

"Sure is," Ivy concurred, and asked Marcelo to continue playing the video.

As they watched, it initially appeared as though Kakalina was alone. Or, at the very least, in the company of everyone at the club, but no one in particular. Then someone walked up to her, putting a long arm territorially around her slender waist, before he faced the camera. "Freeze it!" Logan commanded. Marcelo complied and Logan focused on the person, and recognized him, causing his heart to skip a beat. He could barely believe his eyes. Clear as day—or at least clear enough for Logan to make a confident assessment—the man Kakalina apparently went out with last night was none other than Elena's brother, Tommy.

IT WAS ALL Logan could do to remain mute on the identity of the male seen in the video with Kakalina Kinoshita, given what was on the line. It was a line that Logan knew he was dangerously close to crossing, due to his involvement with Elena. Especially with Ivy staring at the video, determined to identify and locate the man. For his part, Logan was just as keen on talking with Elena's brother, Tommy, who was now the chief suspect in Kakalina's disappearance, short of her showing up alive and well before Logan had a chance to speak with him. But he wanted to do so first, before it became official, as a courtesy to Elena. Surely, she wanted to get to the bottom of this, too. Even if it meant the case may be much closer to home than she could have imagined.

Logan had managed to buy himself a little time by

making an excuse to pursue another angle, while hoping, if possible, to smooth things over with Ivy later. He left her to study more surveillance video, including footage outside the club that could lead to identifying Tommy's car and license plate. *Hopefully, he'll be able to shed some light on Kakalina's absence without being guilty of any wrongdoing,* Logan thought, as he headed over to Elena's house. He had texted her to say he was coming, adding that it was official business and leaving it at that. Some things needed to be said face-to-face.

After parking, Logan headed to the main house. But not before having a peek at the *ohana*, where Tommy was staying. Noting that a black Volkswagen Atlas was parked by it, Logan assumed he was home, which may or may not be indicative of a person with something to hide. Could Tommy be keeping company with Kakalina Kinoshita, who could have been hiding out here for her own reasons? Resisting the desire to find out, Logan stuck with the plan to inform Elena first. Before he could ring her bell, she opened the door. "Hey," he said in a controlled tone, ignoring the sexual vibes that were still working overtime in her presence.

"Hey." She favored him with a curious, uneasy gaze. "What's going on? Did you locate the missing woman?"

"Can we talk inside?" Logan didn't want to tip his hand, in case Tommy was somehow able to overhear them and was planning to make a run for it if he knew something bad had happened to the missing Kakalina, and that he was responsible.

Elena moved aside and waited for him to enter. Once she closed the door, she faced him and asked point-blank, "Why the cryptic texting? What aren't you telling me…?"

He sighed and smoothed an eyebrow, as though he needed to. "The missing woman's name is Kakalina Kinoshita," he told her. "Her parents informed us that she went out last night with a male friend. We were able to establish that Kat, the nickname she went by, was last seen at a place called the Southside Pub. The person she was with was seen on surveillance video." Logan paused. "It was your brother, Tommy."

Elena sucked in a deep breath. "So what are you saying?"

"I'm saying that, as someone who may have been the last person to see Kat before she went missing, your brother is a person of interest." At this point, Logan didn't even want to think about the implications of a missing Hawaiian woman in relation to the recent murders of native Hawaiian women attributed to a serial killer.

"Tommy would never have hurt her," Elena insisted, as if reading his mind, her voice dropping an octave out of despair. "There must be some other explanation—"

Logan could see that Elena was visibly shaken by this. But there was something more to her reaction. Did she know something? "What is it?" he asked.

She stared at him for a long moment and her voice shook as she answered. "I saw Tommy with Kat last night."

"Where?"

"At the *ohana*. I went there to borrow something for our meal, just as they were headed out to go dancing..." Elena's gaze fell. "Tommy is in a band with her, playing for a hula show at the mall. I got the feeling they were pretty cozy and probably ended up back at his place afterward."

Logan reacted to this disclosure. He wasn't sure if Elena's knowledge of Kakalina was a helpful sign that Tommy was not guilty of anything other than possibly harboring the missing woman. Or if this compromised Elena as a witness to a possible crime in the making. "I need to talk to Tommy," he told her forthrightly. "It would make things a lot easier all the way around if Kat's there with him. I came here first to give you a heads-up."

Elena bristled. "I'd like to go with you."

Logan wavered. "Not sure that would be a good idea."

"He's my brother, Logan," she pleaded. "If Tommy is in some kind of trouble, I need to be there to help him face up to it."

Against his better judgment, but not wanting to burn his capital with her, Logan agreed. "Just so you understand, I'll be questioning him as a police detective. If I determine a crime of any kind has been committed, I'll have no choice but to arrest your brother."

"I understand," she said coldly. "Let's go to see Tommy."

ADMITTEDLY, ELENA HAD butterflies in her stomach as she walked with Logan in stilted silence through the lava-rock-walled entry yard toward the *ohana*. The idea that the woman who supposedly went missing was actually Kat was bad enough. Much worse to Elena was if something bad had actually happened to her and Tommy was somehow responsible for it. She could only imagine what was going through Logan's head. Any missing woman of Hawaiian ancestry was automatically linked to the so-called Big Island Killer, and would make the detective likely suspicious that one thing could have led to another and, as such, her brother could be a serial killer. Elena didn't believe that for a moment. Tommy couldn't possibly have done the things said to have been done to those poor women. And Kat was someone she could see that he genuinely liked. It seemed as though they had chemistry. Much like Elena felt she had with Logan. But could that be in peril, as the man she'd made love to less than twenty-four hours ago was now bent on questioning her brother regarding Kat's whereabouts? Elena could only hope there was a simple explanation that Tommy—and perhaps Kakalina—would be able to clear up.

Elena knocked on his door, feeling tense as Logan stood beside her, not as her lover and former client, but as an officer of the law looking for answers from her brother that Tommy may or may not have. When he opened the door, fully dressed, she could read the shock in his face as his eyes darted from her to Logan suspiciously.

"What's going on?" Tommy leveled his gaze at Logan.

"Detective Ryder would like to ask you some questions about Kat," Elena told him, curious herself as to how he would take this.

Tommy hoisted an eyebrow. "What about her?"

"Why don't we go inside," Logan said, making it clear that it wasn't a suggestion.

Tommy didn't argue the point, and allowed them in. Elena was hoping that Kat would be right there, wondering what all the fuss was about, and would let them know that she was perfectly fine and had chosen not to confide in her parents as to her location. But there was no sight of the missing keyboard player, causing Elena's own blood pressure to rise out of concern.

"Will someone tell me what's going on?" Tommy peered at Elena. "Why does he want to know about Kat?"

Before she could answer, Logan said edgily, "Kakalina Kinoshita's parents have reported her missing. Seems as though Kat was last seen hanging out with you last night at the Southside Pub. Where is she now, Tommy?" His eyebrows knitted as Logan gave him an implacable stare.

"I have no idea," he claimed, ending any such thoughts in Elena's mind that he was hiding her in the bedroom. "After we left the club, Kat and I got into a fight—not physical or anything," Tommy emphasized. "Verbal. I told her that flirting with every Tom, Dick and Harry that looked at her twice wasn't cool. She disagreed."

When he paused, Logan said thickly, "You still haven't told me where she is."

Tommy sucked in a deep breath and ran a hand ruggedly across his mouth. "She asked me to let her out of the car," he asserted. "We both probably had too much to drink at that point, so I did as she asked. Then I left and went home."

Elena pursed her lips. "What were you thinking, Tommy?" she admonished. "Why would you leave Kat out there alone knowing there's some psycho going after Hawaiian women?"

"It was only about two blocks away from her house, okay," he retorted. "How was I supposed to know she wouldn't go home?"

"Did you kill her?" Logan moved up to him, gritting his teeth.

"No, never!" Tommy responded. "She was very much alive when I left her, I swear it." He faced Elena. "Look, I screwed up. I should've driven her home, but I can't go back and change things. I'm sure she found someplace else to chill for the night and, once she's past the hangover, she'll let her parents know she's all right."

"For your sake, you better hope so," Logan warned, and added, as though it didn't go without saying, "I'd advise you not to make any plans to leave the island until this is cleared up, one way or the other."

Tommy gave him a mock salute. "Got it, Sergeant. Now if there's nothing else, I'd like you to get out of my house!"

Logan's jaw tightened. "Whatever you say." He angled his hard gaze at Elena and walked out the door, leaving her behind.

She shot Tommy a disappointed look. "I'll talk to you later."

"I'm not going anywhere," he assured her lowly, masking what Elena saw as concern for the welfare of Kat.

Elena went after Logan, feeling as if she was caught in the middle. In reality, she knew it went far deeper than that, with stakes that couldn't be higher all the way around. She reached Logan at the gate, calling out to him. He rounded on her, almost seeming like a stranger. "If your brother has done anything to harm Kakalina, I won't be able to run interference in keeping him from facing the consequences."

Elena scowled. "No one's asking you for a get-out-of-jail-free card for my brother, Detective Ryder," she shot back.

"Fair enough," he conceded contritely. "We just need to find Kat, make sure she's unharmed."

Elena couldn't agree more. "Whatever you may think of Tommy, and I know he's far from perfect, he did not hurt Kat. It's not in his DNA." In spite of his faults, Elena felt she knew her brother well enough to know that he would not intentionally harm someone. She recalled a time when Tommy had risked his own life to rescue a female swimmer who'd gone under. He refused to be called a hero, insisting that he only wanted to do what was right. That wasn't the sound of someone capable of committing an act of violence against someone he obviously cared about.

Logan's features softened. "I hope you're right about that."

"I'd like to help in the search for her," Elena offered. "Kat could have fallen and hit her head, or worse—"

"We're not quite at the point of needing to put together a volunteer search team," he said. "And while I appreciate the offer, if it should come to that, it probably wouldn't be a good idea for you to get involved on multiple levels. Tommy is still a suspect in Kakalina's disappearance. That alone would create a conflict of interest, no matter how well-intentioned your offer." Logan met her eyes in earnest. "Apart from that, there's still a serial killer on the loose. I'd never want to see you put in danger, any more than you already are by fitting the characteristics of the unsub's victims."

At least he's differentiating the Big Island Killer from Tommy, Elena told herself, feeling that was a positive thing of sorts. It also illustrated Logan's concern for her, over and beyond his investigating her brother. But was that enough, considering? "You better go continue your search for Kat," she told him stiffly. "The sooner you find her, the sooner Tommy can get out from under a cloud of suspicion. And maybe choose a woman without such a roving eye for others."

"Yeah." Logan paused, seeming to mull things over. "Assuming your brother was being straight with me, we'll focus our official search for Kakalina in the area near her home and see what we come up with."

Elena put a hand on her hip and tried to think positively about the situation. What other choice did she have? "When you learn something…"

"I'll let you know." He scratched his neck. "Look, I'm sorry about all this, Elena," he said sincerely. "I hope you know I'm just doing my job."

"I know," she conceded, holding his steady gaze. "And I'm just looking out for my brother. That's what family does."

Logan nodded. He started to say something, but seemed to think better of it and walked away. Elena watched him briefly, wondering if her mention of family had the unintended effect of diminishing what she thought they had. And just what exactly was that? Was there any chance of building a relationship with Logan as long as he was going after Tommy, and possibly trying to hang Kat's disappearance on him, and more?

Chapter Eleven

I probably could have handled things differently, Logan thought with regret after leaving Elena's property, given the look of distress on her face, as if she had been betrayed by his appearance. The last thing he wanted was to throw up a roadblock in whatever it was that they had going. It wasn't like he'd planned to make Tommy a suspect in a missing woman's case. As it was, Logan felt he was treading on thin ice in trying to balance an investigation into Kakalina Kinoshita's vanishing act with protecting the woman he had developed feelings for. But as long as he was a police detective, he was duty-bound to take what was handed to him and see where it led. He hoped Elena wouldn't hold that against him. Especially should things take a turn for the worse for her brother. But since she presumably knew him better than anyone and was convinced Tommy's only mistake was bailing on his date, for now Logan intended to go on the assumption that Kakalina Kinoshita was still alive. They just needed to locate her and reunite her with her family.

Logan hung on that last word—*family*—as if it was something that had managed to elude him in the truest sense of the word for much of his life. Elena clearly had that bond with her brother and Logan envied her for that. Someday, he hoped to be able to have a family of his own where the bonds of love and loyalty would be unbroken. There was still a chance that this could come with Elena. But Logan sensed that the road might be a bumpy one at best, if they were to drive down it at all as a united front. He allowed that thought to linger for a moment or two, before phoning in a directive to begin searching for the missing woman along Hawaii Belt Road.

Half an hour later, a team from the Hawaii PD, including a K-9 unit, had arrived and the search commenced, starting approximately two blocks from the residence where Kakalina Kinoshita lived, and going in both directions. This included stretches of open acres and farmland, where a body could have been dumped. Logan hoped it didn't come to that. In the best-case scenario, Kat would emerge from a neighbor's house no worse for wear, aside from being hungover. Better yet would be to get a call from her parents informing them it was a false alarm and their daughter was fine.

When Ivy showed up, the look on her face told Logan she had latched on to information he knew was inevitable. "Surveillance video in the parking lot of the Southside Pub indicated that Kinoshita left the club with the unsub and got into a black Volkswagen Atlas. We were able to get a look at the license plate. The car is registered to a Tommy Nagano—"

"I expected as much," Logan said matter-of-factly. He paused, weighing what would come next. "I spoke to Nagano less than half an hour ago."

Ivy cocked an eyebrow. "What am I missing here?"

"I recognized him from the surveillance video, but needed to be sure."

"Sure about what?" she asked questionably, a hand on her hip.

Another pause and then Logan continued, "I've been seeing his sister, Elena Kekona."

"The grief counselor?" Ivy's mouth hung open.

"Yeah," he confessed awkwardly, wishing he had come clean earlier. At least she was privy to the required therapy with Elena in order for him to keep his job.

"You're still seeing her professionally?"

"Actually, it's morphed into more of a personal relationship." Logan wondered if that was still the case after leaving Elena with things unsettled between them. "Nagano lives in an *ohana* on her property. Keeping that in mind, I went to talk to them both—see what he was willing to say about Kakalina."

"And…?" Ivy asked anxiously. "Don't hold back."

"Nagano admitted to going out with her last night and leaving the club together," Logan said evenly. "He claims he and Kakalina got into an argument two blocks from her parents' house, where she asked to be let out of the car. Nagano complied and drove off with her very much alive and unhurt."

Ivy rolled her eyes skeptically. "Do you believe him?"

Logan jutted his chin, while considering Elena's unwavering faith in her brother's innocence. Though it was admirable, experience told Logan that kinfolk were not always the best judge of character, no matter how close they were. "I'd rather reserve judgment until we have more to go on, such as the missing woman materializing."

Just then, they were approached by a grim-faced bald officer, who said sourly, "We found something…"

Logan held his breath as they were led to a nearby vacant lot about three blocks from the home where the missing woman lived. About an acre wide, it wasn't dissimilar to Logan's property. Walking across the grassy, mostly flat land, he heard the police dog barking as if sizing up its next meal. When he saw the fully clothed body lying on its back, and the beautiful face tortured in death and surrounded like a halo by wavy, long dark hair, it didn't take much for Logan to realize his worst fear. He was staring into the face of Kakalina Kinoshita.

"MY INITIAL ASSESSMENT is the victim died as a result of blunt-force trauma to the head area," Dr. Bert Swanson, the forensic pathologist, said glumly. He flexed the black nitrile glove covering his hand. "Consistent with the deaths of the three other women, ostensibly at the hands of the Big Island Killer."

"Can't say I'm surprised at your preliminary finding." Logan furrowed his brow. All the indicators fit like a perfect embroidery. A corpse laid out like yesterday's leftovers. A lead pipe left behind by the killer, bloodied from going to work on the victim as if her life was worthless. The deceased's personal effects, including her cell phone, strewn about the lot, as though to add substance to the crime scene. And perhaps, most importantly, like the others, Kakalina Kinoshita was a native Hawaiian, a telltale sign that she'd been targeted for that very reason. Even if the specifics for such a cruel ending remained a mystery to Logan. As did the identity of the unsub, though Tommy Nagano had moved to the head of the class as the person in the hot seat with respect to her death.

"It's not much of a head scratcher," the pathologist said succinctly. "Your serial killer has struck again, Detective Ryder. The real question is, can you and your colleagues force the perpetrator out in the open before more damage can be done to other Hawaiian women?"

Could be we already have, Logan told himself reluctantly, but he hoped it was otherwise. If only for Elena's sake. "We won't stop trying," he responded, knowing the words were empty without concrete action to back them up.

He watched as crime-scene photographer Martin Campanella methodically took pictures from every angle of the victim, as well as the surrounding area, as potential evidence of the crime—all of which could be used against the unsub once they had him in custody.

"Did I miss anything?" Campanella asked, pointing his lens away from the crime scene.

"Probably not," Logan told him. "But get a few more pics, anyway, including on the road and to the right and left for anything the unsub may have left behind."

"I'm on it."

Logan watched him work for a moment and then turned to the sound of Aretha Kennedy muttering to herself. Then, she said more clearly, "Judging by the location of the body in relation to the victim's home address, I'd say that either Nagano lied about where he says he dropped off Kinoshita, or someone else—the serial murderer—picked her up afterward and drove the victim to this spot before beating her to death with the lead pipe. Different murder weapon. Same MO."

"Maybe someone she knew?" Logan said, hazarding

a guess, as he wanted to give Elena's brother the benefit of the doubt for the time being. He couldn't envision even an inebriated Kakalina willingly entering the car of a stranger. Unless it was one whom she viewed as nonthreatening. Given that the immediate area was unlikely to reveal much through home-surveillance videos, their best bet was that a camera might have picked up Kakalina getting out of Tommy's car. Short of that, his story could fall flat.

"Or someone who forced her into the vehicle at gunpoint," Ivy said, tossing out another possibility. "These things happen. Especially if the perp had followed them from the club and seized on the opportunity."

Aretha frowned. "Could be a hard sell, Detective. Particularly when we have a clear suspect in the onetime missing woman's death who admitted getting into an argument with the victim that could have easily gotten out of control." She glanced at the deceased, who was now being carted away under the authority of Bert Swanson. "You heard the forensic pathologist. We're looking at the work of the Big Island Killer. Do the math. Two plus two women bludgeoned fatally equals four and counting…"

It was something Logan could not turn his back on, even if he wanted to. The facts spoke for themselves. He would be interested to see if the victim's cell phone yielded any clues, now that it was being analyzed forensically by the CSI unit. But at the moment, the spotlight was squarely on Tommy Nagano as Kakalina Kinoshita's killer.

"A BODY WAS found in a vacant field," Logan informed Elena in a video chat on her laptop, legs folded beneath as she sat on the vintage cherry accent chair in her great room. He hesitated just long enough for her to read what was coming next. "It's been tentatively identified as Kakalina Kinoshita…" He paused again. "She was murdered in a manner similar to the victims of the Big Island Killer…"

Elena put a hand to her mouth as the implications became loud and clear, and there was a pounding in her ears. "Oh, no, you don't think Tommy killed her… and the other women?" She knew this was exactly what was registering in Logan's strained facial expression. He was insinuating that her younger brother had progressed from some minor skirmishes with the law to suddenly becoming a violent serial-killer psychopath in Hilo. "He didn't do it," she insisted, knowing that her brother would never have so coldly taken another's life, much less several lives, as though undeserving of being among the living. No matter the bleak picture that was painted on a dark canvas.

"So you say." Logan gazed at her coldly. "Whether I believe you or not is immaterial at this point. Given the fact that he was apparently the last person to see the latest victim alive—and now she's dead, not far from where he claimed he dropped her off—we're going to have to bring Tommy in for a more formal interrogation regarding Kakalina's murder, as well as the other murders attributed to the Big Island Killer."

"When?" Elena asked with trepidation.

Logan sighed. "Detectives are on their way to pick him up even as we speak," he warned straightforwardly. "I need you to keep him there until they arrive. The worst thing for Tommy would be if we had to issue a BOLO for his apprehension."

Elena was appalled that he was asking her to be involved in the arrest, in effect, of her own flesh and blood…for murder. *How can Logan expect me to turn him in?* she asked herself. The answer came just as swiftly. As a dedicated detective for the Hawaii PD doing his job, how could he not expect her to do the right thing even if it seemed so wrong? If Tommy was truly innocent, wouldn't they be able to figure it out? If he wasn't, would she be doing him any favors in helping him become a fugitive from justice at the expense of future victims of a serial killer?

"Fine," Elena stated acquiescently. "I'll do my best to make sure Tommy doesn't try to make a run for it." As she realized that suggested he was guilty of something other than letting Kat get out of the car prematurely, she added firmly, "Not that he would, as someone innocent of committing any murders—"

"Good," Logan said simply, seeming to focus more on the first part of her response than the last. He tilted his head caringly. "Will you be okay?"

"I guess that all depends, doesn't it?" She held his gaze. "I just want my brother to be given a fair shake."

"He will be," Logan promised and waited a beat. "I'll let you go talk to him."

Wanting to say more, but unsure what she could do to alter the course of events at this stage, Elena merely nodded before ending the chat. She closed the laptop and sucked in a deep breath, knowing the hard part came now—preparing her brother for becoming the primary suspect in the death of his girlfriend and bandmate. And, even worse, being questioned about any knowledge or involvement in the homicides perpetrated by the Big Island Killer.

SHE PHONED TOMMY and asked him to come over, wishing they could just make this go away. But that wasn't an option. At least not until the authorities questioned her brother and were satisfied that they were reaching for something that wasn't there. Surely, Logan and the police department weren't under so much pressure with the Big Island Killer case that they would seek a shortcut to ending it, even if it meant railroading an innocent man?

The moment Tommy stepped into the house looking bedraggled, as though he hadn't been able to rest all night and day, Elena figured he knew something serious was up. "What is it?" he asked, peering at her.

She sucked in a deep breath and cut to the chase. "They found Kat—"

For an instant, Tommy looked relieved. This was replaced by a sense of dread. "Is she…?"

"She's dead, Tommy," Elena said, finishing for him sorrowfully. "Someone murdered her."

He put his hands to his face and muttered an expletive. "Where did they find her?"

"In a vacant lot a few blocks from her parents' house." Elena's lower lip quivered. "She was beaten to death in a way that's similar to the murders of the other Hawaiian women blamed on a serial killer."

Fear registered across Tommy's face. "Do they think I killed Kat?" His voice broke. "The others?" He gazed at her. "They do, don't they?"

"It doesn't matter what they think." She was trying to be supportive, even if believing otherwise. "We both know you're innocent. They will, too, after you talk to them."

His brow furrowed as he pondered things. "So the cops—and your boyfriend—are coming to arrest me?"

"Logan's not my boyfriend," Elena countered, but knew that the nature of their involvement was ambiguous. Neither had truly defined it, though she realized they had something between them that went beyond sex. But even that was imperiled by the current situation. Her thoughts turned back to the question posed. It deserved a candid response. "I'm afraid they're on their way."

Tommy began pacing. "The cops are going to try to pin those murders on me."

"Just tell the truth about last night, Tommy," she pleaded. "They can't charge you with anything if the evidence isn't there."

"You don't know that," he responded, agitated. "They do that all the time, put people away to make themselves feel better—guilty or not."

"That's not true. Not in this instance." Elena had heard about the occasional person being set free after faulty evidence, shady witnesses, or DNA exonerated them. But most who were convicted were guilty as charged. She was convinced that it was the truth that would get the authorities to back off her brother. But not before they would probably put him through the wringer. Until such time, she would stand by him, as any loyal sister should. Elena heard the car drive up, indicating that the police had arrived. The idea of seeing her brother possibly being hauled off in handcuffs made her stomach turn. Worse, though, was having this cloud hanging over him while the real killer of Kakalina, very likely the Big Island Killer, was still on the prowl.

Chapter Twelve

Logan regarded the suspect through the one-way window as Detective Miyamoto and Agent Kennedy interrogated Tommy Nagano. Against his better judgment, Logan had stepped aside in leading the interrogation of the suspect, given his own conflict of interest and needing to do this by the book, whatever the result. He only wished Elena's brother hadn't been dragged into the Big Island Killer probe by way of his involvement with murder victim Kakalina Kinoshita. This, quite naturally, put Logan at odds with Elena, whom he had developed feelings for that had nothing to do with the investigation. Something told him she didn't exactly see it that way. He was left to wonder if they could get past this when all was said and done.

"You did the right thing in letting Miyamoto and Agent Kennedy run with this one," Chief Watanabe remarked beside him. "Hard to imagine that Elena's brother is wrapped up in this murder investigation. Worse yet is the notion that we could be looking at our Big Island Killer in Tommy Nagano."

Logan flinched. "Elena doesn't believe for one second that he's guilty of anything, other than being at the wrong place with the wrong person at the worst possible time."

"I would expect her to defend her brother to the death," Watanabe said sensitively. "All people tend to believe the best of their blood relatives while dismissing the worst, as though their lives depended on it."

Logan didn't disagree. "The search warrant on Nagano's *ohana* and vehicle came up with nothing to connect him to the Big Island Killer homicides, such as a hoodie or other potential evidence. Or to indicate the premeditated murder of Kinoshita."

"So maybe he got smart and dumped anything and everything that could tie him to the crimes."

"Doesn't seem likely." Logan begged to differ, since he was familiar with the unsub's MO. "If Nagano is our serial killer, he wouldn't have necessarily thought we were on to him to get rid of the evidence. Moreover, using forensic tools for mobile devices, we were able to unlock the victim's cell phone and found no unusual communication between her and Nagano to indicate they had a toxic relationship, or otherwise gave him a reason to want Kinoshita dead."

"Hmm…" Watanabe scratched his pate musingly as both listened in on the interrogation of the suspect, who had yet to ask for legal representation after being advised of his rights.

"Do you really expect us to buy that you just left Kinoshita by the side of the road and went on your merry way?" Aretha asked, peering at the suspect.

Tommy didn't waver. "That's what happened. I wish I could go back and change things, but I can't."

"You mean change beating her to death?" the FBI agent said tartly.

"No way!" he insisted. "I would never have done that to her."

"And yet she was found dead just a few short blocks from where you claimed you let her out of your car." Ivy planted her hands on the table separating them. "How do you explain that?"

"I can't." Tommy put his hands to his head. "Obviously someone else came along and...killed Kat—"

"Doesn't that sound just a little too convenient?" Aretha furrowed her brow. "After all, you've already admitted to being jealous that she was flirting with other men. Is that why you killed her—you just couldn't take it anymore? If you couldn't have her, then no one would?"

"That's crazy!" Tommy's chin sagged. "I didn't kill her. Why don't you find out who did? Or don't you care about getting to the truth?"

Ivy took a breath and changed course in the questioning. "We all want the truth to come out, Nagano. Especially with four Hawaiian women dead, all the victims of blunt-force trauma. We believe they were murdered by the same assailant. Given your direct connection to the latest victim, Kakalina Kinoshita, why should we believe this was just happenstance and you're not the Big Island Killer?"

Tommy's eyes dropped before he said in a defeated tone of voice, "Maybe this is where I ask for an attorney—"

Logan cringed at the thought of a much more drawn-out investigation should a lawyer get involved. The last thing they wanted was to let a serial killer loose. But just as bad would be devoting time and resources to harassing an innocent man. Logan turned to former

FBI profiler Georgina Machado, who had come in to assess the suspect. "What do you think?" he asked her.

Georgina wrinkled her nose. "I'm not feeling it with Nagano being our serial killer," she said bluntly. "His story about dropping off an inebriated Kinoshita short of her residence strikes me as a bit weird, but I don't see him as a sociopath. The Big Island Killer has no sympathy for their victims. Just the opposite. This person feeds off their suffering and eventual deaths. Nagano, on the other hand, clearly shows remorse in his actions and the aftermath that resulted in the death of Kakalina Kinoshita." Georgina ran a hand through her hair. "I think we may be looking in the wrong direction here..."

"You may be right." Logan was inclined to agree. But they needed more than gut instincts and profiling before letting Elena's brother off the hook. "Why don't I see if Nagano will agree to take a lie-detector test?"

"If he's really innocent," she said, "that would be a better way to show it than lawyering up."

Taking that cue, Logan stepped into the interrogation room. Ivy and Aretha looked at him curiously. Tommy glowered, his lips pursed in anger. Logan wasn't sure if this was for being there against his will. Or a misguided belief that by virtue, he was somehow betraying his sister. Logan got right to the point. "Would you be willing to take a polygraph test, Nagano, before you call your lawyer? It could go a long way in getting us on the same page in establishing your innocence."

An hour later, Pauline Alvarado, a licensed polygraph examiner for the State of Hawaii, arrived to administer the lie-detector test. In her early forties and slender, with dark hair in a wedge cut with bangs, she told Logan coolly, "Let's just see if Mr. Nagano is being truthful or not…"

"Do your thing," he said to her in earnest, and watched along with Aretha, Ivy and Georgina through the one-way window as the polygraph examiner entered the room where Tommy was sitting alone. She explained the procedure, and got him set up.

After she went through the basic questions, such as name, age and occupation, Pauline got to the nitty-gritty when she asked the suspect, "Did you murder Kakalina Kinoshita?"

"No," Tommy said succinctly.

"Do you know who murdered Ms. Kinoshita?"

"No."

"Did you kill Liann Nahuina?" Pauline asked evenly.

"No, I didn't," he said flatly. She didn't like his response and repeated the question, and got a simple no for an answer.

"Did you kill Daryl Renigado?"

Tommy kept his cool. "No."

Pauline waited a beat, then asked pointedly, "Did you murder Yancy Otani?"

"No," he answered solidly.

The polygraph examiner drew a breath and looked him in the eye squarely. "Are you the Big Island Killer?"

Without hesitation, Tommy declared in no uncertain terms, "No!"

Pauline asked a few more questions, analyzed them and left the room. Logan and the others on the team eagerly awaited her findings. "Let's have it," he said professionally.

Before she could utter a word, Logan had already sensed her conclusion on the suspect in Kakalina

Kinoshita's death. "He passed with flying colors," the polygraph examiner asserted. "Unless Mr. Nagano has figured out a way to beat the system, he is neither the killer of Ms. Kinoshita nor the one you are calling the Big Island Killer."

"I suspected as much," Georgina said. "The unsub is much too clever to go down so easily."

"I suppose," Aretha conceded. "Still, we needed to push Nagano to rule him out as the unsub."

"Now that we have," Ivy said, "it means the perp is more dangerous than ever in the ability to track a target, kill with the slimmest margin for error and get away."

Logan's forehead creased. "It also suggests a sense of desperation, which, with any luck, will lead to the unsub's downfall," he said confidently, as the victims of this crazed killer flashed through Logan's mind. But at the moment, he knew they could at least take Tommy off the list as a serial-killer suspect. "I'll drive Nagano home."

THEY RODE BACK in silence for the first few minutes. Then Logan decided he better say something. Whatever it took to try to smooth things over between them. After all, he fully expected they would be involved in each other's lives to one degree or another, if Logan had anything to do with it, considering his desire to be a big part of Elena's life moving forward. In spite of the hit their relationship had taken recently, through no fault of his own. Or hers, for that matter. "Your sister never stopped believing in you," he told him supportively.

"I know that." Tommy was riding in the front seat, which Logan had offered as a courtesy, having been empty for the most part since the death of his partner. "Too bad I had to be hauled down to the police station like some common criminal. Or worse, a murderer."

"It was never anything personal," Logan insisted, keeping his eyes on the road.

"Was to me."

He's going to make this difficult, Logan thought. "Look, Tommy, we're dealing with the cold-blooded murder of someone I presume you really cared about and played music with. I would think that you, of all people, want to see Kakalina's killer caught."

"Yeah, of course."

"In order to do that, we needed to believe your story about dropping her off on the road, so as to concentrate our efforts on the true killer. Do you get that?"

"I suppose." Tommy's tone became more conciliatory. "I never wanted that to happen to Kat." He paused. "Or to those other women killed by this Big Island Killer."

"We're singing from the same hymn there," Logan said, seizing the moment. "But it did happen to Kakalina and the others," he stressed. "Getting to the bottom of it is a priority for the police department. Sometimes that can mean having to put an innocent person through the wringer to eliminate them from suspicion."

Tommy sighed. "Yeah, I get it."

While he believed that, Logan also felt that Elena's brother still had a chip on his shoulder regarding the police, whether warranted or not. "I know you've had your issues with law enforcement in the past, Tommy, but just so you know I'm not your enemy."

He nodded. "Okay."

Good first step, Logan thought. He waited a moment

or two and got right to the heart of the matter. "I care about your sister."

"I gathered that," Tommy said sardonically. "She seems to care about you, too."

"Elena deserves to be happy," Logan added.

"Yeah, she does." Tommy left it at that. Logan believed they had turned a corner. At the very least, they could be cordial to one another moving forward, if not friends, as Logan worked toward regaining any ground he had lost with Elena.

IT HAD BEEN hours since Tommy had been taken into custody and Elena hadn't heard a peep from Logan or anyone else in the police department. Not that the man she had slept with, leaving her longing for more, had any obligation to keep her informed on the fate of her brother as a murder suspect. *Or maybe Logan did owe me that courtesy*, Elena told herself, pacing around her great room like someone who was far too unsettled to be still. If they had anything solid on Tommy as a murderer, didn't she have a right to know? Even if he was presumed guilty, her brother was entitled to legal representation. Elena tried to figure out how she might be able to help him pay for a good lawyer. Though she had managed to do well for herself through savings and investments, along with a large sum from Errol's life-insurance policy, lawyers didn't come cheap. But she would do whatever she needed to be there for Tommy, as she knew he would if their situations were reversed. That notwithstanding, Elena clung to the belief that her brother was incapable of inflicting the type of violence on innocent women as had been done by the Big Island Killer.

Her thoughts were interrupted when she heard a car drive up. A peek through the window and Elena recognized it as Logan's official vehicle. Her heart skipped a beat as she wondered if he was there to throw more negative news her way. Or could he actually have something positive to tell her? Only after focusing did Elena realize someone else was in the car with him. A man. It was Tommy.

She watched as both men got out and approached her house, illuminated by the driveway lighting and tiki lights that lined the pathway leading to the door. Tommy did not have on handcuffs or appear as though he was coming to say goodbye as a courtesy from Logan. Racing to meet them, Elena opened the door. Both men stood there with stoic looks on their faces.

"I'm no longer a suspect," Tommy told her measuredly. He looked weary but surprisingly energetic.

As if to double down on that, Logan said in an official manner, "Tommy is free to go about his life."

Elena was practically speechless. In that instant, she wanted to hug both men. Instead, she hugged one—her brother. "I'm so glad to hear that." She pulled away and met Logan's steady gaze, needing more information.

Tommy said perceptively, "I'll let Detective Ryder fill you in on the details. Right now, I could use a hot shower. Maybe a bath, too." He chuckled tonelessly. "I'm going to the *ohana*. We'll talk later, sis." He made eye contact with Logan, shook his hand and said plaintively, "When you find Kat's killer, I want to be there to see justice served."

Logan nodded in agreement and Elena watched as her brother headed off toward the open gate to his place. "Mind if I come in?" Logan asked hesitantly.

She gave him space to do so and he walked by her, then Elena closed the door to face the man who had been her lover and suspected her brother in his girlfriend's disappearance and murder. Now it appeared as if Logan was responsible for getting Tommy released from custody, for which she was grateful. Elena gave him a quizzical look. "So what happened?" Her voice was more inquisitive than demanding.

"Tommy passed a lie-detector test," Logan told her simply. "Apart from that, the search of his premises and car came up with zilch." He met her eyes sorrowfully. "Things just didn't add up in terms of your brother being guilty of anything beyond poor judgment. We had to let him go."

"Mahalo for that," she said, unable to help herself, while resisting a repeat of the I-told-you-Tommy-was-innocent statement that Elena had felt in her heart and soul. She was thankful the authorities came to realize that before it was too late for her brother. "I'm glad Tommy was cleared of any wrongdoing."

Logan moved closer. "I hope you realize that I was only doing my job in investigating Tommy. As the last person, apart from the killer, to see Kakalina alive, I would have been derelict in my duties as an officer of the law if we overlooked him as a suspect. At the very least, we needed to clear him so we could better focus on other potential unsubs."

"I know. I get it." Elena found it difficult to argue with his logic. In her heart of hearts, she understood that in order for Tommy to be removed from the equation, he had to walk through the fire to get to the other side. "You did what you had to."

His features relaxed. "So we're good then?"

She took a moment before responding positively, knowing she didn't want to lose him. "Yes, we're good."

Logan grinned. "Great! That's all I needed to hear."

Elena smiled back thinly. As much as she was thrilled to continue their journey, she still felt as though they were being weighed down by his serial-killer investigation. It had almost pulled her brother under. Would the case prove to be more than their relationship could handle? She asked, "With Tommy no longer considered a person of interest, where are you now in the search for Kat's killer?"

Logan scratched an ear pensively. "Well, for one, given the manner in which she was murdered, we're going under the assumption that her death was caused by the Big Island Killer. That alone gives us more insight into the unsub and the risky moves being made by this person to fulfill this sick need to brutally murder Hawaiian women. Kakalina Kinoshita was unfortunate enough to fall into this deadly trap, with your brother being caught in the undertow."

Elena cringed at the thought of what the women had to endure. "Will this nightmare gripping Hilo ever end?" She was sure he was asking himself the same question.

"Yes, it will end." Logan's voice was forceful. "No killer, no matter how cunning and cruel, can keep it going indefinitely. This one is no exception. When the unsub slips up in the slightest, we'll nail them and bring this case to a close."

Eyeing Logan and the determination in his hardened features, Elena couldn't help but believe him. And stand by him, even with the recent strain that had been put on their relationship. Though she wanted to ask him to stay the night more than anything, it seemed like the wrong way to go, maybe for both of them. "I think I'm going to go to bed," she told him unenthusiastically. "It's been a long day and even longer night."

"I understand," Logan said dolefully, making no attempt to use his charm to talk her into anything he wanted. "I won't keep you any longer."

Before he could turn to leave, Elena cupped his cheeks and did what she had been unable to resist—she planted a firm kiss on his lips. Drawing their bodies even closer, Logan was just as caught up in the moment in giving as much as he received, which made her go weak in the knees. Using all the strength she could muster, Elena managed to detach herself from him and uttered breathily, "Good night, Logan."

He lifted her chin satisfyingly. "'Night, Elena."

She watched him leave, touching her swollen lips, and Elena again found herself fighting to keep from going after him. But in the end, she trusted herself enough to believe that what they had was real and worth waiting for.

Chapter Thirteen

The following morning, Elena took a short hike with Tommy to Peepee Falls, an 80-foot waterfall fed by the Wailuku River and surrounded by lush vegetation and lava rocks. She considered this as nature therapy for her brother, who was in the midst of the stages of grief, even if unaware. Losing someone he was close to in such a violent manner was something he would need to deal with and she wanted to be there to help him get through it.

"It's tough," Tommy groaned, kicking at some rocks. "Robin is torn up about it, too." Robin Oyama was the other male member of their band and played the hula drum. "Kat didn't deserve to go that way."

"No, she didn't." Elena did not pull any punches in emphasizing the nature of the tragic death. Tackling what had happened head-on was the best way to accept and come to terms with the grief her brother was experiencing. "But then, neither did the other victims of the serial killer." Logan had made it pretty clear that the task force investigating the crimes believed that it was all but certain that Kakalina Kinoshita's death was carried out by the Big Island Killer. "Kat and the other women had their whole lives ahead of them before they were snuffed out by a maniac."

"I blame myself for what happened to Kat," Tommy lamented ruefully. "I should never have let her get out of that car."

"As I recall, you only did what she asked," Elena pointed out. "You had no way of knowing that she would meet up with a serial killer that close to her house. Neither did she. We can't control some things that are simply beyond our control." She knew it was more complicated than that. Drinking had played a role in their decision-making on that fateful night. And in that respect, both parties had to bear the blame. Sadly, only one of them had lived to talk about it, and with deep regret.

"How does one get past something this terrible?" Tommy asked. "Or can you really ever get past it?"

"Yes, you can." Elena watched as he kicked more small rocks. "It's never easy and it certainly won't be in this case. But you're young and strong, and can weather the storm of such a loss."

He looked at her. "You mean like you did when Errol died?"

"Yes. His death was not a violent one, but no less painful as someone I loved and never imagined I'd lose so soon."

Tommy put a hand in his pocket musingly. "How are things with you and Detective Ryder?"

Elena raised an eyebrow, not expecting him to ask. "We're trying to get back on track after—"

He cut her off. "If you like him, don't mess things up on my behalf. We talked things through and I believe he's a good guy. Maybe even the right man for you."

"You think so, do you?" She could barely believe her ears. How had Logan managed to convince her sometimes stubborn little brother to cut him some slack as a detective and a man? It certainly made things simpler as Elena thought of possibly building a future with Logan.

"I'm just saying…" Tommy gave a little chuckle.

"Duly noted." She smiled warmly, while hoping that after some time had gone by, he would be able to get past this and his penchant for playing the field, and find someone he could fall in love with and have a family of his own. Elena turned the topic back to dealing with his grief. "You need to go see Kat's parents."

Tommy frowned. "Not sure I can do that."

"You have to," she persisted. "They need closure, too. The only way her parents can get that is if you help them by showing sympathy and letting them know how much you cared for her."

He mulled this over. "All right, I'll talk to them."

"Good." She put a hand on his broad shoulder. "You'll feel better afterward. And if I can be of service to them as a counselor, I'll be happy to help."

"Mahalo, sis." He gazed at the waterfall, as did Elena, as she pondered her next get-together with Logan.

ON MONDAY MORNING, with Tommy Nagano no longer considered a suspect in the murder of Kakalina Kinoshita, the task force was doubling their efforts to home in on others who might be lurking in the shadows as the Big Island Killer and going unnoticed. To that end, Logan and Ivy were pouring over more surveillance video from the Southside Pub, where Kat spent her last night before leaving with Tommy. "See anything?" Logan asked, scanning the image that showed people coming and going, including Tommy and Kakalina.

"Nothing or no one that jumps out at me," confessed Ivy. "Maybe if we take it back further…"

"Wait," Logan said when he spotted what looked like someone in a dark hoodie moving away from the camera. "There—" He pointed at the screen.

"I see the person." Ivy asked Marcelo Tahutini, the club owner, to zoom in on the hooded one. He did and all they could see was the back of someone who was tall and slim. Then the person faded from view. "Rewind," she ordered, hoping to find a different angle.

When that failed, Logan had the owner switch to the outside camera and timed it for when Kakalina and Tommy first left. For maybe thirty seconds there was no indication of anyone else leaving the club. Then someone moved out swiftly, head bent down in what Logan thought was a clear attempt at concealment. It looked to be the same person wearing a hoodie inside the club. Frustratingly, the unsub moved out of view.

After Tommy's car drove off, it wasn't long before another vehicle sped away in their direction. The video was rewound and frozen to reveal what looked to be a late model black Buick Envision SUV. The driver could not be seen, but Logan believed it could be the possible killer of Kakalina Kinoshita and a string of other Hawaiian women.

They were able to get a read on the license plate and found that the vehicle belonged to Julian Gaskell, who lived at a residence on Haili Street. With time of the essence and a search warrant in hand, police personnel, including the Hawaii PD SWAT team, and FBI agents converged upon the address, hoping to catch a serial killer before he struck again. Logan and Ivy, armed with their Glock pistols, and Aretha, carrying a SIG Sauer P226 sidearm, led the way. They moved past mature sugi pine trees and the SUV parked in the driveway, and approached the front door of the mission-style house.

It opened almost on cue, as if the occupant sensed trouble, and Logan found himself face-to-face with a dark-skinned male about his height and in his midthirties. He had short black hair with a balding crown and a hipster beard. "Whoa…" The man raised his hands immediately, as shock registered across an oblong face. "I think you've got the wrong house."

Logan still had his gun pointed at the man, not convinced his claim was accurate. "Are you Julian Gaskell?"

"Yeah." He flashed Logan a questioning look. "What's this all about?"

"Step outside the house," Logan ordered, hoping the suspect didn't make a wrong move. "Keep your hands up where we can see them."

"All right," he agreed, keeping his arms up while stepping onto the lanai. "Don't shoot!"

Once the suspect was frisked by Ivy and determined to be unarmed, Logan lowered and put away his own weapon and said tonelessly, "I'm Detective Ryder, Hawaii PD." He didn't bother identifying anyone else, but was sure the suspect got the point that they were all law enforcement. "Is there anyone else inside?"

"No, I live alone," Gaskell indicated. "Is someone going to tell me what it is I'm supposed to have done?"

Logan ignored him for the moment while giving the team the nod to check the residence for other occupants or evidence suggesting a serial murderer lived there.

While they were at work and the SWAT unit was ready and waiting, he shifted his attention back to the suspect. "Is that your vehicle?" Logan eyed the Buick Envision.

"Yeah," he responded nervously.

"Anyone else been driving it lately?" Aretha asked, taking a crack at him.

"Just me," Gaskell insisted. "Why do you ask?"

"Were you at the Southside Pub last Friday night?" she asked him directly.

"Yeah," he admitted quickly. "Did I break any laws in going out to have a good time?"

"That remains to be seen," Logan told him with reservations. He allowed the suspect to lower one hand in presenting the search warrant that covered the house and vehicle. "Your car was seen following another vehicle from the club. One of the occupants of that vehicle, Kakalina Kinoshita, was later found beaten to death in a vacant lot. Do you know anything about that?"

Gaskell's jaw dropped. "Not a thing!" His voice rose an octave. "I had nothing to do with any murder. I saw such brutality when I was deployed as a member of the US military in Iraq and then Afghanistan. I would never do anything like that as a civilian. I have no idea who this Kakalina Kinoshita is. If I followed the car she was in from the club, it was by chance and nothing more."

Logan couldn't knock his service to the country, if he was telling the truth on that score. Turned out, Logan's own father was a US Air Force veteran. Sometimes soldiers came back messed up and took it out on innocent people. Did that happen here, in the form of a serial killer?

"Where did you go after you left the Southside Pub?" Ivy asked the suspect sharply.

"To my girlfriend's place," Gaskell responded swiftly and surely. "Spent the entire night there."

"Her name?"

"Lorraine Fuentes. She has a condo on West Lani-kaula Street."

"We'll check it out," Logan promised. He then got the word that there was no one else inside the house and a search of the Buick Envision turned up nothing suspicious. After the suspect's alibi held up and with no other reason to believe he'd played any role in the death of Kakalina, it became clear to Logan that this was a false alarm. Julian Gaskell was not the Big Island Killer.

"I WAS WONDERING if I can take another shot at making you dinner tonight?" Logan asked Elena in a cell-phone video chat that afternoon. "Figured after the drama that happened involving Tommy, you could use a break. Or at least a home-cooked meal where you aren't the one doing the cooking."

"Just dinner?" She gave him a teasing look, while sitting in her office.

"Well, now that you mention it, I thought that maybe afterward we could take a hike. There's a great trail right outside my property, and since that's something we both enjoy, it might be a good way to unwind."

Given the tenseness she'd felt lately, Elena didn't have to think about it twice before answering enthusiastically. "Yes, I'd love to have dinner with you and go hiking." Both would give her an opportunity to get to know him better in his own environment.

"Great." He gave her a polite grin and quipped, "This time, if it's all the same to you, I think it's best we avoid meeting at the farmers' market beforehand."

Elena laughed, even if the thought of being robbed and hitting her head on the ground was anything but funny. She appreciated his dry humor anyhow. "That works for me."

"Somehow, I thought it would." He laughed generously.

"This time, I'll bring the wine," she said jovially.

"Wouldn't have it any other way." The smile on his face faded like the vog that polluted the air on the Big Island, courtesy of the emissions coming from the Kīlauea volcano, which was nothing new for residents. "Well, I'd best get back to it so I don't screw things up this time. See you later."

"You will," Elena promised, and disconnected from the chat. She was tempted to ask him for the latest on the investigation into the death of Kat, which was connected to the Big Island Killer case. Especially now that Tommy had been part of the probe, though since removed from any involvement of a criminal nature. But she'd decided to hold off on that for now, not wanting to put a damper on what she hoped would be an evening to remember more for their spending time together rather than talking about a serial killer in Hilo.

When she arrived at Logan's gated house, Elena was suitably impressed, if not a tad nervous, to be taking the next step in their relationship in his neck of the woods, no pun intended, as the property bordered the Waiākea Forest Reserve. Still, she embraced the opportunity, wanting nothing more than to get past the strain between them after Tommy's detainment. Logan greeted her at the doorway, looking dapper in a casual way in a form-fitting golf shirt and chino pants.

"Hey." He offered her one of his charming smiles

and gave her a once-over, causing Elena to blush. With the hike in mind for later, she had put on a tank top and cropped jeans to go with her sneakers, while putting her hair in a loose ponytail.

"Hey." She smiled at him as her heart fluttered under the weight of his nearness.

"Welcome." He moved to the side. "Come on in."

Elena stepped through the door and handed him the bottle of pineapple wine she brought. "Hope this will do."

"Yes," Logan assured her. "Excellent choice. I'll set this in the kitchen and give you a quick tour of the place before we eat."

"You're on." She followed him around and marveled at the interior. The architectural style and Hawaiian furnishings definitely agreed with her, and Elena could actually imagine living here, even with her current house and the memories made there with Errol. But maybe new and lasting memories were meant to be created with a new person in her life.

As if to play on that theme, Logan stopped the tour when they reached one spacious room and said coolly, "This is the master suite."

"So it is." Elena hummed interestedly, as she took in the bedroom with tropical furniture and a wrought-iron four-poster California king bed.

"You like?" He brushed up against her shoulder and Elena felt a tremor throughout her body.

"Yes," she confessed, a fresh surge of desire threatening to overtake her.

"Hoped you would." Logan gave her a teasing look and said, "Why don't we step onto the upstairs lanai so you can take a peek at the landscape."

"I'd like that." Frankly, Elena welcomed the distraction from the man himself. On the lanai, she admired the property's lush acreage and wondered if he planned to do anything with it. Or did that depend on whether there was someone steady in his life to help with the decision-making? "It's amazing," she told him.

"Yeah," he agreed thoughtfully and faced her with earnest eyes. "You're amazing."

She flushed. "You really think so?"

His response was to kiss her and Elena welcomed it wholeheartedly, before Logan broke the spell. "Better get back downstairs. Wouldn't want the food to get cold."

Elena licked her lips, wanting him now. "You sure about that?"

"Not really." He stepped back into the room. "I think the food can wait."

"Yes, it can," she uttered, not being able to take off her clothes fast enough, and neither could he.

They made love with the same sense of urgency as before, throwing themselves into it carnally and with a kind of familiarity with each other's bodies that left Elena breathless and contented. Logan left little doubt that the same was true for him. Dinner came afterward. While eating *kalbi* ribs, ahi poke salad and grilled pineapple, and washing it down with wine, they kept the conversation mostly light. Neither seemed too interested in talking about the Big Island Killer investigation, as if avoiding it would somehow make it go away. At least temporarily.

They ended up back in bed for more of each other's intimate company, and when they finished the satisfying sexual bonding, Elena asked in a giggly voice, "Whatever happened to the hike you promised?"

Logan laughed. "Something more important came up."

"Agreed." She chuckled. "Much more important."

"But if you're willing to spend the night," he began, "we can take that hike in the Waiākea Forest Reserve first thing in the morning."

As she had nowhere better to be and no one she wanted to spend the time with more, Elena accepted his invitation to stay the night, knowing that neither of them was likely to get much sleep or complain about it.

Chapter Fourteen

They were up bright and early to hit the trail. Walking through the misty forest, with its breathtaking views of Mauna Kea, Logan welcomed Elena's company. Last night had been incredible and only made it clearer to him that he wanted her in his life on a much more regular basis. They had gotten over the hump in his business with Tommy, and now Logan wanted only to get past the Big Island Killer case and concentrate on developing a relationship with someone for the first time since Gemma. He had high hopes that this could happen with Elena, who seemed every bit as receptive to building upon the advances they had made.

"I could get used to this," she remarked as they headed down the trail, no one else in sight.

Was there a double meaning there? Logan asked himself. "So can I," he said, leaning more toward waking up with her each and every day, with an active lifestyle together a bonus. "Gives us something to shoot for."

Elena smiled. "Always a straight shooter, I'm sure," she teased him as they made their way down the path surrounded by rich vegetation and exotic trees.

He smiled back. "I try to be."

"Then I'm with you." The sparkle in her tone told Logan she meant what she said, which put even more pep into his own steps in taking this journey toward the future with her.

When Elena suddenly gasped, Logan first thought she might have spotted injured wildlife. Or another hiker in distress. Then he followed the angle of her eyes and homed in on an area off the trail. Sprawled atop foliage was the fully clothed body of a dark-haired female. Judging by the condition of the remains, she had been there for some time. He noted what looked to be a rusty sledgehammer nearby. Acting on his protective instincts, Logan held Elena close to him, sparing her from seeing what he feared might be the work of the Big Island Killer.

"MY GUESS IS she's been dead for a week or more," Bert Swanson, the forensic pathologist, said in his preliminary assessment of the deceased at what had been labeled a crime scene. "The injuries to her head and face are eerily similar to those inflicted upon the other victims of our serial killer."

Logan cringed at the thought. Based on identification found near the body, she was tentatively identified as thirty-two-year-old Paula Hekekia. He had already ascertained from the moment he'd seen her that she was a victim of foul play. Now it appeared this was from blunt-force trauma, the MO of the Big Island Killer, with the murder weapon being the sledgehammer that had been bagged as evidence by Forensics and would be analyzed for fingerprints and DNA. The fact that Elena discovered the body was equally disturbing to Logan—he hated she had to come face-to-face with this kind of death. Not wanting her to be involved any more than necessary in the investigation, he'd called in the crime and then taken Elena back to his house to await his return. She was shaken, but doing her best to remain strong under adverse circumstances.

Aretha peered at the corpse and, frowning, said petulantly, "This is certainly the Big Island Killer's work. Somehow, the unsub managed to strike and keep the murder from being discovered until now."

"Not sure that was the game plan," Logan offered. "More likely, it wasn't the perp's intention to go this long without the discovery of the remains. Somehow it just worked out that way."

"And could have prompted another kill," the FBI agent speculated on the murder of Kakalina Kinoshita.

That thought occurred to Logan, as well. If true, it had set in motion not only Kakalina's death, but also the inadvertent involvement of Tommy in the case. "Does it appear as though the victim was killed where the body was found?" Logan queried, given its proximity to the often-used hiking trail in the forest reserve. "Or could it have been put here by someone?" If so, this would have required some doing and put the unsub at greater risk for detection.

Swanson examined the corpse with his gloved hands, turning her over and back. "In the absence of any visible indications that she was dragged or perhaps tossed into transportation to bring her here, some distance from the entry to the park, I'd have to say that the victim was likely struck at or around her present location. I'll know more after the autopsy."

"I'll touch base with you then." Logan didn't want to wait that long for some answers as to how Paula

Hekekia ended up being murdered. And who may have wanted her dead, assuming the crime was planned before the fatal attack was carried out. There had been no other reports of a missing woman recently that would have drawn the PD's attention. And possibly saved the life of the victim. Logan needed to get to the bottom of this if they were to have any hope at all in solidly linking the homicide to the unsub.

TAKE A DEEP *breath to calm your nerves*, Elena ordered herself, as she sipped on a cup of oolong tea at the soapstone breakfast bar in Logan's kitchen. Just as they had started to bond with nature on a personal level, the last thing she expected was to come upon a dead body in the Waiākea Forest Reserve. Especially one that had all the earmarks of being someone who died violently. With the victim's features distorted with time since her death, and perhaps being further victimized by animals and insects, it was hard to know if she was a native Hawaiian like the others murdered by a serial killer. Or if her death was an entirely separate incident. Either way, it pained Elena to think that the woman, who had long dark brown hair with caramel highlights, she imagined—based on her style of clothing—was probably around her age, with a long life ahead of her, had been murdered. Ending any chance for a worthwhile future life. *All I can do is hope that Logan and the police department find out who killed the poor woman*, Elena told herself, *and bring some type of peace to her loved ones*.

When the front door opened, Elena flinched, as if the killer had zeroed in on her as Logan's lover and houseguest, and was planning to add to his victim count. She relaxed upon seeing that it was Logan himself entering the kitchen. "Hey," he said in a gentle tone, moving right up to her. "Are you all right?"

"I'm alive," she answered sardonically, considering the fate of the woman they located. Elena knew, though, he was only concerned for her welfare. "That will have to suffice for the time being."

He held her sturdily in his strong arms. "I'll go along with that."

"Why was she even there in the woods in the first place?" Elena asked, recalling that her clothing did not appear as if she was dressed for hiking.

"Could have been any number of reasons," Logan answered. "Just taking a leisurely stroll or maybe she liked the environment."

"Do you think she went to the forest reserve willingly with the person who killed her?"

"That's a possibility. And it's just as possible she went there alone and was accosted and killed by a stranger."

Either way, it unnerved Elena. "Someone must have been looking for her."

"You'd think so. But that might not have been the case." He released his grip on Elena and said thickly, "We'll get the person who killed her."

Elena raised her chin, reading his thoughts. "You think it was the Big Island Killer, don't you?"

Logan paused. "It's a good possibility."

She recoiled while picturing the ghastly remains. "I was thinking the same thing," she admitted, sure it came as no surprise to him, considering the serial killer on the loose on the island.

He didn't try to sugarcoat it. "The MO is the same and the time frame corresponds with the other deaths.

We'll know more soon. In the meantime, if you'd like to stay here, chill out for a while, you're more than welcome to."

While under other circumstances Elena might have jumped at the chance to spend more time at his house—in his bed, keeping it warm and ready for him to join her—now she preferred to be under her own roof as this homicide investigation unfolded. "Thanks, but I should go," she told him gently.

"Okay." Logan ran a hand along her cheek and gazed at her keenly. "Just be careful. As long as this case is still active, don't take any unnecessary chances in what you do."

"I won't," she promised, knowing that he had given her a whole new reason to live. She would not let that be threatened by her own actions. "I would ask the same of you. Now that we have something to build upon, your health and well-being is just as important as mine."

"Fair enough." He flashed a sidelong grin and kissed her softly. "I'll be careful out there. I have you to remind me of what I have to lose."

Smiling, she lifted up on her toes and gave him another kiss, ignoring the ominous feeling of danger that suddenly came over her like a shroud threatening what they had.

"THE DECEASED'S LAST known address was a house on Laukona Street," Ivy said as she and Logan walked toward his desk at the station. "According to her landlady, a few weeks ago Paula Hekekia simply dropped out of sight. Apparently, she was unemployed and struggling to pay the bills. The landlady believes Hekekia became homeless."

"Which could explain how she ended up in the woods," he suggested. "Or maybe she just wandered there from the streets and was latched on to by the unsub, who tracked her like an animal, found the right moment to go on the attack and then bludgeoned her to death before making an escape."

Ivy's brow furrowed. "The victim was there long enough to have attracted attention, if the pathologist's preliminary estimates are correct. So why did it take you and Elena to discover the body?"

"I'm still trying to figure that out," Logan admitted. "The most likely thing I can think of is that she was simply missed by hikers, with just enough distance from the main path and shrubbery to block the remains from view."

"Probably not exactly what the unsub had in mind. The killer seems to feed on making a statement, if you will, with the display of the victims of blunt-force trauma."

Logan couldn't disagree. He feared that this would only propel the unsub to act again. And it wouldn't stop as long as there were more women who had the desired characteristics, with seemingly no one able to prevent the murders from occurring. This was something Logan was determined to change, with the alternative being more than he wanted to imagine.

Ivy stopped as they reached the desk. She took out her cell phone. "Paula Hekekia's landlady showed me a photo of the victim that she left behind. Fits right in with the other Hawaiians the unsub has gone after."

When Ivy pulled it up, Logan stared at it. The victim had a long, thin two-toned hairstyle with wispy bangs. Her features—big olive-brown eyes and a dainty nose with a full mouth—were remarkably similar to Elena's, perhaps more so than the other murder victims, causing him to wince. What if she had been the one who crossed the killer's path in the woods? The very thought of Elena meeting her end in such a terrible way was almost more than Logan could even imagine.

Ivy cocked an eyebrow. "What's up? You look like you've just seen a ghost…"

"It has nothing to do with the supernatural." He scratched his chin reflectively. "Let's just say I'm more determined than ever to put an end to the Big Island Killer's murder campaign." Logan left it at that, while steeling himself for the battle ahead to protect Elena from a potential date with death.

"SORRY YOU HAD to see that," Tommy said as he consoled his sister.

"No more than I am," Elena told him honestly, having dropped by the *ohana* after a shower and change of clothing.

"I'm just glad Detective Ryder was there to get you through it."

Me, too, she thought. She was becoming more and more comfortable with Logan's strong presence in her life. The fact that Tommy seemed to find it acceptable as well made the promise of tomorrow all the more exciting. But today was a different matter altogether. Hawaiian women were still dropping dead like flies and the authorities seemed no closer to catching the culprit than after the first woman was killed. Or perhaps she wasn't being fair to those tasked with solving the case. Surely, they were pursuing angles toward that end that Elena was not privy to. Could she expect Logan to let her in on every single detail of the investigation? Even if she did have a vested interest, in more ways than one, as a Hawaiian female who was also romantically involved with the detective. "We were both able to come to terms with the reality of the moment," she pointed out. "It was frightening, to say the least. But there was nothing I could do to keep from finding the body."

"If you hadn't, who knows when someone else might have come along and been observant enough to do the same?" Tommy put a hand on her shoulder. "Just don't stress out about it."

"I'll try to heed your advice." Elena kept her voice level. She didn't want to crack, knowing that he was still dealing with the death of Kakalina and needed her to remain strong.

"So does Logan believe the woman was murdered by the Big Island Killer?" her brother asked, curious.

"He thinks it's a real possibility," she told him candidly.

Tommy sucked in an uneven breath. "Is this nightmare going to go on forever?"

"I keep asking myself the same question." Elena paused, then, in realistic terms, said, "I guess it will end when the killer runs out of steam. Or the police gain the upper hand in putting the killer out of commission." She wasn't placing bets either way, but bracing herself for whatever came next.

The following day, Elena attended the funeral of Kakalina Kinoshita with Tommy. In spite of the drizzle, many people showed up to pay their respects, including their bandmate, Robin Oyama. Elena felt for Kat's parents, grieving for a loss that never should have happened, but had, anyway. She offered them her services as a grief counselor, letting them know she was Tommy's sister. He had owned up to his part in inadvertently opening the door to a killer. They had forgiven him and welcomed him to be there in memory of Kakalina and in the spirit of all Hawaiians, who came together during times of need.

Gazing at the mourners, Elena couldn't help but wonder if Kat's killer could actually be among them. Didn't they say that some serial killers got a perverse thrill out of being present when burying their victims, as if pulling one over on law enforcement by hiding in plain sight? Would the person be so bold as to be there? She scanned the faces, trying to identify the culprit. Realizing it was a hopeless effort, Elena tried to relax and refocus on the service, and get through the rest of the day. It wouldn't be easy, as long as the Big Island Killer remained at large, putting other lives in danger.

Chapter Fifteen

"We got what appears to be a hit!" forensic analyst Shirley Takaki exclaimed, as she stood before the large screen display in the conference room the following morning.

Logan's eyes lit up at the news as he looked at her, with Ivy, Aretha and other members of the task force on hand. "Go on…"

Shirley used the remote to click at the screen, showing a sledgehammer. "We were able to collect DNA, apart from the victim's, from the handle of the hammer found at the crime scene where you discovered Paula Hekekia's body, Detective Ryder. The forensic unknown profile came up with a match in the state database with arrestee and convicted offender profiles. It belongs to a Mark Teale, who was arrested a year ago for trespassing, but the charge was dropped."

She put his mug shot on the screen and Logan saw a white male in his early thirties with blue-gray eyes and long, scraggly dirty blond hair, parted in the middle. Was this their serial killer? The pathologist had confirmed that Hekekia was murdered, had died from blunt-force trauma to the back of the head. Her injuries matched with the sledgehammer as the murder weapon.

Shirley continued evenly, "We put Teale's DNA profile in the Combined DNA Index System to see if anything came up and struck pay dirt! The forensic DNA record corresponded with a DNA record of the suspect in the database. Teale had an earlier run-in with the law in California for drug possession." She drew a breath. "As to the DNA found on the sledgehammer, at this point, we don't know if it could have somehow ended up there before the hammer was used as a deadly weapon. Or if the DNA belonged to the assailant—"

"I'm betting on the latter," Logan asserted, even if the suspect's arrests were for nonviolent offenses. He wanted to hear much more about this Mark Teale. "A DNA match and an identification is music to my ears…"

When Shirley seemed to hedge and eyed Ivy surreptitiously, Logan got an uneasy feeling in the pit of his stomach. He watched as Ivy took over from there. She uttered bleakly, "Before any of us get too excited about the suspect being the Big Island Killer, there's just one small problem…"

"Don't keep us in suspense, Miyamoto." Logan raised his voice intentionally. "What is it?"

Ivy blinked. "Six months ago, Mark Teale died by suicide at the age of thirty-four." She put an image of a newspaper article on the screen with the headline, Disgruntled Man Dies at Hawaii Volcanoes National Park from Self-inflicted Gunshot. "Apparently, Teale was depressed and decided to check out by putting a stolen .357 Magnum semiautomatic pistol in his mouth and pulling the trigger," Ivy said, frowning. "So unless Teale was able to come back from the dead as something akin to a homicidal vampire, he couldn't have killed Paula Hekekia in spite of the DNA found on the murder weapon."

"I don't believe in the supernatural," Logan muttered humorlessly, his disappointment evident. "Especially where it concerns murder." He was not quite ready to dismiss the dead man in relation to the crime that had occurred in Logan's backyard, in effect. "What else do we know about Teale?"

"Not much, at this point," Ivy admitted, "though the name sounds familiar. From what I've been able to gather, he meandered between being homeless and working odd jobs on the island, before taking his life."

Logan zeroed in on the crime-scene DNA profile. In his mind, it had to be more than coincidence that it happened to belong to a dead man. "Could Teale have a twin brother?" he asked.

"It's possible." Ivy scratched her head. "Why? You think the DNA could belong to someone else?"

"Someone who may have the same DNA," Logan said speculatively. He directed his attention to Shirley and asked, "Isn't it true that identical twins have the same DNA?"

The forensic scientist responded with authority. "Yes, essentially. A standard DNA test on monozygotic or identical twins will come back with a 99.99 percent similarity, leaving little room for differences."

Logan's eyes widened. "Meaning that if Teale does have a twin brother, there's a good chance the DNA left on the sledgehammer used to kill Paula Hekekia belonged to him and not Mark Teale."

"Yes," she conceded, "that would certainly help clear up the mystery of the DNA and a dead suspect."

"And give us a viable living one," Logan said fervently, "who just may well be camouflaged in clear view as the Big Island Killer."

ELENA WAS ADMITTEDLY curious when Logan phoned to say that there was an interesting development in the case regarding the dead body they found. Without giving anything away, he asked her to meet him at Audra's Coffee House on Kinoole Street. He was already seated when she arrived, but stood before Elena got to the table, giving her a light kiss on the cheek.

"I took the liberty of ordering us green coffee," Logan said, having learned that it was one of her preferred healthy drinks.

She smiled. "Thanks, that was thoughtful of you."

"My pleasure." He waited for her to sit before taking his seat across from her. "I wanted to keep you in the loop with the latest news in the investigation into the death of the woman we found at the Waiākea Forest Reserve…"

Elena picked up her mug with the steaming coffee. She wondered if they had a lead on the killer. If so, were they certain that the perpetrator and the Big Island Killer were one and the same? "What's happening?" she asked eagerly.

"She's been identified as Paula Hekekia, age thirty-two. According to the autopsy report, she's been dead for about ten days, a victim of foul play." Logan tasted the coffee, waiting for it to go down. "Apparently, she's been homeless for a while, which is likely why no one reported her missing. But we don't believe she was living in the woods at the time of her death."

"How sad, on multiple fronts." Elena pictured her in life, while unfortunately picturing her in death, as well. "Do you think she was a victim of the serial killer?"

"The timeline indicates that Hekekia was killed before Kakalina Kinoshita and Yancy Otani," he said, musing. "But the MO fits. When you add that with other elements of the case, I'd say that we're almost certainly talking about the work of the Big Island Killer. We just happened to miss discovering Hekekia's remains before the unsub could strike again."

Elena couldn't help but wonder how the perpetrator had been able to so easily slip between the fingers of law enforcement and the public, who were on guard against the attacker to the extent that they could be. Could there be more bodies out there, unknown and unclaimed, with the killer gloating?

Logan broke into her reverie when he said evenly, "There's been a break in the Big Island Killer investigation that will either give us what—and who—we're looking for or prove to be another disaster insofar as cracking the case."

"Tell me…" she urged him, feeling the strain he was under in dealing with an elusive monster on the Hawaiian island.

"Identifiable DNA has been pulled from the sledgehammer found near Hekekia's body. That's the good news." Logan's chin sagged. "Bad news is that it has been linked to a man who died by suicide six months ago. Now we're left to wonder if the DNA had been left over from when he was still alive. Or if he could have an identical twin brother, which we're looking into even as we speak."

"Wow!" Elena's gaze grew wide with wonder. "What are the odds of that happening?"

"Not very good," he allowed, raising his mug. "But stranger things have occurred. If this doesn't pan out with the brother, then the DNA will prove to be totally irrelevant to the murder of Kakalina Kinoshita, and the dead man, Mark Teale, can rest in peace. At least insofar as being involved in any way in this homicide."

Mark Teale, Elena repeated in her head. It rang a bell. But when and where? Then it registered. "I know that name... Mark Teale—" she practically shouted.

Logan cocked an eyebrow. "How?"

"Mark was a client."

"Really?" Logan leaned forward, his face intense. "Tell me more."

"He came to see me...about seven months ago," Elena recalled. "Mark was feeling depressed about his life. I knew he was troubled, but never expected it would reach the point of suicide." She tried tasting the coffee, but lost the desire to drink. "I only wish I had been able to better read the signs before it was too late, maybe recommend that he seek mental-health treatment beyond what I could give."

"Did Teale happen to mention anything about a twin brother?" Logan asked.

"No." Elena looked him in the eye contemplatively. "Mark said he had an identical twin sister named Marlene."

"Twin sister?" Logan repeated the words as though it had never dawned on him. "He used the term *identical* twin?"

"Yes," she said with certainty. "Mark claimed it was an anomaly, but true. According to him, it was Marlene who was the source of his problems. Apparently, she saw them as being tied at the hip, emotionally if not physically, and was clingy and controlling to the point that he simply couldn't take it anymore. Mark even claimed he had a girlfriend, whom he believed was in danger, given his sister's obsessive behavior. He felt trapped and didn't know where to turn."

"Hence, he came to see you?"

"Yes." Elena's eyes fell. "I did my best to help him. Obviously, it was not nearly enough."

"You can't blame yourself for the man taking his own life," Logan told her. "These things happen. Whatever hold Teale's sister had on him, it was powerful enough to make him want to check out rather than remain under her thumb."

It was a scary thought, but Elena knew Logan was right. Still, it left a sour taste in her mouth. "This is all so weird," she said.

"Yeah, I know." He rested his arm on the table. "Did you happen to meet the sister?"

"No. I did attend Mark's funeral and saw a tall, attractive woman dressed in black from a distance, but we never spoke." Elena paused. "I thought of offering my services as a grief counselor to help her deal with the loss, but somehow it didn't seem appropriate."

"Maybe not."

She eyed him. "How do you suppose Mark's DNA ended up on the sledgehammer?"

"Not sure it did," Logan remarked straightforwardly. "It's possible that because Teale and Paula Hekekia were both homeless at times, they could have intersected on that front. But that still doesn't tell us how his DNA would find its way to a murder weapon that connects Hekekia's death to a string of other murders of Hawaiian women."

"You think the DNA could have come from Marlene?" Elena asked, reading between the lines. "How's that even possible? Aren't true identical twins always of the same gender? Especially where it concerns a DNA match?"

"That's what I need to find out." Logan's voice lowered with fortitude. "Could be that we've been looking in the wrong direction all along in assuming that the Big Island Killer was a male."

"But why would Mark's sister go after these women?"

He shrugged. "Why does any serial killer kill? Maybe it was some form of sick obsession with her dead brother that somehow went too far in taking it out on those targeted. But before I get too carried away with theories, why don't we wait and see how this unfolds."

Elena nodded, restraining her own eagerness to get answers, putting her trust in him and the investigation. She rose. "You'd better get going."

"Yeah." Logan got to his feet. He put his hands on her shoulders and gazed down at her. "Keep your eyes open. If the sister is involved with these serial homicides, there's no telling how far she might go in her warped mind. That includes going after her brother's grief counselor."

Elena was chilled at the thought, but tried not to show it. "I'll try to stay alert at all times," she promised.

"Okay." Logan kissed Elena on the mouth and they walked to her car, where they kissed again a little longer before she broke the lip-lock. They would have plenty of time to kiss and much more, once they were no longer under a cloud of murder and mayhem threatening to rain down on the entire island.

Chapter Sixteen

At the Hawaii Police Department's Scientific Investigation Section, Logan stood at the workstation of Shirley Takaki. He had tasked her with determining whether or not the DNA extracted from the sledgehammer found at the Waiākea Forest Reserve crime scene could possibly belong to Mark Teale's supposed identical twin sister, Marlene, since they didn't have an actual sample of her DNA.

"Well, what have you learned?" Logan pressed his lips together, wondering if this was a wild-goose chase—trying to link a serial murder case to a blood relative of a deceased suspect for whom the DNA lined up. "Give me something we can work with."

"I think I can, to one degree or another." Shirley smiled as she sat at a laminate-top science table in an ergonomic lab chair. She glanced at her laptop and back. "I've been doing some research and have found that virtually all cases of identical twins are the same sex. Or to put it another way, in 99.9 percent of boy-girl twins, they are nonidentical or dizygotic twins."

Logan didn't like those odds one bit, yet he had to believe there was a method to the madness that could still add up in their search for a killer.

Shirley moved hair from her face. "But here's the rub—in very rare instances, a genetic mutation can occur in which identical twins develop from an egg and sperm that started out as males, in which they shared the XY chromosomes, before losing a copy of the dominant Y chromosome in changing into a male-female pair. The condition is known as Turner syndrome."

"So you're telling me that it's actually possible that a female can be the identical twin to a male and carry the same DNA?" Logan asked, while wrapping his mind around the notion.

Shirley hesitated. "Yes, I believe this is a possibility based on what I've just outlined," she explained, "in relation to the DNA found on the sledgehammer that's mostly likely not from the deceased Mark Teale. Of course, the only way to know for certain is to get a DNA sample from his sister and see if we can match it to the crime-scene DNA profiles."

"That, we can do," he said confidently, knowing that a judge would likely sign off on a search warrant. But first, they needed to locate this Marlene, wherever she might be, as a potentially dangerous and unstable serial killer.

An hour later, Logan had assembled members of the task force into the conference room to discuss this latest twist in the Big Island Killer investigation. He allowed Shirley to present her findings on the DNA evidence and its relationship to a deceased suspect and his twin sister, before Ivy spoke. "I was able to dig up some interesting information on Marlene Teale, the identical sibling of Mark Teale. Seems as though the thirty-four-year-old Ms. Teale has been in and out of mental institutions for much of her life with various personality disorders and anger-management issues. She was last hospitalized two years ago for psychiatric evaluation after threatening the life of her brŏther, Mark, who had taken out a restraining order against her."

Ivy pointed the remote at the large format display, bringing up an image. "This is what Marlene Teale looked like at the time." Logan regarded the suspect, who was average-looking, with an angular face surrounded by a short, choppy blond hairstyle with side bangs. She wore glasses and had blue eyes. He wondered if this could actually be the face of a serial monster.

"Ms. Teale's last known address was on Pulima Drive," Ivy continued. "With any luck, she still lives there and we can pay her a little visit. Or track down the Chrysler Pacifica registered to the suspect."

"While we're at it," Logan added unsmilingly, "we can compel her through a search warrant to give a sample of her DNA, assuming she won't supply it voluntarily. Then see what else she may be hiding relevant to our investigation."

"The idea that this Marlene Teale is our serial killer, based on shaky forensic evidence, is a bit of a stretch, don't you think?" Aretha asked dubiously.

Logan faced her, expecting that he would get some pushback on the theory yet to be substantiated, all things considered. But his gut instincts, combined with the unusual nature of the DNA analysis, told him they were onto something. Now he only needed to back this up with hard evidence. "What I think, Agent Kennedy, is that we've had one dead end after another. As long as this one is still possible, if not necessarily plausible, we'll work with it and see what happens."

She relented. "You're the lead investigator, Detective Ryder. With the deaths mounting, if you can thread the needle and stick it in the newest suspect, go for it."

"Appreciate that." He nodded, acknowledging her tacit support. Eyeing her former FBI mate and former criminal profiler Georgina Machado, he asked curiously, "Care to weigh in?"

"Sure." She smiled, then observed the picture of the suspect still occupying the screen. "It's quite a fascinating prospect of an identical female twin of a dead male being the Big Island Killer, based on slipping up and leaving controversial DNA evidence. The long odds notwithstanding, far be it for me to rule this out. On the contrary, in spite of the fact that males are predominately more likely to be serial killers, females are still well represented in the annals as serial killers. We're talking about Martha Beck, Rosemary West, Judy Buenoano, Charlene Gallego, Karla Homolka... Shall I go on? Be it profit, jealousy, obsession, revenge, hatred—you name it—women have all the same excuses as men and can be just as deadly. Let's see if Marlene Teale is a red herring. Or a cold-blooded killer just waiting for us to finally figure it out and take her into custody."

"That's good enough for me," Logan told her respectfully. It had better be, he knew, given that the stakes were never higher for ending the state of terror inflicted upon the citizens of Hilo. With Hawaiian women on the front lines of danger.

Ivy got his attention when she announced on cue, "We've got the warrant to go after Marlene Teale."

"Let's not waste any time," Logan responded decisively as they moved into action.

"HMM… I THOUGHT I recognized the name Mark Teale," Ivy said from the passenger seat as she rode with Logan. She was holding a tablet computer.

"What do you have?" Logan glanced at her while driving.

"Seems as though Teale's name came up when we were investigating the death of Liann Nahuina, the first identified victim of the Big Island Killer. Apparently, the two had been cohabitating before Teale's suicide, which resulted in us taking him off the list of suspects."

"Interesting." Logan's mind was churning. "Wonder if there's some symmetry between the two deaths? A cause and effect, if you will?"

"You mean as in the twin sister of Teale going after Nahuina in some sort of misguided attempt at revenge or unnatural grief over his death?"

"Why not?" Logan mulled over the notion. "Sounds far-fetched, but no more so than different-sex twins sharing the same DNA, one of which left some on the sledgehammer used to kill Paula Hekekia."

"True." Ivy took a breath. "But if Nahuina was the primary target of Marlene Teale, why kill the other women?"

"Maybe because of the similar features," Logan said, and thought of Elena, who had the same traits as an attractive Hawaiian female. "Or just to throw us off."

"If so, she succeeded," Ivy argued. "And if not, we've still got a devious unsub on the loose."

"We'll find out soon enough." Logan only wished it had come before Paula Hekekia was murdered, only to have Elena go through the trauma of discovering the body. He sensed that her fortitude as a grief counselor had played a big role in allowing her to better process the experience. That didn't mean she wasn't still in harm's way, with the killer yet to be taken into custody.

He brought the car to a stop on Pulima Drive and they got out. The bungalow-style residence sat on a corner lot with a few bamboo palm and rambutan trees dotting the landscape. A carport was empty, making Logan believe the occupant was not present. But taking no chances, the team, including Agent Kennedy, was armed and ready should they encounter a threat or any resistance. With his Glock pistol out, he led the way, with Aretha and Ivy on his heels. They would request backup, if needed. Stepping onto the lanai, Logan listened for any sounds coming from within. Hearing none, he banged on the door and announced their presence, mindful that the suspect was still innocent until proven guilty.

When no one answered after repeated knocks, the order was given to break the door open using a Halligan tool, after which Logan barreled inside, unsure what they might find, but sensing it would be some answers. They fanned out across the driftwood flooring of the cottage-like home with an open floor plan. It was sparsely furnished. A mildew scent permeated the air, as if the place hadn't been lived in much of late. Logan wondered if the suspect still lived in the house. Or was someone else occupying it?

"We're clear," Ivy shouted, indicating that there were no threats to their safety inside.

Logan put away his firearm as he continued to make his way around, when he heard Aretha make a cryptic comment. "You may want to take a look at this, Ryder."

He followed her voice to the master bedroom, where

the FBI agent was hovering by the closet. "What have you got?"

"What haven't we got is more like it?" Aretha motioned him over, as Logan noted that below the ceiling fan, the full-size bed was made. A large window, facing the backyard, was closed, making it even stuffier inside. "Looks as though someone has been stockpiling the tools of the Big Island Killer in here…"

He gazed into the closet and Logan saw aluminum baseball bats, wooden mallets, lava rock, lead pipes and sledgehammers—all of which had been used to murder five women with blunt-force trauma. His eyes widened with shock. "Guess we've come to the right place," he muttered humorlessly, even if they hadn't confirmed that it was occupied by Marlene Teale. "No wonder the perp didn't bother to collect the murder weapons, knowing there were plenty more where those came from."

"Meaning that the killer was just getting started," Aretha said grimly. "Unless we stood in the way, no telling how many more women would be targeted."

"I wouldn't want to even speculate," Logan said, frowning at the mere thought, with Elena in mind. "We need to get Forensics here in a hurry." He believed that, aside from the treasure trove of circumstantial evidence, there should be DNA evidence that would link the occupant to the DNA found on the sledgehammer that killed Paula Hekekia.

"I found something." The sound of urgency in Ivy's voice got Logan's attention. They followed her to a second room, where she said, "From the looks of it, Marlene Teale still lives here, at least part of the time. More disturbing is what the lady's been up to and who she's now targeting…"

Logan gazed at a white wooden L-shaped desk against the wall. On it was a photograph of Mark and Marlene Teale that looked to have been taken in the last year or so. Next to it on one side were pictures of the Big Island Killer victims: Liann Nahuina, Daryl Renigado, Yancy Otani, Kakalina Kinoshita and Paula Hekekia. Each face had an *X* across it, as if to indicate elimination; along with premeditation in staking out the victims beforehand. Logan inhaled a sharp breath, as his eyes turned to the other side of the center photo of the identical twins and saw the picture of Elena. There was no *X* on it, but the fact that she was there at all told him that the killer was planning to hunt her down and kill her.

"Elena's next on Teale's list," Ivy said, a catch in her voice, but he'd already figured it out.

"I have to warn her." Logan's heart pounded in his ears, knowing the woman he had fallen in love with—and he was ready to admit it—was now in danger for her life.

"With Marlene Teale being the Big Island Killer and apparently mad as a hatter," Aretha began, "we need to move fast to find her before she can get to her next target."

Ivy nodded in agreement, getting out her cell phone. "We'll issue a BOLO alert for Teale and the Chrysler Pacifica she's driving."

With his own phone, Logan took a picture of Marlene Teale's face to send to Elena, so she would be aware and could avoid the dangerous woman at all costs. Until such time, they would place Elena in protective custody, to keep her safe and sound, so long as Teale remained on the loose. Assuming it wasn't too late.

ELENA LEFT THE office to wait in her car for Tommy to show up. They would ride together to have lunch at a seafood restaurant in Downtown Hilo, at which time he planned to tell her about his newest adventure as a tour guide. She was happy to see him try to get on with his life, following the death of Kakalina. Elena knew there would still be good and bad days, but felt that time would lessen the blow and allow him to return to some semblance of normalcy. Just as had been the case for her after Errol's passing. She had managed to get beyond the grieving and find a new love. *Did I just say love?* Elena asked herself, repeating the word in her head. Even if the thought was a little scary and she was unsure if Logan felt the same way, the heart knew what the heart knew. She did love Logan Ryder and would have to muster up the guts to tell him.

Just as Elena opened the door to her car, she felt a presence behind her. Turning around, her initial fear of an attacker was abated somewhat when she recognized the person. It was Marybeth Monaghan, one of her clients. "Hi, Marybeth," she said politely.

Marybeth gave her a friendly smile. "Hey."

Elena lifted her eyes curiously. "Did we have an appointment for today?"

"Not really." She touched her glasses demurely. "I was still having some issues and decided I'd take a chance that you'd be around."

"I'm sorry, but I have a lunch date, so…" Elena hated to disappoint her, but she didn't want to cancel getting together with her brother, feeling it was important that they do what was needed to strengthen their own bond after recent challenges. Surely, Marybeth would understand? When her cell phone rang, Elena lifted it from her pocket and saw that the caller was Logan. Her heart skipped a beat at being able to hear his voice. She sensed, though, that the call could be an important update on the case instead of what she meant to him. Glancing at her client, Elena said softly, "Excuse me, but I have to get this…"

Marybeth gave a halfhearted smile, but did not budge. Suddenly feeling uneasy for some reason, Elena turned away from her and answered the phone. "Hey," she uttered.

"Mark Teale's sister is the Big Island Killer," Logan said in a panicked tone. "Her name is Marlene Teale and I think she's coming after you."

"Really?" Elena's fear radar shot up at the prospect of being in the crosshairs of a serial killer. Even if she had no idea why, other than that she resembled the other victims.

"Yes," he snapped urgently. "I'm sending you a picture of her. If you see this woman anywhere, stay away from her until I can get there…"

When she got the photo, Elena stared at a face she recognized, save for the different shade of hair. Marlene Teale *was* Marybeth Monaghan, the woman standing behind her. Before she could react and reveal to Logan that she was in serious trouble, Elena felt something slam against the side of her head. Without even realizing it, she blacked out, not knowing if she would ever get the chance to express her true feelings to Logan.

Chapter Seventeen

Elena opened her eyes with a splitting headache. What happened? Where was she? How did she get there? Then it began to come back to her, groggy as she was. She had been hit hard on the head by someone. But who? She strained to remember, before it clicked like a light bulb flashing in her brain. She had been assaulted by Marlene Teale, the woman Elena knew as Marybeth Monaghan. Only it had been an alias to hide her true identity as the sister of Elena's former, and now dead, client, Mark Teale. And, according to Logan, a serial killer.

It took another moment or two for Elena to realize that she was bleeding on the side of her head—the warm blood had trickled down her left ear and cheek onto her neck. She further recognized that she was seated on a wooden cross-back chair with her hands tied behind her back with rope. *Where has she taken me?* Elena pondered worriedly. Clearing her vision, she saw that she was near a cottage-style beige-colored wall in a small living room with gray laminate wood flooring and an open concept. The place was lightly furnished with rustic reclaimed barnwood furniture. Double-hung windows were covered by faux-wood plantation blinds, with the source of illumination a small vintage glass lamp that was sitting on a three-sided cream-colored corner table.

As she assessed the situation, Elena tried to wrest her hands free with no luck. She had to get out of there. Alert Logan that she was in peril. Or was he already looking for her and trying to rescue her? Along with trying to take down a stone-cold killer? But how on earth would he know where to look? Something told Elena that her kidnapper had taken her somewhere not easily found. But for what purpose, other than to kill her with a slow, torturous death?

When the front door burst open and her abductor entered, carrying a black duffel bag, Elena wondered if she should pretend to still be unconscious or not. She opted for the latter, figuring that Marlene Teale was not likely to fall for it.

"So you're finally awake." Marlene dropped the bag on the floor and walked up to Elena with an amused look playing on her lips. "Sorry about the conk on the head." She laughed mockingly. "Actually, I'm not. Unfortunately for you, I'm not done with you yet. By the time I am, believe me, you'll be glad when it's over, because you'll be dead."

I have to say something to this seriously disturbed lady, Elena told herself, trying her best to remain calm. "Why are you doing this, Marybeth?" she asked, pretending to still only know her by her fake name. "What have I ever done to you, but try and help?"

"Save the act, okay?" Marlene narrowed her eyes behind the glasses. "I know you know my real name's Marlene Teale. I saw the picture of me your cop boyfriend sent to your cell phone. He's on to me and, I'm sure, what I've been up to. But that won't help you at all. While you were snoozing, I got rid of your cell phone so it can't be used to track your location. No one knows you're here. It's my secret hideaway, so don't count on being rescued by him or anyone else."

Realizing it was not going to do her any good playing dumb, Elena felt that the next best thing was to try to get some answers out of her while stalling for time. "Yes, I know you're Mark Teale's identical twin, Marlene," she confessed. "What I don't understand is why you would want to hurt me? I did everything I could to help Mark. It wasn't my fault that he took his own life."

"Is that what you think?" Marlene laughed hysterically. "If you want to know the truth—and it doesn't matter at this point, since you'll never live to tell a soul—Mark didn't kill himself."

Elena's eyebrows cocked in surprise, notwithstanding the threat to her own life. "What?"

"I only made it look like he had," she said, bragging. "My brother wanted to cut off all ties to me, as if I meant nothing to him anymore. Can you believe he actually fell in love with someone, or so he claimed, for the first time in his life? Her name was Liann Nahuina. After all I did for him, we were supposed to always be there for each other. Have each other's backs, through thick and thin. Then he wants to kick me, his twin sister, to the curb—for what, her? I couldn't let that happen. So I put on a convincing act to get him to meet me at the park to say our goodbyes, where I used a gun stolen from my married former lover and shot Mark in the head. I put the gun in his hand to make it look like it was self-inflicted. Everyone believed it. I hated to lose the only person who truly got me, but he made me do it."

She really is unhinged and obviously homicidal with jealous rage in a sibling-attachment way, Elena told herself, shuddering at the thought that she had murdered her own twin brother as if it was just a walk in the park. *Who does that?* Elena wondered what else she could get her kidnapper to reveal that could later be used against her. Now that the cat was out of the proverbial bag, there was no reason for her kidnapper to deny who and what she was. "What about those poor women? Did you kill them, too, as the Big Island Killer? And, if so, why?"

Marlene hardened her face. "Yes, I killed them, like I'm going to kill you," she replied tartly. "Why? The first one, Liann, was Mark's girlfriend and the reason he turned against me. She needed to pay for that. She made it easy to take her life away, living off the grid as she did, in this very cottage…"

Elena scanned the place again, as she mulled over this revelation. Could Logan possibly figure out that this was where she had been taken? Or was Marlene right in that there was no escape from her maniacal plan to kill her?

"The others were meant to throw the police off any possible trail to me," Marlene continued, as if proud of herself and the deception. "The fact that Liann happened to be Hawaiian, it wasn't that difficult to locate some other Hawaiian women with similar features to dispose of. I decided to kill each of them with a different object to confuse the authorities even more. But the funny thing is, I started to feel good about it with each killing. I came to realize that I liked having the power to take away lives. It seemed like killing was in my blood.

Too bad it took killing Mark to make me realize this."
She paused, as if a flicker of regret hit her. Then the
steely cold countenance returned. "But I'm just getting
started. The Big Island Killer, as they chose to name
me, has more tricks up her sleeve in targeting others
who don't look like Liann. That will really confound
the police as a wickedly clever serial killer."

"What do you want from me?" Elena had hesitated
to ask, even as she continued to try in vain to break her
hands free. Why hadn't she killed her already? *Or do I
really want to know?* Elena thought. "Why the ruse in
pretending to be Marybeth Monaghan?"

"The Marybeth part was simply a way to get to you
without giving myself away. After I learned that Mark
went to you for counseling, I wanted to see for myself
who it was that he poured his heart out to. Though I
lied about my mother passing away recently, she really
did die from pancreatic cancer—only when Mark and I
were six years old. Without a father ever in the picture,
we were then placed in foster care." Marlene sighed,
sadness in her eyes, but her face hardened once again.
"Imagine how surprised I was to discover that you bore
a strong resemblance to Liann. It was almost too perfect
as someone who had interfered with the kinship I had
with my brother. I knew then that it was only a matter
of time before you would die, too. That time is near
and there's absolutely nothing you can do about it—"

Elena fought hard not to believe her chilling words,
which made any possibility of getting out of her predic-
ament seem hopeless. Dying before reaching the age of
thirty-three, before having a chance to have a life with
Logan, wasn't what she'd bargained for. Certainly not

at the hands of a mentally unstable, but still quite capable, serial murderer. "Just let me go and I won't tip the police off." She doubted her kidnapper would buy that, but wanted to make it sound believable, anyhow.

Marlene crouched down so their faces were lined up and inches apart. "Sorry, but no can do," she growled. "You have to die like the others. Mark would want that, too. After all, he chose to bring you into the picture that, as his identical twin, made me a part of it, as well. The only reason you're still breathing, with probably a massive headache, is because you're a grief counselor and I wanted to get some final therapy of sorts in memory of my brother, as a parting shot to your demise."

Elena swallowed the lump in her throat, as she had to come to terms with the reality that her abductor seemed to hold all the cards. Meaning that her life hung in the balance. Unless she could find a way to prevent Marlene from carrying out her plans to murder her.

LOGAN GOT A bad feeling in his gut when Elena's phone suddenly went dead in the middle of their conversation. Had it been merely a lost signal? Or something more ominous? Such as Marlene Teale getting to her before they could pick up the armed and dangerous suspect in the murder of five women. Before he could wrap his mind around the unsettling possibilities, Logan got a call from Elena's brother.

"Hey, I'm standing in the parking lot next to Elena's car outside the office complex where she works," Tommy said, concern evident in his tone. "We were supposed to get together for lunch. Only she's not here, but her car door is open…"

"Did you try calling her cell phone?" Logan strained not to panic. "Maybe Elena forgot something in her office."

"Yes, I called her. There was no answer." Tommy's voice cracked. "I'm freaking out here, thinking that something bad may have happened to my sister."

I'm thinking the same thing, Logan told himself, but had to keep it together for both their sakes. "Let's not jump to conclusions," he said evenly. He had to believe that Elena was still alive, whatever the case. "Maybe there's an explanation as to why she isn't there. Hang tight, I'm on my way. In the meantime, keep trying to reach her and don't touch the car. It may now be an official crime scene."

"Okay." Tommy hung up and Logan was left with a sense of dread as he turned to the others at the bungalow where Marlene Teale had been staying. "I think Teale may have Elena." He explained why, while resisting the more morbid thoughts that if the serial killer suspect had kidnapped Elena in broad daylight, her chances for survival were bleak, at best.

"If she does," Ivy told him steadfastly, "we'll find her."

"One can only hope." Logan refused to think otherwise. Now that he had found Elena as a woman he had a future with, losing her to the Big Island Killer was not an option as long as there was an ounce of breath in him.

"With the BOLO out, we're in full pursuit of Teale," Aretha reminded him. "She no longer has the element of surprise on her side. Or maybe places that she can go."

"I know," he said solemnly. "That's what I'm afraid of. If Teale feels cornered, there's no telling what she's capable of." He considered that she might try to use

Elena as a bargaining chip to get away. That was assuming the twin sister of Mark Teale hadn't already harmed Elena, given her MO. "I'm heading over to the parking lot where Elena apparently was abducted. Send a forensic team over there to look for evidence. Also, let's see if we can use cell site location information and GPS data to triangulate the location of Elena's cell phone." Even in seeking the information, Logan suspected that if Elena had been kidnapped, her abductor would likely have disposed of the evidence near the point of abduction. Still, they had to exercise every means to locate her, as Elena's life depended on it with every excruciating second counting.

"I'll get on it," Ivy assured him. "And we'll check parks, trails, woods, vacant fields, anywhere Teale could have taken her."

"Good." Logan knew he could count on her and the entire PD and FBI to do everything in their power to try to prevent another human being from being murdered by the Big Island Killer. But would any of that be enough to save Elena?

He raced to the scene of Elena's disappearance, and spotted Tommy pacing in the parking lot of the office complex on Waianuenue Avenue. Logan pulled up near Elena's Subaru Outback and got out. He winced, picturing her being accosted by a killer and how terrifying it must have been to be in that situation. Adding to his uneasiness, he saw what seemed to be drops of blood just outside the car. Elena's? Apparently, Tommy had failed to notice it. Probably a good thing, Logan believed. He hoped Elena was strong enough to withstand whatever Teale dished out until he could get to her.

"Did you check Elena's office?" Logan asked her brother.

"Yeah. It was locked and no sign she was inside."

"I doubt she was," Logan admitted sourly.

"What's going on?" Tommy narrowed his eyes agitatedly. "What aren't you telling me?"

Locking eyes with him, Logan responded straightforwardly, "We think Elena may have been abducted."

"By who?"

While hating to spill out the words, given the obvious implications, Logan felt that Elena's brother needed to know the seriousness of the situation that they were up against. "The Big Island Killer."

The color seemed to drain from Tommy's face and Logan could almost read his mind. First Kakalina Kinoshita. And now Elena. "Are you saying that this serial killer has Elena and has murdered her...?"

"I'm saying that neither of us should panic at this point," Logan told him, while trying hard to practice what he was preaching. "Until we know for sure, we have to assume that Elena is still alive."

Tommy went stone-cold silent as the crime-scene technicians arrived. Logan insisted that Elena's brother go home and wait until there was news, or in case she miraculously showed up. He complied begrudgingly and Logan went to the office complex's security office to get a look at the parking-lot surveillance video. The security coordinator, Diego Holokai, in his sixties and bald-headed, wasted little time in pulling up the video with the sense of urgency attached to it by Logan.

"Okay, let's see what we've got," Diego said.

Logan watched as the video slowed down and zoomed in to when Elena stood by her car talking to a woman he recognized as Marlene Teale. The way Elena was conversing with her, it appeared as though they were not strangers. Could the killer have gone under-cover as a client in order to get a read on her target be-forehand? Logan saw Elena turn away and talk on her cell phone—presumably to him. It was after he sent the picture of the suspect that Elena was hit in the head by Marlene with what appeared to be a piece of lava rock.

"What the…?" Diego's voice cracked in disbelief.

Logan cringed in horror as Elena seemed to lose consciousness right away. He only wished he had been able to reach her five minutes earlier, kicking himself at the timing misfortune. Before she could fall to the ground, Elena was caught by Marlene and dragged out of view. "Pan the video out," Logan ordered, needing to see where the kidnapper took her.

"You've got it," the security coordinator said, com-plying.

Peering, Logan saw that Marlene was now wearing a dark hoodie over her head as she tossed Elena into the passenger seat of a silver Chrysler Pacifica, match-ing the one registered to the suspect. Then Marlene ran around the vehicle, got behind the wheel and took off. It was obvious to him that she had planned this in ad-vance and, frighteningly, it had gone off without a hitch.

Diego frowned. "Where is she taking her and why?"

"Have no idea on the first question." Logan hated to admit it, feeling helpless in his quest to avert another tragedy. "As to the why, she's a serial killer and is plan-ning to commit murder—if we can't find her."

"I hope you do," he said sincerely.

The clock was ticking, Logan thought miserably, knowing that if he didn't get to Elena soon, she was as good as dead. "I need a copy of that video. I'll send someone to pick it up later."

"No problem."

Logan left him to get back to the search for the woman he intended to ask to marry him, if he ever got that chance. After conferring with detectives on the scene in what had become an active case of kidnapping, Logan climbed back in his car, not able to stand idle while Elena was out there somewhere alone with a madwoman and serial killer, with Elena unsure if she would survive her ordeal or not. *I'll never stop trying to find you as long as there's any possibility you're still alive*, he thought to himself.

When his cell phone rang, Logan answered, putting it on speaker. "The car Teale's driving was spotted a little while ago on Komohana Street heading toward South Hilo," Ivy informed him. "We've dispatched all available vehicles to the area."

A bell suddenly rang in Logan's head. "Wasn't the cottage where Liann Nahuina's body found off of Komohana Street?"

"Yes, I believe so," Ivy confirmed. "Why do you ask?"

"Call it a hunch," he told her thoughtfully, "but the off-the-grid cottage seems like the perfect place for Teale to operate and lay low as the last location her brother called home, at least part-time, before his death."

"You could be right about that."

"Only one way to find out," Logan said, pressing his foot down on the accelerator. "I'm not far from there." If his instincts were correct, he didn't have a second to spare.

"I'll alert the SWAT unit and head over there myself with Aretha and other reinforcements," Ivy stated decisively.

"I was counting on that." He disconnected, not about to wait for backup. Not this time. Not when Elena meant far too much to him to depend on anyone to come to her rescue but himself. If Marlene had kept her alive, it wouldn't be for long. But maybe just long enough, Logan believed, to do whatever he needed to neutralize the threat and make sure Elena was safe and sound.

He drove the car to the side of the road, just far enough from the cottage to not announce his arrival to the kidnapper. Stepping outside, where it had started to rain, Logan removed the firearm from his pocket holster and approached the location he believed Elena had been taken to. He moved silently across a brown field and spotted a silver Chrysler Pacifica parked in the back. The license plate number corresponded with the vehicle registered to Marlene Teale, giving more credence to Logan's belief that Elena was there.

With his gun drawn, Logan checked for any signs of her in the vehicle. Seeing none, he approached the side of the cottage, careful not to tip his hand, not knowing if the suspect had a firearm or not. He wasn't willing to take any unnecessary chances when it came to Elena's life. Gazing inside a dirty side window while ignoring the rain pelting his face, he could see Elena sitting in a chair. Her hands appeared to be bound. At first, there was no movement and he feared the worst. But then she jerked her head and seemed to say something. *She's alive*, he thought, feeling a sudden adrenaline rush to make sure Elena stayed that way.

Logan's vision turned toward the kidnapper, who was hovering over Elena like a mighty conqueror enjoying her position of power. She didn't appear to have a gun in her possession. But even if she wasn't packing, he didn't doubt that she had other potentially deadly weapons within reach, as Logan thought of the lava rock used to assault Elena. Not to mention the cache of lethal items found in the closet of Teale's residence, similar to the ones used to murder five women. Marlene clearly planned to kill Elena, perhaps after extracting information from her. *Not if I can help it*, Logan thought, ready to make his move to avert disaster.

"You don't have to do this," Elena pleaded with her kidnapper, hoping to buy time, if nothing else, as she heard the rainfall. She sensed that Logan was out there somewhere near, doing his best to extricate her from the desperate situation she was in. In the meantime, Elena had finally begun to feel the rope loosening, but still not enough to break free.

"I'm afraid I do," Marlene taunted her. "I need to finish this for Mark. The sibling bond between us is unbroken, even with his death. I should think you of all people would understand this. You have your own sibling bond. It's Tommy, isn't it?" Elena reacted to the familiarity with her brother. Marlene made a snickering sound, as if pleased with herself. "Yeah, thought so. You know, I didn't realize he was your brother when I followed him and the lady from the club. I thought I might have to go against the grain and kill her inside her house, along with anyone else who got in the way. But then Tommy let her out of the car and she was only too happy to hitch a ride with me, drunk as Kakalina was. I doubt she ever realized what was happening to her, until it was much too late. Never considered that your brother might be taken into custody for the crime. Lucky for him that I wasn't about to let Tommy take credit for what I was doing. If the police hadn't released him, I might've had to come after you sooner. Then your cop boyfriend would have realized too little, too late, that they had the wrong person under lock and key."

"You're sick," Elena uttered contemptuously, feeling queasy at the thought that she might already be dead, never to see Logan or Tommy again, had it not been for a twist of fate. She only wished someone else didn't have to die in the interim.

"I suppose I am," Marlene admitted, a delirious chuckle cracking through the air. She halted it on a dime. "But sane enough to finish what I started in killing you. Unlike the others, though, out of the goodness of my heart—or maybe to make it sporting—you'll get the choice of how you're to die…" She went to the duffel bag and removed several items, including an aluminum baseball bat, lava rock, lead pipe, wooden mallet and a sledgehammer. She laid them out on the floor, as if on display. "Pick one," she demanded.

"I can't," Elena choked out, not wanting to play her insane and evil game.

"Do it!" Marlene's voice echoed venomously throughout the room. "Otherwise, I'll do it for you and, just maybe, choose two of them to attack you with— one to start, the other to finish—"

So, this is it, Elena thought resignedly, twisting her hands every which way frantically to get them loose, while frightened beyond belief. Not so much in dying before her time. But in not getting the chance to say goodbye to Logan, the love of her life. And Tommy, the only relative she had left. She couldn't go down without a fight. Elena finally freed her hands, knowing she had only one shot to get out of this alive. She uttered submissively, "How about the lava rock?" She sensed that was what the serial killer had used to hit her on the head in the parking lot.

"Good choice." Marlene laughed maniacally. "Might have chosen the same myself, had I been in your situation. Especially considering the alternatives."

When she turned to the killing tools, Elena sprang up, catching Marlene off guard. "I won't become another victim of yours."

"Oh really?" Marlene quickly overcame her surprise that Elena had freed herself. "We'll see about that." She grabbed the lead pipe and approached her. "Guess I've been left to make the choice for you in how you'll die…" She swung the pipe, hitting nothing but air.

Elena's blood ran hot as she dodged the attempt to hit her in the head. Putting her kickboxing skills to the test, she raised her leg and landed a hard kick to Marlene's face, knocking the serial killer off balance. The woman yelled an expletive, shook off the pain, regained her balance and again swung the pipe at Elena's head, but she managed to avert it with quick foot action. In the blink of an eye in a countermove, she brought her leg up and kicked Marlene solidly in the pit of her stomach, and in the same motion put a foot solidly to the side of the kidnapper's head. Marlene's glasses flew from her face as she staggered and shrieked.

Feeling as though she was gaining the upper hand, Elena's pulse raced as she lifted both feet off the ground. She struck her assailant's face with one foot, knocking the pipe out of her hands as Marlene fell hard to the floor, before Elena landed back on her feet firmly. Just as it appeared as if it was over and she was victorious, Marlene grabbed the sledgehammer, rose and started to charge Elena with a crazed look in her eyes.

Backpedaling, Elena lost her balance and fell onto the floor. Her heart beating wildly, she struggled to stand, fearing that if Marlene got on top of her, the serial killer would do as she intended in bludgeoning her to death as another victim of the Big Island Killer. The front door suddenly burst open and Elena watched in amazement as Logan barreled in, his gun aimed squarely at Marlene.

"Drop it!" His voice was commanding. "I said, drop it, Marlene. It's over. Now!"

The murderer's features contorted like a rabid animal, as Marlene turned away from her and faced Logan. Instead of obeying the detective's order, she charged at him with the sledgehammer as if she had nothing to lose, and Logan fired one shot, then another, before the serial killer went down.

Bypassing the unconscious Marlene, Elena rushed toward Logan, who put his gun away with the threat brought under control, and wrapped her arms tightly around his neck, almost wishing they could remain that way forever. "That was a very close call," she said, catching her breath. "Thanks for showing up just in time."

"Nice to see you, too," he said wryly, holding her closely in his arms. She could feel the wetness on his body from the rain. "You're bleeding," he noted with concern.

Only then did Elena remember the pop on the side of her head and the fact that there was blood coming from the gash. "Nothing I can't overcome with a few stitches, a hot shower and a good night's sleep."

"Good." Logan kissed her temple. "Kickboxing,

huh?" His voice was tinged with amusement. "I caught some of the action through the window before I came in."

She blushed. "It has its moments."

"I can see that."

Elena released her hold on his neck and gazed into Logan's unblinking eyes with curiosity. "How did you find me?"

"Teale's car was spotted in the area," Logan explained. "I had a feeling that she might have been using the vacant and out-of-the-way cottage her brother shared with Liann Nahuina before his death as a place to hide out...and, apparently, perpetrate more violent crime."

Elena felt a drop in her blood pressure as she turned to the fallen serial killer and back. "She killed him..."

Logan's right eyebrow shot up. "What?"

"Marlene confessed to murdering Mark in some sort of jealous-sibling spat that morphed into homicidal revenge," Elena told him. "She made it look like suicide."

"Why am I not surprised?" Logan took an exaggerated sigh. "Especially given the odd twists and turns of their symbiotic relationship as identical twins." His forehead creased. "Too bad she felt the need to go after and murder five innocent women in the aftermath."

"That's a whole different story." Elena mused about her own harrowing experience at the hands of Marlene and how much different the outcome could have been, considering the victims who didn't pull through.

Logan seemed to read her mind and, staring deep into her eyes, said in earnest, "Fortunately, we were able to draw the line there. If something had happened to you that there was no coming back from, I would never have been able to truly tell you how I feel."

Her heart skipped a beat. "And just how do you feel?"

"I'm in love with you, Elena," he said plainly, "and I'd like you to become my wife and mother to as many children as you'd like."

She put her hands to her mouth as the powerful words registered in her ears. It was just what she wanted to hear and, for a little while there, she'd feared she might never have been afforded the opportunity. "I'd love to marry you, Logan." She minced no words in expressing how she truly felt about him. "Especially since I've fallen in love with you, too. And I can think of no better way to show it than by becoming your wife and the mother to as many children as we decide to bring into this world."

"Mahalo." Logan beamed ecstatically. "Shall we seal the deal with a kiss?"

Elena laughed. "I'd be pretty disappointed if we didn't."

"So would I." On that note, he slanted his face just right and gave her a passionate kiss that had Elena seeing stars. Something told her Logan was seeing them as well, as they planted the seeds for a lifetime together, built on love, trust, respect, adventure...and, yes, parenthood in paradise.

Epilogue

Six months later, Mr. and Mrs. Logan Ryder were walking hand in hand on a sunny afternoon along the black sand beach at Hilo Bayfront Beach Park on Kamehameha Avenue, a popular park just a short distance from downtown Hilo. They were celebrating their two-month anniversary as husband and wife, leaving Elena still breathless and overjoyed to have found her soul mate and second love of her life in the handsome detective. Not wanting to wait to begin their union, she had moved into his house two weeks after Logan proposed to her, prompted by his urging and promise to do whatever was necessary to make it their home. Instead of putting her own house on the market, while holding onto the precious memories of her life there, Elena offered the place instead to Tommy at a bargain price. He gleefully accepted, while turning the *ohana* into a rental property.

"What's happening in that pretty little head of yours?" Logan asked, breaking into her daydreaming with interest.

"Oh, just thinking about what a difference half a year can make," she told him musingly, while staring at the murky waters of Hilo Bay with the ocean as the backdrop. "I feel as if a great weight has been lifted off our shoulders, allowing us the opportunity to recalibrate."

"Yeah, one's whole world can change in a short time." He held her hand tighter. "For the better, I might add."

"Definitely." Elena beamed, rejoicing in their blissful relationship and exciting plans to add to their family. But then she thought about those who were less fortunate. Specifically, the six murdered victims of Marlene Teale, the woman who gained infamy as the Big Island Killer. She had survived her injuries and was currently in jail, while showing no signs of remorse. Including the killing of her own twin brother. Elena couldn't imagine doing such a thing to Tommy, no matter how great their differences. But if there was a silver lining to Mark's death, it was that he didn't take his own life as had originally been thought. Elena felt relieved that this also meant she needn't bear any guilt that she could have played a role in his suicide as a counselor. On the other hand, she certainly could not have conceived that Mark's obsessed sister would not only murder him, but also come after her for merely trying to help him and happening to look like his girlfriend. Elena raised her eyes pensively to meet Logan's. "So what's going to happen to Marlene?"

"That will be left for the courts to decide." He flashed a look of frustration. "Right now, the lawyers and psychiatrists are sparring over her competency to stand trial. Who knows how long that will take? The PD and task force did our job in identifying and apprehending the kidnapper and serial killer. The rest is out of our hands. As of now, Teale's sanity is in serious doubt, given the unnatural attachment she had to her identical twin and her willingness to commit fratricide in some act of vengeance. Not to mention, turning her jealous rage on Mark's girlfriend, Liann Nahuina, and four other women who had the misfortune of looking like Liann." His jaw set as he gazed at Elena. "Make that five women. Thankfully, one was able to survive." Logan sighed gratefully.

"We were both blessed in that way," she uttered, knowing it could just as easily have gone in the other direction and left him without the love he deserved in a partner.

"Yep." Logan released her hand and wrapped his long arm around Elena's shoulders protectively as they continued to walk on the beach. "Everything I said about Marlene Teale's mental fitness to go to trial could just as easily work against her as someone who was obviously cognizant and calculating enough to commit a string of blunt-force-trauma homicides and keep the authorities at bay for as long as she did. The good thing is that whichever way this goes, Teale's not likely to ever see the light of day again in the free world."

"Amen to that." The thought was comforting to Elena, for herself as a victim and in memory of those who didn't make it. Not to mention other Hawaiian women who might have been unjustly targeted for death by the unstable and evil serial killer. Elena lifted her chin and kissed Logan heartily, then, with romance on her mind, said, "Let's go home."

"If you insist," he said, grinning from ear to ear.

"Oh, yes," she assured him passionately, taking a peek at the two-tone gold wedding band on her finger, with its shimmering diamonds, that cemented their love. "I do."

* * * * *

COMING SOON!

We really hope you enjoyed reading this book.
If you're looking for more romance, be sure to
head to the shops when new books are
available on

Thursday 1st
September

MILLS & BOON

THE HEART OF ROMANCE

A ROMANCE FOR EVERY READER

MODERN

Prepare to be swept off your feet by sophisticated, sexy and seductive heroes, in some of the world's most glamourous and roman locations, where power and passion collide.

HISTORICAL

Escape with historical heroes from time gone by. Whether your passion for wicked Regency Rakes, muscled Vikings or rugged Highlanders, av the romance of the past.

MEDICAL

Set your pulse racing with dedicated, delectable doctors in the high-pre sure world of medicine, where emotions run high and passion, comfor love are the best medicine.

True Love

Celebrate true love with tender stories of heartfelt romance, from the rush of falling in love to the joy a new baby can bring, and a focus on emotional heart of a relationship.

Desire

Indulge in secrets and scandal, intense drama and plenty of sizzling ho action with powerful and passionate heroes who have it all: wealth, sta good looks…everything but the right woman.

HEROES

Experience all the excitement of a gripping thriller, with an intense ro mance at its heart. Resourceful, true-to-life women and strong, fearles face danger and desire - a killer combination!

To see which titles are coming soon, please visit

millsandboon.co.uk/nextmonth

LET'S TALK
Romance

For exclusive extracts, competitions
and special offers, find us online:

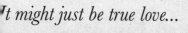

GET YOUR ROMANCE FIX

Get the latest romance news,
exclusive author interviews, story
extracts and much more!

MILLS & BOON

Desire

Indulge in secrets and scandal, intense drama and plenty of sizzling hot action with powerful and passionate heroes who have it all: wealth, status, good looks…everything but the right woman.

MILLS & BOON
MEDICAL
Pulse-Racing Passion

Set your pulse racing with dedicated, delectable doctors in the high-pressure world of medicine, where emotions run high and passion, comfort and love are the best medicine.

MILLS & BOON
True Love
Romance from the Heart

Celebrate true love with tender stories of heartfelt romance, from the rush of falling in love to the joy a new baby can bring, and a focus on the emotional heart of a relationship.